DAVID GILMAN

DELACORTE PRESS

Text copyright © 2011 by David Gilman
Jacket illustration © 2011 by Owen Richardson
Jacket photograph © 2011 Shutterstock Images
Book design by Heather Daugherty

All rights reserved. Published in the United States by Delacorte Press, an imprint of Random House Children's Books, a division of Random House, Inc., New York.
Originally published in paperback in Great Britain by Puffin Books Ltd., a division of the Penguin Group, London, in 2009.

Delacorte Press is a registered trademark and the colophon is a trademark of Random House, Inc.

www.randomhouse.com/teens

Educators and librarians, for a variety of teaching tools, visit us at www.randomhouse.com/teachers

Library of Congress Cataloging-in-Publication Data
Gilman, David.
Blood sun / by David Gilman. — 1st ed.
p. cm.
Summary: Desperate to uncover the secret of his mother's death, fifteen-year-old Max Gordon, pursued by enemies, travels from the bleakness of Dartmoor to the rain forest of Central America, where the environmental devastation hides a sinister secret.
ISBN 978-0-385-73562-9 (hc) — ISBN 978-0-385-90548-0 (lib. bdg.) —
ISBN 978-0-375-89809-9 (ebook)
[1. Adventure and adventurers—Fiction. 2. Survival—Fiction. 3. Rain forests—Fiction. 4. Environmental protection—Fiction. 5. Dartmoor (England)—Fiction. 6. Central America—Fiction. 7. Mystery and detective stories.] I. Title.
PZ7.G431B1 2011
[Fic]—dc22
2010005169

The text of this book is set in 12-point Goudy.

Printed in the United States of America
10 9 8 7 6 5 4 3 2 1

First U.S. Edition

FOR DES,
THE BEST OF MEN .

ACKNOWLEDGMENTS

My appreciation to my guides Joe Awe and Hilbert Tut in Belize for sharing their knowledge of the rain forest, and for Joe's rich history of the Mayan culture. Thanks to Keith Chiazzari for double-checking all things about boats and planes; naturally, any errors, deliberate or otherwise, are mine alone. James McFarlane continues to be a constant source of help with flora and fauna and many other things. I'm grateful for the kindness and help offered by staff of the Anthropology Library at the British Museum's Centre for Anthropology, who guided me toward various academic research papers on the history and culture of the *Quipu,* which I have chosen to write in its alternative spelling of *khipu.*

MAYAN PROPHECY

When the last tree falls, so too will the stars.

1

Darkness devoured him.

Eyes wide with terror, he saw only the gaping void, heard his desperate breathing hammering through his skull as the rasping one-eyed monster pursued him. Beneath his feet, death's slippery tongue glinted dully in the belly of the beast.

A faint signal beat through his mind, a rhythmic note that was his own voice. *Don't fail. Don't fail. Don't fail.* To do what? His thoughts were in tatters. He tried to scan the memory banks embedded in his brain. Terror gushed chemicals through his body. He couldn't remember! Legs and arms pumped him deeper into the tunnel as crackling sparks of cruel laughter gained on him. The monster's beam of light could not see him yet, his dark clothing morphing him into the nothingness. A grinding, pulsating sound of metal on metal. Arms flailing, he felt his coordination begin to fail. Always so strong, always so capable, and fit and young.

Young. Yes, he was. He remembered that. And voices from the past—echoing in his head. *Never give up. Keep going. You're one of the fittest boys here, Danny.* Danny! That was his name. He was too young to die. He knew this as surely as he knew that the blackness suffocating him was now the beginning of the end. Blood began to seep from his eyes, nose and ears. Like the tears of a clown, it dripped down his cheeks.

He fell forward, and in those two seconds it took before he hit the ground, lightning flashed behind his eyes and a rippling wave of enormous power reached up to him from the blackness, pulling him to his death. His muscles loosened; the coarse brown envelope he had been clutching fell from his fingers. His body jerked convulsively as the power surged through him.

The approaching London Underground train's impetus created a vacuum that sucked air out of the tubelike tunnel. Rubbish scattered. Old crisp packets and a brown envelope addressed to Max Gordon at Dartmoor High School tumbled and fluttered their way to the platform.

The train shuddered over the unseen body now lying to one side of the electrified line, but the boy felt no pain or fear. He had already sunk into the vortex of death.

The brain worm had finally eaten its way through his skull.

A black Range Rover purred down the rain-slicked strip of tarmac, over gorse hills and around granite tors. As it crested each rise, the onrushing clouds skimmed above the roof of the vehicle. Hard rain pebbled against the windscreen as the road dipped and twisted through the folded hills. The driver wore black denim jeans that crumpled onto suede desert boots. A dark-blue T-shirt hid beneath a hooded sweatshirt that sported a San Francisco 49ers logo, and the leather jacket had cost a lot of money. Half-gloved hands teased the steering wheel round a snaking bend as the big Rover squeezed across an ancient bridge. Swirling copper-colored water, rich with peat, churned below the supports, threatening to spill onto the road. He pressed the accelerator; the four-wheel-drive pulled power effortlessly from the V8 engine, and a whiff of steam hissed from the spray that slashed against the exhaust.

"Godforsaken place," said his companion, a man similarly dressed, of similar age and in exactly the same profession. He shifted in his seat, the 9 mm semiautomatic catching his ribs. He eased the pressure.

The two men seldom spoke. Training and a natural tendency to stay silent meant their brains weren't picking up pieces of useless flotsam to make small talk. The driver said nothing. He liked the bleakness of Dartmoor, the shifting light and the threatening power of nature that could catch the unprepared and kill them. Nature could be as efficient a killer as he. Besides, years ago, he had trained for many long months in conditions like these, being tested beyond his limit. It was a trial he had relished and overcome. He reckoned that the boys who attended Dartmoor High had that same instinct.

Weighted with rain, the clouds sucked any light from the sky. The road twisted across the side of a hill, rose up, and there in the far distance, barely visible between darkened earth and impenetrable sky, was a building hewn from granite.

A Victorian fortress held by claws of black rock. Once a harsh prison constructed on the remains of Rome's XX Legion's outpost, it had housed the criminally insane, but the wardens had been unable to stand the terrifying nights of banshee winds and the tormented cries of the incarcerated.

It had been converted into a school a hundred years ago—a place where a boy's intelligence was challenged as much by the no-nonsense education as by the demands of physical pursuits. With commanding views, the place was a solitary image of unyielding steadfastness in the face of the storms nature threw at it.

The driver smiled. No wonder the boy who died in the tunnel had given them such a long, hard chase. He had been from Dartmoor High.

Fergus Jackson, the headmaster, stood in the tiled entrance hall. Crumpled corduroy trousers, a rough knitted sweater over a checked shirt and a stout pair of hiking boots gave him the appearance of a moorland farmer. Callused hands would pull through a shock of gray horse-mane hair in a troubled response to any question he was uncertain how to answer—or when he wanted to buy time. It made him come across as a bit of a bumbler. Whoever thought that did not know Fergus Jackson. This was his smoke screen while he assessed those in his presence—what he was doing right now with the two men who stepped into the entrance hall as he closed the oak doors behind them.

He had observed them from his study window before answering the insistent doorbell. Two young men. Fit, strong. They moved almost lazily. Short-cropped hair and rough stubble on their faces. They ignored the flurries of rain when they stepped down from the Range Rover.

As he ushered them inside, he took in their every movement and gesture, saw their eyes scan the school's entrance hall, watched as they turned back and caught each other's gaze—a quick look that said each had checked the place with a professional eye.

"Sorry it took me a while to get to the door—it's half-term. We've only a few teaching staff around, and the boys who are still here probably made a determined effort to ignore the doorbell. I'm Fergus Jackson. Headmaster here. Though I'm supposed to say 'head teacher' these days. We haven't quite caught up with political correctness. All a bit silly, really, isn't it?"

Another glance between the men. They'd get the information they needed from this old dinosaur without too much trouble. Mr. Jackson extended his hand in greeting. Each of the men shook it. Neither took off his half-fingered leather gloves.

Ill-mannered, Jackson decided. Men who don't care what people think of them. He saw the band of skin under one man's wrist, between glove and sleeve. A tattoo, three words, but only one word of the three was visible; the others were fragments: . . . nnia—*Velvollisuus*—*Tah* . . .

"We don't get many visitors out here. Are you lost?" Mr. Jackson asked innocently.

The man who had stepped down from the driver's side of the Range Rover pulled out a small leather wallet.

"Mr. Jackson, sorry to disturb you. My name is Stanton

and this is Drew." There was a hint of an accent. Mr. Jackson couldn't place it, but he guessed the man had spent some time in the Nordic countries.

Stanton flipped the wallet open and handed it to Mr. Jackson, who patted his chest for his spectacles, thrust his hand beneath his sweater and pulled out the glasses from his breast pocket. The men waited as he scanned the identity card.

"Security Service? MI-Five?"

The driver smiled and took back his warrant card. As he returned it to his inside pocket, his jacket eased back, exposing the speed-rig shoulder holster and the semiautomatic that nestled against his ribs. The black nylon clamshell gripped the body of the weapon, allowing a fast draw when needed.

"We're here to make inquiries about a former pupil, Danny Maguire. The boy who died on the London Underground a couple of days ago?"

"Yes, tragic. Absolutely tragic," Mr. Jackson said. The television news images of ambulance and rescue crews as they recovered Maguire's body replayed themselves in his mind's eye.

"We think he might have been trying to contact one of the boys here. A Max Gordon," said Drew.

No foreign accent here. British. Southeast England.

"Really? I see. Well, perhaps we should go through to my study," Mr. Jackson said. He stepped to one side, aiming his arm toward the left-hand side of the corridor that ran each side of the main staircase. A couple of boys pounded down the stairs. Mr. Jackson shouted, "Boys! Come here!"

Obediently they slowed their exuberant descent. "Just because you are here during term break does not give you the right to behave as if you were at home." He took one of the boys by a shoulder and turned him to face the two men. "Morris, take these two gentlemen to my study, and put a log on the fire while you're at it."

Mr. Jackson smiled apologetically at the two men. "I have to speak to this other boy while I have him at my mercy. Morris here will show you the way, and I'll be right behind you. Just a minute or so. Off you go, Morris."

The two men were momentarily caught off guard, but there was no reason for them to be suspicious, so they followed the boy. As they stepped away, they heard Mr. Jackson raise his voice as he castigated the younger boy. "I have told you, time and time again, that this kind of behavior will not be tolerated at Dartmoor High. You are going to learn one way or the other, or I will speak to your mother!"

A heavy door closed behind the men as Morris took them farther down the corridor. Mr. Jackson immediately lowered his voice and held Sayid Khalif's shoulders squarely.

"Sayid, listen to me. In five minutes I want you to phone my study from Matron's office. Say one of the boys has cut himself and that Matron wants me to have a look. Got it?"

Sayid nodded.

"I'll put you on speaker phone so they can hear. And get down to the mailroom and see if there's anything waiting for Max. If there is—hide it!"

With that final command, Mr. Jackson turned and walked quickly toward his study. Sayid knew Mr. Jackson must have a very good reason to make such a strange request. Something was wrong, and his best mate, Max Gordon, was in trouble. Again.

Torchlight cut through the darkness of the moor. Soldiers. A hunter group was after Max. Wind-whipped rain would help his escape, but now he lay absolutely still. The men were barely visible in the darkness; camouflage-pattern clothing broke up their silhouettes, and the mist and rain that swirled in and out of the gullies made them half-seen specters. But now they were getting closer, quartering the ground—a methodical search pattern. Max had watched them for the latter part of the day, saw them start wide a kilometer away and gradually tighten the search zone until it was barely a two-hundred-meter semicircle. The net was closing.

Max shivered. He'd give anything for a hot drink right now. That would improve his energy, take the cramp from his aching muscles and boost his morale. He had barely slept for two days. Always on the move, aware that others had already been trapped and caught, he had slithered his way through gorse, heather and mud, keeping a low profile, remembering tips his father had given him over the years: *If you're being hunted, stay below the skyline. Move at night. No fires, no torches. The tiniest speck of light can be seen for miles. And if you want the best chance to stay undetected, crawl into the biggest thornbush or the dirtiest, smelliest place you can find.*

Well, Max hadn't found a thornbush, but on the first night, he had come across a sheepfold scooped out of the ground, high on the moor. It was a bitterly cold night, exposed to the northwest wind that howled in from the coast. The small, half-walled stone shelter was virtually invisible to the naked eye. It stank of sheep droppings, which the rain had turned into slurry. Max had secured one edge of a ground-sheet under the wall's top stone, laid rocks on the other, laid a smaller sheet in the sludge underneath, then crawled into this shelter inside his lightweight sleeping bag. The place reeked of sheep urine, but he felt sure that if the hunter group had tracker dogs, this stench would throw them off his scent.

He hadn't cooked a meal since he'd escaped from the army truck when this whole thing started, but had lived off dried fruit and water. Hunger would play a role in his survival, and he needed to keep the gnawing pangs at bay. If you knew where to look, *Lathyrus linifolius*—known locally as heath pea—would be invaluable. Max had gone straight to a shaded area of moss and heather, where the small tubers grew about ten centimeters belowground, and scrabbled beneath the thin surface of turf. He ate the tubers raw. They tasted bitter and smelled of licorice, but they were an appetite suppressant, which would halt his body's craving for food.

The first two days saw him cover the most distance in avoiding the patrols, but then, as others were captured—a flare lit the sky every time one was taken—more troops came into the area to hunt for survivors. Max had covered more than fifteen kilometers over difficult terrain the previous day, and that night he saw a light flicker far across a valley. Another boy had succumbed and risked a hot meal. Max waited, lying shivering in the wet. Sure enough, the smell of food drifted across the valley. He watched, unmoving, staring intently into the darkness, searching out every sway of grass and heather, certain he could see shadows emerging from the deep gorse. Max's instincts felt as though they sat on his skin—an animal waiting for the least vibration to alert him to danger.

And then a shout and a parachute flare shot into the blustery sky—it swung crazily in the wind, drunk with success.

How many of those being pursued like Max were left out there? He didn't care. He was going to survive. After the sheepfold hideout, he set off before dawn and jogged along animal tracks, scars in the heather—uneven underfoot, but a good way to put distance between himself and those giving chase. The gorse needles covered the tracks at shin height, and they pierced his lightweight cotton trousers, pricking his skin, but they also stopped anyone seeing his footprints. Now, at the end of the third day, he ran on a bearing, zigzagging across the open moor, using his compass.

Dartmoor was notorious for its rainfall. Bogs and mires dotted the landscape. Water squelched underfoot, seeping down a grassy hillside. There was a crawl space beneath a slab of granite resting on a smaller rock, like a smaller cist—one of the ancient boxlike burial chambers that dotted prehistoric settlements on the moor.

Five hundred meters up the hill behind him was a cairn and a trig point. With the absence of any prominent structures, such as church towers, on the open moor, Ordnance Survey trigonometric stations were built, short concrete pillars used as map references. Max didn't need his compass for that one. When dawn came, he would have a clear line of sight toward Dartmoor High and would find the most concealed route home.

After three days of living rough and being chased by these hardened soldiers, he ached and shivered whenever he stopped running.

Now they were almost on him.

Max squirmed through the mud; if he got up and ran, he could be out of sight for at least two minutes—that was all he needed. He flung his groundsheet across the gorse and secured it by twisting bungees at each corner round the roots, ignoring the wasplike stings of the gorse needles on his hands. Water seeped into his already sodden cargo pants as he crawled under, reached in and dropped his beta light. Its dull glow barely registered, but it would draw the soldiers like moths to a flame.

He could already hear their labored breathing.

Max left his kit and leopard-crawled down a sluice. It was an animal track barely as wide as his body, probably a badger or a fox run, and the ferns and gorse offered a low canopy of concealment—provided he stayed down. As he dug knees and elbows into the ground, fear gushed through him. In those few moments, he felt a huge sympathy for animals pursued to their deaths by huntsmen.

"There he is!" a voice cried.

Max stopped, holding his breath. Boots crushed the ground to the left, less than a meter from his face, and then to the right. He wriggled forward, almost between the two men, who saw nothing because they were focused on the dull glow up ahead. The wind shook fern and gorse, and another squall whipped rain across their vision.

"Come on out, boy! It's over!"

The voices were behind him now, and the torchlight

scanned the area he had drawn them to. Like slimy sewage, animal droppings and fouled water slithered under his clothes; his shins scraped rock, and his arms caught sharp-edged gorse sticks—he ignored it. Time to break cover.

Shadows loomed.

They had trapped him!

The men with the torches were the distraction; like any good hunter group, they had a second ring of men behind the first. They were the outer defense—and they didn't use torches.

Max barreled into the dark bulk of one of them. The man cried out, swore, kicked and squirmed and grabbed Max's ankle. Max couldn't recover; someone else pinioned him, and his breath got knocked out of him. Something deep inside him exploded, a surge of power; an animal cry echoed through his mind as he gulped air and twisted free, slamming a third man in the chest as he leapt like a wolf.

Then he was gone into the storm with long, open strides, feet barely touching the ground, carrying him into the darkness.

2

"We seem to be out of chocolate biscuits," Mr. Jackson apologized as he poured hot water into cups. "And it's only instant, I'm afraid," he said, handing the scalding mugs of coffee to the two men. He wanted them out of his school as soon as possible and had no intention of making them comfortable. "Now, where's the sugar? I'm sure these boys sneak in here and help themselves."

The two MI5 officers were in no mood for hospitality either. Stanton cursed under his breath as the hot liquid spilled. "We're hoping Max Gordon can help us with information," he said testily.

"I have to say," Mr. Jackson said quietly, "that I don't quite understand how the suicide of a former pupil on the London Underground can involve either this country's Security Service or Max Gordon. Danny Maguire left here when he was eighteen, and that was well over a year ago, closer to two, in fact. He certainly hasn't been in contact with anyone here, as far as I know."

Drew quietly inhaled to ease his impatience. This was supposed to be a straightforward "get in, check the kid and get out" inquiry. And here they were, sitting in overstuffed chairs in front of a blazing log fire in a room crammed with so many books it looked like a country-house library. Fergus Jackson seemed to have a cozy number here, probably whiling away his days until retirement. Soft, cosseted academics. What did they know about the real world?

"Police agencies in South America picked up a flagged word a few months ago during a regular intel sweep of Internet traffic," he said.

"Intel?" Mr. Jackson asked, looking perplexed, knowing full well what the word meant.

"Intelligence," Stanton replied. "Look, Mr. Jackson. This is just a routine inquiry. If we could just speak to Max Gordon . . ."

"I wish I could help, I really do, but he's on holiday. Half-term. He's not here. He went to Italy with a friend and his parents," Mr. Jackson lied. "But what kind of intelligence?" he asked, trying to momentarily divert interest away from Max.

The man answered patiently, humoring Jackson, not wishing to appear too eager to get to Max Gordon. "We think Danny Maguire might have been involved in drug smuggling."

"Rubbish!" Mr. Jackson couldn't hold back his incredulity. "Maguire? The boy barely took a headache pill when he was here."

"I didn't say he was taking drugs but that he might have been trafficking them. So, if we could at least have a look at Gordon's room?"

"Of course. What a shocking business. We will endeavor to assist your inquiries as far as possible. Drug smuggling. Who'd have thought it?"

The men stood in anticipation, pleased at last to get past this dithering idiot of a headmaster. The phone rang. Mr. Jackson raised a hand to settle them back down again. He pressed a button. "Yes?"

"It's Khalif, sir," Sayid's voice said into the room.

"I'm very busy on important business, boy. I don't want to be disturbed. What is it?"

"Matron says that Harry Clark has cut his foot on broken glass."

"Well, tell her to deal with it. I'm not a doctor. It's what we pay her for," Mr. Jackson said, convincingly grumpy.

"She said you might have to call an ambulance."

"Oh, for heaven's sake! Very well, I'll be right there."

Mr. Jackson ended the call. "This'll take only a minute," he said apologetically. "There are some macaroons in that jar. Do help yourselves."

Moments later he lifted the phone receiver in the staff room and patted Sayid's shoulder as the boy reported back. "Nothing for Max in the mailroom, sir."

"Well done. Go and check his room. Make sure there's no recent mail there. If there is, hide it in your room. And take his laptop as well. Be quick."

Sayid closed the door behind him as Mr. Jackson dialed a number. The soft voice of a pupil's father responded.

"Ridgeway."

"Bob, it's Fergus. I need your help."

Robert Ridgeway was a senior man in Britain's Security Service, and his youngest son excelled at just about everything at Dartmoor High. He knew the value of Fergus Jackson's care for his charges, and a phone call from him was not something to be taken lightly. He listened to Jackson's requests, asked him to wait a moment and in less than a minute came back with definitive answers.

There was no known investigation into the death of the Maguire boy by MI5 and no record of any intel on his Internet traffic. As Fergus already knew, officers often dressed scruffily if they were working undercover, so the men's appearance hadn't aroused any suspicion, but there were no field operatives by the name of Stanton or Drew. Even if they had been what they'd said, MI5 officers did not have any personal choice of handguns, certainly not the kind of heavy-caliber chromed weapons Fergus had described. And the tattooed name, *Velvollisuus*? Ridgeway had never heard of it, but it sounded Eastern European, possibly Russian. He would check. In the meantime, he would alert the local police firearms unit to get to the school. These two men were clearly impostors.

"No, don't do that, Bob. I don't want armed police here; that might escalate the situation. I'll get rid of these people. I'll get their number plate and pass that on so you can check it," Jackson said.

"As you wish. And what about Max Gordon? Is he in danger?"

Like a huge firework, the mortar flare rocketed into the sky. It burst with a fluttering crackle, and despite the gusting conditions, it would be seen for miles, which was the intention.

Max watched. The road—a curved snake of wet tarmac that led to the soldiers' assembly point—was clear. Half a dozen army lorries and a hot-food wagon were parked as forty or so soldiers stamped their feet, pleased the whole thing was over as they lined up for hot stew and a mug of tea. Mobile arc lamps flooded light across the men.

He was so close to them he could hear their banter, the crackle of their radios and their slurping of tea.

A good hunter would stalk his prey as near as he could, and Max had wanted this final hour to test himself. How close could he get to the men who had hunted him for the past three days without being seen? Max had broken the outline of his body by snapping off gorse and fern, jamming it into his shirt and belt and the tops of his boots. With stealth and patience, he crawled ever closer, past soldiers who moved across the perimeter, around men whose legs were so close he could have reached out and touched them.

Finally he stood up from the gorse cover, barely five meters from the officer in charge, who carried a clipboard and had a radio operator at his side. Max's body was covered in slime, his clothing was sodden and his hair matted with something disgusting. His eyes were red-rimmed from lack of sleep and flecks of dirt. And he stank.

The officer was momentarily taken by surprise at the

apparition that emerged from the bogland. Then he smiled. "Lads! He's here!"

The soldiers jeered and cheered, shouted insults and encouragement—all meant to welcome the boy as he pulled the bits of camouflage free.

"You took your time!"

"Don't stand upwind, mate!"

"We almost had you."

"Look what the cat dragged in."

"The Creature from the Black Lagoon."

"You're not coming in my lorry smelling like that!"

The flare had been the signal that the exercise had ended. Escape and Evasion, the paras and special forces called it. Cast adrift out on the moor without any means of shelter, food, money or weapons and issued with the most basic clothing, potential recruits were dropped off to be hunted down and captured. Then they would face another two days of intense physical and mental interrogation. Thankfully they didn't do that with the schoolboys and girls who had passed the tests to get on to this exercise. And they allowed them basic rations and groundsheets for shelter. Only five schools in the country could compete, and Dartmoor High had always had an entrant. All schools wanting to participate had to have competed in the annual Ten Tors competition, administered by the army, where four hundred teams of six teenagers would face the grueling task of marching for two days, anything up to seventy kilometers between the ten nominated Tors. Those teenagers had to be determined and self-sufficient. Backup teams of the army, Royal Navy and Royal Air Force were always on hand to help.

But despite the Escape and Evasion exercise taking place in a demarcated area, this challenge was tougher. You were treated as the enemy and hunted down. And the colder it got and the more exhausted the competitors became, the more real it seemed. On the run, in enemy territory. Even hardened soldiers had died out here on the moor, and it was a huge risk for youngsters—they were on their own, no one else in a group to help if they got injured or lost. On the third night, at 2100 hours, the survivors *had* to report to this assembly point.

That was what the mortar flare meant. ENDEX—end of exercise. If anyone was left out there and didn't report, then a major search and rescue would be undertaken within the hour. But so far all had been captured. Only one boy came in under his own steam.

The last survivor.

Max Gordon.

Stanton and Drew looked through Max's room while Mr. Jackson stood in the doorway. They made little fuss and barely disturbed anything. The room was small. There was a bed, a small table that doubled as a desk, a bookshelf and a small trunk for bits and pieces. On the shelf were a few artifacts Max's explorer-scientist father had sent him over the years. A Cook Island figurine, a rock crystal from the Himalayas, an amber teardrop from Russia that was a hundred million years old.

"Do you know where he'd keep his computer?" Drew asked, breaking Mr. Jackson's thoughts of faraway lands.

"He would have taken it on holiday with him. You said

you have already checked Maguire's emails—is there any evidence that he sent any to Gordon?" Jackson asked.

"No," Drew said, and gave a reassuring smile. "We just wanted to double-check. We think Maguire might have sent him something in the post."

"In the post? That's a bit unusual for his generation. Text, email and network sites are what they all use nowadays. Must say I can't quite get the hang of it myself."

"Still, if he had received something in the post, it'd be here, right?" Stanton asked.

"Absolutely. The boy's been away for a few days, so anything delivered would be on his table or his bed. When might it have been sent, do you think? The last few days? Before, or even on the day of Maguire's death?"

"Yeah. Probably," Stanton said.

"Is it a letter you're looking for? You never said," Jackson asked.

"A letter? Have you seen one?" Drew queried.

Jackson shook his head. "No, but if poor Maguire took his own life, I was wondering if it might have been a suicide note. Something to explain why he did what he did. Danny Maguire was such an articulate and positive-minded boy— if he was so distressed as to take his own life, I feel sure he would have explained himself. His death really is a shocking mystery."

The two men didn't answer right away. Jackson had asked the most obvious question. "No," Stanton said, "we don't think it would be a suicide note."

"But one wasn't found?"

"No."

"Nothing on his body?"

"No, we made sure."

"You were there, then? You examined his body yourself? Or would that have been the police who checked for that? So what is it you're looking for?"

Stanton hesitated. Jackson had gleaned quite a bit of information without their realizing it at first. He had learned that in all probability, they had had Maguire under observation; otherwise, how would they have identified the fact that he had something to post? They had also admitted to scanning his emails. They might well have been close to the boy at or soon after the time of his death, because had there been a suicide note, they would have found it. Maybe Jackson wasn't as dithering as the men had thought.

"We're not sure—maybe a small package," Stanton said.

"Then it would have been put in here, and as you can see, there's nothing. But why don't we go and check the mailroom to make sure?" Mr. Jackson said helpfully.

From his room, Sayid watched Mr. Jackson escort them downstairs.

They moved lightly, their bodies trained for fast reactions. Sayid had seen men like them before and they scared him.

A medic wrapped a space blanket around Max, and an army cook shoved a mess tin full of stew into his hands. Max suddenly realized just how chilled he was. Blowing briefly on each spoonful, he shoveled the food into his mouth as fast as he could. The warmth seeped down to his frozen toes as if someone had turned on a hot-water tap inside his body.

"We need to check your feet, Max, make sure there's no trench foot," the officer said. "Then we'll get you back to Dartmoor High."

"I know how to look after my feet, sir," he spluttered through the stew.

"I'm sure you do. But we're going to check anyway." The major nodded to the medic, and Max sat down obediently on a haybox, used for keeping food hot in the field, and allowed the medic to haul off his boots.

"They're a bit mank," Max apologized for the squelching, black-water-soaked socks.

"Mank? We could use these as a secret weapon, son." The medic smiled.

A soldier shouted in the background. "Can you go around us, mate? Unless you don't want to get mud on your nice car!"

Soldiers laughed. Max and the others turned. A black Range Rover had come down the tarmac strip and was unable to negotiate the army vehicles that were reversing and forming up for the return to barracks.

Drew grimaced as he watched the narrow gap Stanton was edging them through. "What the hell is this? Army maneuvers are the last thing we need. They're not supposed to be in this area," he said.

Stanton weaved the big 4x4 through the obstructing lorries, Land Rovers and trailers. "Relax, they don't have weapons. This is something else."

Max saw the men in the Range Rover give a thumbs-up

and nod to the gathered soldiers; then the driver turned the steering wheel and went effortlessly off-road.

"Let him through," the officer instructed the pockets of men as the beast of a vehicle edged toward them. It passed within a couple of meters.

Stanton concentrated on avoiding the paraphernalia but caught sight of a bog-soaked kid wrapped in a space blanket. He looked as though he'd been pulled out of a sludge pit. Shivering, barefoot and clutching a mess tin of food, the boy looked wretched in the glaring floodlights. Except for his eyes. They seemed to bore straight through him.

"Must have been some kind of rescue operation," Drew said. "These kids are so dumb. They have no idea how dangerous places like this are."

Stanton got a clear run, then gunned the V8 engine, and the black beast made short work of the difficult ground.

Max watched it power away across the moor and then disappear from view. It was unusual to see anyone out here at this time of night. They weren't tourists; that was for sure. Maybe they were bonus-heavy stock traders from London on their way to a shooting weekend, but the way the driver had handled the heavy 4x4 showed a subtle skill. Most city people had no idea how to drive off-road. So, who were they? And what were they doing all the way out here? Max's natural curiosity teased him. Maybe he should stop being suspicious of anything that seemed out of place, he told himself. *But maybe recognizing the out-of-place is what survival is all about,* his thoughts answered.

* * *

Sayid was in Jackson's study. The door closed firmly behind him. Were there any letters anywhere for Max? Satisfied there were not, Jackson gave Sayid strict instructions not to mention the intrigue of the men who had visited.

As if.

Mr. Jackson would decide when to tell Max.

Yeah. OK.

Did Sayid understand?

Of course he did. What? He wasn't going to tell his best friend everything the moment he laid eyes on him? Maybe Mr. Jackson had never been young.

"You've done extremely well, Max," Mr. Jackson said as the major delivered his soggy charge back to Dartmoor High. "Away with you now and sluice off that muck. Are you hungry?"

Despite the army stew, Max's stomach felt like a punctured football. "Starving, sir."

"Right. We'll rustle something up once you're in a more civilized condition. Off you go."

The major shook hands with Max. "Well done, son. I bet your parents will be proud of you."

He didn't catch the flicker in the boy's eye. Max's dad, Tom, was in a specialist nursing home, unable to distinguish between dream and reality. Max was desperate to see and speak to him. There were tough questions that needed answering, but he could do that only when the nursing home contacted Mr. Jackson. It had to be the right time for a visit—

a time when the father might recognize his own son. Mr. Jackson understood. He saw Max's momentary hesitation and gave him a brief nod of encouragement.

"Thanks, sir," Max said to the major. "It was great fun, but I'm glad it wasn't for real."

He squelched up the granite stairs. He heard Mr. Jackson offer a nightcap to the major, who declined, saying he needed to get his men back to barracks.

Sayid peered round the balustrade, careful not to be seen by Jackson.

"Hey!" he whispered urgently as Max reached the top of the stairs. He quickly fell into step down the long corridor that led to their rooms. "There's been some really spooky stuff going on! What *have* you been rolling in? Anyway, something's up, but I'm not sure what yet. All I know is these two men came here, really tough-looking blokes, and Jacko was acting like he was in the end-of-year play. He's not exactly Johnny Depp, but he had them convinced."

"Me? I'm fine. Hundred percent. Oh, did I mention I was the last one to stay out there, so I won the competition? Thanks for asking, Sayid."

"All right, keep your shirt on. Well, perhaps not. You know you're gonna have to burn your kit. You'll clog the washing machines with sludge."

"Sayid, stop beating around the bush and let me shower, get some nosh and sleep for a week."

"Who's Danny Maguire?"

"Why?" Max became immediately more alert.

"*That's* what I've been trying to *tell* you. He's dead."

*   *   *

Grime sluiced away around Max's feet. The hot water pum-
meled his muscles. He stood in the shower, head down,
watching the muck swirl and disappear down the drain.
Scratches and abrasions stung, but the pain helped drive
away the numbness he felt after hearing about Danny's
death—and made Max feel alive. Very alive and very anx-
ious. Max's heart had gone up a gear. Had Maguire sent him
something? Sayid hadn't known much about the details other
than that those men were looking for a letter or a packet. But
where was it? Maybe he hadn't managed to post it before he'd
died. If he had, how many days for it to get here? Danny
Maguire's death shocked him, because Max's instincts yelled
at him that it was not suicide, as Sayid had said.

Maguire had been murdered.

Max's thoughts swirled like the water. Was he being irrational? There was no evidence that Danny had been murdered. Sayid had told him there had been no mention of
violence. No one had raised any alarms—except Max's gut
feeling, which told him otherwise.

Max had barely known Danny Maguire when he was still
at Dartmoor High. He was four years older and a senior boy.
Almost two years ago, he had left for an extended field-
experience trip in Central and South America before contin-
uing his studies at university in England, where he hoped to
graduate as a forensic anthropologist—digging up the past
and finding the truth behind ancient civilizations and the way
their people had died. Max hadn't known any of this until
quite recently, when he'd delved into Danny's background

26

after receiving an email from him that promised the only real lead to finding out the truth behind Max's mother's death. Danny had answered Max's cry for help over the Internet. A hundred others had plagued Max's alias mailbox—eagle@ high-tor.co.uk—that he had set up on a server, but this one meant something.

A cryptic message. Of no interest to anyone—unless they were deliberately looking for it.

Eagle. Dr. HG. Something unusual. Have last known location. Will be in London, 1 month. Will contact. Wolfman

One email out of hundreds and it had taken his breath away. It could have been from anyone or anywhere, but its source was an ex-Dartmoor pupil.

There were four houses at Dartmoor High: Otter, Badger, Eagle and Wolf. Max belonged to Eagle House, and when he'd first arrived at the school and found his natural ability to compete in long-distance races across the moor, one older boy had stood head and shoulders, both physically and academically, above the others. Danny Maguire. He could have been an Olympic runner, but he had planned a life of adventure. Two years later and Maguire had grown a beard, and that, combined with his long hair, amazing running abilities and position as head boy of Wolf House, earned him the sobriquet of Wolfman.

Dr. HG was Helen Gordon, Max's mum.

Max's father had met Max's mother in South America, where she had been researching environmental damage caused by illegal logging in the rain forests. Tom and Helen

Gordon both had reputations for fearlessness. Their integrity made them many enemies. They and the privately funded organization they worked for challenged governments to reassess their environmental credentials and forced many companies that endangered the environment to close. Max's parents were known and respected by everyone associated with science and ecology. These brave, pioneering troubleshooters were quietly acknowledged as being at the forefront of the fight against corruption. But four years ago, Max's mum had died in the Central American rain forest. His father had barely spoken of it, other than to explain to Max that she had fallen ill and that they had been so isolated he could not reach help in time to save her. His father's pain seemed even deeper than his own, and their shared grief brought father and son emotionally closer together. Until Tom Gordon's closest and best friend, Angelo Farentino, betrayed him.

Max had recently been caught up in a violent conflict in the French Alps, and fate had brought him face to face with Farentino. The Judas bargained for his life when Max could have abandoned him to a cruel death in the desolate mountains. Max could see his face, hear his screams as Farentino begged the boy to save him.

Your mother! I know how she died. How she really died!

The memory inflicted the same cutting pain now as when he had first heard the bitter accusations.

She died alone, Max, because your father saved himself! And he can't live with the shame! Why do you think he stuck you away in that boarding school? Why do you see so little of him? WHY? Because he ran and left her to die! He knows he killed your mother!

"No!" Max yelled, unable to keep the shout of denial in his head.

Was it the hot water or the tears that stung his eyes? He slid down the shower wall and sat huddled, arms round his knees.

Max had endured a lot of violence when he'd tried to save his father in Africa. Now the tormented whisperings of his mind—that his dad, whom he loved so much, might have betrayed them both by lying to him and abandoning his mother to die—was a poison eating away his insides.

Max stayed hunched until the racking sobs and tears ended; then he washed the snot from his face and turned off the shower.

The open window allowed steam to escape. Cold air prickled his skin. He didn't mind. He felt better now. Cleansed of the moor's grime. Emptied of self-pity. Stronger.

He needed food and sleep.

Then to find out if his dad had really lied to him.

And why Danny Maguire had been killed.

3

Max fell asleep at the long, scrubbed table in the school's kitchen before he'd finished his meal. Fergus Jackson left him where he sprawled, threw an old multicolored blanket from his study over the boy and let him be.

He'd been relieved when Max had volunteered to take part in the Dartmoor exercise when an older boy could not compete due to an injury, because Max Gordon had started behaving erratically. His temper was short, his attitude often sullen. Jackson knew teenagers got like that: all part of "growing into your skin" is what he told them. But this was something different. Max was carrying a burden, and he wasn't sharing it. It was probably something to do with his injured father.

Sayid Khalif and Max were as thick as thieves, but Jackson's questioning of Sayid had yielded nothing to explain Max's recent behavior. And Jackson suspected that Max Gordon had not shared whatever was bothering him with even his best friend.

"Get your elbows off the table, bog rat!" A boot kicked the chair and Max tumbled onto the floor. He rolled instinctively, protecting his head, and quickly found his balance.

Baskins!

The older boy grinned—it was what he would have done to his best mate, Hoggart, if he'd been there instead of Max. But Hoggart's parents had dragged away their protesting son to spend time together on a stupid holiday, on a beach somewhere abroad where there was nothing, absolutely nothing, to do. Baskins had managed to avert a similar fate with his family and had opted to spend the half-term at Dartmoor High, where at least there were enough boys remaining for seven-a-side.

"Don't bog rats' mothers teach them table manners?" Baskins teased as he raided the fridge, foraging for breakfast.

Sometimes when you open your mouth and say something, the warning bells don't ring loudly or quickly enough. Baskins just about managed a look of regret before Max's lunge took the heavier boy rolling across the kitchen floor. Pans clattered. The big milk jug on the table couldn't resist gravity and shattered on the stone floor. A chair splintered.

Max straddled Baskins's chest, twisting his rugby shirt in a double grip that threatened to choke him. Baskins was stronger than Max, but he couldn't kick free. Giddying splodges of light blurred his vision. He was starting to black out. Spittle rattled in his throat; his eyes were bulging. He hit Max on the side of the head with his fist. It made no impression.

Max Gordon was going to kill him!

Fergus Jackson burst in, grabbing one of Max's arms as Mr. Roberts, the sports master, held the other.

"Max! Enough! Let go, Max!" Jackson shouted. For a moment, they could not loosen his grip, and Max shot a look at him, which sent a shudder through Jackson. Something other than rage and intent glinted in Max's eyes—it was as if a wild animal had been snared and was about to fight for its life.

Then Max eased his grip slightly, Jackson's commands breaking through his blinding haze of anger. Between them, Jackson and Roberts hauled Max off the gasping boy.

Max crouched, ready to attack. Jackson was scared. He had never seen Max behave in such an uncontrolled, aggressive manner. No one moved; then Roberts put himself between Max and Baskins, a warning hand raised.

"Enough!" Roberts shouted.

"Max," Jackson said more quietly. "Max, it's all right, boy. It's all right." They could see Max physically relax and come out of whatever zone he'd been in. He nodded.

"Sorry, Baskins," he said dutifully, but the look he gave Baskins as he left the room allowed no doubt in anyone's mind that the fight had been stopped just in time.

"What did you say to him?" Jackson asked.

"Nothing, sir. Well, I just gave him a poke to wake him up and asked if his mother hadn't taught him any manners." He pulled a face. "I forgot about his mum."

*　*　*

Max walked down the corridor with Mr. Jackson. He really
hadn't wanted to apologize, but his parents' influence and his
own sense of shame pushed those feelings aside. His dad had
always told him that only unthinking thugs attacked without
provocation. Baskins mentioning his mum seemed perfect
justification to Max, though he knew it wasn't. Besides, he
hadn't wanted to let Mr. Jackson down.

"Apology accepted," Mr. Jackson said. "Do you want to
talk about it?"

"I don't think so, sir."

"All right. Well, you know you can whenever you wish."

Max nodded.

Mr. Jackson pulled a coat from a long row of hooks.
"Come on, let's get some fresh air."

Max grabbed his jacket and followed Mr. Jackson, who
had already pulled open the side door to the cobbled yards at
the back of the school. It was ear-nippingly cold, but the various outbuildings broke the wind's direct assault.

"I want to tell you something, Max, and I don't want to be
interrupted while I do so."

Max waited. Jackson looked as though he was about to
break bad news. "One of our ex-pupils died a few days ago.
His name was Danny Maguire."

Max had to fake it: "Sorry to hear that, sir." He listened as
Jackson recounted the visit by the MI5 impostors. Was Max
in trouble? Was there any connection between Maguire,
these men and Max? Did he know anything about drug smuggling? Max denied all knowledge of anything Jackson asked

him. Telling the truth might hinder his investigation into what had really happened to his mother—and why Maguire had died.

"And you have received nothing in the post from Maguire?"

"Like what, sir?" Max said, hoping Jackson might know something more.

"I don't know. Anyway, I shall be speaking to the police about this matter, so think hard and long about whether there is anything that might tell us who those men were. I'm not at all sure what's going on. Now, don't take this the wrong way, but I want you to stay in school for a couple of weeks."

"Like a prisoner, sir?"

"Only until I have some answers. I appreciate that your life is not how you would like it to be, but you have good friends here, and I hope you know that all the staff, myself included, hold you in the highest regard."

Max nodded. There was no denying that Dartmoor High had become his home. There was nowhere else for him to be.

Mr. Jackson put a fatherly arm on the boy's shoulder. "If I can arrange it, would you like to speak to your father on the phone?"

He was surprised to see a look of doubt touch Max's face. The boy idolized his father.

"Yes, sir. Thank you." He knew he had to speak to his dad soon—in fact, he really needed to see him—but he was dreading it.

"I'll see what I can do. All right, Max. Off you go."

Max's dad had endured mind-wrecking torture at the hands of a madman in Africa. The fist of trepidation thumped into Max's stomach at the thought of challenging his own father, who had become a stranger with only fleeting moments of recognition of his son. Max would confront him to dig out the truth from his mind, as a firefighter digs through the rubble to save a victim's life. Max needed to know everything about his mother's death.

He left Mr. Jackson wandering around the courtyard. He was obviously thinking about matters—he seemed impervious to the cold.

Max headed to Eagle House's common room. Some of the boys were playing computer games. He could hear the electronic crackle of gunfire and the hoots of joy as the boys made a "kill." It all felt so phony. After what Max had been through in the past, having experienced real violence where people had done their best to kill him, Max couldn't bring himself to play anymore.

The boys had noticed this and just thought he was going through some sort of rough time. Except Sayid. The common bond he and Max shared was that each had experienced the terror of real gunfire, the swirling confusion of attack and the heart-crushing loss of a loved one. As Max came across the room toward him, Sayid was wedged into a window seat reading a book, but was now distracted by the leaden sky that had sunk lower across the high ground. The forecast was for snow.

"Hello, mate," Max said quietly, pushing himself into the narrow space next to Sayid.

"You all right?" Sayid asked.

"Yeah. Just a bit strung out—one thing and another. Sorry if I've been a bit of a pain."

"Easier having a tooth out than being around you these last few weeks."

"You want a written apology?"

"That'd do, yeah. Sure you're OK?"

Max nodded. "I need your help."

Sayid didn't know whether to smile or cry. Helping Max could be bad for your health—but he really wanted to be back in his best friend's confidence after these weeks of him being withdrawn and uncommunicative. Despite the conflicting thoughts, he realized he was already nodding.

The day Danny Maguire died, Jasmina Dhokia had run down the escalator to catch her train for work. Her usual bus was delayed by roadwork, and she was not familiar with the Underground station. She took a wrong turn, realized her mistake and went back just in time to see her train move smoothly away.

The deserted platform was a lonely place. Fingers of cold air sneaking out of the tunnel tugged at her coat. She wished she could be home with her family, where it was warm and dry and people laughed and smiled more easily than they did here. But this country had been good to her and she was grateful. She was very fortunate to have a good-paying job that allowed her to send money back to help her family. Curiosity made her pick up the small padded envelope that lay on the edge of the platform near the mouth of the tunnel. It was already stamped. Someone must have dropped it. She tucked it into her shoulder bag. She would post it as soon as she could, as she trusted someone else would do if she had dropped an envelope.

Like her own letters, this one might be carrying words of love between a parent and a child.

Where the land rose in the fold of hills, the Range Rover nestled against a tor's slabs of precariously balanced granite. Black sheen against black rock. At first glance, the big 4x4 would be indistinguishable from the boulders around it. In the distance, Dartmoor High was shrouded by the confused mist and rain, but the wet tarmac that ribboned its way around the vales and rock outcrops was still visible.

Drew looked through binoculars. "Nothing. What a place to send your kid to school. If it were me, I'd hate my parents for the rest of my life," he moaned. "Let's get out of here."

"Stop complaining," Stanton said quietly, keeping his gaze on the view through the windscreen.

"A good whine makes me feel better," said Drew.

Stanton was silent. They'd give it a few more hours. Then, if it was obvious that Maguire had not sent Max Gordon any information, they could call it a day. He checked the radio signal: it was clear and strong. Who knew how long it would be before someone found the listening device they'd planted in Jackson's study when he'd left the room to attend to that injured kid? He had already heard Jackson speak to the nursing home inquiring about Gordon's father. Then he gave instructions to another teacher that he was to bring the post directly to him when it arrived.

"Kid on a bike," Drew muttered, binoculars still clamped to his eyes.

"Is it Max Gordon?"

Drew looked at the photograph they had stolen from Max's room, then, concentrating on the figure in his lenses, said, "Nah!" He snorted. "He probably *is* away like Jackson said. This looks like a boy making a break for it! I know I would. Place looks like a Victorian prison."

Sayid pedaled his mountain bike as fast as he could. Stinging rain pecked his face. It was six kilometers to the nearest road junction that bisected the moor. An ancient stone clapper bridge straddled a turbulent stretch of the river there. By this primitive drover's crossing was the Packman's Horse, a pub popular with seasonal holidaymakers. It was a rough-and-ready place where walkers could take their dogs and riders could tether their horses while their owners enjoyed a warming drink.

Just like the postman.

Max sat reading a book, eyes skimming pages as his MP3 player's music rattled around his brain at the same time. Neither engaged him. They didn't have to. Tucked into the pages of his book were the last photographs he had of his mum— half a dozen pictures taken in different areas of the rain forest.

Max was considering what to do next. Besides trying to find connections to Danny Maguire, he wanted to confront his dad. Why did Max's heart still harbor the terrible accusation made against his father? Perhaps it was because he knew that Tom Gordon had different sides to his character. There was the strong, kind man, passionate about ecology and making sure that the people who harmed it were brought to justice. But Max knew that as a younger man, before he'd become an explorer-scientist, he had been trained as a hardened soldier. Max had to admit there had been times when he'd been scared on their holidays together off the beaten track. His father had averted frightening situations by using his courage to confront violent people. He had pulled a gun against pirates when they sailed in the Indian Ocean, had shot up their engines and left them floundering in shark-infested waters. Facing drunken men spoiling for a fight in Greece, he had talked them out of attacking his family. He seemed to have the ability to close the door on fear and become almost another person.

So who was Max's real dad? Snow began to tumble. The book and music were forgotten. Out of the dreamlike storm, the small red postal van appeared.

"Anything?" Drew asked, shoving a stick of chewing gum into his mouth.

Stanton pressed his earpiece. "They're shuffling stuff. Letters. Jackson is moaning about junk mail. He's asking if that's everything . . . if there's anything for the Gordon boy. The other teacher's in there with him. Says no. That's it. OK. Now he's telling him to take everything to the mailroom and make sure the kids get their letters."

Drew looked at Stanton and shrugged. "Well? If the dead

kid didn't get to send anything, it's all hunky-dory. Let's get back to London. I can't stick all this fresh air."

Stanton was less impatient. Maybe they should wait out the day. But what was the point? If Maguire had sent anything before he died, it would have been delivered by now, and nothing Jackson had said suggested it had. Drew was right. Job done. Time to go back.

Something wasn't right, though, and Stanton didn't know what it was. He nudged the hood out onto the narrow tarmac, but his thoughts were still held by this Max Gordon. He hadn't laid eyes on the boy, so why did it bother him so much? He swung the Range Rover across the hillside and felt it tilt as it angled downward. It righted itself as the wheels found the path. Snow sluiced off the windscreen.

"Look out!" Drew shouted.

Sayid squinted against the snow as it caught his eyelids. His ski beanie was pulled across his ears, and his scarf was tucked up to cover his mouth. Pushing his legs to keep going up the incline and balancing the wheels against the settling snow, he crested the rise with a decent turn of speed. As he angled his face away from the wind-driven flurries, he failed to see the black boulder of a car as it eased down from the sheltering tor and nudged into the road.

He jerked the handlebars away from the looming 4x4 and felt the front wheel slide. Boy and bike separated and crashed down into the snow, skidding along for a few meters until his twisted body thumped into one of the small raised banks that flanked the roads across the moor. His last thoughts were of sliding toward the front radiator grille of the 4x4—a monster's jaws. The impact on his back knocked the wind out of him. A sudden pain shot through to his chest and darkness closed over his mind.

Drew was already out on the road. He bent down, eased Sayid's body gently so it lay flat and quickly felt for any broken bones.

Stanton stood next to him, looking left and right. It was highly unlikely any other vehicles would be using this isolated strip of road, but if they did, he would not hear their approach in the snow's blanketing silence. He stayed alert.

"Is he dead?" he asked Drew.

"No, out for the count."

Drew was still on one knee and twisted to look back at Stanton. The two men stared at each other for a moment. Both knew there was a decision to be made. The cyclist was obviously a boy from the school. Had he seen them when they'd visited? If he had, would it appear suspicious to him that the men in the Range Rover were hanging around? They couldn't just leave him, because he or one of the teachers might consider the vehicle driver responsible and report the accident to the police.

Breaking his neck would solve the problem.

It would look like the boy had fallen on the slippery surface and landed badly. Snow was already covering the Rover's tracks.

"Well?" Drew asked, knowing full well the thoughts they both shared.

The boy groaned.

Stanton shook his head. "Help him up." And as Drew eased the fallen rider into a sitting position, Stanton righted the bike. It wasn't damaged.

"You OK now, son?"

Sayid nodded groggily.

"Your bike's all right. You came over the blind hill like an Olympic skier," Stanton said, subtly shifting the blame onto the boy. "We didn't have a chance to see you."

The man who first helped him put an arm under his shoulder. Sayid recognized the two men, and he didn't want them staring too closely at his face. His beanie was still intact, and he pushed himself up, getting to his feet. He took his bike from the other man. The snow flurries were now a blessing; he could avert his eyes from their faces as if shielding himself from the wet flakes.

"Sorry I gave you a fright. My fault. I should've been more careful," Sayid said, but thought that he should go one better to make sure the men didn't suspect he recognized them. "Are you lost? Are you looking for somewhere?"

Drew and Stanton glanced quickly at each other. "The Country House Inn," Stanton said. "Yeah, we're lost."

Sayid settled himself back onto the bike. He mustn't panic now.

"The Country House Inn? No, I don't think there's anywhere called that on this side of the moor. Sorry, can't help."

"Not a problem," Stanton said. He had made up the name. Now he was satisfied. If the kid on the bike had come up with a set of false directions, just to get the men away from him, his suspicions would have been alerted.

They watched a moment longer as the boy's tires cut a furrow through the snow, then banged their boots clear and climbed back into the 4x4. The wheels creaked over the powder, and they turned their backs on the cyclist and Dartmoor High.

Sayid sped down the final stretch of road, hands tightly gripping the handlebars, desperately wanting to look over his shoulder to see if the men were still there. But he didn't, because he was scared and did not want them thinking he knew anything, because if they thought he did . . .

His imagination was running away with him faster than the wheels beneath him. He did a satisfying skidding halt at the bike sheds and didn't even bother to kick the snow from the mountain bike's tires. There were more important things to do.

At the pub, he had spun a line to Phil, the postman, about his birthday present from his parents being late, and as this was half-term, he was going to his aunt's place in a nearby village. Could Phil check for him? The postman had no doubt the boy was from Dartmoor High and obliged him.

Sayid crunched across to the school building. So, if those two men were looking for Max and for the letter Danny Maguire had sent him, they didn't know how close they'd come to having it in their hands.

There was a satisfying crinkle of the envelope tucked under his arm beneath the jacket.

4

Sayid breathlessly told Max about the men who had nearly run him over.

"They must have been watching the school," Max said as he fingered the envelope, suspicion making him wary. What if this was a letter bomb? That was a stupid anxiety, he decided. It was more the anticipation of what lay inside it that was making him nervous.

"They must have been watching for you," Sayid said.

"Or for this being delivered. That's what they came here for, isn't it? A letter from Maguire to me?"

"But they were out at Hunter's Tor. You're not going to see Postie deliver a parcel with your name on it from there, are you?"

Max knew it didn't make sense, but right now it was this envelope that was important. Max suspected Danny Maguire had died trying to get it to him.

The two boys sat on Max's bed. A bold, strong hand had written Max's name and Dartmoor High's address on the packet in block letters, so there could be no mistaking for whom it was intended. He carefully cut open the padded envelope, and a tangle of string fell out.

"What is that?" Sayid asked.

"I've no idea. Are you sure this was the only thing Postie had for me?" Max said.

"Yeah."

"Well, it must mean something. It's not just . . . string. Is it?" Max teased the strands apart. The pattern across was as big as the palms of his hands side by side. A top strand of coarse string had several other pieces tied on to it, like a small skirt. Each of the dangling strings had knots tied in it at various places along the strand. A few turns in the string were dyed red.

Max rubbed the rough strands in his hand. Was this what Danny Maguire had died for? A handful of string?

He pressed a button to bring his laptop out of hibernation, then keyed in "string messages." Google said there were 877,000 bits of information and started with string messages in Java computer language.

"You think there's any link between this and computer code?" Max asked Sayid.

Sayid watched as Max scrolled down. The links continued in the same vein: protocol and error messages. "Maybe. This might be something you're supposed to decipher. Y'know—one knot means something in the binary of a specific string that he's laid in somewhere. Has he sent you anything by email that we could look at?"

Max shook his head. "Only that he was coming to London and he'd be in touch. That was a month ago."

"Well, this is going to take some kind of genius to work it out. I'm happy to have a go at it."

"Nothing like modesty, Sayid. Who appointed you chief scientific officer?"

"Someone's got to try."

"This hasn't got anything to do with computers; I'm sure of it. He was doing field studies in South America. This has something to do with where he was. What is it he's trying to tell me?"

Max scrolled down the screen. There was nothing apparent. String instruments of South America, shoestring holidays . . . nothing that indicated what he was looking for.

The door burst open. Max slammed the laptop's lid down. It was Baskins, as subtle as a bull in a china shop. "Hey, Max, I need one more for seven-a-side. Be great in the snow, yeah? Oh, hi, Sayid. You up for it, Max? Come on, it'll be raining again soon, and where's the fun in that?"

"No, thanks. I'm busy."

"Ah, come on! I need some speed and muscle on my team. Look, I'm sorry for what I said, OK? No hard feelings—you caught me a good one. My ears are still ringing. Why've you got a khipu?" Baskins rattled on, never drawing breath as he picked up the tassels of string.

"A what?" Max said.

"Khipu."

"How would you know what this is?" Max said.

"We did a whole thing on South America with Mr.

Peterson last year. Hoggart called 'em *kippers* when the bloke came down from the university and told us about them. Hoggart's such a prat at times. It was all about ancient stuff. It was so boring except for the sacrificial bits. That was cool. They used to disembowel their victims and—"

Max took the strings back and cut short Baskins's gory recounting of blood sacrifices. "What's it for?"

"Apparently, Incas used them for keeping tabs on things. Y'know, how many bags of corn they had, information and stuff, shorthand or something. Look, I dunno. Are you coming or what?"

Max eased him out the door. "I can't right now. Thanks, you've been a great help."

Baskins had never been a great help to anyone before, so the compliment needed some thought. By the time he'd reached the top of the stairs, he still had no idea what he'd said that was so useful, but he remembered someone else as a replacement for Max. He pounded down the corridor to press-gang the boy.

Max tapped another query into the computer: "k-e-e-p-u." That made no sense at all. He reached for his dictionary. He couldn't see anything that spelled what Baskins had said.

"Let's try Incas," Sayid said as his fingers quickly touched the keys. "Here we go!"

They scrolled down the information bars. Incas: pre-Columbian tribes, distinct language, located in Peru, Ecuador and Chile.

Max clicked on one of the links: *British Museum: Sun God Exhibition*. A series of photographs spread themselves across the screen. Figures carved into stone tablets, double-headed snakes made of jade, burial masks, temples, figures decorated in plumes of exotic birds.

Sayid double-clicked another link. "Stand back—genius at work."

They had found the correct spelling. Max read the paragraph on the khipu, which described it as an abacus, but then went on to explain that khipu knots might well be arranged in a binary code, which meant they held more information than a simple memory aid.

"Y'see, I was right," Sayid said. "Binary. You send an email or anything and what you see is really eight-digit sequences of ones and zeros. Then that gets translated by the computer that received your text."

"Then maybe there *is* a message here somewhere."

"Well, you're good with knots."

"I've never seen any like these, though. And what's this got to do with Mum?" Max inadvertently asked the question aloud that echoed around his mind.

Suddenly, what had been upsetting Max recently was becoming more apparent. "This is about your mum?" Sayid asked carefully.

Max nodded. He fished out the half-dozen photographs and gave them to Sayid, who thumbed through them.

"But she was in Central America when she . . . when she died, wasn't she? I thought Maguire was doing his field trip in South America," Sayid said.

"That's right," Max said, taking the pictures back, regretting mentioning his mother. "But there has to be a connection. I'm just not sure what it is."

"Do you want to tell me what this is all about?" Sayid asked.

"I just want to find out more about her, that's all. I put a thing out on the Net. Danny Maguire said he knew about her." Max did not want to tell even his best friend about the accusation against his father. That he had left his mother to die alone in the jungle. That in fact even Max did not know exactly how she had died.

"But your dad must know all that stuff."

"But how do I get it out of him? The way he is, I mean."

Sayid did not press his friend. It was obvious Max was being cagey, and given his recent unsettled behavior, he did not want to risk pushing any wrong buttons, as Baskins had done earlier. Word had zipped around the few boys left at the school that Max Gordon had lost it big-time.

"Maguire's death was suicide," Sayid said gently.

Max gave him an "oh yeah?" look.

Sayid shrugged. "Well, OK. The guys who came here were pretty creepy, and maybe it is a bit of a coincidence. But they thought Maguire was involved in drug smuggling. We don't know for sure."

Max pulled his backpack down and began folding clothes. "I'm going to see my dad. And I need a couple of things."

"Like what?"

"A school letterhead, and Mr. Jackson's signature."

"Max, that's crazy. It's impossible."

"Nothing's impossible, Sayid—you should know that. Anyway, that's the easy bit. I need my passport."

"To go where?"

"I'm not sure yet."

"Well, your passport's in the vault. End of story." It was a flat statement of finality.

The vault was 133 steps below Dartmoor High's granite walls. Each boy had a safe-deposit box, and in each box, which could be opened only by a key that Mr. Jackson held, was that boy's life. A passport, a legal guardian's letter, a parent's last words. If anything fatal happened to any of the boys' parents, Mr. Jackson would take him down into the gloomy cavern, open the box and hand the boy a prerecorded message on an MP3 player. It was a final act of love from a father and a mother to their child—the last words the boy would hear from his parents.

The vault gave everyone the creeps—it was as if the dead were waiting.

Max had almost finished rolling T-shirts, cotton shorts and cargo pants. He pulled the compass cord over his head and let it sit below his sweatshirt.

"I know. But I have to get it."

"Just like that? You get caught and they'll kick you out."

"If *we* get caught, they'll kick *us* out," Max said, giving Sayid a comforting smile that the other boy did not find reassuring.

Stanton had changed his mind. Why would Jackson have phoned the nursing home to inquire about Tom Gordon? Stanton's people had already checked the place out, and there had been no sign of Max. That was understandable given his father's condition. So why phone? To reassure a boy about his father? He had underestimated the possibility that Jackson might be canny enough to be suspicious of them.

Jackson had lied; Stanton was beginning to be sure of it. He was protecting one of his pupils. Max Gordon was somewhere in that school, and if somehow Maguire had managed to get any kind of message to him, what would he do? Try to find answers.

Under cover of darkness, Stanton edged the Range Rover beneath the overhang of a hollowed-out rock face. The night shadows swallowed the 4x4 easily, and the shelter allowed a brief respite from the cutting wind. The rain had not come, but a scarring north wind had frozen the last snowfall. From their vantage point, he and a less-than-happy Drew gazed across the hills, beyond the moon-white river, toward the fortresslike Dartmoor High.

Wind crept and growled. Oak beams, hundreds of years old, creaked and twisted, moaning their discomfort like trapped ghosts. In the darkness of the school, only a couple of dim lights glowed at the end of each corridor.

Max's headlamp cut a wedge into the blackness. Sayid followed him down the stairs, a constant whispering of apprehension, teasing Max's ear like a draft from below the heavy-paneled doors.

Max stopped. "Sayid," he said quietly, "shut up."

"Sorry. But it's two in the morning and I've never liked the dark. And all this creaking and groaning gives me the creeps."

A door banged closed somewhere. Max turned off the

light, grabbed his friend's arm and pulled him into the blackness of the stairwell.

Footsteps. Leather shoes creaking. A cough. A door opening and closing. Somewhere to the left. Max whispered close to Sayid's ear. "Probably Mr. Chaplin. He's the only one who wears leather-soled shoes. And he fancies a hot chocolate before he goes to bed."

"Which is where we should be," said Sayid, grimacing.

Max led him down the corridor, eased open a set of swing doors, careful not to let the hinges squeak, and finally squatted down in front of Mr. Jackson's door with his prized multitool pocketknife.

Metal scraped metal inside the old mortise lock. He eased the handle, the lever clicked and he scurried into Mr. Jackson's office with a huffing and puffing Sayid behind him. He was scared and it made his breathing ragged.

Max gestured. *Stay at the door. Listen. Watch.* Max knelt in front of the safe. Like the granite of Dartmoor High, it looked solid. It was about the size of an undercounter fridge, had one opening lever and a combination dial. The best plan when robbing a safe is to steal the whole thing and then blow it up later, but Max couldn't see that happening with only Sayid's bike for transport and a few bangers from last year's firework display. A half-empty Pot Noodle cup stood on a shelf next to the safe. Max could just see Mr. Jackson mooching around his bookshelves, putting the container down and forgetting about it.

Memory carries smells and tastes, and as Max pressed his hands against the cold steel, his mind flooded with both.

Hong Kong. Rich spicy food, the soft misty air of steaming

noodles. A cacophony of sounds. A trip when he was eleven to meet his parents, who were investigating the massive contamination the Chinese government was inflicting on the rivers and coasts of China. Tom Gordon had been banned from the mainland, and what was supposed to be a few days' holiday turned into a daily round of arguments between his parents and government officials. He didn't know the exact details of what was going on, but his mother woke him in the early hours one morning and told him to get dressed. She was packing their holdalls. Where was his dad? he had wanted to know. In the manager's office sorting things out, she had told him, putting a finger to her lips. The moment her back was turned, Max ran down to the darkened reception area.

A night doorman, feet propped up, snored behind the desk, and a soft glow of light crept beneath the manager's door.

Max turned the handle and came face to face with his dad, who was kneeling in front of a safe. For a moment he thought his dad was going to strike him—he had moved so quickly. Faster than a striking cobra. It was the trigger of recognition that stopped him from finishing the attack. He quickly closed the door behind Max and eased him to the safe.

"Our passports and laptops are in here. The manager's been told that the police are coming first thing to interview us. Which could prove awkward," his dad said, and smiled.

Max was in awe of his father. Everything he did seemed to have such a definite purpose. He just nodded while his dad kept up a whispered running commentary as his fingers delicately tweaked the safe's dial.

"You have to find the contact points on the lock. You listen for the click. That tells you which way the lock's drive cams—its levers and arms—are balanced inside." He had pulled Max's face to the safe, turned a notch and let him hear the soft click. Max nodded enthusiastically. This was great stuff. Safecracking with his dad!

"Old hotels, old safes. Not that difficult. Look . . ." There were a hundred numbers on the dial, and his fingers turned the pointer to rest on the number sixty. "That's called parking the wheels, aligning the clicks you heard, and then you have narrowed down what the combination is."

His dad caressed the wheel with his fingertips. "Now, when I move the dial, these drive cams click out of place again, left or right. Find which way"—he listened again, head pressed against the safe door—"and you should . . . get in."

Max heard a final accepting click. His dad opened the safe and hauled out their papers and their laptops, shoving them into a backpack.

"How did you learn to do that?" Max remembered asking his father when they had finally found the safety of the plane home.

"My dad taught me," Tom Gordon said, and smiled.

"Max! How did you do that?" Sayid asked as Max opened Jackson's safe.

"It's a long story," he whispered, subduing the prickling emotion he felt at his father's memory. He found the name-tagged keys he was looking for. "Come on, let's go."

"What about the safe?"

"We leave it open. I've got to get this key back."

"We're coming *back?*" Sayid felt the wall of his stomach

twitch. His family owed so much to Max and his dad. His own father had been assassinated in the Middle East, and it was Tom Gordon who had rescued Sayid and his mother. It was Tom Gordon who'd secured a home in England for them because of the brave work his own dad had done—and because Tom Gordon was a sworn friend, almost like a brother, to his father. His mother taught Arabic at Dartmoor High, and Sayid had never felt safer. Max was his very best friend. There was nothing he wouldn't do to help him. But he did not want to be caught and kicked out. It was not just his own life that might be ruined—it was his mother's too.

Max saw the doubt flicker across Sayid's eyes.

"It's a piece of cake. You'll see. Come on."

But Sayid shook his head.

"Sayid!" Max insisted.

"I can't. Anything happens and I've messed up Mum's life."

There was an uncharacteristic look of anger on Max's face. He needed Sayid to keep watch for him. Now he was chickening out. He checked himself. Sayid was right. He had to look after his mother. He was all she had. Max nodded, patted his shoulder.

"Off you go, mate. I can do the rest and—"

Shrill, heart-stopping ringing tore through the stillness, cutting off Max's words. An alarm? Had he triggered something? The thousandth-of-a-second thought was immediately dismissed. It was Jackson's phone.

Sayid flinched. Max nearly dropped the keys as he scrambled to pull Sayid between the safe and office door. A light flickered on in the corridor. Mr. Jackson's private quarters were down the hall.

Scuffling feet got closer, the door opened and a bleary-looking Mr. Jackson, wearing pajamas with a hastily thrown-on dressing gown, walked straight to the desk, flicked on his desk light and picked up the phone.

Max had squeezed them both into the corner. The open door shielded them, creating a small enclave of darkness next to the safe. He could feel Sayid's heart thumping as they huddled like two monkeys in a rainstorm.

"Jackson," the headmaster said into the receiver, unaware that he had walked straight into his office without having to unlock the door.

Max peered round the edge of the safe. Mr. Jackson's back was to him, but Max could see that the safe door was open enough to be noticed when Jackson turned back to leave the office.

He stretched out, his fingertips catching the heavy door. If the old hinges squeaked, Jackson would surely hear it.

"Bob, what's wrong?" Jackson said the moment he heard Ridgeway's voice. The MI5 man worked very unusual hours despite his seniority, but phone calls from anyone at this time of the morning always meant bad news.

Max strained; the safe door edged onto his thumb, the weight of it telling Max that was as far as he could close it. He and Sayid scrunched themselves as small as possible. They could hear only one side of the conversation, but if it was serious, then it might have Jackson's adrenaline pumping—and that would make him more alert.

"Have the police been to see you yet?" Ridgeway asked.

"The police? No. There's only a local constable, and

there's enough rural crime to keep him busy. He'll get here in due course."

"And Max Gordon—is he at school?"

"Max? Yes. He's here."

Sayid flinched. Max felt his muscles tighten. The phone call was about him! At this time of the morning? Was it something to do with his dad? Was he ill? He suppressed the urge to cry out to Jackson and ask what was going on. Sayid's clawlike grip on his shoulder told him his friend was just as tense.

Jackson was listening to whoever it was on the other end of the phone.

"We've got a field office a couple of hours away in Bristol," Ridgeway said. "I've just dragged one of the agents out of bed and told them to get down to you and have a chat first thing."

"Oh? That sounds ominous."

"Precautionary. Don't be too alarmed, Fergus. I would have left this till a more decent time, but I thought you should know I had some feedback on that name you gave me. *Velvollisuus*."

"Yes?" Jackson replied cautiously.

"It's part of a motto."

"Ah," Mr. Jackson said, not really knowing what else would be an appropriate response. Mottos and MI5. Perhaps not too strange a mixture.

"*Kunnia—Velvollisuus—Tahto*. It means 'Honor—Duty—Will.' It's the motto belonging to the Finnish Rapid Deployment Regiment. Special troops."

"I see," Jackson said, though he didn't really. "And what on earth would they be doing here? Training, do you think? Along with our chaps?"

"No, Fergus, it's nothing like that at all. We have a list of known assets, people who are in place to carry out covert dirty work for whoever pays the highest. You said the name on the man's warrant card was Mark Stanton."

"Yes. That's right."

"Real name, Markus Sutinon. Goes by the code name of Riga. Trained with their special forces and went private. Did some rather nasty work for the Russians last time we heard. He speaks perfect English. We don't know who's paying him, but if he's posing as one of us, it must be something big. We haven't pinpointed his current partner yet. He tends to go through them. They have a habit of dying—violently."

"I see," Mr. Jackson said again, the edge of fear now creeping into his voice. "Can you trace him?"

"Doubtful. He'll have a dozen passports in as many different names. The question is, Fergus, what's the connection between Danny Maguire, Max Gordon and a hired killer? Charlie, that's my officer, will be there tomorrow to speak to you and the Gordon boy."

"Right. I'll make sure Max is here."

Mr. Jackson replaced the receiver, bowed his head in troubled thought for a moment, switched off the light and without a glance left or right, turned on his heel and closed the door behind him.

After a moment the hall light went out.

Max and Sayid sighed like two deflating balloons.

Stanton nudged Drew. The sleeping man was instantly awake but made no sound.

"I was right. He's there. He's just busted into the safe in Jackson's room. I heard two kids talking. Then there was a phone call and they stayed quiet. Jackson answered. Something about the local cops being expected. Sounded low-key to me."

"So you think there was something in the old man's safe after all? Maybe Maguire's letter got here earlier than we thought and he stashed it?"

"Don't be stupid. We've already heard Jackson asking someone if there was anything delivered for Gordon. No, Max was going after something else in the safe," Stanton said.

"Maybe there's money in there," Drew suggested. "Something may have warned the kid and he needs cash."

"Perhaps," said Stanton, unconvinced but not knowing what it was Max was after.

Drew put a pair of night-vision binoculars to his eyes. Nothing moved. An owl cut across his vision, and a pony shifted its weight as it slept beneath a thorn tree.

"OK," Drew said. "We'll wait. If he's spooked, he'll run."

5

The air was dry from the school's geothermal heating unit as Max ran quickly down into the pit of darkness. The vault lay buried like an Egyptian tomb. Deeper and deeper the steps went.

He reached the bottom. His headlamp scanned the boxes. Opening his own flooded him with memories of the last time he had been down here. His father had gone missing in Africa, and someone had tried to kill Max. Taking his passport then had been the start of a frightening adventure that left his dad's mind wrecked and Max a changed boy. He took what he wanted from the box and began the muscle-burning exercise of running back up the stairs.

He had tried to eliminate the self-defeating anger he had felt over the past few weeks by hard physical activity. The sickness of suspicion and doubt had threatened to depress him as it ate away at his love for his father. Nothing could really shake that love—nothing except the thought that his mother had died because his dad had abandoned her in the jungle.

Now, as he pounded up the steep incline toward the faint glow of the corridor far above, he felt as though he had a focus for his pent-up emotions and energy. Danny Maguire was dead but had somehow managed to post the khipu to him. It was a message that needed an expert to decode it.

Max had just taken the first 133 steps toward finding out the truth about his mother's death.

He closed his laptop's lid, shoved it into its case and handed it to a waiting Sayid. He had done as much as he could to prepare for his journey.

"Keep this out of the way for me. Once they know I've gone, they'll search this to see what they can find. Don't lose any sleep over it, Sayid, but keep them guessing for a few hours, yeah? Then give it to them."

"OK."

"You remember everything I've asked you to do?"

"My name's not Baskins."

"Sorry, mate. Right. Time to get out of here."

"You're going now?" Sayid shivered and yawned. It was still dark, and the early hour meant Sayid's bed beckoned. Unlike Max, he did not have the capacity to ignore the need for sleep or the crushing tiredness fear can bring.

"I have to get across the moor, Sayid," Max said, pulling on his gloves. "It'll be light in a few hours. If I hang around, I bet Mr. Jackson will have one of the masters keeping an eye on me, and they'll find plenty of things to keep me busy until whoever's planning to come and see me turns up."

He zipped his fleece, then tightened the Velcro tab on his waterproof leggings. He'd be running part of the way, and the ground would be muddy despite the frost. He pulled his wool cap down over his head, but only to the top of his ears—he needed to hear clearly.

"Thanks for the extra cash," Max said.

Sayid had raided his sock drawer and pulled out every note he'd stashed there from doing odd jobs on people's computers. Max had his own small savings pot and the credit card his dad had set up for emergencies. But Max had wanted to avoid using that until the last minute.

"I'll come downstairs with you," Sayid said.

"No. Kill the lights and I'll get going."

Sayid knew Max was right. His friend could move more easily without having him to worry about. The two boys embraced.

"Take care, Max."

"I will. Don't worry, I'll be in touch. I just have to sort this out."

Sayid switched off the room's light as Max settled his backpack onto his shoulders, left the room and walked quickly and silently toward the back door that would lead him to the yard.

Within minutes he had skirted the dark edge of the building, finding clear ground that would leave no footprints. He lifted Sayid's mountain bike onto his shoulder, edged around the outbuildings and found an animal track etched through the gorse and heather. He ran, balancing the bike as best he could. Clouds were pushing in, hurried along by the north wind, its chill biting through his cargo pants. Tears from the cold filled his eyes.

For the next twenty minutes or so, it would be almost as bright as daylight, a chance to make fast time. A bomber's moon, his gran had called a full moon on a clear night. As a child, she had endured saturation bombing in the Second World War, and whenever there was a beautiful, cloudless night, she would hastily close the curtains in her modest home. Well, he was glad of the moon. The sky's glow helped Max see exactly where he needed to go. Within minutes he would drop out of sight from the school; then there was no chance of anyone who might still be awake seeing his shadow flit across the white-topped land.

Except that the threat did not lie in the school behind him.

Drew ran steadily on a bearing that would cut Max off. There was no need for night-vision goggles or binoculars: he saw the boy's dark shape cut in and out of the folding ground. Somewhere behind him, and over to one side, Stanton would have the Range Rover ready to plunge through the night if for any reason Drew could not catch the boy.

Max was already more than a kilometer from school. Sweat ran down his back, his T-shirt clinging to his skin. As the track became a path, he climbed onto the mountain bike and kept his legs pumping. At this rate he would make good time.

If his plan was going to succeed, he had to be in the city before the commuter rush hour started. He was so busy projecting his thoughts, following the plan in his mind, that he failed to see the rock in the path. The front wheel hit it awkwardly, the handlebars twisted and, because he was riding out of the saddle, using his body weight to power the bike along, he fell sideways into the gorse, rolling a couple of meters into the undergrowth.

Frozen snow and gorse needles scratched his face. He swore, picked up the bike and was immediately grateful for the accident. As he got to his feet, he looked back the way he had come. Across the low hill to his left, a shadow came on relentlessly. It was a big man, less than three hundred meters away. A determined energy powered the spectral figure forward, jumping and dodging any small obstacles like the inconsequential nuisances they were.

The shock of seeing the man momentarily stunned Max, but he recovered, kicked down on the pedals and felt the tires bite into the frozen sludge. Sucking in air, he kept going as fast as he could. Gran was right! A bomber's moon brought the enemy right down your throat! Where were those clouds?

He dared a look over his shoulder. The man was closer. A horrible sensation gripped Max. The man pursuing him with such relentlessness must be superfit. Not only had he kept a fast pace going across difficult ground, but also he had increased his speed. He obviously had untapped reserves of stamina.

Max knew he was not going to outrun this man.

Know your ground, use your mind. Survival needs more than

guts and strength. Dad whispered in his mind like a guardian angel.

Max knew where he was. He had run these hills and paths ever since his dad had placed him in school here. Dartmoor had dozens of danger zones. Military no-go areas, old mine shafts, bogland—there were plenty of nature's traps ready to snare the unwary.

Where to go? Max's mind raced faster than his legs. *Get off the path! Make it difficult. Make him look where he's going! Make him take his eyes off you!*

Cold, raw air scoured his lungs. *Pedal harder! No need to turn and look now.* He could hear the man's boots brushing aside the frozen gorse. Carrying the bike again would slow him down, but he had to take the risk. He couldn't ride here. The crossbar dug into his shoulder. He dipped left, downward past an outcrop of knuckle-like boulders, saw the edge of the moon smiling its farewell as clouds crawled all over it. Darkness! He needed darkness. Another twenty meters. In the distance, the woods, spiky grassland in front, a last glint of light to help confirm what he saw in his mind's eye. He veered right, banged his shoulder on an unseen fist of rock. It threw him off balance. But he was almost there. Now he ran straight, right out into the open where the man could not fail to see him.

He turned and faced his pursuer. Like a cornered rat.

"Who are you? What do you want?" he yelled, shaking with exertion, offering himself to the predator, who was less than fifty meters away. The man was expressionless. His eyes locked on to the seemingly helpless boy.

Max saw the ground in his head, remembered it in

daylight, watched his finger trace the map as he took part in orienteering. Saw the places to avoid.

The mantraps.

As the darkness blanketed the moor, Stanton watched through night-vision binoculars. One of the ghosts had stopped. The other, a silvery, fast-moving apparition, raced toward it. And then floundered, half of its ghostly image disappearing from view.

Drew was down.

Stanton turned the ignition key.

Max gasped in air, letting his lungs settle, watching as the man spluttered and gagged on the foul bog water. The craters were deep, some of them bottomless, according to local legend. This was Blacksnake Mire, one of the primeval pockets of sludge, camouflaged by a covering of vegetation.

The man was trying to clamber out, but there was no means of reaching the edge. He trod water, except there was no buoyancy. The glutinous liquid was like quicksand.

"You're going to die. You can't get out of these mires unless someone helps you," Max said evenly, surprised at the objective tone of his voice. Death was part of nature, and this hunter was about to be taken into a foul grave.

Drew spat out vomit-inducing mud and swore at Max with an even more evil spewing of expletives.

"Why were you chasing me? Tell me!" Max demanded.

Drew stayed silent. He was convinced he had the strength to get out of this, but the mire was sucking him down. Maybe he wasn't going to make it.

"Gordon! Get me out, kid."

Max was surprised to hear the man call him by name. "Tell me!" Max yelled. He could hear the purr of a powerful engine some distance away. It wouldn't be a farmer. Their old workhorses coughed and spluttered through thirty years of use. This was controlled power. Like a Range Rover. Exactly! The one that nearly hit Sayid. These were the same men and they were still out here.

Drew had sunk down to the top of his chest; there was no chance of using his arms except to spread them out—to delay the inevitable.

"I dunno, boy. Your pal Maguire. He found out stuff. . . ."

"What stuff?" Max asked desperately. The sound of the engine was closer; it must be just over the rise of the hill behind them.

"Dunno! Kid! C'mon! Throw me something! Hurry, dammit!"

"What did he find out?"

A beam of light cut through the night sky. Whatever it was coming across the hills wasn't using its headlights yet, but it had a powerful searchlight. The kind lampers use to hunt foxes.

Drew never thought he would die like this. Not chasing a kid on Dartmoor. Not being swallowed alive. "They don't tell me things like that! I don't get the details! Y'understand? Please!" Drew had heard men beg before they died but had never expected to hear a plea for life escape from his own lips.

A part of the hillside moved, its lightsaber beam sweeping across them. Max clambered onto the bike.

"Your mate can save you!" he yelled, hoping the man's rescue would buy him time. And then he was gone into the night as Drew spluttered a desperate cry.

"No, he won't! Kid! He won't! He won't help me!" But Max had moved quickly and was already out of earshot.

Moments later the Range Rover stopped. Stanton swung the side-mounted searchlight across the landscape. There was no sign of Max Gordon. He brought the beam to bear on the deceptive land. He couldn't drive any closer, but he could throw Drew a rope and haul him out.

The light settled on his partner. Drew was up to his neck. Gasping.

"Riga, c'mon! Get me outta here!"

Stanton ignored the use of his professional name. It made no difference what anyone called him. He was who he was.

Drew was choking now. The slime was over his chin; his arms reached for the night sky. The beam of light blinded him.

"Pl . . . ea . . . se . . . For God's . . . sake . . ."

Stanton watched the last slurp of foul liquid take the man's face. His fingers curled in a final desperate clutch at life. And then they, too, slid below the surface.

"Maybe now you'll stop whining," Stanton said quietly to himself.

Exeter St. Davids was the mainline station to London Paddington. Some of the trains labored for hours from Penzance at the tip of the country. If they were lucky and everything was working as it should, passengers might have had a hot bacon roll and coffee from the buffet car. By the time the train, its tinted windows veiling the dull glow of light from inside the carriages, rolled into Exeter, Max was waiting—and the smell of the cooked food made his mouth water as the carriage glided past.

Thirty minutes earlier he had stood at the ticket desk, aware that a CCTV camera was in the corner. With barely a glance over his shoulder, he kept his back to the cold-eyed lens. There were others at various points on the platform. Max had already stored Sayid's bike, making sure the padlock and chain were in place. Now all he had to do was mingle with the crowd of commuters.

The train squealed to a halt. Doors opened; a few students, who used the intercity as a local train for a few stops, got out. Doors slammed. The train manager waved to the front of the train, and the driver eased the brakes. Two minutes after arriving, the train was gone.

And so was Max.

Fergus Jackson paced his study. Bob Ridgeway's MI5 agent would be here any minute, and Mr. Jackson was even more worried than the previous night. Max Gordon was missing. Jackson had assembled the twenty or so boys in the staff room under the watchful eye of the four teachers who had stayed on at the school during half-term.

Sayid Khalif had denied all knowledge of anything Max might have done or where he might have gone. Even Sayid's mother could not get any information from him. No one knew anything. Limbo. That was where Fergus Jackson felt himself to be. Schoolboy honor and friendship closed doors against the adults who were trying to help one of their own. Although Jackson grudgingly admitted to himself that of all the boys at Dartmoor High, Max Gordon was probably the one who least needed help.

He heard the slick-engined motorbike before he saw it. So did the boys in the staff room. They crowded the windows to see the rider crest the hill over the still-frozen approach road.

"Look at that!" one of the boys said as the rider wobbled at speed, corrected the spin and then opened the throttle again. It was a big, heavy machine, and the slightly built figure looked as though he would have trouble lifting it if it fell. Which probably meant he didn't lose control too often—an expert rider.

The black-clad figure wore a full-face helmet, and the leathers had creases of red in the gussets. It looked as though flames sneaked from the side vents on his jacket, like a Spitfire's engine used to spout flame.

Now the rider downshifted, and the sweetly tuned engine idled. He wore a body-hugging backpack that matched his leather gear. Racking the bike onto its stand, he turned and looked directly at the boys' faces. The smoked Perspex helmet hid the rider's features.

"That's awesome," one of the boys muttered.

"That's a liquid-cooled, six-hundred-cc, four-cylinder, four-stroke, sixteen-valve engine, giving one hundred twenty-five bhp at thirteen thousand five hundred revs. Zero to sixty in three seconds, zero to a hundred in about six. Top speed one hundred sixty-five miles an hour," said Baskins, almost drooling.

The rider pulled off the helmet. A purple and crimson head emerged. Jackson was momentarily lost for words. The highlighted tufts of hair were chopped short, there was a stud in the rider's nose and once the gloves came off to shake his hand, Jackson could see she wore Goth jewelry.

She.

"Charlotte Morgan," she said, and smiled, extending her hand. "Great place you've got here. Roads were rubbish. M5 was terrible. A lorry had slipped its load—took me longer than I thought. Wouldn't half mind a cuppa."

She was already pulling a slimline laptop from her backpack and peeling off her leather jacket to reveal a T-shirt hidden by a sweatshirt that sported a Sundance logo. At least, that was what it appeared to be to Mr. Jackson. For all he knew, it could have been an advert for a grunge band.

"Tea. Ah. I have coffee on the go. . . ."

She smiled. "A cup of tea would be ace."

"Yes. Of course. Forgive me. I'll . . . er . . ." He reached for the phone, pressed a button and asked if one of the teachers could rustle up a pot of tea from the kitchen. The young woman was keying information into her laptop. She pulled out a file from the backpack and laid a mobile phone on his desk.

He replaced the phone. "You're not quite what I expected, Charlie."

"That's what most people say. I find that helps."

"Understandably," he said.

She turned her computer round so he could see the screen. Hash marks crisscrossed it; a small red dot blinked.

He watched as she bent down and ran her fingers under

the edge of his desk. She pulled out what looked like a Shreddies square, dropped it on the floor and crushed it under her boot heel.

"Cheap as chips, no pun intended, but effective up to about a couple of Ks."

"Pun?" Jackson said.

"Microchips," she said. "The phony guys bugged you."

Stanton and Drew's intrusion felt all the more grubby. They'd been eavesdropping! Had he said anything that could have endangered Max?

"OK. Let's speak to this Max Gordon and see what he can tell us about Danny Maguire," Charlotte Morgan said.

"Well, Charlie, that's where we have a problem."

There was no sign in the frozen snow of anyone using the road that led in and out of Dartmoor High. *So Max Gordon must have gone cross-country. To where? It would take at least six hours of hard slog to get to the nearest railway station, which could be either Exeter or Plymouth. Could any of these boys hack that in these conditions?* Morgan wondered.

She scanned the files on Max Gordon. Definitely, was the answer she came up with. In two hours she had looked at everything to do with Max Gordon. There was no direct relationship or even friendship noted between him and Danny Maguire, and that was confirmed by Jackson. She sweet-talked half the boys who would have told her anything had they known, but the boy who had fought with Max, Baskins, was worth interviewing.

Charlotte watched as Baskins straddled her bike. Its body

contour demanded a low-profile riding position. Baskins could see himself screaming along at 150. Wait till he told Hoggart about the babe on the bike.

He'd realized he'd dropped Max in it when he mentioned the khipu. She had smiled and turned away. She'd lured him in and trapped him. The bike didn't feel that great anymore.

Charlotte Morgan declined to speak to Gordon's best friend, Sayid, until she had more information about him. She needed a lever. Now the information had been downloaded. No more Miss Cool Nice Person.

Sayid and his mother sat in Mr. Jackson's office.

"Why has he run, Sayid?" Charlie asked.

"I don't know," he answered.

"Mr. Jackson told me he might have been expecting a letter or a package. Did he get anything?"

"I checked the postal deliveries myself. Nothing came for Max," Jackson told her.

"Sayid, I'm here to help Max. There are some dangerous people out there who might want to hurt him."

Sayid shook his head and shrugged. "I don't know anything. Max keeps things to himself."

"Then where did he get the khipu?"

Baskins! Sayid couldn't believe the oaf had blabbed. Well, actually he could.

"I don't know. He just had it."

She looked at the laptop screen. "You and your mother were rescued by your late father's friend, Max's dad."

Sayid's mother looked worried, and Mr. Jackson placed a reassuring hand on her shoulder. "I don't see what that has to do with anything," he said.

"Sayid's father was a vital link for work that was being done in the Middle East. It was his good standing that allowed Tom Gordon to get Sayid and his mother into this country." She paused and made a quiet but pointed comment. "I don't know just how secure that status is or whether there is a case for deportation."

Sayid's mother pushed her hand against her lips. Sayid looked panicked. Exactly what Charlie wanted.

"That's a terrible threat to make to this family. How dare you. I'll speak to Ridgeway about your behavior. He offered help, not intimidation!" Jackson said.

The girl was unperturbed. "You can do whatever you want, Mr. Jackson, but since you contacted my boss, he's had a lot of heat put on him from people in our own government. He's been told not to get involved in this matter. A boy's death on the London Underground has now triggered something entirely different, and we don't know what it is. Mr. Ridgeway does not like being squeezed by faceless bureaucrats. We're the ones who are supposed to know everything. We're the spooks. So I want information and I want it quickly. This now has as much to do with Max Gordon as it does with Danny Maguire's death. He knew something important, and we want to know what."

She looked at Sayid.

"You can save your mother a lot of heartache if you tell me."

Keep them guessing for a few hours, yeah? Then give it to them. Max's voice in his head calmed Sayid's anxiety.

"I've got his laptop," Sayid said.

Robert Ridgeway listened to his field agent. Max Gordon had broken into Jackson's safe—and how did the kid ever do that?—and taken his passport from a place called the vault. He had also made a dozen online inquiries about flights to Peru, which was where khipus came from. Trouble was he could get to Peru from a dozen local airports via Europe. Charlie had no idea where he might leave from. There was also a composite letter on Gordon's laptop, forged by pasting elements of the school's website information pack, which had Fergus Jackson's signature on it. It was written as a letter of authority confirming that the underage Max Gordon had permission to travel. A second letter was addressed to the British consul in Lima, asking that all assistance be given to the boy while he undertook field studies at a volunteer program in the Andes. The boy had everything planned.

"Then he's been too clever by half," Ridgeway told her. He would scan all the airports' ticketing systems. Sooner or later, Max Gordon's name would appear; then they would have him.

Morgan finished her report: a certain university lecturer in Oxford should be checked. He was the one who had visited the school and given a lecture on the Peruvian khipus. If Max Gordon had one of those things, then odds were he'd head there first. And then he would have easy access to Luton or

Stansted airports, which had flights to Europe. That all seemed to fit neatly.

"I'm going to check CCTV at the most likely train station. If he's heading anywhere by train, we'll find him," she said. "The London train stops at Reading. He could connect to Oxford from there."

"Or the main London airports," Ridgeway suggested.

"Maybe."

"All right. We'll get an alert at all passport controls," Ridgeway told her. "For some reason, this boy has, or is able to obtain, information that people want. And until I know more, I don't want another boy to die under suspicious circumstances."

"Why? What makes you think that, boss?"

"As soon as we knew about Riga, we tried to double-check Danny Maguire's cause of death, but we can't; his body has gone missing. If Danny's death was something other than suicide, Max Gordon might well be their next target."

6

Max's thoughts raced as he jogged round the perimeter wall of St. Christopher's. Would they find him? He had laid a false trail, but was it enough? Sayid would keep them at bay for a while as far as giving out information was concerned. Baskins was bound to blab. How carefully had the authorities checked on Max's escape?

Max had watched all the CCTV cameras at Exeter station out of the corner of his eye. Overcrowded trains made it difficult to spot anyone easily, and as people struggled with cases and backpacks onto the London train, Max ducked round the rear of the Victorian-era waiting room—and waited. It was a blind spot for the cameras. And anyone tracking him would stop watching the CCTV footage the moment the train left.

He gave it another twenty minutes, then made his way back across to the other platform. A slower train bound for

Waterloo station, via Salisbury and just about every small town in between, shuddered into view. St. Christopher's, his dad's nursing home, was just outside London, and this would take him there.

Now, three hours later, Max's need to know about his mother was like hunger. It drove him on as it had done since he first learned of the doubt surrounding her death. When Mr. Jackson had phoned St. Christopher's, they had asked him to call again in a couple of days, because right now Tom Gordon was not in good enough mental condition to see his son.

Jackson would have informed anyone asking about Max's dad of the man's condition, which might also have bought Max a few hours. As for the rest? He didn't know. The killers on the moor were still around. They were hard characters. His dad had told him about men like them before. They took to violence like a bird to the air—effortlessly, unthinkingly— a natural state in which to exist. There would be no reasoning with killers like that. *You're not a thug, Max. You don't fight because you can't control yourself. You'll know when to strike first. It will be in their eyes. And then, God help you, but you have to do it. You'll know when they want to kill you.*

Dad.

Almost there. The knot in his stomach tightened. There was no sign of anything unusual at the gates of the old mansion grounds, at the driveway or at the entrance of the house itself. Max lowered the small 8x20 rubberized binoculars from his eyes. Everything seemed normal, but if the people chasing him were as determined as they seemed, then odds were they'd have someone, somewhere, watching the main entrance.

He checked his watch, unconsciously wiping its face—it had been to the top of the world. His dad had worn it when he climbed Everest. Now Max's emotions were as daunting as that climb. *Concentrate!* He scanned the perimeter, searching for anyone concealed in the shadows. He knew his dad's schedule by heart. In trying to heal a man's mind, the care-givers had established a definite routine. Scattered thoughts were placed neatly into a timetable.

The patients here were well looked after. Some of them, because of their government work, might be at risk. Max studied the grounds and remembered walking the parkland with his dad, whose old habits, learned at the sharp end of life, still made him ever watchful. *They won't always let you come to see me. See that corner? See where the two cameras cross each other's line of sight beneath the tree branches on the corner of the wall? That's a blind spot. There's always a way through. Don't forget.*

Max found a foothold and eased himself across the top of the three-meter wall. In the distance, there were one or two people sitting in the late-afternoon sun or walking the grounds. A few sat in wheelchairs, a blanket across their legs. Max crouched, then dropped down between the trees, glancing over his shoulder at the diagonally placed security cameras and hoping he'd learned the lessons his father had taught him about concealment. He pressed himself against the bole of a tree, mentally scolding himself to be patient.

Then he saw his dad. Max's heart thumped.

He was with a big man, taller than his wiry companion. They jogged effortlessly round the grounds' outer limits.

Ex–Royal Marine Marty Kiernan stood 1.83 meters tall and weighed 112 kilos. As a combat medic, he had saved others, but he had paid the price fighting in Afghanistan. Bullets had slammed into his huge frame and ripped away his right arm. Now he worked with men whose injuries were psychological—and Tom Gordon was one of his patients.

Max watched as the two men, sweat glistening on their faces and staining their running vests, passed thirty meters from where he crouched. Max stifled the yell that almost burst out of his chest. *Dad!*

He just had to play this cool and get his emotions under control, but, like trying to keep a pack of hunting dogs from tearing their prey apart, it was impossible.

He swallowed the bile that soured the back of his throat. His stomach twisted in anxiety. He was about to confront the man he loved more than anything in the world.

Max ducked beneath the low branches and ran quickly into the shadows. He did not see the man watching him through a pair of binoculars more powerful than his own. The observer stood in a raised road-maintenance platform, dressed as a workman, pretending to fix a streetlight a couple of roads away. His view between the houses gave him a clear line of sight toward St. Christopher's. He pressed the fast-dial button on his mobile.

"The boy is here."

Riga sat in a coffee shop in London. He had placed his own men around the nursing home. The boy was bound to turn up sooner or later.

"Wait till he comes out. Then deal with him."

"I can finish him inside the grounds. It's like a park. Outside is busy. The kid sneaked in. He doesn't want anyone to know he's there."

"Then do it. Damned boy is a nuisance."

Robert Ridgeway did not have the resources for his Security Service agents to be tracking down Max Gordon, but a rogue assassin on the loose, and a carefully placed word of warning from someone in his own government to leave alone that which he knew nothing about, agitated him. All governments had secrets—even from their own people. All governments told lies—*especially* to their own people. The less individuals know, the better; the truth could be a burden. But Ridgeway wanted to know more. What was it about Danny Maguire's death that was causing concern? Why was his body taken from the mortuary, and by whom? And just what had Max Gordon stepped into? Whatever Ridgeway decided to do, it had to be done quietly. and, he realized, unofficially.

Charlotte Morgan was due some leave. This tough, nononsense agent would not think twice about going it alone. She could find Max Gordon and help unravel the mystery.

As he picked up the phone and dialed her number, he felt a chill of apprehension, a sixth sense that years in the spy business had imprinted on his DNA. He hoped he was not sending the girl to her death.

* * *

"Max, how the hell did you get in here?" Marty Kiernan asked as he opened the door.

Max smiled, but his eyes quickly moved to his dad, who stood slightly behind the big man. Both men were breathing heavily from their last hard sprint on the run, and Tom Gordon looked uncertainly at the boy stepping into the middle of his room.

Would his father recognize him?

No one spoke for a moment. Then Tom patted Marty's shoulder.

"Don't ask daft questions, Marty. My boy could break into the Bank of England if he had to."

He stepped forward and hugged Max. Max smothered his face in his dad's shoulder and held him tightly, wanting to capture every moment of the embrace. The smell of the outdoors, mingled with sweat, seeped into his nostrils. It was an earthy scent that he remembered from other shared times with his dad.

Tom Gordon eased Max away to arm's length and looked at him. The moment of recognition began to flit away like a sun-chased shadow.

"Tom?" Marty saw and understood the look. He needed to emphasize Max's name again to embed it into his patient's mind. "Max has come a long way to see you."

Tom Gordon smiled and nodded. "Max," he said, as if reminding himself. "Yeah. Of course he has. Stick the kettle on, Marty. Let's have a brew."

The one-armed man winked at Max as he stepped through to the small kitchen. His dad should be all right for a while longer.

Tom Gordon gestured for Max to follow him through to the bedroom. He peeled off his running vest and toweled the sweat from his body. There wasn't much heating in the rooms—Max's dad preferred it that way—but he made no concession to the cool air as he pulled on a clean T-shirt.

"They said I couldn't come and see you, Dad. Mr. Jackson phoned, but they said . . . well, y'know."

His father nodded and put an arm round him. "Some days are bad. I just don't know who's who or what's what. It's horrible. I'm sorry. I know it hurts you."

A wave of emotion swelled in Max's chest. It was like having his dad home after a long absence. His father understood the uncertainty and pain he must feel. The gentle words stroked his anxiety away. Just as Max's mother used to stroke his hair when they all sat on the big sofa in the house they once had. When all three of them would splutter popcorn as they laughed at a crazy movie. When the log fire burned, when the world was warm and safe. When she was alive.

Mum.

Max swallowed, took a deep breath and almost whispered the question. "I want to know how . . . Mum . . . died."

Painful memories creased his father's face. "You know all that, son. I told you."

"No, you didn't. You said she died in the jungle. That she got sick."

"That's right."

"You've never taken me to see her grave. You said we could go one day. . . . I don't even know where it is. . . ."

Max's dad struggled with the memory. "It's a difficult . . . remote place."

Max shook his head—he had to get rid of the horrible thoughts implanted by the man who once had been his father's best friend.

"Dad, when I was in the French Alps and I saved Angelo Farentino's life, he said . . . he said . . ."

He couldn't bring himself to say the words that the Italian had desperately whispered—that he had loved Max's mother, that Max's dad had abandoned her to die alone. Vile images.

A tap on the door. Marty stood there. A concerned look both for his patient and for Max. "Tea's brewed. It's on the table. I'm just outside if you need me," he said, looking at Max. The boy wasn't supposed to be there; he hadn't come through reception, and the look of anguish on Tom Gordon's face meant something was going on between them. Whatever the relationship, Marty Kiernan could not allow any distress to his patient.

Max nodded. He understood what the ex-Marine was saying.

Tom Gordon moved past his son into the main room, where late-afternoon sun caught the blemishes and smears on the small panes of glass in the French doors. Outside, trees morphed into silhouettes as sunlight dipped lower in the sky. Max's dad sipped the mug of tea and watched the branches shudder in the breeze.

"What did Farentino say?" he finally asked.

It was easier talking to his dad when he wasn't looking at him. Max told him everything, spilling the words out rapidly, wanting to rid himself of the poisonous thoughts. How Farentino's love for Max's mother eventually caused hatred for his father. How she had spurned their friend's advances and how the bitterness of that rejection finally oozed hatred in Farentino's heart like an abscess weeping pus.

"You think I abandoned your mother?" his father asked with an edge of uncertainty at his own memory.

"He said you left her to save yourself. You were there. You were with her in the jungle, somewhere in Central America. I remember you coming home and telling me she'd died. Soon after that, you put me in Dartmoor High . . . and went away again."

Tom Gordon shook his head, like a man unable to find his way out of a dense forest when daylight is fading, panic creeping up his spine and smothering any rational thought.

"No . . . ," he whispered, reaching for the edge of a chair.

Max, scared his dad was going to collapse, stepped forward to help him. "No!" his father suddenly commanded, and sat down carefully, as if his bones would shatter under the strain of movement. "Your mother was ill. . . . I remember . . . she fell so ill. . . ." The words tumbled from him as he tried to see the memory. "The jungle swallowed her. It took me days to reach the ocean, and our people got me out."

"The organization you worked for? Did they know what happened to Mum? Dad, please. Tell me what happened!" Max tried to shake the memory loose from his father's mind.

"I tried to save her. . . . I don't remember. . . . I . . . I ran . . ."

"You ran away?" Max couldn't bear it. The lies were twisting themselves into truth.

"I ran. Yes. I ran. Through the jungle. I ran," his father said quickly, as if seeing the event in his mind's eye for the first time. Surprise and fear embellished his words. His hands trembled and then covered his face. A low moan came from his throat. It settled like an animal whimpering in pain, and then Tom Gordon crumpled in on himself. A dark star imploding.

"Dad," Max whispered, going down on his knees in front of his father, barely able to stop the tears that threatened to blur his eyes, frightened at the change that had come over his father. He held his dad's hands in his own, like a child begging not to be torn away from a parent.

"Please, Dad, don't cry. It's all right. It'll be all right."

Tom Gordon wiped a hand across his face. Tears dried, eyes glaring, he stared at the boy in front of him. "Who the hell are you? Why are you asking about my wife?"

All recognition had gone.

Max felt as if he'd fallen from a boat into the ocean—the boat sailing away, leaving him helpless in the vast expanse of loneliness. A shudder racked his muscles. He stood up quickly. He and his father were suddenly like two men facing each other in a dark alley, neither willing to give way. "You ask too many questions! I don't know you!" Tom Gordon was on his feet.

"Dad! Come on! Please! Cut it out. You're scaring me now!" Max shouted in his father's face. Tom Gordon snatched out a hand and grabbed a handful of Max's jacket. This was the side of his father Max had only occasionally glimpsed—a determined fighter who could respond immediately to any threat.

Before Max could do or say anything, Marty Kiernan swept into the room, stood behind Max's dad and wrapped him in a gentle one-armed bear hug. Tom Gordon resisted for a moment, but Marty was whispering, gently calming his patient. "All right? Yeah? All right now, Tom?" Max heard him finally say louder.

Tom Gordon nodded. Marty released him and eased him gently onto the sofa, where he lay down, as if exhausted from a punishing ordeal.

Max's dad gazed at the ceiling, locked in his own torment.

"What happened, Max?" Marty said. "What did you say to him?"

"I just wanted to know about my mum, whether he'd tried to save her or not."

"Course he did. He's your dad. He'd move heaven and earth to help his family."

Max shook his head vigorously, but the images wouldn't free themselves. They clung like leeches to his mind, sucking all the love out of him. "He ran away and saved his own skin!" Max yelled.

"Keep your voice down. Remember where you are. Now, you listen to me, son. Your dad has never run away from anything in his life. He's one of the bravest blokes I've ever known, and I've known a few. Don't think of your dad like that. You've got it wrong."

Marty had placed his hand gently on Max's shoulder, but the boy pulled away. He grabbed his backpack and pushed open the French doors.

"Marty, he told me! He ran! Farentino told the truth. My dad ran away and left my mum to die."

"Never! Your dad's confused. He doesn't remember things—you know that. Wait!"

Max ignored the big man's plea and sprinted straight

across the open lawns toward the trees, no longer caring whether he was spotted.

Marty glanced quickly at his patient. Tom Gordon had turned on his side and closed his eyes. His breathing was slow and deep. The big man pounded after Max. He couldn't let the boy go without trying to talk to him about his father.

Max reached the edge of the trees; the wall was another sixty or seventy meters away. He ducked below the branches. Evergreens sucked in the light; pine needles cushioned his footfalls and saved his life. The man who stepped out of the shadows rammed his shoulder into Max like a fierce and dangerous rugby tackle. Max's head whipped back as he was slammed onto the ground. If the ground hadn't been so soft, his neck would have snapped.

Max had a blurred vision of the man who straddled him. It was like a slow-motion movie. The man said nothing, grabbed Max's hair and raised a fist. One thing Max knew without any doubt was that, unlike in the movies, when someone hits you in the face, a real punch can shatter bones and kill. This was real.

He squirmed and bucked, twisting his body. Split-second convulsions powered from somewhere deep inside his brain. Max reared up, baring his teeth like an animal, spitting in the man's face.

The man was too heavy to push off, but it made him falter. Then, in the moment that he regained his balance, a tree trunk moved, blotted out the faltering light and fell across him. Max's assailant was crushed and made only the briefest sound as the air wheezed from his lungs. The tree trunk stood up. It had only one arm, but it yanked Max to his feet.

The ex-commando dragged Max and held him effortlessly against an old oak. "Quiet," he whispered, his eyes scanning the uneven shadows. Satisfied there was no one else out there, he let Max go.

"Thanks, Marty. I dunno who that bloke is, but he's the third nutter who's had a go at me."

Marty was still cautious, but the danger seemed to have passed. No doubt security cameras would have picked up something. He could probably convince the nursing home staff that the man who lay prone was the intruder—Max would be long gone by then.

"What are you into? Tell me."

Max knew he could trust his dad's caregiver, and there was no time for long-winded explanations.

"The truth about my mum. Someone sent me a message. I'm gonna find out what it's all about. Some phony MI-Five guys came to the school. A friend of mine was killed. Everyone thinks it was suicide. I don't think it was."

"Bloody hell, Max. You don't half get yourself into trouble."

"*It* finds *me*. Marty, I have a lead. I've got to try and sort this out. Please. If I go to the police, they'll laugh at the evidence I have. Meanwhile, someone out there is trying to stop me."

"All right. Look, you're wrong about your dad. There has to be an explanation."

Max said nothing, the anger still sitting like acid in his gut.

Marty nodded. "OK. Get out of here. My guess is the cops'll get nothing out of this bloke. You call me when you need help. You get the info about your mum, and I'll bet you'll find out what really happened to your dad. Go on."

Marty gave Max a push into the darkness. He ran for the wall, hit it at a run, reached up, grabbed the top and belly-rolled down the other side. Then he was back on the street. A bus turned the corner. He ran to the stop, flagged it down and jumped aboard.

It didn't matter where it was going; it got him away quickly and anonymously from the area—away from any other prying eyes. Once he reached the city, it would be time to contact Sayid to see if he'd done what Max had asked.

Riga's second man, whose job it had been to cover a different section of the nursing home's wall, sprinted to the corner just as Max's bus turned away. He swore aloud in frustration. However, had anyone been passing, they would not have understood the Serbian.

This was not good. This was going to upset Riga. He pressed a button on his mobile phone.

"Max Gordon has escaped, and Yevko has not come back. There are two police cars driving onto the grounds. What shall I do?"

"Pray I am in a good mood when you return," Riga said.

7

Max found a hole-in-the-wall café. Barely large enough for a couple of tables, it offered milk shakes and sandwiches the size of a brick.

He checked his phone—a single text message: two letters.

MW

That was Sayid's signal. Max had told him not to phone but to leave a message on the networking site **DTYP**—Don't Tell Your Parents—and drop the information that Max needed into that. If anyone was going to start digging through Max's computer, which he was sure the authorities would already be examining, then they wouldn't find much. Except, of course, the information he had downloaded on Lionel Blacker, PhD, senior lecturer in South American studies at the University of Oxford: the man who had visited Dartmoor High and given the lecture on khipus.

It was only a matter of time before a trail to the Oxford lecturer would be picked up. How long did Max have? The man he wanted to speak to was a block away. It was dark now, and he needed somewhere to sleep, but he couldn't afford anywhere in the city. If everything went according to plan over the next few hours, he would get to the airport and sleep on a bench.

"Is there an Internet café anywhere around here?" he asked the woman from behind the counter who was fastidiously cleaning his table.

"Two streets left, scruffy place, on the corner."

Skunk Alley was the name of the Internet café. There were ten computers sitting on grubby Formica tops, and it cost a couple of pounds to access his webmail. The girl at the till had a glaze across her eyes that told Max she might have been inhaling more than the city's car fumes.

MW. Magician's Web. That was what held the information. He clicked on the exploding star logo, settled the headphones on his ears and saw Sayid's face appear.

His friend was agitated. The connection wasn't great—Sayid's features flickered and the audio faltered—but it gave Max everything he needed to know.

"Tickets are booked just like you asked. There are two file attachments I've put with this vid. An MI-Five agent came and questioned us. She was horrible. Her name's Charlie Morgan. She's young, short black hair, purple and red tufts, stud in her nose, Goth jewelry. Looks like she could go undercover in a zombie film. Scary. She threatened me and Mum."

Max said a silent apology to his friend. Sayid and his

mother had suffered enough at the hands of extremists. He hated the thought that a British agent would stoop to that kind of questioning, but that was the real world, not some kind of fantasy computer game. That was what grown-ups did—came on so heavy you couldn't fight them.

"So I gave them your laptop. Everything else just as you planned. The man you wanted to see is expecting you tonight. I phoned him. He's cool. Seems a nice bloke. I did those letters you wanted—they were on your laptop when they took it." Sayid gazed at the webcam. Max could almost feel his concern as his friend pushed his face closer, as if whispering. "Max, Mr. Jackson is really upset. He thinks he's let you down by not keeping you here. I haven't said anything— I can't, can I? Because if I do, Morgan will blackmail me, yeah? I told him I knew nothing about you cracking the safe. I'll play dumb. Don't worry." Sayid fell silent for a moment. "Max, I don't know if any of this is gonna work. They could be waiting for you." He nodded, gave a brave smile and a thumbs-up. Then he reached out and switched off the webcam.

Now all Max had to do was get to the man who was expecting him and who, he hoped, could decipher the khipu.

Max felt a surge of hope and excitement. He was sure he would learn more about Danny Maguire and how the dead boy could have known about his mum.

Charlie Morgan broke every speed limit to get to Oxford. A few well-placed phone calls had cleared her path down the motorways. Frustrated traffic cops watched her blitz by but grudgingly acknowledged they didn't have a car fast enough to catch her. Traffic cameras would pick up her plate, and the courts could decide whether anyone was above the law or not. It had to be something important, though, for such a high-level clearance.

She parked the bike and made her way toward the pillars, flashing her warrant card at the security guard on the main door.

The boy was obviously after answers. Professor Blacker had visited Dartmoor High and given them a lecture on khipus. She would wait in the library. Blacker didn't have to know anything more than that they were looking for a runaway boy. And when Max Gordon turned up, she would be there. She wasn't going to risk losing him—it appeared he was a tough little rat.

Max angled his way through the narrow lanes. He had checked the city street map earlier, but the crisscrossing alleyways still caught him out. He needed a quick fix on his direction. He looked up to the rooftops. Television satellite dishes in the UK point south. He was on track. Moments later he found the small Museum Street, and at the end of it was the imposing building he was searching for. The huge pillars proclaimed the building's status—a seat of civilization and knowledge.

There were still people about, even though it was getting late. He took his time, found a darkened area behind one of the huge pillars and looked around. Security guards lingered at the main entrance, a few tourists huddled in small groups and academic-looking types flitted across the main yard toward the east end of the building. That was where the offices were. Was the man he'd come to see in there?

He unfolded the city tourist map. There were more than thirteen acres of buildings, and the place he wanted was not shown. He did not have time to search for it. They would be closing the doors to the public in less than half an hour. Max approached a security guard.

"I'm looking for the Anthropology Library," he said.

The man, used to questions all day, simply nodded, pointing through the huge main doors. "Across the central hall, through room twenty-four, down the north stairs. It's there. And it's about to close," he warned.

Max was already moving. A massive Roman lion built of stone, standing meters high, guarded the entrance. Maybe it once stood at the gates of the Colosseum, watching bloody fights to the death. He moved into the building's central hall. It was vast, the size of Wembley Stadium. Max hoped there were no modern-day gladiators waiting to attack him.

The skeleton framework forty meters above his head supported the glass ceiling, but the opaque glass now stopped any semblance of city lights coming through. A honeycomb roof, trapping everyone below. Max felt like a worker bee desperately trying to complete his task. Huge wooden doors stood open before him. Other side rooms were being closed by the security staff, heavy chains and padlocks rattling through handles, securing interleading glass doors. Max lengthened his stride. He dared not miss this meeting. He ran through the gallery, past the exhibition cases. The room was labeled LIVING AND DYING. He hoped that wasn't a bad omen.

Max found the north stairs. The last few tourist stragglers were making their way out of the building's rear entrance. Another security guard stood ready to lock up. Max had left it too late. The glass doors to the library were on his left and they were locked. Max rattled them. A keypad was the only way in. There were still lights on inside, but no sign of anyone.

"Hey!" the security guard called. "It's closed."

"I have to see someone. I have an appointment. He's expecting me."

"Not at this time of night, son. C'mon. Think you'd better be off."

Desperation triggered a surge of energy. Max rattled the glass doors, pushed his face against the slim join between them and shouted into the book-filled room. "Please! It's Max Gordon! I must speak to you!"

"All right! That's enough." The security guard moved quickly toward him. A shadow appeared behind Max. An older man, wispy hair unkempt, wearing a rather dilapidated jacket over a faded cardigan, unlocked the door.

"Evening, Freddie," he said to the guard. "My fault. Entirely my fault. I was expecting this young man." He waved the guard away in gentle dismissal. As he ushered Max into the library, Max noticed there were crumbs clinging to his front; some lay captured by the spectacles hanging from a cord round his neck.

"I was just having an Eccles cake and a cup of tea while perusing an extremely boring unpublished manuscript on the elongated shape of Mayan heads. The writer thought such deformed heads indicated they were originally extraterrestrials. Any fool knows they bound their children's heads to misshape them." He brushed a crumb from the corner of his mouth. "I *was* expecting you, wasn't I?"

"Yes, sir. My name is Max Gordon, and I wanted to talk about Danny Maguire."

The old man straightened up. Any guise of dreamy forgetfulness suddenly cleared from his eyes.

"And you have brought the khipu with you?" he asked eagerly.

Charlie Morgan watched Professor Blacker stack manuscripts and files into the crook of his arm. He switched off the library lights and made his way to the door where she waited.

"I think you may have wasted your time, Officer," Blacker told her as he clicked the door closed. "I doubt this boy you're looking for is coming here. Certainly not tonight."

"And he has made no contact with you?" Morgan said.

"None. Bit of a wild-goose chase by the sound of it. Well, I'd better be off. Papers to mark before tomorrow. Good night."

Morgan gnawed her lip. Max Gordon would have been here by now.

"He's fooled us," she muttered to herself. "He's laid a false trail. Where is he?" She called after Blacker, "Professor, is there another academic who might know about khipus?"

* * *

London groaned and coughed with the millions of people who lived, worked and visited. Dozens of languages whispered in the back alleys, called to friends, shouted in argument or promised undying love to another.

But where Max sat in the Anthropology Library of the British Museum, all was quiet. The museum had closed; the lights had flickered down, leaving shadows of giant statues watching blindly over the great halls.

Sayid had done his homework, just as Max had asked. He'd hacked into the school's mainframe computer and found the man who had sponsored Danny Maguire's request to spend a couple of years in South America: Dr. Raymond Miller, curator of South American ethnography at the British Museum.

When the efficient and threatening Ms. Morgan had swept quickly through Max's files at Dartmoor High, she had seen no mention of the curator's name. It had been tucked away in a cyber-vault by a fourteen-year-old boy who felt a warm glow at getting his own back.

"Khipus are devilishly difficult to decipher," Dr. Miller said as he fingered the knotted cords. "Some of them are the size of grass skirts. Huge things. The main cords can often be five or six meters long. Specialists have spent years and years getting to grips with the messages they hold. But this one . . ." His fine-boned fingers teased the cords apart. "This is quite simple. It is, I should say, not genuine, but made, I am sure, by our young friend Danny Maguire."

"Then he *was* trying to tell me something," Max said.

"It is crude and amateurish, but that is not a criticism. It is a fact. One could expect little else, but it was a clever thing to do. Young Maguire must have known there were people wanting this information—why, we cannot say—so he did his best. Bless him. I liked that boy."

Max could barely restrain his impatience. The academic was taking so long to tell him anything, but he did not want to rush the elderly man, desperately hoping his knowledge would be the key.

Dr. Miller rambled on about how a khipu's main cord was always thicker than the pendants tied on to it. How the different knots meant different things, how the colors dyed into the knots were significant. *Come on! Tell me!* Max shouted in his head, but sat on his hands in case his irritation began to show.

Fancy loops and dangles, entwined knots and subsidiary cords all made up a fascinating and confusing intricacy from an ancient people who were thought to be illiterate. Not so, Dr. Miller assured him. Finally he gave a sigh and a grunt of understanding at what lay between his fingers. He pushed his spectacles back up the bridge of his nose. He looked at Max and saw the boy's controlled agitation.

"Forgive me. I've been going on, haven't I? I'm sure you don't want an anthropological explanation of khipus' origins. This is important to you; I can see that. Look here, these knots are stained red. Traditionally that means 'soldiers' or 'armed men.' The arithmetic is simple. Each knot means ten; joined knots like these three mean thirty. Thirty armed men—here." He fingered another knot. "A temple. These other knots denote men and women. These mean clusters of children. Or so it would seem. One can never be certain. Khipus guard their knowledge like sacred secrets."

Max tried to picture the message in his head. Armed men near a temple where there were women and children. Though it seemed the children were separate. What did this have to do with his mum?

"Danny was trying to tell me something about my mother. But she was nowhere near Peru, where Danny was studying. She was in Central America."

"Is this about your mother?"

"I think so. I hope so."

"Where is she now?"

"She's dead."

Dr. Miller grunted. "Oh, I see."

Max pulled out the photos taken of his mother in the rain forest. "These are the only clues I have."

The professor settled his glasses and quickly thumbed through the pictures, then handed them back to Max. "Right, come on. I'll show you something."

He ushered Max back into the corridor, up the stairs that led out onto Montague Street and through the room Max had crossed to get to the library. It was dark now, except for the exhibits' distorted shadows looming grotesquely up the walls.

The interleading doors to each of the galleries left Max's head spinning. He was losing all sense of direction. Even though he followed Dr. Miller's rapid footsteps, it felt as though he was being led into a labyrinth. A moment of re-gret tugged at him. He wished he'd picked up a museum map from the visitors' desk. *Don't go blindly into a place of danger. Wherever possible, know your ground*—Dad's words as he once pointed out a difficult route on a map. *That's what maps are for.* Max's thoughts swirled. His dad hadn't needed a map when he ran away and left his wife to die!

Dr. Miller stopped. Breathless, he tapped his chest. "Indigestion. Too many cakes," he said, then fumbled a small bunch of keys. The doors to the next room were bolted by a heavy-duty chain and padlock. Max heard a movement behind him as the clanking chains rattled through the door handle. A shaft of light caught them both like animals blinded on a country road.

"Hey!" a voice commanded. "What the hell are you doing?" The torchlight barely wavered as the figure moved quickly toward them. Dr. Miller turned. Waved and rattled his keys.

"It's Dr. Miller. I need to get into room twenty-seven for a few moments. Sorry to disturb you."

The night security guard was right next to them but refused to take his torch from Miller's face until he was certain of the curator's identity. Finally he lowered the beam.

"You should tell us when you're working late, Dr. Miller," the man said officiously. "I'll have to make a note of this in the log."

"Of course you will. Quite right too. Don't worry, we won't be long. Good night to you."

There was no mistaking Dr. Miller's dismissal. The man turned away, switched off his torch and faded back into the shadows.

"They get a little jumpy at night. Imagination is what does it mostly. Things tend to take on a life of their own.

I don't blame them, of course. I've worked late here myself and definitely seen statues shift position."

"You're not serious?" Max asked.

"That depends on one's imagination."

There was sufficient light to see the old man's face crinkle into a smile. He pushed open the doors and led the way into a room full of Central American artifacts.

Max gazed into the emerald-green eyes of a black beast. Misshapen, but unmistakably a big cat, it glared back as if Max had just come face to face with the black jaguar in the dense undergrowth of the rain forest.

It was an ancient carving hewn from black volcanic rock. The ragged edges gave the beast a sense of movement, as if its fur was being brushed by the breeze or a low-lying branch. The open jaws displayed white bone teeth, carved to match the shape of incisors and canines. It was powerful and ferocious. It loomed, ready to strike, ears flattened, fixing its glare on him.

The dim light in the room seemed to fade even more. Max smelled the musky cat fur and the carnivore's stale breath, and heard the resonant growl from somewhere deep within the predator's chest. It was frightening. Frightening and glorious. Max felt the sigh escape from his lips as he reached forward and touched the beast's flanks.

A part of Max ran free. Claws dug into the bole of a tree, and a canopy of stars beckoned above the treetops.

"Max?"

Dr. Miller's voice returned the statue to its role as lifeless guardian of the room's treasures.

The showcases around three of the four walls were lit,

while on the fourth, stone fresco slabs, intricately carved with figures, were frozen in a silent, macabre dance of bloodletting.

"Those are Mayan kings and queens, making sacrifices to their gods."

He stepped farther into the room. Max faltered, his hand drawn to touch the rough stonework, as if willing the storyboard to unfold through his fingertips. A loud buzzing alarm startled him. Yanking his hand away, the sound stopped immediately.

"Electronic beams scan those lintels," Dr. Miller said. "They're ancient, so we can't have every child on a school tour rubbing their hands over them, can we? But never mind those for a moment. Now, where are we . . . yes, here."

In the exhibit's half-light, he pointed out the history of the Mexican and Central American people. Different colors stained the map as Miller walked around the room, following history. He stopped. "The Maya—250 BC to AD 1000."

Max gazed past his reflection in the glass and pressed his hand against it. It felt like a contact between him and his mother. She was there, still there, among all those marks and symbols on the ancient map.

Dr. Miller spread out the khipu on an exhibit's plinth.

Max heard movement somewhere deep in the silence. "I heard something, back there," he whispered.

Dr. Miller took his attention away from the knotted cords. A questioning look.

"A flat, dull sound. I don't know what it was," Max said, unable to identify the muffled movement he had heard.

They listened for a moment longer, but it was silent. Dr. Miller turned back to the map. "It will be one of the night

103

security people. Now, see here," he said, ignoring the fact that Max stayed focused on the channels of darkness reaching into the endless halls. His instincts prickled. The sounds were a whispering movement. Not the almost-silent tread of a bored man on night duty whose long hours stretched out before him. These were like rushes of air across the cold, hard surface of the museum's floor, like rats' whispers.

Instinct warned him to stay alert, but he knew it could also be his imagination—he hoped. He forced himself to concentrate on what Dr. Miller was looking at on the map. The narrow strip of land between South America and Mexico was pockmarked with symbols.

Dr. Miller carried on without further hesitation. "Here. This is where Danny Maguire passed through on his way to Mexico. He contacted me several months ago, said he had reached the ancient ruins of Lord Shield Jaguar, who is the king shown on that stone lintel you touched."

"Then Danny went into Central America? He wasn't just in Peru?"

"Absolutely. I was quite concerned at the time. That isthmus is a well-worn path for drug smugglers from Colombia into Mexico and the United States. Danny was traveling off the beaten track, deep into the mountains and rain forest."

Max felt something squeeze the air out of his chest. It was a swell of hope. "My mother died somewhere in the rain forest. Does that khipu tell us anything else? Like where exactly Danny might have traveled in the jungle?"

Miller winced. Perhaps his own enthusiasm to help Max would exceed the boy's expectations. He hesitated, then shrugged. "I did say this was a crude example. A khipu is an information-storage device."

"Like a computer," Max said, remembering Sayid's words.

"Yes. But if someone keys the wrong letters into a computer, then it will not make any sense. So these knots might be the same. Who knows what might have urged Danny to make up this message."

"Dr. Miller. Please. Don't you see? He was responding to my call for help for any information about my mum. He wouldn't go to all this trouble if it wasn't really important. I think Danny was killed because of something he witnessed or because of information he was given. But that bit of knotted string must have more information on it. He was there. Right there. Where Mum died."

Max had raised his voice. He quieted, seeing the look of concern on the old man's face. He lowered his voice. "I'm convinced Danny died trying to get this to me. I've already been attacked. Is there anything, anything else at all?"

Dr. Miller fingered the knots like Sayid fingered his misbaha, the prayer or worry beads inherited from his father.

"I can only speculate," Miller finally said. "In truth, Max, I do not think this khipu has anything to do with your mother. There is nothing to suggest it. It has more to do with a state of affairs that is dangerous and involves children."

He took Max's hands and laid them on the khipu. "Close your eyes and feel the knots," he said gently.

Max did as he was told. The man's smooth palms brushed across the back of his hands and then lifted away. In his mind's eye, Max saw the knots through his fingertips. In that moment of stillness, his mind caressed every fiber. Since he had received the khipu, he had been so focused on finding answers that he had not stopped and held the dead boy's legacy.

There was a rhythm to the strands of cord. The looped and curled knots felt different from each other. The spaces between the knots and the lengths of each pendulum string felt like a pause in speech. It was deliberate. It carried meaning and inflection. But the mystery remained exactly that. He could have no hope of understanding.

Miller's voice guided him like helping someone stumbling through a pitch-dark room. "That gap you feel there is, I think, a vast open tract of land. The curls and loops in the knots indicate disruption. Damage of some kind. Devastation. Perhaps now, perhaps then. I think it is near a volcano. Possibly the temple is near a volcano where the armed men are. I think there is also great fear."

Max opened his eyes. The old man was gazing at the map, his finger hovering near the center of the land mass. "And your mother's photographs could well have been taken in this area. There are pyramid temples hidden in the jungle there, and borders between the countries in the Yucatán Peninsula are imprecise. Those valleys and mountains in Belize and Guatemala, many of them are impenetrable. They're dangerous areas where superstition and ancient beliefs can still hold sway."

Miller turned to gaze at the stone lintel that depicted Lord Shield Jaguar pushing what looked like a needle through his tongue.

Body piercing was one thing; this was something else.

Miller sensed for the first time the seriousness of Max's quest. "Blood sacrifice," he whispered.

"Move!" Max yelled.

He pulled the startled Miller out of the grasp of the shadow that lunged from the darkness. A man dressed in black, eyes glaring, face covered by a balaclava, jumped at them.

Max realized too late that here was the source of the noises he'd heard earlier: the whispered rush of a search.

Dr. Miller fell. Max rolled across him to stop the harsh boot kick aimed at his head. The blow caught Max's backpack. Hands snatched at him. He twisted and slid across the floor like a break-dancer.

"Help us!" he yelled. "In here! Help us!" He was already on his feet, desperate to find any weapon, but there was nothing. The shadow was coming for him. Max sidestepped, dug his shoulder into the man's midriff and heard him grunt, but he knew from the hard muscle he'd made contact with that he'd barely caused the man any pain. It merely bought him a few seconds.

His attacker stumbled into the corner of a plinth. The man lost his balance, went down on the floor, rolled and came up ready to fight. But Max saw that the impact had injured his leg, and the man's ragged breath told him he was hurting.

Max dived for one of the stone lintels, striking it with his fist. The alarm buzzed. Someone out there must hear that! He struck it again.

"In here!"

The man swung out at him. His fist connected with the backpack's shoulder pad, but the shock wave tore into Max's ligaments. Pain seared through his arm. He was lame. And defenseless. He went down, pushing himself backward across the floor as quickly as he could, trying to escape the on-slaught.

His shoulders and neck hit the wall. Max felt the wave of agony suck him down into a whirlpool of blackness.

The last thing he saw was a jade-encrusted skull, cut-stone eyes gleaming madly, broken teeth leering at him.

Welcome to hell.

8

Marty Kiernan had no choice but to tell the police Max had been at the nursing home. It would be suspicious if the security tapes showed Max running across the open lawns and Marty hadn't mentioned it to anyone.

It was easy enough, though, to explain the man carried away in an ambulance under police escort as no more than an opportunistic thief. When Marty's big fist had applied pressure to the conscious man's nerve points, he'd squealed but told Marty nothing. He gabbled in a foreign language that Marty knew to be Serbian. The police had responded quickly, so the ex-Marine had gained no information of any use. Now at least he would be held long enough for his immigration status to be checked. It was a fair bet he was illegal, given that he was being used to attack fifteen-year-old boys.

Marty picked up the phone to call Fergus Jackson. He decided he would tell him that Max had visited his father but would say nothing more. Max was Tom Gordon's son and had the same spirit as his father. Marty knew that no one could persuade him not to do whatever it was he'd set his mind on.

Jackson watched Sayid's face. Khalif had that ability to appear totally innocent of any wrongdoing.

"I've had a couple of phone calls, Sayid," Mr. Jackson said, handing the boy a mug of hot chocolate and nudging his old Labrador-lurcher away from the hearth of the study's fire. "Max went to see his father. He was very upset—both of them were, actually—and he did a runner. People who are trying to help Max—"

"What? Like that horrible woman? Misery Morgana the Witch?"

"Now, Sayid," Jackson chided gently, "she is an MI-Five officer who is trying to help find Max as a favor to me."

"That's not a powerful motorbike she's riding. It's a specially designed broom handle."

Jackson smiled. "Yes, you're probably right. She was certainly heavy-handed, but she is on our side. Anyway, we all thought Max was going to see the chap who came here to give that lecture. But he didn't." Jackson smiled again, and this time it seemed to say, *Though you knew that, didn't you?*

Sayid did his blank expression, something he found particularly useful when his mum had one of her agonizing "I'm a single mother doing the best I can for her son" moments, when it was no good saying anything. When her pain passed, he would let her hug him. That calmed her down and gave her some kind of assurance about something. So was there any way he was going to tell Mr. Jackson where Max had gone, that he was trying to find info on his dead mum?

Sayid shook his head. "Then where did he go?" he asked, forcing a note of surprise into his voice.

Jackson couldn't tell if it was genuine. Max had cracked his safe, stolen the keys to his vault and lifted his own passport. Just how much was Sayid implicated in all of that?

"The Oxford professor told Ms. Morgan that one of the curators at the British Museum was an expert on khipus. She has alerted the police and is on her way there herself."

"Then maybe everything is going to be OK," Sayid said.

"Perhaps I shouldn't tell you this, but they are also alerting all the airports, because his laptop suggested he was going to travel to South America. Did you know that? Please, Sayid. We need to confirm this."

Sayid agonized for as long as he could. He squirmed a bit, hid his face in the mug and swallowed. He looked a bit guiltily at Jackson, who watched him intently, searching for the very signs that Sayid gave him.

"Peru, actually," Sayid lied, looking as stricken as he could.

"So he *is* trying to get there. Lima? We found a forged letter."

"Did you, sir? Oh. Well, yes. Max was pretty determined. I shouldn't have said anything, I suppose, but . . . it sounds as though he's in more trouble than I thought."

"That's all right, Sayid. Now that we know for certain that's where he's going, we can do all we can to stop him. You're a good friend to help him, and you *are* helping him by telling us. Thank you."

Sayid gave a rueful smile, as though he was uncertain. What he knew for sure was that his best friend needed time to make his escape, and his lie had just bought Max more of that precious commodity.

But, knowing Max, he probably didn't need any help.

Riga walked calmly through the museum's side entrance. The intruder alarms had now been turned off, the few night security staff dealt with. No serious harm came to any of them, except for the one who had to be subdued quickly. His body had crumpled from the swift blow to his neck, but he would recover.

By the time the day shift arrived in the morning to find their colleagues trussed up in one of the staff rooms, there would be a few small stickers left prominently on doors and exhibition cases.

ACT WAS HERE.

ACTION AGAINST CULTURAL THEFT.

It would be assumed the raid was by a new group of previously unknown activists who objected to the British Museum holding so many artifacts from around the world. There would be more than enough time wasted to allow Riga and his men to be long gone. And hopefully have nothing more to do with Max Gordon.

Riga's employers were paying a substantial sum of money for this job to be completed, but it was becoming tiresome. Being paid to find another boy was almost below his dignity. Danny Maguire had been tracked and chased, his body now destroyed, but pursuing this Max Gordon kid was like trying to corner a feral dog. The boy seemed to have a guardian angel. Well, not tonight. Riga could blast guardian angels out of the sky like a hunter on a pheasant shoot.

"Max! Max! My boy!" An urgent whisper. Max felt someone tapping his face gently. He came to. His blurred vision cleared. He was propped against the wall with Dr. Miller at his side. The jade skull still grinned in the exhibit case, and on the floor, the attacker's body lay prone. Miller still held the hefty chain and padlock in one hand.

"Ah. My boy. Good. Good. Come along, we have to get out of here."

Max clambered to his feet, looked at the fallen man and then at the academic.

"I may be getting old, but I'm not afraid to stand up to thugs like that. Though I hope I didn't hit him too hard."

Max nudged the man with his toe, and he groaned. "He'll be all right. Where do we go?"

Dr. Miller was limping. It was obvious he had been hurt in the scuffle. "I fell badly on my knee," he explained, catching Max's glance. "I'll manage. We must get to a phone."

"I've got a mobile."

"It's no good down here."

Max took Miller's arm across his shoulders and helped him to walk. The pain in his own shoulder from the attacker's punch still hurt, but he kept silent; this was no time to moan. Shadows flitted and fast-moving footfalls padded quietly but urgently in the background. Dr. Miller's breathing was labored.

He stopped and leaned against an exhibition case. They had barely managed a dozen meters. Miller was trembling, his face drawn, his breathing becoming more strained. His face grimaced in pain.

"Oh dear . . . Oh God . . ."

Max tried to ease him gently to the floor, but his weight was too much to control. Dr. Miller slumped hard and tore unsuccessfully at the constriction of his shirt collar. His eyes seemed glassy and unfocused. Max touched the man's face. It was clammy. Something more frightening than the assault gripped Max's stomach. The edge of panic threatened to take control. Dr. Miller was having a heart attack.

Max's mind raced. He had done first aid; he knew what to do. He eased Miller's body over, tore off the man's tie and ripped open his shirt. Anything that might help him breathe.

There was a look of fearful surprise on Miller's face, and then the muscles relaxed and he sighed. His eyes half closed. He was dead.

Max desperately felt for a pulse in his neck, but there was nothing. *Do NOT do this unless you know what you are doing,* an instructor's warning shouted in his mind. Max knew. He KNEW! He checked Dr. Miller's mouth—there were no false teeth to worry about. He quickly wiped away the spittle that had dribbled from the corner of the old man's lips and wiped the bubbling froth of pink blood from his nose. Max could save him. He could save him. COME ON!

He laid the heel of his hand halfway down Dr. Miller's chest, leaned on it, felt the ribs give a little. *How much? Remember? About forty millimeters.* With one hand on top of the other, he quickly compressed the man's chest. *Twelve, thirteen, fourteen, fifteen* . . . He stopped, eased open the man's jaw, pinched his nose, covered his mouth with his own and blew steadily into the man's lungs four times. More compression. *Nine, ten* . . . *thirteen* . . . *fifteen* . . . Max covered his mouth again, blew again. Dr. Miller's chest rose a little. Max felt a surge of hope. But there was no pulse. Compress. Breathe. Compress. Breathe.

How much time had passed? Max checked his watch. Three minutes. It felt like three hours as he made the frantic attempt to save the man. How quickly a life could slip away. Max shook from the exertion of his first aid and the nervous tension of the old man's death. A death that would have been avoided if Max had not come here. And he had tried and failed to save him.

No!

"No!" Max screamed, and heard the echo bounce down the halls of the uncaring statues.

Feet pounded toward him. Someone shouted something. Two torch beams slashed through the darkness in the distance.

Max touched the gentle man's clammy hand. "I'm so sorry. Forgive me," he whispered. He reluctantly pulled the small bunch of keys off Dr. Miller's belt clip and jumped to his feet.

For a second he stood stock-still, closed his eyes, pictured the way he had come into the building, where he had rushed through to reach the Anthropology Library, and how he had dogged Miller's footsteps to get here. He saw the pictures in his mind's eye—and ran. He knew where he was in relation to those doors, but he needed a map to get out, and they were only to be found on the information desk near the main entrance across that huge open space. That was just too dangerous. He would have to adapt and tackle each problem as it came. All he knew was that the main offices were east, and there were loading bays to the west. And that was how he was going to get out of the building.

Max quickly flipped open his mobile, pressed a button and ran—away from the approaching sounds of running feet. The torch beams had ducked and weaved as the men checked each side room, cabinet and cranny.

"This is Max Gordon. I need help. I'm in the British Museum." He paused. "I don't know where exactly. Help me!" He paused again. "Listen, I can't talk. They're close. I reckon there are at least three men." He closed the phone.

Max pounded up the stairs.

A shadow gave chase.

How close?

Max could hear the man's breathing.

Arms pumping, legs fueled with escape juice, he gained a few meters. The man gasped a breathless shout. "Here!"

Voices echoed. A beacon to another deadly night shape that came from the adjoining room from which Max had escaped. The other man came at him now. He could see his eyes and the snarl on his face. Two of them. He could beat them. He knew he could.

Running scared but running alert, Max saw a third man. Waiting. Right where Max was heading. This man seemed totally unperturbed, as if he knew his victim was being driven to him for the kill. Where to run? Central stairs curved upward, turned at the top and came down the other side. They led nowhere except to a closed restaurant. If he bounded up there, they would simply follow and box him in.

Max was trapped like a monkey being chased by lions.

Monkey see, monkey do.

Climb, Max!

On pure instinct, he ran for the looming shadow that disappeared high into the dull gloom reflecting from the glass roof. It was like a massive, limbless tree about ten or twelve meters high.

Carved, grimacing faces snarled at him. A gruesome mask with a whale's tale in its mouth sat squashed at the bottom. It was a totem pole. Coarse, hacked wood, its paint long gone from a hundred years of North American weather, allowed a firm grip as his feet dug into the swirls and shapes of the carvings. Creatures of a Native American spirit world. He heard men swear below him as he clambered higher. Monkeys climb and monkeys jump, but this was so high he didn't even want to look down into the murkiness below.

A shout: "Get after him!"

Max dared to glance down. One of the two men went higher after him, the second scorched the darkness with his torch beam, but the third just stood and watched. Silent and unmoving. Figuring out what Max could do once he reached the top of this man-made tree. There was nowhere to go.

Trembling with exertion and the fear that came from being pursued, he felt the gentle vibration through his fingertips, the urgency of the man climbing up behind him. The totem wobbled. Max was at the top.

He had expected them to chase him up here. Added weight made the pole unstable, and Max was going to make sure it became even more unsteady—he had to if he was going to survive, but if he got it wrong, the fall could kill him.

Gripping a gnarled creature's sculptured face, he leaned backward. It didn't give. He threw his body weight forward, hauled back again and felt a tremor of movement. It began to rock. Max grunted with effort, felt his leg muscles straining against the force needed to shift the center of balance.

"Hey! Kid! Cut it out! You'll kill us both!" the man yelled, five meters below him. He was gaining fast, but the rocking motion made him grip the pole tightly and cling desperately.

Max was in no mood to do as he was told. "Go to hell!" he shouted back, and threw himself into the momentum. It almost tipped. Max cried out in effort. One more pull and push should do it.

Too far! The pole's momentum was going backward. Max hugged the sharp-beaked face that glared at him. It was like embracing a monster.

"Come on!" Max yelled at the top of his lungs, forcing every fiber of his body to hurl his energy against the momentum. Like a giant, felled tree, the totem pole creaked, shuddered and fell.

The man screamed. He'd lost his foothold and grip. Bones would shatter when he hit the floor. Another agonized scream confirmed it.

But Max's attention was fixed on the stately fall of the totem until gravity took his breath away. He would have to let go at any moment. The wall of the building loomed toward him, and then the shuddering pole slammed into it—taking the decision out of his hands, literally. The impact bounced him off the totem. Max threw out his arms, grabbing the ridge of concrete pediment that ran below the skeletal roof. Feet scrabbling, he found the edge of the totem again and used it to push upward. Then there was nothing but thin air below his feet. His weight wrenched his shoulders, but he brought his knee up onto the narrow ledge, felt the concrete dig into bone, ignored the pain and clung like a limpet. Sweat slicked his hands and face. He risked a downward glance. The dark-eyed man gazed up at Max. Then he sprinted for the hallways and stairs that would bring him up to Max's level.

Max grunted and heaved himself along the fingertip ledge, his badly aching shoulder protesting. Pain took his mind off the fear of falling. At last he reached a small balcony, hauled himself over and tried to calm his breathing so he could hear any sounds of approaching attackers. Max held his breath. His heart would not stop banging in his ears. He couldn't wait. He took a chance and ran down a narrow corridor.

Glass doors, chained and bolted like all the others, blocked his way. He was trapped. He saw the dark-eyed man reach the top of the marble staircase, turn and sprint toward him.

Max fumbled with Dr. Miller's key ring. *Don't look at him! Concentrate!* There were only three master keys on the ring. A one-in-three chance to escape. Max's mind picked the one that looked more like a padlock key, pushed it in, turned it and felt the surge of relief as the padlock sprang open.

The man was running flat out toward him now.

Thirty meters.

Max heaved the chain free, pushed through the glass doors and shoved his hand through the handles on the other side.

Fifteen meters.

Max tightened the chain, pushed the padlock through and snapped it closed.

Bang! Max staggered back. The man had thrown his shoulder against the solid glass doors just as the padlock clicked.

The man seemed unhurt and never took his eyes off Max. There was less than an arm's length between them. Max looked at Riga and their gaze held for a moment. In that split second, both recognized the other from that night on Dartmoor. Max saw the man's jaw muscles clenching. He was really fired up.

Being scared gives a high-octane boost, and Max was about to take off, but so was the other man. He could run through the next corridor and corner Max. To hell with him. Max smiled and raised his middle finger.

Then ran like the devil was after him.

There were stairs at the end. A narrow lift door tempted him, but going inside there would be like handing himself over. Nonetheless, it might help to cause a brief diversion. He pressed the button to summon the lift, turned and ran. And stopped. Now he could hear the sound of pounding feet. He ducked into an alcove. This area behind the exhibit's glass was boxed, creating a false wall.

Max heard the lift doors ping open in the background.

He slid to his haunches—*keep a low profile*—eyes scanning every shade of light. Someone had run past the end of the corridor, heading toward the lift. Max's fingers had already slid out the SIM card from his phone. He reckoned there were only seconds left now.

He was heading the right way: west. There were the stairs. The final exhibit at the end of the corridor was of a cave, with two skeletons lying in the dust—the Jericho Tombs, a sign told him. Max unhooked a fire extinguisher and placed it in position where the glass case ended and the wall started. He was out of sight from each end of the corridor.

He pressed a button on his mobile and slid the phone across the floor. It skittered like an ice-hockey puck.

He could just about balance one foot on top of the fire extinguisher, enough for him to reach up and grasp the top of the exhibit's roof. He heard his own voice echoing across the halls from the message he had recorded. "This is Max Gordon. I need help. I'm in the British Museum." There was a pause as if he were listening. Then, "I don't know where exactly. Help me!"

Max was on the roof. He risked a peek over the rim. The man who'd almost had him at the glass doors now held a short stabbing knife. As his jacket flapped, the butt of a chromed semiautomatic pistol glinted in the half-light. He ran past the tomb toward the sound of Max's voice. "Listen, I can't talk. They're close. I reckon there are at least three men."

The dark-eyed man looked this way and that, then bent down, found the phone and turned. Max ducked. It was as if his pursuer's instincts told him exactly where Max was hiding. He held his breath. Would the fire extinguisher on the floor arouse any suspicions?

Max heard someone call from below. "Riga!"

Riga. Was that the man's name or some kind of warning in a foreign language?

"Riga!" the voice demanded. "Police. C'mon! We gotta get outta here!"

Max dared not move. He lay as flat as he could on the exhibit's roof and hoped it would bear his weight; otherwise he would fall into the Tomb of Jericho and end up dead—just like the skeletons.

"I'll find you, Max Gordon!" Riga called.

Max's blood froze. His throat dried. The man knew his name and was cool enough to take his time and issue the warning.

"You're a smart kid. But I'll find you. Don't think I won't. You can't get away. Not from me. You remember that."

Footfalls pounded into the distance. Unintelligible voices, scrambled words filtered up from downstairs somewhere; then it was silent. Blue light twirled across the walls. The police. What were they doing here? Had a passerby seen something? Had a security guard got free and phoned them? Max heard the throaty growl of a motorbike. Its engine was cut. Doors banged open. And a woman's voice took command of the darkness.

"Search the place! See if the boy's here!"

Uniformed cops ran up the stairs.

Unbelievable. Now Max had to escape from the police.

9

The paramedics covered Dr. Miller's body with a blanket and eased the stretcher out through the doors. Charlotte Morgan stood in the room. There was no doubt that there had been intruders in the British Museum or that the man had had a heart attack. And there was evidence that someone had tried to save him. Who? She did not believe for one moment that the vandalism was caused by these ACT people. Not after being told of Riga's involvement at Dartmoor High.

She studied the room carefully, walking around the exhibits behind the glass. There was no evidence of any connection with Peru or South America. Light caught the glass and she saw the smudges. They were fingerprints, plenty of them. Most were low down. She imagined small children pressing their hands against the invisible wall.

Higher up were other prints. She stepped back, checked

the maps behind the glass that showed the history of the Toltecs, Aztecs and Mayas. Why had Dr. Miller been in here? It seemed obvious that it must have been with Max. In Oxford, Professor Blacker had told her that there were two other experts who could understand khipus. One was in Edinburgh, the other at the British Museum. Max Gordon could go to either. Charlie Morgan had mentally tossed a coin. Heads or tails? Heads. London.

Her eyes scanned the glass. Among all the smudges was a full handprint at shoulder height, as if someone had wanted to touch the very place shown on the map. She opened a small pack of what looked like cellophane peel-offs, pressed one against the glass and lifted the fingerprints. If these prints were by any chance Max Gordon's, then she knew he was not going to Peru, where Danny Maguire had been working, but to Central America. Why? What was there?

"Officer Morgan!" The irate voice echoed down the corridor into the room.

Charlie looked up, annoyed to have her chain of thought broken, but by the look of the wildly beckoning figure marching back outside, it looked like she was going to have to do even more thinking. And fast.

Four police cars, lights flashing, stood guard over the museum's main entrance gates. Uniformed officers were coming and going, still searching the grounds and buildings for Max. Paramedics attended to the security staff. Charlie Morgan walked out into the courtyard. Crowds of faces pressed against the gold-tipped iron gates. There were always so many people on the streets even at this time of night.

"Who's paying for all of this?" the red-faced inspector demanded.

"What?"

"Police time! You've pulled four area patrol cars and a dozen of my officers off the streets. This is not a major incident. A half-baked bunch of activists making fools of the security here is not worth my people's time! I'm leaving one officer to take statements." He turned on his heel.

Damn. Charlie needed these people for another few hours, but he was right—she had no authority to use his officers, and there was always the question of who paid for what in this bureaucratic world. How far could she go before this was blown out of all proportion? There was only one way to find out. "Inspector! This comes from the top. The Home Office. We think it might have been a practice run by terrorists. We have good information. They're using a boy to get past security," she lied. "We think he's still inside."

Mention the word *terrorist* and the world freezes. At least the inspector's did. Was he going to take responsibility for letting an extremist escape?

"Is he dangerous? Do we need an armed team here?"

This was where it got tricky. Just how far could she go? Fear is a wonderful instrument to control people. She didn't hesitate. "That would be a very good idea. Thank you."

Now the inspector felt important. He was part of a bigger, more dangerous picture. He nodded. "I'll bring sniffer dogs in as well. You can have them till the morning."

He turned away. Charlie sighed. Whoever had caused havoc in the museum was already gone. Eyewitnesses had seen a car with four men inside pull away from the side entrance just before the police arrived. Two of the men were injured. There was little point in tracing the number plate; it would be false. Perhaps CCTV could track where it went.

But those were men. Where was the boy? Where was Max Gordon? All her instincts told her he was still inside.

Max waited until the initial shouts, lights and the sound of running feet had faded into a more industrious and less frenetic pace. The voices were more measured now, and it was obvious they were searching for someone. It did not take a great leap of imagination to guess who.

The false wall behind the exhibit case of the Tomb of Jericho was a space for pipework, most of which was as thick as his forearm. Old, solid, Victorian-era conduits. The gap was narrow, but if he held his backpack in one hand and a pipe with another, he could ease himself down. By the time he reached the bottom, he was in a network of underground pipes and cables. A service tunnel. Max knew he had been close to the west stairs when he hid but had no idea where he was now. It was almost pitch-black down here. Max did not like dark, enclosed spaces. He could feel it close around him, like an invisible night monster suffocating him.

It's your mind. Ignore it. It's only fear, and fear can't hurt you. He tugged out his compass, found his beta lamp and watched the needle swing. He followed the direction west, stumbling, barking his shins on unseen pipes. Cobwebs caught his face and hair, and as he moved deeper along the tunnel, he heard scratching sounds scurrying before him. Rats.

The service tunnel led to a set of iron steps that went up into the back of the museum's loading bays.

Max breathed in the cold night air and exhaled the fear he had bottled inside him. Now there were lights. Police cars blocked all the gates, officers came and went, and to the front and to the left of the loading bays, a woman wearing biker leathers was talking to a police officer. She had tufts of colored hair. She was pretty in a funky way. But tough-looking. She never smiled. That was the MI5 woman Sayid had told him about. And she had the place sewn up. There was no way Max could make a run for it.

At the end of the loading dock, an ambulance waited. It was almost as if it was not part of the activity in the nearby courtyard. Doors opened behind him and two paramedics wheeled out a blanket-covered body. They went down the side ramp, opened the vehicle's doors and began to load Dr. Miller's body—*Who else could it be?* Max reasoned—into the ambulance.

Max followed in their footsteps, and as they clambered out, he waited until they noticed him. His sadness was not really an act, but he had to make sure they believed him.

"Excuse me," Max said.

"You all right, mate?"

"That's my granddad in there. We were in the museum together when he . . . fell down."

"Oh, I'm really sorry, son."

"I tried to save him," Max said.

"Yeah, we saw someone had had a go. Look, there's nothing you can really do in a situation like that. Even if we'd been there, we probably couldn't have saved him either."

Max nodded and took genuine comfort from the paramedic's consolation. "I've just spoken to the police. They said if it was all right with you, I could go with him. My mum and dad are on their way to the hospital."

The female paramedic looked at her partner, who seemed uncertain. "You sure you want to?"

Max just nodded.

They closed the doors. Max sat on the opposite stretcher to Dr. Miller's body. The ambulance smelled of disinfectant— a cold, functional place created to save lives. Or to ferry the dead on to the next stage of their journey.

The ambulance stopped at the gates. A police officer waved it through, giving it safe passage through the gawping crowd. It slipped away quietly. No flashing lights or siren needed. There was no need to trumpet a man's death.

Max watched the police activity recede beyond the city streets. He reached out his hand and laid it on the still form in front of him.

"Thank you," he whispered.

The trail had gone cold.

There was no trace in the database of the fingerprints Charlie Morgan had found in room 27 at the British Museum, and the search was called off by the time it opened the next morning.

Ridgeway had spoken to Fergus Jackson, but, despite his most persuasive efforts, had failed to convince him that taking fingerprints from Max's room could aid in tracking him. Jackson was adamant. Such an act would be an infringement;

he had no desire to have an innocent pupil's fingerprints on a police or Security Service database.

No one is innocent, Ridgeway wanted to say, but did not.

Now Ridgeway faced a defeated, gum-chewing Morgan in his office.

"We might have to do this off the record," he said, finally airing his thoughts.

"All right, boss," she said. She didn't care. Rules were for the guidance of the unthinking and the masses. The two were not mutually exclusive.

"I had a brief and robust conversation with a senior member of the civil service who had Jonathan Llewellyn as his shepherd dog."

Llewellyn was a higher-up in MI6, the Secret Intelligence Service. "Does Six have an interest in Max Gordon?"

"Not him. Riga. He's international and seems too big a hitter to bring in to get involved with the Gordon boy. I've now been told officially to keep my nose out of it unless, or until, the security of the nation is at risk from an internal threat. Which, from this particular incident, it is not."

"I've got some leave due," she said, knowing full well the suggestion for any unofficial activity had to come from her. A tacit understanding between professionals. What someone does in their own time is their business, not the department's.

"Good. I'll let you know when to take it. There's absolutely no sign of Max Gordon leaving the country. Passport control at all regional and international airports and ferry terminals has been flagged. I don't know where he is. I don't know what his involvement is with Riga, nor why Danny Maguire's body was mistakenly cremated in a supposed mix-up with another boy at a funeral parlor. I don't know why I've been warned off by our government and Six. But I do know that I want to find out."

"Can you speak to his headmaster? See if there's a connection with Central America?"

"Not Peru?"

"Don't know for sure; it's only a hunch. And I've just remembered. I've got his laptop. His fingerprints will be all over it."

She blew a bubble with a satisfying burst. She didn't need anyone's permission to lift those.

In the early hours of that morning, Max Gordon had walked away from the busy clamor of a city hospital. Easily lost in the crowds, he was minutes from an Underground station.

By the time the automated voice advised passengers that the train's doors were closing, he was on a seat, his head nodding in exhaustion onto his chest. A woman with a big suitcase squeezed next to him. She nervously held on to her case's strap, though Max reasoned it would take some effort to steal it in a hurry. It was obvious by the travel labels that she was going to Heathrow. He asked if she'd wake him when they got there. Then, with an arm hooked through his backpack, he fell into a deep and desperately needed sleep.

Max stood beneath the glistening ceiling of London's Heathrow terminal five. Vast wings of glass, held fast seemingly to keep them from flight, spanned the concourse. There were a couple of hours to go before he boarded. Sayid had already checked him in online when he made the flight bookings. He could not risk using public email or phone to contact Sayid. It was down to the wire now. He had either got away with it this far or he hadn't.

If anyone had rumbled what he had done, or if they had interrogated Sayid too strongly and forced his best friend to tell them everything, then Max would be picked up the moment he got to the boarding gate. He would soon find out. In the meantime, he needed a wash, food and a pharmacy. Not necessarily in that order.

Sometimes the small things in life help give you a boost—the airport cost five billion pounds to build, and the showers were pretty good. Max let the steaming water sluice away the grime and sweat. He stood for a long time, letting it pound his skin, allowing his mind to settle. He still had so much to do. And he wished there were a compass that pointed him in the exact direction he needed to go. He would use Miami as a gateway to fly down into the Caribbean and then strike inland through Belize, where he would try to find one of the remote border villages. Someone there had to know what had happened to his mother; a foreigner's presence would not have gone unnoticed. Danny Maguire must have come close to finding out—and had paid the ultimate price. Max took heart from the fact that he had got himself this far.

By the time he presented himself at the boarding gate, he felt a different person. He had inverted his reversible jacket and settled the cheap reading glasses that he'd bought in the pharmacy onto his nose. He hoped that the brown color tint he had washed into his hair would not stay forever—the bottle's label had promised him it would not.

He caught a glimpse of himself in a reflection and returned the counter clerk's smile as she checked him through.

"Enjoy your flight to Miami, Mr. Lewis."

Joshua John Lewis: eighteen years old, a final-year pupil at Dartmoor High. Max had also taken Lewis's passport the night he broke into the vault.

Max Gordon had ceased to exist.

10

Riga went to an office in Canary Wharf. It was high up in one of the new towers that proclaimed themselves to the world as being very modern, very important and very expensive. None of which impressed Riga.

He waited while the ordinary-looking man spoke on a cordless phone. He stood with his back to the mercenary, making no concession to his presence. The balding head had close-cropped gray hair, barely covering the man's scalp, but there was still a light dusting of dandruff on the crinkled suit. The man reminded Riga of a teacher who had taught English at his school in Finland. If you passed him in the street, you would not give him a second glance. Little did Riga know at the time that the mumbling teacher was a government agent, someone who kept an eye out for promising young men who would work for the state with blind obedience. Young men who could be trained to superfitness and given unpalatable tasks. And, like that teacher, this man speaking softly into the telephone wielded enormous power. Never judge a book by its cover. Never pick a fight with a stranger. Never believe the obvious. Riga had learned his lessons the hard way, and he knew that the man who now turned to face him was answerable to even more powerful people.

He replaced the phone and faced Riga with an ambivalent expression, giving nothing away. A professional. There was a hint of a German accent when he spoke, but Riga knew he was Swiss and that after this conversation, the helicopter on the roof of the building would whisk him away to another building in another city in another country. The extent of these people's influence was global. His name was Cazamind.

"The Gordon boy is still in the country. Our people have double-checked the computer logs on all airline bookings," Cazamind said.

"So why pursue him? It's a waste of time," Riga said, checking out the view, knowing he could speak freely because his services were so valued.

"I do not know the full details, but our friends"—he laid emphasis on the word *friends*—"feel it essential that their activities in Central America be kept private." Cazamind brushed the dandruff from his shoulders and blew it from his desktop to the floor.

Riga wondered if anyone ever took him out to a restaurant and if the sight of that small snowstorm put diners off their food. He kept those thoughts to himself. He could stand his ground on any issue relating to his employment, but to discuss personal hygiene with the man who represented such powerful people would be a breach of etiquette. Even professional killers need good social skills.

"Gordon doesn't know anything. It doesn't look as though Maguire got any info to him," Riga said.

"We cannot be certain. Not yet. He approached the man at the British Museum who was Maguire's mentor; perhaps something passed between them before the old man died. What do you think of him? The boy." Cazamind paused and, like a Swiss banker studying a balance sheet, gazed at Riga— reading between the lines, looking for anything not quite right. "Your professional opinion," he said finally.

Riga gazed down at the bankers and traders scurrying out of their offices and into the man-made oases of food and drink. This was a small city-state created especially for the people who made the country's wealth. In moments they would be jam-packed into expensive restaurants where they would have to shout to be heard in a conversation. Then an hour later they would surge back to their computer screens and play the equivalent of high-stakes poker with other people's money. Meanwhile, Riga was a free man. Like the kid. Max Gordon was out there on his own, running scared maybe, being hunted, gone to ground, surviving. Riga respected that. He did not respect the moneymakers. Their risk was not the same as his and Max Gordon's.

Riga turned back to Cazamind. "He's resourceful. He's got guts. He's tough. He doesn't give up. He knows how to survive, and he's got a brain between his ears. If he has anything, anything at all that compromises the people you represent, the kid will exploit it. In a couple more years, I could train him up. He'd be an asset."

"And you think that is even a remote possibility?"

Riga shook his head. Of course not. The boy did not have the instinct. He would not be able to stand the smell of a man's fear as he moved in to kill him. He shook his head again.

Cazamind sighed, his palms opening in a small gesture of inevitability. "Then, if he is that tenacious, we should assume the worst-case scenario. We must find him, wherever he is." He fixed his eyes on the mercenary. "And have you kill him."

Twelve hours later, in Florida, a bus lurched, a car swerved and there was a scrape of metal. The drivers swore at each other. A man who had obviously been living rough threw up in the back of the bus, and the stench was foul. Passengers shouted abuse at him. The driver turned and called to everyone.

"OK, folks, take it easy. End of the line. I have to call this in. There'll be another bus along in a few minutes."

The driver eased himself down the aisle, muttering apologies to his passengers, most of whom he knew by name. His belly pushed against his trouser belt. Maybe that was why he wore suspenders as well, Max thought, just in case the belt snapped one day and, like a dam bursting, his belly disgorged and smothered everything in its vicinity. Max was surprised the man was as good-natured as he was, considering his bus had just had an accident, a bloke had puked all over the backseats and it was hot.

Miami.

Hot, bustling, big sky and brightly dressed people in floral shirts. It looked just like a travel poster. Except down this part of town. This was where the opulent lies of television and movies stopped. There was no glamour around here. There were poor people living on welfare who caught buses. Some of the shops were boarded up.

They stood in the heat while the drivers exchanged details. A Miami–Dade County police car arrived, but there was no sign of a replacement bus. Max turned to a woman who waited in the queue with him. "Excuse me, can you tell me where Backpackers' Big House is?"

She looked at him for a moment as if an extraterrestrial had suddenly appeared next to her. "You English?"

"Yes," Max said. "And you're an American."

She laughed. "You got a smart brain, son. What you doin' all the way down here? This is no place for sightseein', hon. This is the *baad*lands."

"My friend in England booked me into a place called Backpackers' Big House."

"He wou'n't be no fren' o' mine, he did that to me. I can tell you. No, sir."

Sayid, what have you done?

"Still, I guess mebbe you kids've gotta have somewhere to stay, and it's better'n bein' on the streets."

"I guess," Max said.

"Well, you go three blocks south, two blocks east and it's down there near the docks."

"Thanks."

"You sure you heard what I just said?"

"I've got a compass. I'll find it, thanks."

"What are you, some kinda Boy Scout? Son, this ain't

cowboy country—this is hostile territory. You get to this place you lookin' for, you lock your door and don't go out at night, you hear?"

"Yes. OK. Thanks for your help."

"You're welcome." She watched Max walk away. "Damn fool kid's walking into a mess of trouble. But do they listen? They do not," she said to herself, and then yelled at the driver being questioned by the police. "Clarence! Where's this damn bus you said was comin'?"

At least the room at the Backpackers' Big House was halfway clean. There were only a few cockroaches scurrying around the bare floor. A solid, old-fashioned bed, with a well-worn but laundered sheet and a cotton bedcover on the mattress, was the only furniture. There wasn't even a wire coat hanger to hook over the back of the door for his clothes. There was a bathroom down the hall. Smelly, industrial-sized rubbish skips, or Dumpsters, as the desk clerk had called them, were below his first-story window. It was the only room the guy at the desk had available. He wore a bandanna over his head, a Grateful Dead T-shirt and a gold earring. White whiskers clung like cactus spines to his face. It was no good Max's arguing that his friend in England had made a booking—there was no trace of it, and a whole tour of German backpacking kids had reservations, taking all the rooms. But they hadn't arrived yet, so why couldn't he have a room that wasn't over the Dumpsters? Max wanted to know. Because, the man said slowly, the bookings had all been paid for with a deposit. It was the room above the Dumpsters or nothing.

There was no key in the door lock. That was because, Cactus-Face told him, some dumb kid had lost it. If Max wanted to pay for a new lock, he could have a new key.

Max had slept in worse places. He took his backpack into the bathroom down the hall, where there was a lockable door, and showered. The hair color didn't wash out. Back in his room, he pulled the bed across the door. He could hear the belly-growling blast of a ship's horn not too far away. He had enough food and drink he'd picked up at the airport to keep him going until tomorrow. Just as well, looking out at those bleak streets. It was obviously not the kind of area renowned for family diners.

Max lay on the bed fully dressed, dismissing the idea of leaving his clothes on the floor. He hated doing nothing. It was like being in a hide, waiting for an animal to appear and having to find that stillness inside himself. Just as he'd done with his dad when he had taken him to Scotland and they sat next to a sea loch in a camouflaged hide waiting to see the wild otters. He and his dad had barely spoken, because they had had to stay silent, but they shared the same passion. Father and son on a small adventure together. Well, not anymore. His father had abandoned his mother, and now Max was on an adventure on his own.

He calmed himself as the adrenaline pumped at the thought of his dad. He needed to take every day as it came. He fingered the khipu, wishing his thoughts could show him the pictures the knots represented. He was warm, and safe from anyone pursuing him. All he had to do was get up early and reach the airport for the connecting flight to Central America.

He pulled out the wallet that held the half-dozen dog-eared

pictures of his mother. Her hair was tied back, her tanned face smiling. Max pored over every inch of her. She wore a jungle fatigue shirt, its sleeves rolled halfway up her arms, and an army-style floppy hat. She looked so beautiful. Each picture was in a different location in the rain forest. A waterfall, a ruin—which Max now felt certain was a Mayan site—some huts and a cloud-shrouded mountain. The plume of cloud looked like a smoldering volcano.

A volcano was exactly what it was. That was what Dr. Miller had translated from the khipu. He kissed his mother. Now he felt stronger. The message was accurate. Jungle and volcano. It was as if his mother's memory were calling him. *Come to me. Find out the truth. I'm waiting, Max.*

"I will, Mum, promise," he whispered.

He tucked the photos back into the wallet and buttoned it into his shirt pocket. He wanted her close to his heart.

Knowing he had evaded those who pursued him enabled him to control his fears and uncertainties and allowed his thoughts to settle. He closed his eyes, set his mental alarm clock, which always worked, and drifted into sleep. His final thought was that he was safe.

For now.

Fergus Jackson ran down the corridor. The few boys on their way to various activities scattered. When Mr. Jackson ran, his arms flailed like a drowning man, but he could put a fair pace on that uncoordinated body.

"Yes?" he gasped down the phone that he'd been summoned to.

"Fergus. It's Bob Ridgeway."

"You've found Max?" Jackson said hopefully, praying the boy was safe.

"Can you check something first before I go into details?"

Mr. Jackson listened, did as he was asked and within ten minutes, having run down and then back up the 133 steps, confirmed Ridgeway's question.

"Yes. Josh Lewis's passport is missing from the vault. The boy's at home in Herefordshire with his family. How did you know Max had stolen it?"

"Our friends in the FBI and Homeland Security run biometric fingerprint checks on all visitors to the States."

"Max is in *America*?"

"Miami."

"What on earth is he doing there? Have they caught him? Is he all right? How did you know he was there?" The questions tumbled out of Jackson's concerned thoughts.

"They responded to our request to keep an eye open for Max's prints."

"But how did you get his fingerprints?" Jackson demanded, since he had denied them access to Max's room for the very reason he did not wish Max's personal data to be entered into a police computer system.

Ridgeway hesitated, then said, "We got a print off his laptop and circulated it. Thankfully, the FBI dislike the CIA as much as we tolerate MI-Six, so they kept it to themselves. The bureau likes to help their English counterparts whenever the occasion arises."

Fergus Jackson berated Ridgeway even though the means might, in this case, have justified the end. "Max will be a criminal by entering America under a false name using stolen documents. This could irreparably harm the boy's future, Bob."

"He knew what he was doing."

This was no time to argue with the security official. "What happens now? Can you find him? Can you bring him home?"

"We're the Security Service, not MI-Six. We have no authority beyond these shores. Anyway, I thought you would like to know we've tracked him. I'll pull whatever strings I can, I promise you. We'll have people pick him up at Miami airport when he checks in again. Your boy has booked a flight onward to Belize."

"Belize."

"What's the connection with Central America?"

Jackson quickly explained what he knew about the Gordon family background. "This is all about his mother," he said. Another, more worrying thought occurred to him. "What about the mercenary?"

Ridgeway did not have an answer. Riga had dipped below their radar. "I don't know where he is," he admitted.

"Then Max is on his own without any protection from us."

"Yes. I suppose he is," Ridgeway said, ending the call.

From his office window, the MI5 officer gazed across Lambeth Bridge and the River Thames. The rise and fall of the tide was a certainty, unlike intelligence gathering. But there were times, as in the river at low tide, when muddy secrets might be revealed.

He turned to face Charlie Morgan. "If *we* know Max

Gordon is over there, then so might the people chasing him. How do you feel about a spot of leave in a warmer climate?" he asked.

Despite the clatter and hydraulic hissing of the garbage collection in the early hours, Max slept soundly. Nor did he wake when a ship's horn bellowed repeatedly into the night; distant police sirens barely penetrated his dead-to-the-world slumber. What snatched him from his sleep at four in the morning were the screams and gunshots.

They boomed. Terrifying blasts that reverberated throughout the building. Screams and shouts of alarm shattered the air like an exploding bomb. Feet pounded up the stairs. Someone was yelling, banging on doors along the corridor. A young voice. "¡Por favor! ¡Socorro! ¡Alguien! ¡Por favor!"

A cry for help. Max nudged the bed away a little, peered through the crack of the doorframe and saw a boy about his own age, maybe older. Hard to tell. He had an underfed, skinny look. His long, black hair caught across his face with sweat. He wore shorts, trainers and a T-shirt, and his hand clutched his side, stemming a flow of blood. He staggered, fell, got to his feet, leaving a blood smear along the wall. He was terrified. Max could hear someone pounding up the stairs after the wounded boy.

Max's actions leapt ahead of any rational thought process. He heaved the bed aside and stepped into the corridor. The boy's slight frame was easy to support. The look on his face said it all. A mixture of surprise and gratitude that someone had come to help him.

143

As Max dragged him to the door of his room, the gunman reached the top of the stairs. Latino twentysomething, bandanna on his head, bling jewelry round his neck and a big handgun in his fist. He snarled, screaming something in Spanish Max couldn't understand. The shooter was in a blood rage and obviously after the wounded boy Max was now pulling into his room. Max was in the wrong place—again—at the wrong time—again.

A chunk of plaster exploded, followed by another terrifying boom from the handgun. Max threw the boy roughly to the floor of his room and wedged the bed back, ducking as part of the door splintered from another shot. Max's hands shook with fear, but he hauled the wounded boy up, pushed open the window and lifted him out. He held him by his arm and dropped him onto the top of the Dumpster. No sooner had he let the boy fall than he jumped himself. His feet hit the curved lid. Legs together, he fell forward into space and tucked into a roll as he hit the tarmac.

The Latino kid was bleeding, but because he was so weak, his limp body had slithered from the top of the Dumpster and flopped onto the ground. Shock was getting to him now. Max quickly eased the boy's hand away from the wound. It was a messy scrape of a flesh wound just above the hip bone, so there was nothing broken, and it looked worse than it was. Max clamped the boy's hand back over the wound and took his weight. The boy pointed toward the darkened streets and alleyways, nodded enthusiastically, speaking rapidly, words Max didn't understand. But there was no misunderstanding the danger. The gunman was at Max's window, firing wildly at the garbage area.

Three shots quivered through the air in quick succession—
zip, zip, zip—and the heavy bullets thudded into the Dumpsters. Something in Max's mind clicked. The shooter was
using a revolver. It must have six rounds. The gunman had already fired three inside the building. He was reloading.

Max pulled the boy to his feet, grabbed his arm over his
shoulder and ran into the night. Fear powered his legs. His
mind screamed at him. *Idiot! You've left everything in the room!*
But survival was more important now. Max might have only
minutes to live if that gunman had friends down here on the
street. But now at least he had covered ground and moved out
of sight.

He heard the sound of a big-engined car approaching.

Then two more gunshots. Different from the gunman's.
Car tires squealed round the corner, full-beam headlights
holding Max and the wounded boy like a searchlight. The
driver was going to run them down.

Max had nowhere to hide.

He braced himself for the inevitable impact if he couldn't
jump aside with the injured boy at the last second.

Chances? Rubbish.

The big American SUV shuddered to a halt. Scorched
rubber smoked the air. Two men piled out of the car. They
were in their twenties. They wore jackets and jeans, and had
automatics in their hands. The driver stayed put, engine
revving. They looked Mexican or South American. It didn't
matter. Max was going to die. The nationality of the man
who pulled the trigger was irrelevant.

A third man climbed out of the passenger side. His
leather jacket, black T-shirt, gold necklace and cowboy boots

seemed to proclaim him the leader. He eased a wicked-looking revolver from his waistband and pointed it at Max.

Max desperately looked around for any escape route. There wasn't one. The wounded boy was on the street behind him. Max stood his ground, fists clenched, ready to fight for his life if given the chance. Shuddering fear and expended energy made him gasp for air. He did not want to die. *Let me fight. Give me a chance! Don't just kill me!*

"We haven't done anything!" Max yelled, exploding his own tension and wanting the man to think for a split second before pulling the trigger. "This boy. He's hurt. Look! He needs help." He scrambled for Spanish words. "Hospital. *Ayuda.* Help him. Call an ambulance. *Un médico—una ambulancia.*"

All of this happened in seconds. Then the boy on the ground opened his eyes and spoke rapidly. Max caught the word *amigo*. The man lowered his weapon, then barked orders. His two companions grabbed the wounded boy and put him onto the backseat. Police sirens wailed somewhere in the distance. Were they coming here or not? They faded. Max and the gunman faced each other. He raised his gun again. Max was a witness.

Then he hesitated and spoke in English with a heavy Latino accent.

"You saved my stupid brother. I owe you. Get in!"

The SUV swung away into the night. Within minutes they had crossed a causeway, leaving the city's glistening tower blocks behind. The driver killed the headlights and drove fast through the semidarkness. Canyons of shipping containers loomed next to iron skeletons of cranes guarding the docksides.

Max hung on as the SUV swerved, evading anyone who might be giving chase. The two men in the back had a first-aid pack open. One spilled a clear liquid that stank of antiseptic onto the boy's wound. The boy winced, gritted his teeth and seemed a lot tougher now he was in the men's company. The other quickly mopped the wound dry with a wad of gauze, then sprinkled a white powder over the gunshot. Using butterfly clips, they pulled the gash together. Finally they taped a clean dressing across it.

Max could see they had done this before; gunshot wounds were evidently not uncommon in their business.

The boy grinned. He was OK now. He reached out his hand toward Max. The boy's grip was strong enough. His blood was already smeared across Max's clothes. They both looked as though they had been in a war zone. The boy spoke in broken English.

"You save me. We friends now, yes? I am Xavier Morera Escobodo Garcia. What is your name?"

"Max, just Max will do fine."

11

The boat thundered across the flat, calm water with a roar like a jet engine. Max was strapped in, Xavier by his side. The breathtaking power kept Max from screaming with exhilaration. These men were not going to kill him; they were taking him on a heart-stopping journey into the unknown. There was no doubt they were on the wrong side of the law, but Xavier had promised Max that no harm would come to him. They were going home—somewhere in Central America—and Max was going with them. Their common destination offered some comfort, at least.

Dawn's needles of cold light splintered the sea. They were in warm waters, but the air still chilled him. Especially at this speed. Max looked behind him. The land was out of sight; the surging power wave crested and fell.

"It's called a go-fast boat," Xavier had told him when they

reached the tucked-away boatyard in the Miami dockland. "Is very fast."

Max had recognized what he'd always thought of as a racing boat: deep V hull, narrow beam, huge thousand-horsepower engines and nearly twenty meters long.

This was not just fast; this was breathtaking. Xavier's brother eased the power controls forward, the boat's nose lifted slightly and the engines bit deeper into the water—doing a wheelie would never be the same again.

Max could see the GPS-based speed readout in front of Xavier's brother. They were doing 180 kilometers per hour. Max had been in planes flying slower than this.

Xavier shouted above the engines' roar and the wind. "We go fast now. The Americans"—he pulled a face—"they don' like us. They try and catch us all the time." He grinned. "But they have to get very lucky, yes? They don' have boats like this."

"Was it the Americans who shot you?" Max shouted, pushing his face next to Xavier's ear.

The boy shook his head. "Another gang. We are taking business away from them. My brother, Alejandro, he is ambitious."

Max did not want to ask the obvious question, but he needed to know for sure.

"Drugs?"

"Sí. Plenty. Big business. From Central America to Miami. Very nice money."

They could not talk for long—the buffeting slipstream was too powerful. The far horizon, the open sea and the speeding bullet of a boat created an overwhelming sense of helplessness. Max was alone and defenseless in this vast ocean, ricocheting across the marble-hard water. *Always be careful what you wish for*, a voice said in his head. *You might not want it when you get it*. He had wished hard and long to get to Central America, but he had not figured on becoming embroiled in a gunfight, saving a drug runner's brother and being at his mercy. Not only had he stolen a passport and entered America illegally, but he was also now part of a vicious gang—and had no proof of identity or a plane ticket. He did not know which would be the worst fate: being taken to the drug runner's home base or being intercepted and arrested by the authorities. He was no better off than a refugee or a fugitive. But at least he was heading the right way.

Max concentrated on the trouble he was in. He was in no immediate danger. What would his dad have done? He allowed his father's image to settle in his mind, pushing away the stab of anger he felt. Rule one—don't panic. Rule two—be patient: watch and listen. Rule three—be ready, and when the time comes, pick your moment.

And then?

Escape.

Like the plowed water behind the boat, Max was leaving his own turbulent wake.

Charlie Morgan sat in Miami airport's security room with two FBI agents. Security cameras scanned the passengers coming and going, but there was no sign of Max Gordon masquerading as Josh Lewis on any of the screens. Nothing was flagged showing he had checked in at the departure gates. The Belize flight had already left without Max on board. The airline staff had been briefed and would press a control button to alert the agents, but no such alarm had been raised.

Did Max have yet another false identity?

"Where *is* he?" she asked no one in particular.

The FBI were doing Bob Ridgeway a favor by stopping Max from leaving America, but they could not extend their time beyond this act of professional courtesy.

"We can check every reservation and every young man who's checked in already," one of them said, "but if this kid is as smart as you say he is, then maybe the Belize thing is a red herring."

"Maybe," Charlie said, "but he doesn't have unlimited resources. He moved fast. He needed to smoke screen us long enough to get out of the UK—that was all. We know he's here in Miami, and he has to get to Central America somehow."

The men ran through the options Max could have taken. He might have caught a bus and traveled to another state airport and taken the Belize flight from there. He could have gone way across Florida and Texas and slipped through Mexico.

"Let's check all the airline bookings and the bus station. Can we do that?" Morgan asked.

The men shook their heads. "That's a lot of legwork," one of them said.

"And the kid's got at least twelve hours' start on us. I dunno, Charlie. That's a big ask," the other added.

It was time to charm the two young men, using the smile that made her look vulnerable enough to ask for the guys' help—like she used to do when she was a schoolgirl. "Just the main bus terminal, then. Maybe if there's time, we run the computer checks. What do you say?"

They nodded. They'd do as she asked.

Men always did.

An hour later, Charlie Morgan watched the television monitor at the bus station. "A suspected drug shooting last night involved a British boy. Police found the body of a known drug dealer in a Dumpster beneath the room rented by the boy. Two passports and personal effects were discovered. It is thought the British boy was using false identities and is involved in a drug-smuggling gang."

Charlie and the FBI had found Max Gordon thanks to a ravenous-for-news TV station on a quiet day. A visit to the Miami police headquarters, barely five miles from the airport where they had waited so patiently, confirmed the facts.

The questions Charlie Morgan could find no answers to were: where had Max been taken, who had taken him, and why would gunmen snatch him? She was convinced he'd been taken because someone as smart and quick on his feet as Max would never leave his passports and backpack behind if the shootings had not involved him. More questions: Had the man found dead in the rubbish bins been after Max? Who was the second boy? There were no answers, but these FBI men were officially involved now. Kidnapping—especially of a minor—was a major offense, and that was their jurisdiction. And now they needed her because she was the link to Max Gordon. She wasn't asking for their help anymore; they would be asking for hers. She felt good. Back in control. She just knew in her bones she was going to find Max—but whether he would be dead or alive was another matter.

Xavier's brother eased the throttles back. The wind had picked up on the open ocean and small waves lapped the hull. Alejandro nudged the subdued engines forward toward a fishing boat and shouted in Spanish to the two men aboard who caught the ropes thrown by his men.

When the engines were cut and the boat was tied alongside, the silence was complete.

Max stayed where he was. This was no place to jump ship. They weren't even in sight of land, and they had been pounding the ocean for hours. At those speeds and with the boat's extra-long-range tanks, they must have covered hundreds of kilometers.

Xavier looked nervous.

"What's happening?" Max asked him.

"We do the drugs run. We need boats out here to refuel us. This is our gas station," he said, and smiled. But his eyes scanned the skies. What was it that scared him? Max wondered.

Alejandro's men seemed unconcerned about anything other than feeding a fuel line into the tanks, and then Max heard the muffled thumping of a generator below the fishing boat's decks.

The fishermen handed over a cold box. Alejandro's men opened it and passed out food. Cold meat, sausage, chicken, flat bread, beer and soft drinks. Max made no move toward it, although he was ravenous. He was in an unpredictable situation and felt it best to be as low-key as possible. Stay still. Stay silent. He did not want to tempt fate and have Alejandro dump him out here. Even if he'd spared his life because of the debt he owed Max for saving his brother, he could easily leave him on the fishing boat to be eventually taken ashore.

"Kid," Alejandro said, offering Max bread and meat, "eat. There's enough." He nodded at Max as if enticing a nervous stray dog forward. Max took the food gratefully and had no concern for whatever it was that he ate. It tasted good—salty and tough—and made the juices in his mouth run.

Bobbing in a boat on the deep blue sea, with barely a cloud in the sky and a warm trade wind scuffing the surface, he could have been on a picnic. But he kept his eyes on the gang leader and his gunmen. Max would not be lulled into any false sense of security.

He turned to Xavier. Now that the battering speed had stopped, the boy seemed more subdued. "You all right? Your wound? Does it hurt?" he asked.

"It hurts, but it's OK."

"Where are you taking me?" Max asked, daring to prize information from them.

"Yucatán. South."

Yucatán! Max kept the gasp of excitement locked in his chest. That might take him close to the border with Belize. If he could get ashore and make his way inland from there, he might have a chance to pick up Danny Maguire's trail.

"Down the cays. Plenty reefs and islands," Xavier said, his mouth full of food. "You will like it there. We get into the jungle and no one can find us. No one. Out here"—he scanned the horizon again—"there are Coast Guard boats and their helicopters."

"American patrols?"

"Maybe. We are out of American waters now. But the Yanquis, they pay good money for our people to hunt us down. They all hunt us."

Max tugged a shred of meat from between his teeth. If government patrol boats found them, he would be repatriated. He would never get to the rain forest and find out what had happened to his mother. His thoughts whirled. Escape now seemed impossible. Even if they got within sight of land, he would not be able to jump ship. Like jumping out of a fast car onto a motorway, hitting the water at the speed the boat traveled would be no different from landing on concrete.

He would go all the way with these men and pray that as soon as he got ashore, he would be able to make a run for it. That was the best bet. But run where? He did not know that yet.

One of the smugglers lifted a shrink-wrapped carton of water bottles onto the boat. With a slash of his knife, he cut free the plastic and handed them out. Everyone drank thirstily. Saltwater spray encrusted Max's face and hair from the accelerated ride, and after swallowing as much as he could, he tipped the remainder of the bottle over his head and face. Once the sticky film was sluiced away, he immediately felt better. Wind-burned and tanned, and now with a full stomach and his thirst quenched, he felt stronger and more able to tackle whatever lay ahead in the next few hours.

The man who'd ripped the plastic wrap free from the

bottles threw it into the sea. Without thinking, Max shouted at him, "Hey! Don't do that!" The generator stopped, the water lapped and the breeze made a hollow echo in Max's ears. That was the only sound as the men stared at him in disbelief.

"Dolphins and turtles die because of that kind of stuff," he mumbled. *Big mouth, slow brain.* Why had he chastised a man who looked as though he could rip him apart with his bare hands? But no one made a move toward him; instead, they looked to Alejandro.

"He's right, Carlos. The boy is right. What are you, an ignorant peasant?" Alejandro said.

"*Sí.*" The man nodded.

"You let a fish die slowly because you throw away a piece of plastic?"

The man shrugged.

Alejandro kicked open the lid of a box, and Max could see it was packed with grenades and snub-nosed machine pistols. Alejandro reached down and took out a grenade, testing its weight like a bowler with a cricket ball. Max felt the lump of food he'd just eaten regurgitate. He swallowed hard. Xavier's brother looked every inch the kind of man who could cause you very serious harm. There was no humor in his eyes. Probably never had been. He yanked the pin, flipped the grenade and everyone ducked—except Alejandro.

A softened *boom!* and a geyser of water rocked the boat. Spray covered them and Max saw twenty or more fish float to the surface.

"I am a kind man. I bring death quickly. Yes? You think I care about fishes in the ocean?" asked the man who helped destroy thousands of lives with his drug smuggling. Alejandro and his henchmen laughed, but Xavier and Max did not. Max averted his eyes from the drug smuggler's. Push a man like that a sliver over the edge and he would forget any sense of obligation or family honor. Max would be fed to the fishes with a grenade tied round his neck.

Alejandro shouted at the men in Spanish. They were obviously commands to cast off and release the fuel lines. No sooner had the boat been pushed free than the monster engines bellowed, churned water and hurled the boat forward. Max was slammed back into the seat. He saw Xavier's look of concern. The boy raised a finger to his lips and shook his head. The message was clear. Don't ever challenge his brother.

Cazamind's power reached far and wide. He had the support of a vast complex of government and corporate infrastructure. Police in Miami were somewhere near the very bottom of authority and power, but Cazamind's contacts had been busy. The news of Max Gordon being involved with drug gangs was immediately backed up by intelligence reports that a known drug dealer, Alejandro Escobodo Garcia, had been in Miami that night. And someone had contacted the Drug Enforcement Agency to cut a deal. Complete immunity for Alejandro in exchange for information about the drug-shipment routes that flowed up from South America and their dispersal points from Central American countries. It looked as though Alejandro wanted to get out while he still could. It was an excellent opportunity for the American intelligence agency.

Drug dealers were of no interest to the Swiss master planner. The secret he was protecting was more terrifying and dangerous than the international drug trade. Within hours of Max's disappearance, Cazamind had tracked police and FBI reports, collated all the information and concluded that Max Gordon had stumbled into this very scenario. For whatever reason, the smugglers had taken Max with them.

The Drug Enforcement Agency had issued an intercept command to the U.S. Coast Guard's Helicopter Interdiction Tactical Squadron to chase down Alejandro Garcia and to arrest and detain him.

It would be a clean sweep that snared a turncoat drug dealer.

Arrest and detain.

If they did that, Max Gordon would be found and sent home. Was it better that way? From everything Riga had told him about the boy, he would keep on trying to uncover the secret of his mother's death. He would have to be dealt with in England if he returned. A risk worth taking?

Cazamind picked up the phone. The intercept command must be changed.

Arrest and detain was insufficient.

Locate and destroy.

In Alejandro's world, millions of dollars changed hands, and buying information was easy. There was always someone who needed a new car, a health plan for their children or a means to pay off their own bad habits. There were informers at every level, and people like Alejandro Garcia had them in his pocket.

Now one of them told him that he had been betrayed.

Alejandro braced himself against the boat's controls, the satellite phone pressed tightly against his ear. He eased back the power, spoke quickly and turned to look behind the boat, across the plumes of water.

"Carlos!" Alejandro's man stepped forward to take the controls.

Xavier flinched as his brother stared at him in disbelief. "*Usted me traicionó. You betrayed your own brother?*"

Xavier cowered into Max. Alejandro had not made a move toward him, but the man struck fear without raising a hand.

Alejandro gestured to Carlos, who eased back the throttles.

The boat slowed quickly and then settled into the ocean's swell. The silence was frightening; the engines' roar had at least muted Alejandro's anger.

Xavier turned to Max and spoke rapidly in English as if the foreign language might disguise his guilt.

"They said they would take us and give us a new life!"

"Drug smuggling is a death sentence!" Alejandro yelled.

"No, no! They come for us now there is no trouble. We are going home. We have no drugs on board. You see? They cannot charge us with anything," Xavier pleaded. "This is not a life, brother. We can live in America. They will look after us. They promised!"

The men stood silent, dumbfounded by the discovery of the traitor in their midst, but they could make no move against their leader's brother. If the boy was to die, and surely he must, then it had to be by Alejandro's hand.

"It *is* a way out," Max said, wanting to break the imminent threat of the violence he knew was about to be inflicted. "They can't charge you with anything."

"You are wrong. Kidnapping is a life sentence," he said. And then he gave a sorrowful smile and shook his head. "Xavier, you are a fool. You made your deal before he came aboard," Alejandro said, pointing at Max.

Xavier looked confused.

"Do I kill him now?" Alejandro said. "Tip his body in the water? Then there is no kidnapping, eh? No evidence?"

Max was ready to jump, but knew he could never survive the gunfire that would surely follow.

"He saved my life!" Xavier cried.

"And I was in his debt. But you are no longer my brother."

Alejandro eased a semiautomatic from his belt, pulled back and released the slide, loading a round into the chamber. It was the moment before their deaths.

"He's still your brother," Max said desperately. "He's your blood. He did it because he loved you. He was trying to protect you."

Alejandro raised the gun and gazed along its barrel.

"It's too late," he said.

He lowered the weapon. "They're here."

The Coast Guard's *Hamilton*-class, high-endurance cutter lay sixty kilometers beyond the horizon, but its attack helicopter came like a low-flying vampire bat out of hell—and it was looking for blood. Precision laser-sighted, .50 caliber rifles, nestled next to M240, 7.62 mm machine guns, lethal weapons that exemplified this unit's special status—AUF, Airborne Use of Force.

Alejandro powered the go-fast boat into a rearing surge, and like a white stallion given its freedom, the boat charged forward. Max held on to Xavier, who fell to the floor, grasping his wound as he slammed into the bulkhead. The boat slewed right, snaked and then headed due west, toward the setting sun.

"He won't outrun a chopper!" Max yelled over the engines.

Xavier shook his head. "He's going for land—for the inlets."

Max squinted against the blurring light and spray. There, on the ragged horizon, was a scribbled pattern of palm trees. Alejandro was taking the straightest route while shouting instructions to his men. They opened the weapons box and armed themselves.

"He's crazy. That's exactly what they want him to do. That gives them an excuse to shoot back."

Xavier's face streamed with tears, but whether they were caused by the buffeting of the wind or by his emotions Max didn't know.

The helicopter was less than a kilometer away now—and so was the shoreline. The waves had disguised the distance between boat and shore, and Max could see the narrow, curved beaches, the rocky outcrops and the headlands. Reefs intertwined like bracelets, settling the swells into narrow strips of calm water.

The walloping downbeat of the rotor's blades flattened the air above their heads. The helicopter was less than a hundred meters above them. The expert pilot shadowed Alejandro's every evasive move. But then Alejandro swung the boat in an almost suicidal maneuver. For a moment it felt as though they would all be thrown overboard. The boat nearly flipped and fell onto its side, engines screaming in the air as they sought the water that fed them. The helicopter zoomed past.

Alejandro turned to Max. "Get ready! I'm going across the reef! You take Xavier." He paused a moment and locked on Max's gaze. "He can't swim. You get him ashore. You saved him once. You save him again. Yes?"

Alejandro was giving him his life. Max nodded.

"He's a fool, but he's my brother," Alejandro said. "Get ready."

A tortured, ripping sound reverberated through the boat as he ran it across the reef. The helicopter was coming in again. Max gripped Xavier's shirt.

"We've gotta jump, Xavier. You stay with me."

Xavier looked bewildered. He cried out in Spanish to his brother, who turned and answered him. Max didn't understand what they said, but he knew that one brother was sacrificing himself for the other.

Alejandro looked at Max and nodded. The engines suddenly slowed; the boat wallowed in its own wake. Max didn't hesitate. He grabbed Xavier and pulled him over the side. As they hit the water, the boat's engines surged, churning the sea into a twisting confusion of foam.

Max was out of his depth but quickly hooked the struggling Xavier under his arms. "Kick your feet! I've got you!"

Max pulled Xavier after him, calming the boy's panic. Beyond the reef, Max could see the boat zigzagging and the helicopter weaving to keep alongside. Alejandro had fooled the pilot, making it look as though they were running for the mangrove inlets and had caught the reef, momentarily losing control. For a few seconds the boat and the wave concealed Max and Xavier, and once Alejandro was back on the open sea, the helicopter crew was focused on him and him alone.

Dark shadows glided beneath Max's legs. Sharks. *Don't panic. They must be reef sharks.* His mind urged him to remember that most predatory sharks were outside the confines of the reef—unless there was a break in the reef wall.

Max felt the sand beneath his feet and the slushy entanglement of turtle grass—soggy strips of lasagne-like kelp. "We're there, Xavier. Come on, we've got to reach the trees."

They floundered, forcing their legs to push against the weight of the water, and fell onto the hard, wet sand, which was darkened by palm-tree shadows and low, overhanging branches. Max pulled Xavier deeper into the shade. The gentle waves lapped behind their heels, but their footprints were still visible. There were barely a few meters of sand, trimmed halfway with a ribbon of seaweed, as light as lace. Max bellied back to the water, brushed the sand smooth and edged up the weed to disguise the scuff marks.

Back in the safety of the tree line, he turned and watched the cat-and-mouse game between boat and helicopter. Max could see the boat was not as maneuverable as the chopper. They must be taking on water. It had been damaged on the reef.

The gentle thunder of waves on the reef muted the cracking of gunfire. Flames spat from the side of the helicopter. Two of the men in the boat pointed machine pistols in the air, fired and then fell back as blood exploded around them, the heavy-caliber rounds smashing their bodies. The other two men were still alive on the boat. Alejandro steered with one hand and fired his pistol with the other.

The helicopter seemed to shudder, then dipped its nose like an angry bull readying to charge. A sudden shattering noise reached Max and Xavier as the violence from the gunship assaulted their senses. Sustained firepower poured into the boat in angry response to its resistance.

A vivid flame blossomed, ballooning outward, then sucked back in on itself as the inferno in the boat's fuel tanks made them explode. Moments later, the sound of the explosion washed over the two boys.

Xavier cried out and ran toward the water's edge. Max grabbed him. The boy fought free, yelling his brother's name.

"They'll see us! Xavier. Wait!"

Max threw him to the ground and pinned him into the wet sand. The wildness went out of the grieving boy's eyes, and Max felt the strength seep from Xavier's body. Max forced him to his feet and pushed him back into the undergrowth.

The helicopter turned like a beast sniffing out another victim.

Max didn't wait for it to find them. He grabbed Xavier and ran him deeper into the trees. Within fifteen meters, they had lost sight of the sea, and the tangled undergrowth made it almost impossible to penetrate any farther.

Scratched, bleeding and soaking wet, they rested, gaping upward through the jungle canopy, involuntarily holding their breath, as if the shadow that roared above the treetops might hear them.

The helicopter turned. Max followed the sound, checking

that Xavier was behind him. They crouched and a narrow window between the low branches allowed them to see the chopper hover over the sea, its blades dissipating the black, choking smoke, blowing it aside, as if the beast had snorted air in search of its prey.

Satisfied that nothing remained alive, the helicopter banked away and headed for its mother ship on the horizon.

"I killed my brother," Xavier said, his body trembling. Shock was setting in.

"If that's true, he let you," Max said. "We'd better check your wound, Xavier."

The boy pulled back. "Leave me alone." Tears welled in his eyes.

This wasn't the time to play field medic. Max saw the glitter of light fade through the leaves. It went dark. He checked his watch—6:20 p.m. They could go no farther. Max was already thinking of how to survive the claustrophobic hours in the jungle when, as if on cue, night sounds erupted. Cicadas chattered in deafening unison, and the screeching pitch of night beetles, like a short-wave radio being tuned, filled the night air. Max pulled Xavier down into the base of a tree whose roots flared out like shields from the trunk. This was not ideal. He did not want to spend the night on the jungle floor. Spiders, ants, snakes and all kinds of animals would be moving.

Leaves rustled.

Creatures moved.

The jungle was alive.

12

Max's eyes were wide open, staring into the darkness. Pulling his knees up, he felt for anything he could use as a weapon. His hand found a stick, and he held it across his body like a sword, giving himself the confidence of having something for self-defense, even though he knew it would be useless if anything dangerous attacked. Creatures were on their night hunt. Rustling and scratching surrounded him, and Max did not know whether he and Xavier were on the menu. Xavier's exhaustion and grief held him in a cocoon of deep sleep. Max had become his guardian but had no illusions that they would survive a predator's attack. He had seen men stalked and killed by lions when he was in Africa. He could never erase the horrendous sight from his mind, or the sounds of the men's screams as they were torn apart. If fear was the key to survival, then Max thought he should live forever.

Survive, learn and never take your own courage for granted.

There are times you have to dig deep to get into the zone that drives you on—that's how you stay alive.

His dad's words came unbeckoned into his mind. He squeezed his eyes closed, torn between the comfort of his father's voice and wanting to blot out the face that came with it. Max grimaced. Time to forget the emotions. Get on with it. If his dad were here, would he be doing this? Was there anything else Max should do? His choices were limited. Stay put and survive till morning and then try to determine a plan of action.

Then, out of the darkness, fingers of light pierced the mangrove forest. An animal's eyes gleamed as the light swooped across them. The slow rhythmic beat of an outboard engine broke the silence. The Coast Guard team was looking for survivors. Max heard their muffled voices. Americans. Their unhurried search faltered once or twice as they found another body in the water. "Here's one of them," a voice called. The engine spluttered as the revs were reduced. Max strained to hear. They were about fifty meters offshore. The searchlight's beam swung crazily and then settled. Max saw the fractured illumination create shadow and form through the low branches. One of the men cried out, "What's that? There!"

The lights swung away from the jungle. "Crocs! They're going for the dead guy in the water!" Two rapid gunshots boomed through the night. Max heard the men whoop with success and heard one shout, "Saltwater croc! Did you see the size of him? Wow!"

Xavier jerked awake as the gunshots reverberated across the water. A cry of alarm escaped from his throat.

Max reached behind him and pushed a restraining hand against the boy's face, whispering urgently, "It's all right. It's all right. They're searching for survivors. They just shot at something, that's all." Max did not have the heart to tell him about the crocodiles and the bodies in the water—it could well have been Alejandro's body the croc had tried to savage.

Someone shouted a command.

"All right, you men! C'mon, get that guy's body aboard!"

A slushing rush of water carried across the surface. Max imagined the estuary yielding the body as it was hauled into the boat. He shuddered. He had been attacked by crocs before, but the thought of them prowling through the night waters of the mangrove swamps, ready to take the corpses of the men from the boat, made his stomach squirm.

"You think the Yanquis come for us?" Xavier whispered.

"No, they'll patrol until daybreak and then do a final search of the area as soon as it's light. Until then we have to stay exactly where we are, but I think we have to get off the ground. There's too much going on in there," he said, nodding toward the dense jungle. The sweeping light from the men's boat had illuminated ropelike vines coming down from the tree's canopy. Max tugged. It took his weight easily. "It'll be OK. We have to climb into the tree. We'll be safer from whatever's hunting down here."

Xavier eased himself from the ground. It was almost pitch-dark, and he reached forward like a blind man stumbling in an unknown place. His hands found Max and gripped his shoulder. "We don' know what's up there. The big cats, they hunt in the jungle. They climb the trees. Nowhere is safe. Maybe we swim, into the river, then around the headland."

Xavier's nerve had broken. He pushed against Max in the darkness, but Max turned his shoulder and shoved hard, forcing the boy back against the tree. Xavier grunted with pain. Max knew he could not afford to fight now. If they started rolling around on the floor, grappling for supremacy, that would attract bigger creatures than the insects that still shrieked around them. There were killers in the jungle, and the men were still nearby in the boats. The boy obviously had no idea how lethal the jungle and mangroves could be. He was probably a small-town kid who hung around bars and ran messages for his brother.

"We can't do that, especially not at night—and not with those men out there." Max could feel the boy's nervousness as well as his own. He had no desire to go wading waist-deep in the dark estuary with saltwater crocodiles cruising. Max knew the boy wasn't thinking straight, and if he panicked, they both might die. There was no choice; Max had to shock him into focusing on survival.

"Don't tell me what to do!" Xavier grunted, trying to push Max away.

"Listen to me," Max hissed, his hand reaching to the boy's shirtfront, twisting it into a knot. He used his strength to hold Xavier back, to stop him from running blindly into the night. "We survive every minute. We can't even think about tomorrow! We can't even think about getting out of this mess tonight. We stay where we are and do the best we can. You want to go out there? I don't like crocodiles or water snakes, and I don't like men with guns. They killed the others. You think they won't kill you?"

Max felt the boy's body relax in surrender. Xavier had

never had to think for himself. Alejandro had shielded him all his life. His thought process was totally messed up.

"I'm thirsty. I am hurting. I need water," he whimpered.

Max pulled him forward and pushed the creeper into his hands. "If we get through tonight, we'll get water tomorrow. Now climb! Get into the fork of the tree. I'll be right behind you."

No sooner had Max issued the command than a blood-curdling wail tore at their nerves. Xavier hesitated, his feet already off the ground, but his hands froze in fear as they clutched the creeper.

"Get going!" Max yelled, forgetting there were men probably within earshot. Like a child's scream, the sound became a banshee wail of fear. And closer! Palms and bushes thrashed as something hurtled toward them from the depths of the night.

Max's hair stood up on the back of his neck, and ice-cold goose bumps tickled his spine. What was it? It didn't matter; there was no time to think about it. Xavier had still not moved. Max punched him hard. The boy shouted in pain, but it did the trick—he scrambled up the creeper. The under-growth shuddered as if a mighty force had been let loose. The sounds of terror escalated, louder and louder until they were almost unbearable.

The searchlight swung into the trees, and Max saw a deep black shadow of a beast, its eyes glaring yellow, its ivory-colored fangs smothered in blood. A black jaguar gripped a paca, a rodent about the size of a small dog, in its unyielding jaws and shook it violently, killing it by snapping its neck. The big cat turned and carried its prey into the smothering forest. The searchlight jerked through the night. Max and Xavier clung to the fork in the tree's boughs. They heard the boat cutting back and forth in the shallow water, the beam of light sweeping across them. But no alarms were raised, no voice called out and no gunshots tore into the jungle. The boat's engine pitch changed as the throttle was opened, roaring louder and then becoming more muffled as it eased away into the surf. The two boys were left with the comparative silence of the chattering insects.

Had the big cat caught their scent? For all Max knew, the hapless paca had come between them and the jaguar, offering a more manageable victim. A clawing, biting attack surging out of the blackness would have been all they'd have known about it.

How close had they been to death?

A few strides?

Despite the cloying heat, Max shivered.

It had been too close.

It was the longest night Max could remember. When the cool predawn light seeped through the canopy, he blearily checked out the ground below. His face was puffy from fretful sleep, his limbs stiff from lying crookedly in the tree. Beyond the strong breeze swishing the palm fronds and treetops, he could hear the sea washing against the shore.

He shook Xavier. The boy groaned, then quickly sat up. Max clambered down the vine and moved toward the sound of the crashing surf. He reached the small beach where they had landed the day before, and now he could see that Alejandro had chosen the only place where they had any chance at all of getting ashore; they were on a spit of land.

Fifty meters away, curving into the estuary, the mangroves cluttered the shoreline. For the two boys to try to make their way through there would have been exhausting, dangerous and probably impossible.

The salt air refreshed Max, but he resisted running into the small waves to wash himself free of the grit and sweat that had clung to his body since they entered the jungle. The Coast Guard cutter was still beyond the reef, while men in Zodiac inflatable boats swept the lagoon, doing a final daylight search for bodies. Max kept a low profile in the undergrowth and scrunched down into the sand. A moment later, Xavier joined him, shivering despite the warm breeze. He had barely slept, evidently. Max looked at the boy's agitated state. Perhaps it was more than fear and grief that Xavier was dealing with.

"Listen, are you on drugs? Are you going through withdrawal?"

Max could see the boy's expression was genuine. "Drugs?" Xavier asked. "Are you kidding me? Alejandro would kill me if he saw me touch that stuff. I need a cigarette. You got any smokes?"

Max was relieved the problem wasn't as bad as he'd imagined. He shook his head. Xavier shrugged and nodded toward the water. "They still here, eh?"

"They won't hang about all day; we've just got to wait until we can move," Max said. He was already planning their escape from the confines of the overgrown peninsula.

"Move? What do you think we can do out here? We're going to die—that's what's going to happen to us. This is the wilderness. Nobody lives here; nobody comes here. Except the drug boats. This is what we do: we wait till they have gone and we light a fire, a big fire. We make smoke. The boats will come for us."

Max didn't look at him, keeping his eyes on the inflatable that weaved its way in and out of the coral outcrops. It seemed to Max that the men were withdrawing to the ship, that they had achieved most of their tasks the night before.

"You can do that, if you want," Max said, "but what exactly are you going to make a fire with? And, if you do find a way, how are you going to survive until someone, maybe, sees the smoke? You have no food, you have no water and you're going to have to stay in that tree for safety. I reckon you'll be dead in less than a week. You think your drug-running friends haven't already heard about the attack? They'll be lying low for a while. They're not going to come out here when there's a Coast Guard patrol in these waters."

Max squirmed back into the undergrowth, Xavier dogging his footsteps. "We need water now; otherwise we won't even get through today," Max said.

They were above the high-water mark, and Max was scrabbling in the sand. He lifted up two or three fan-shaped shells. "Find me some rocks that look like these." Max ran his finger along the ragged edge. "Broken, like this." He beckoned Xavier into the trees and began the search. "We need something that might cut. You want a drink? Find me a cutting stone."

Making sure they stayed out of sight of the patrolling sailors, it took twenty minutes to find half a dozen stones; then Max made his way back to the mangrove. He took one of the jagged rocks and began stripping fibers from a palm tree, twisting and gathering them until they became long and thick enough to act as rough string. Then, finding a piece of fallen wood, he split the string apart near one end with the sharp stone and forced the stone down through the string. Using the fibers, he bound the stick at the base of the jagged rock, then did the same at the top of the split, securing the rough-edged piece of stone. Max had just made a primitive ax.

He pulled down one of the vines and hacked at it. It took three or four attempts, but he finally managed to cut away a two-meter section. He kept his thumb over the end, as you would cover the end of a hose.

"Open your mouth," he told Xavier. Max held the vine over the boy's mouth and released the pressure of his thumb. Water trickled down and Xavier slurped greedily. It tasted slightly woody, but they both drank without hesitation.

"Where did you learn that?" Xavier asked.

Max shrugged. You had to think for yourself. You had to look around and see what might save you. He knew it must have been his father who had told him about water collecting in jungle vines. That thought was interrupted by the sound of the ship's horn blowing. Max ran back to the shore and hunkered down among the small bushes. The American cutter was turning. Mission accomplished.

Xavier muttered under his breath. Max did not need to understand the language to comprehend its meaning; it was obvious that he was cursing the men who had killed his brother.

The boys lay in the sand and watched until the vessel disappeared behind the headland. Max gazed at the sky. A couple of pelicans turned languidly on the wind and settled near the reef to fish. If only he could catch a pelican and tie a rope to its leg, he'd have a perfect fish catcher. A darker shadow blotted the sky. The batlike wings of a frigate bird angled across his vision. Its thin tail moved slightly and the bird skimmed away. But its shape nudged his memory. He would have to be careful out here—there were vampire bats.

Xavier turned to him. "You get water from a tree—you will find a way to make a fire."

"No, I don't want to be rescued. And certainly not by any friend of yours."

"My brother saved your life, not just mine," Xavier snarled.

"Yeah, so I could babysit you."

The two boys glared at each other. But then Xavier, understanding the truth of Max's statement, nodded. "OK, so what do we do?"

Max gazed across the mouth of the river. The tide was turning; there was already a sandbank exposed in the middle. "We're going to make a raft and get upriver; that way we might find a settlement. But first I have to get across there and recover whatever I can from the boat's wreckage. That's where the tide's washed everything."

"You're a crazy boy, Max. Those mangroves"—he shook his head—"I don't know. You get into trouble, I can't help you."

Max stayed fully dressed. That onshore breeze had done them a favor and kept mosquitoes away from them during the night, but it also disguised the fierceness of the sun. He knew that if he stripped off for the swim, his skin would burn badly in the water. And, even though it would be hard going, he wanted the comfort of his boots when he got into those mangroves. Using a fairly straight branch as a pole to help against the force of the undertow, Max edged forward, allowing the shaft to bear his weight as he tested the depth ahead of him.

He looked back over his shoulder, swimming on his side, warily keeping an eye open for crocodiles. He could not bring himself to think about what lay in the tangled roots of the mangroves ahead of him; the fer-de-lance, one of the world's most poisonous snakes, inhabited this area, and a single bite from one of them would kill him. He told himself to control his imagination. Let that run riot and he may as well give up now and float out to sea to die. Wild thoughts could paralyze him with fear.

He had instructed Xavier to start pulling down palm leaves from the smaller trees, tear them into strips and tie the ends of each strip together; they could use this as binding. He caught a glimpse of him sitting on the narrow strip of sand, palm leaf held over his head, shading himself from the sun, watching Max struggling to swim across the estuary and the tide. Max groaned in frustration. This was going to be hard work in more ways than one. If he had had enough air in his lungs, he might have yelled at the boy to get busy, but he needed all his strength to push and kick ahead.

The water became shallower; now he could stand chest-deep, which helped push him on toward the foul-smelling mangroves exposed by the retreating tide. He waited, letting his eyes adjust to the shadows, desperately checking for any flurry of water that would tell him a crocodile had scented his presence. He edged forward, feeling the uneven ground beneath his boots. He stumbled once and went under, then pushed himself clear, gasping. The closer he came to the tangled undergrowth, the more disgusting the smell of the water became.

He could see bits and pieces of wreckage from the boat caught in the unyielding roots. After the explosion, there would be very little left, but some fragments would have survived. He had spotted a long white shape and suspected he knew what it was. It was not as pristine now as when he had sat on it speeding across the ocean. The bench seat's leather cushion was scorched, but the stitching had held, and the foam interior had not been penetrated by any water. It was a good flotation device. Shattered wood from the destroyed boat bobbed beneath the mangroves. A useful length of rope had entwined itself, snakelike, around the roots.

Max had to make a choice—either get out of the water and clamber among the mangrove roots, which were as thick as a man's arm and would take him a long time to negotiate as he picked up the boat's flotsam, or stay in the water and risk the chance of not seeing the telltale ripples of an approaching croc. Being crazy was one thing; being stupid was another. He hauled himself out of the water, grateful for the slimy branches. Gagging at the stench, he clambered from root to root, seeking out anything usable from the wreckage.

Tattered remnants of cotton covers were snagged, caught up in the mangrove branches. A length of wood with a riveted piece of steel attached at its end, probably a part of the boat's fittings, lay wedged in the entanglement. There was little else, except for a bobbing green plastic bottle. Fresh water. Max immediately remembered Alejandro scoffing at his concern when one of the drug dealer's men had thrown plastic overboard. Ecological issues aside, at this moment Max was very grateful for plastic bottles.

Like a beachcomber, he gathered the bits and pieces. The length of wood with the steel fragment on it felt heavy. Perhaps it was from some part of the engine housing, but it would serve equally well as a boat hook or a spear. Either way, he felt more confident that he had something he could use to defend himself. He scooped up the rope while balancing precariously on the slimy branches with his face turned away from the foul stench, desperate to be back on the beach, with the clean sea breezes sweeping over him.

He snagged a couple of pieces of torn cotton cloth, rolled them up and tucked them into the four meters or so of coiled rope he had looped over his shoulder. The water bottle was more awkward to reach, but it was a temptation impossible to resist. He straddled the slippery branch, hooked a leg over it like a commando pulling himself across a rope and reached down. He was balancing precariously on this unstable perch, one arm stretched out in front of him, the other using the length of wood to bring the bottle closer. He caught a movement out of the corner of his eye, and he turned to see Xavier waving the palm branch. He was making a fuss, shouting something, but the wind and the waves breaking on the reef muted his voice. Max figured he'd probably seen him succeed in getting the bits and pieces together. Somehow he was going to have to get Xavier to pull his weight, because Max knew that he couldn't get them out of this mess on his own. He turned his attention back to the bottle, his taste buds already anticipating fresh water. If he could just stretch a little farther.

Xavier shielded his eyes against the glare from the strip of sand and the glistening water. Max had made good progress, stumbling occasionally but soon getting himself back on his feet and moving toward the mangroves.

He screamed and waved, jumping up and down like a lunatic. Max could not see the approaching crocodile from where he lay across the branch. A horrifying memory flashed into Xavier's mind. Once, when they had moored a go-fast boat in an estuary like this, he had seen a troop of howler monkeys moving downriver in the mangrove's low branches. In a terrifying show of strength and speed, a crocodile had powered itself upward, using its tail to propel almost the whole length of its body out of the water. It had snatched an unsuspecting monkey from the tree and taken its screaming victim into the foul, dark depths.

Now there was a crocodile heading right toward where Max lay on a branch, barely three meters above the water. Xavier yelled at the top of his lungs, but Max showed no sign of hearing the warning.

Max stretched down, intent on reaching the water bottle, concentration totally focused.

A little farther.

Careful.

And then the water exploded.

Max yelled in fear.

The crocodile's jaws clamped shut and tore flesh.

13

Sayid twisted and turned through the labyrinth that lay before him. He had written new code and created new trapdoors for anyone following him. Anyone, that is, who had realized that he had hacked into their system.

He had had no word from Max, but Mr. Jackson had relayed the information to him that Max had not been heading for South America after all but had made his way to Miami. Sayid knew all this, of course, but stayed silent under Mr. Jackson's inquiring gaze. What bothered him was that no one had mentioned Max going on to Central America, as had been his plan. Sayid did not know that Mr. Jackson had kept the bad news from him: that Max's belongings had been found in the downtown room but that there was no sign of Max.

Sayid's mother had moaned at him for staying in his room

and absorbing himself with whatever he was doing on his computer.

Helping Max was what he was doing. His friend had asked him to find out as much as possible about Danny Maguire's final hours, and the best place to start was in the Underground station where he had died. For the better part of twenty-four hours, he had concentrated on finding the visual evidence of Danny jumping onto the tracks.

It was easy enough to get the ball rolling. By typing in an inurl code on his browser, Sayid accessed hundreds of CCTV cameras. After hours of changing the search threads, he found the cameras he wanted. He scanned the platforms, determining which camera angle would give him the best view. He could alter these angles on-screen, and he watched, like a fly on the wall, as people scrambled in and out of the Underground carriages. This was real time. What Sayid needed was the past. He had to find out if the images of Danny Maguire on that day had been stored. The police would have viewed the tapes, but they would have already been examined and archived. Where?

Just as Max would wipe out his tracks if he did not want to be caught on one of his outdoor adventure tests, Sayid also had to cover his digital footprints as he weaved his way through the government security network. With everyone on permanent alert because of potential terrorist threats, he knew that the systems were far more sophisticated than they had been. Sayid had sent out word to those who knew of his skills in the hacking community, but he had learned to exercise caution. He had once been drawn into a Black Hat group, who were commonly known as "crackers." Their intent was often the destruction, manipulation and sometimes blackmail of their victims as they clawed into people's websites and security networks. Thankfully, there were experienced senior members in Sayid's own international computer community, White Hat hackers, who helped him out of the mess.

Sayid turned to them for the intricate code that would allow him to view the stored images of Danny Maguire. Finally, he had written a program using open-source software, which lessened the chance of being traced, and Perl, software optimized for scanning and extracting information. The one thing a good hacker should always do is write in clear, concise, correctly spelled English. Sayid was always grateful for what at times seemed a grueling regime in Mr. Dolby's English class.

He scanned the video images of the platforms on that fateful day. The picture quality was poor, and he strained to see the faces in the crowds. But then, as a train departed and the platform emptied, a figure came into view. He was running; his long hair was pulled back, revealing his face. Sayid froze the image and tried to enhance it. He felt sure this was Danny Maguire, and when he hit the Resume button, he could see that the young man running flat out did not hesitate as he jumped off the platform and ran into the tunnel. Minutes later, two men appeared to be in pursuit, but within those minutes, other passengers had moved onto the platform, and Sayid could see that if they had been chasing Danny Maguire, they would not have been able to follow him. There were too many witnesses. Another train arrived, a lot more people got off and the two men became mixed up, almost unidentifiably, in the crush. Sayid concentrated and isolated their images. They were the two men from the Range Rover that had almost run him down on the moor.

Sayid was convinced that Danny Maguire had been chased to his death like a hunted animal. He pressed the Fast-Forward button and watched as police arrived, the platform was cleared and one of the men pointed down the tunnel into which Danny had run. The firefighters and paramedics squeezed onto the end of the platform, but then something more frightening came on-screen. The police ushered through two new arrivals. Like lumbering astronauts, they were dressed in cumbersome protective clothing. They looked like bomb-disposal experts. Clambering down onto the track, they disappeared into the tunnel carrying a stretcher between them. This was no bomb-disposal team, Sayid realized—these people were wearing biohazard suits.

He felt the pulse of nervous excitement. There was something down that tunnel that clearly frightened everybody.

The crocodile ripped and tore at the carcass. Max was almost in the water. The slimy branch slipped through his fingers, but he jammed his knee into a twisted bough as the water churned and pieces of flesh bobbed to the surface. A carcass had been wedged under the mangrove root, and the low tide had exposed the decomposing body. It was this that the crocodile had smelled. For a horrifying moment, Max thought it might have been one of the bodies from the boat, but he saw the hind leg and hoof of a deer, which must have fallen into the river and been carried away and drowned. No wonder there was such a stink by the tree. As the crocodile thrashed in the water, Max hung on for dear life; if he fell now, he would be down there in that horrifying turmoil.

With a huge splash of its tail, the crocodile pulled the carcass below the surface. Within moments, the muddy water was still again. Max gripped the branch with such force it felt as though the bones in his hands were going to break. He had to steady his nerves and control his breathing. His heart was banging so loudly he felt sure the submerged crocodile would hear it vibrating down the tree into the water.

There had been a swirl of ripples, like a small eddy, as the beast had dived and swum away with its prey. The last thing Max wanted to do was to jump back in and swim to the beach. He took a little comfort from the fact that only one crocodile had attacked the carcass. Had there been more about, there would have been an even greater feeding frenzy.

He studied the water. It was time to go. He pushed the white leather seat down onto the surface, where it bobbed for a moment and then began to drift slowly away. *Don't think about it. Keep your eyes open. Ease down, find your footing. It'll be only chest-deep. You'll be OK. There's nothing down there; nothing's going to hurt you. Feet onto the bottom and you'll be back on the beach in no time at all. That's all you've got to do. Into the water. Find your footing. Get back to the beach. Do it.*

Which was worse? Slowly but surely lowering yourself into that squelchy, smelly water, or just dropping down and going for it? If he was lucky, he wouldn't make a splash, and if he was really lucky, that crocodile had taken the carcass to its underwater lair. Enough was enough: he was torturing himself. Left to its own devices, his mind would freeze him in terror. He had to get past his fear. Sliding off the branch, he let himself fall into the chest-deep water. He stretched out his legs and pulled his hands above his head, gripping the metal-tipped shaft of wood as tightly as he could, wanting to be as slender as a knife blade when he entered the water. He clamped his mouth shut. That water was laden with bacteria, and he did not want to swallow a drop.

His feet touched the bottom. Glancing rapidly, he looked left and right, then pushed himself forward, reaching out to grab the floating leather seat. River boulders twisted his ankles. His knees took the strain, and he used the seat at his side, leaning on it almost like a crutch to help keep him stable.

He was still trembling from the crocodile attack. It was an unreal scenario: wading back across a fast-flowing river, ferocious attacks by man and beast, with jungle and mangroves behind and to his front, while a drug runner was relying on him to get them through. When Max had left London, he had been in control, as much as he could be, and now he was alone and vulnerable. The odds against survival seemed stacked too high. But he had got this far. He focused on getting back to Xavier, who stood on the small strip of sand, waving as if greeting a long-lost friend arriving on the *Queen Mary 2*, pride of the seas. Here comes Max Gordon, half swimming, half stumbling, clutching his own pride of the sea—a seat cushion.

Suddenly the water seemed to boil next to him. Bubbles broke the surface. Max froze. The crocodile! In a belching, smelly bubble, the water bottle popped to the surface. Max laughed, releasing his pent-up emotion.

Xavier ran into the shallows and grabbed the bulky seat from Max as he sank to his knees in the sand. "I tried to warn you," he said.

Max upended the water bottle and guzzled greedily. To the victor the spoils. Xavier waited, desperately watching the water spill over Max's chin, but Max left more than half and handed him the bottle.

Max flopped over onto his back. The wet sand smelled of salt, and the sea breeze cooled him under the burning sun. He cackled exhaustedly. "I thought you were dancing," he said.

Xavier guzzled, gasped for breath and belched with satisfaction. "Yeah? That's not how I dance."

He suddenly started moving like an electrified snake. He clapped his hands and shuffled his feet, accompanying himself with a raucous salsa tune. Max laughed, got onto his knees and watched the crazy kid cavort.

"You alive, man! You alive!" Xavier shouted.

He reached out and took Max's hands, making him stand up. Xavier jigged him around until Max also sang aloud. It was gibberish, but it was fun. Finally they collapsed, laughing. Xavier put his hands on Max's shoulders. "You some kinda strange fella. You got angels on your shoulders. Me? I'm with you. You say, I do."

Max nodded. Held out his hand. "It's a deal."

Xavier spat into the palm of his hand and clasped Max's. "It's a deal, gringo!" And he laughed again.

Max knew he had to grasp every positive thing that happened in circumstances like this, so he allowed a sigh of satisfaction. He had managed to get to the other side of the river and back, avoided a horrific death and gathered a few bits and pieces that would help them escape from this place. So the day hadn't been all bad. Max was determined never to lose hope. And he'd never have to spike his hair with gel again— he'd been so scared it would probably stand on end permanently.

Riga had an energy that frightened people. It was not that he flaunted it; it was something that anyone close to him could sense. Nor did he use his physical strength and endurance simply to impress anyone. He had supreme confidence in his ability to survive and preferred, at every turn of his life, to be alone.

From a young age, he had been trained as a destroyer of life and property and had been taught to get close to his enemy so he might understand him better. He held a deep sense of pride in his skills. It was his profession, just as a doctor was attracted to medicine or an attorney to law. It was a calling. He had no sympathy for his victims and was a confirmed sociopath by the age of fourteen. A perfect killer.

Chasing down Danny Maguire had been part of a bigger picture, so Riga's status had not been diminished because his target was young. Cazamind and the people he worked for dealt only with issues at an international level, so when Maguire ran into the tunnel and fell onto the high-voltage rail, it ended one part of Riga's brief. The follow-up, checking on Max Gordon, was like a full stop at the end of a sentence. It was all supposed to end there. Find out if Gordon had received anything from Maguire. He hadn't, as far as Riga knew. End of story.

Not quite.

Cazamind had sounded worried—even, Riga suspected, scared. There were enormous implications for Cazamind's "people." Tendrils of corruption squirmed through the corridors of power in America and the UK, and national interests were at stake. All because a fifteen-year-old boy had outwitted them all. It seemed obvious Max Gordon had learned *something*.

Extreme caution had to be employed. A swift and low-key operation to remove the problem had been sanctioned, and the job had to be done by one man. The money was already in Riga's Swiss bank account. It was more than generous, and he was to have anything he needed—weapons, transport and information.

A private Learjet with long-range tanks was a more luxurious way to travel across the Atlantic, and unlike Charlie Morgan, who had sat cramped in the back of an overcrowded commercial flight, Riga had unlimited resources at his disposal. He was already in Central America in a place of Cazamind's choosing. From his vantage point deep in the rain forest–clad mountains, Riga could strike at Max should he ever reach this inhospitable area.

Riga was not waiting in luxury, however. The palm-leaf roof of the long hut kept the scorching sun off him, but the stifling jungle humidity enveloped everyone like a blanket soaked in hot water.

A decrepit air conditioner whirred noisily, the tatty piece of ribbon tied to the front grille fluttering pathetically, showing that the ancient cooler should have been replaced years ago. But the killer had learned to ignore any personal discomfort. This apparently abandoned airfield cut out of the limestone hillside deep in the forest was used years ago by the CIA for arms shipments to insurgents in Cuba and Central America. Those days were long gone, but secret airfields were still used by the people Riga worked for, as well as by the drug cartels, who needed to move shipments across vast areas of jungle.

Riga's satellite phone beeped. It was Cazamind.

"The boat has been dealt with. They recovered two bodies; the others would have disintegrated when it exploded."

"Was Gordon's body found?"

"No. Two men."

"Then we can't be sure."

"No one would have survived."

"I want to double-check."

There was a pause. "All right, Riga. As soon as it's possible, I'll have the attack helicopter's video surveillance tape downloaded to you. But I think it's over."

Riga liked certainties. It was how he earned his reputation. It was how he stayed alive.

"I'll wait," Riga said.

Xavier followed Max's instructions, just as he had promised, though he thought he was being asked to do girl's work. He sat under the shade of a palm tree plaiting together strips of palm frond into a circle, like a crown. He had seen young girls at village weddings wearing things like that on their heads. It was a decoration! He wanted to protest but did not. It was of no consequence. He would keep his word to *este chico y sus angeles*—this boy and his angels.

Max used his teeth to tear apart some of the cotton pieces he had fished out of the water. They still stank of the fetid mangrove swamp, and he hoped he was not inviting every lethal germ under the sun to invade his body. He tore them into a roughly circular shape and then began ripping strips round the edge. This was going to help them survive the intense sunlight and the flies and mosquitoes. Xavier was muttering under his breath as he painstakingly braided the palm strips. He was clumsy and made a mess of it once or twice, but with grim determination, a tight smile and a shrug, he had continued the task.

It was only a small point, but Max had not told him of the palm crown's use. If Max could get the boy to help without him needing to question and challenge him, so much the better; then the end result would be self-explanatory. Get on; do the job. Save time; save energy.

So far, so good.

Max knew he had to be organized. Tasks had to be performed, one of which was to make the raft. He could have used the animal tracks to help find their way out of this jungle and get inland, but that would be asking for trouble sooner or later. They certainly didn't have any effective means of cutting their way through the dense undergrowth. They might not be able to stay on course; they would make less than a kilometer a day and would be vulnerable to the jungle predators. Max had considered the options and was convinced the river offered the best chance of escape. Sooner or later, he felt certain it would take them to a settlement or a town where he hoped the people might have heard of his mother or Danny Maguire. Then he might have a chance of tracking her journey. But he and Xavier needed food and water, much more than the slender vines offered; otherwise they were not going to be strong enough for what was bound to be an arduous journey.

Following Max's lead, Xavier pulled down thin, twisting creepers that snaked up tree trunks and grubbed up ground roots to bind together the wood that they had gathered. Then Max put a layer of palm leaves on top, which he secured with the fibrous string Xavier had made earlier.

Max pointed. "You should let me see that wound."

Xavier pulled back. "It's OK. I don' want you messin' with it. What? Now you a doctor or somethin'?"

"OK. If it's infected, it's infected. You want to die of blood poisoning, that's your business."

Xavier looked worried. He eased up the damp T-shirt and looked at the wound for himself. "You think it's infected?"

"You don't let me look—I can't tell."

"You won' touch it? Promise?"

"I promise. But you let your brother's men fix you up; you never whimpered then."

"What is 'whimpered'?"

"Moaning like a baby."

"Me? Hey, you look all you like. Here!" And Xavier pulled up his T-shirt and knelt next to Max.

The dressing had long since disappeared, and one of the butterfly clips had torn loose from the skin, which was puckered and looked clean. The salt water might have even aided the wound's healing, but one edge of the wound was discolored, and that blemish was creeping round the boy's side. It looked to Max as if there was some festering underneath the broken skin, which meant that in a couple of days, exposed to the river water, the infection could go right through the boy's body.

"Does that hurt?" Max asked as he pressed very gently on the affected part.

Xavier yelped. "You said you weren't gonna touch!"

Max looked at him. He needed Xavier to feel good—especially for what Max was going to propose. "You're tougher than I thought," he said.

"Yeah? I mean, yeah. I'm tough." And then he thought about it. "Why?"

"It's infected—it must hurt. You didn't say anything."

Xavier wasn't in much pain, but he pulled a face. It was good to let Max think he could handle it. "It don' hurt so much."

"But if that infection gets worse . . ." Max paused and shook his head sadly, turning away from the boy's gaze.

"What? Is bad? You think is bad?"

"I wouldn't be able to get you out of here. I'd have to leave you."

"What!"

"I'll send help as soon as I find it."

"No way! You go, I go. That's the deal. That's what I said. I'm with you."

Max put his arm on the boy's shoulder. "Good, I was hoping you'd say that. Then you'll let me fix it?"

Xavier wasn't certain, but he had talked himself into a corner. Or rather Max had. "OK," he said.

Max turned over a rotten log. Poking it with his steel-tipped piece of wood, he made sure there were no snakes curled beneath it. Then, skimming away the desiccated wood with his new ax, he found what he was looking for. He carefully lifted the wriggling maggots from the trunk and laid them on a palm leaf. Food and medicine.

Xavier lay on his side, his arm covering his eyes. Max had just explained that you could eat maggots for protein, providing you didn't take them from a rotting carcass of an animal. Xavier had squirmed almost as much as the maggots, and the reason he had covered his eyes was because Max had popped two or three of the maggots into his own mouth and crunched, not so happily, away. Max grimaced.

"They're not that bad," he lied. "They'd be much better cooked, I suppose, but beggars can't be choosers."

"I am not going to eat those things. I will puke if you put those squirmy things into my mouth. Puke more than you have ever seen in your life. I would rather die."

"I didn't think you'd want to eat them—I brought these for your wound; I'll find us some food later."

"And you're gonna do what?"

Max knelt next to him, took three or four maggots from the leaf and laid them gently on the festering wound. "Don't look, Xavier. These things could save your life."

Xavier muttered a private mantra—which sounded like a prayer—to keep his mind off the things that were eating into his flesh. He could barely feel anything other than a soft tickle as they dug into his wound. But he refused to look at it and decided to stay somewhere in his head until this crazy English kid told him it was all OK. He should have been in Miami or New Orleans or anywhere else in the big U.S. with a new name and a new identity, money in the bank and he and Alejandro driving open-top sports cars. It would have been a good life, a safe life, and they would have been legal. But it had all gone horribly wrong, and now he lay in the jungle with maggots eating into him. The devil must be laughing somewhere, getting his own back for all the bad things Alejandro and his men—and Xavier—had done.

"I'm going to forage for food," Max said, interrupting his thoughts.

Xavier propped himself up and looked toward the dense undergrowth. "You forgettin' what's in there? How many lives you think you got? Just 'cause that big cat killed somethin' las' night, you think he still ain't hungry? Maybe he has a friend and say to him, 'Hey, amigo, you hear about those two kids down near the beach? They got no water; they got no food. They're just two dumb *chicos* stranded in the middle of nowhere. They got meat on their bones, and they got nothing to fight with.'"

"Jaguars hunt alone and at night."

"So how come you know everything?"

"I read books and my dad told me."

"Uh-huh. Your daddy lets you come all the way out to Miami where you help a drug smuggler from gettin' whacked?"

"I didn't know you were a drug smuggler."

"So? If you'd known, you'd have let that crazy guy kill me!"

"If I had, I wouldn't be in this mess," Max said.

"Hey, *chico*, I saved your ass from Mr. Happy Snappy Crocodile."

"I don't think so. You didn't shout loud enough."

"You got all that mud and water in your ears—tha's not *my* fault. OK. I *tried* to warn you. Don' you ever say thank you for nothin'?"

"Thank you, Xavier Morera Escobodo Garcia, for trying to shout loud enough."

"You're welcome. But you get into trouble again, you on your own."

Max left him in the shade of the palm trees. He knew he wouldn't move. The jungle was one place Max did not want to be injured or ill; it was bad enough being fit and strong and having to cope with the energy-sapping heat, which was why he had some sympathy for Xavier.

Max scoured the jungle for any berries, seeds or nuts that he thought were safe to eat. Some he was uncertain of and let them rest on his tongue before spitting out the acid taste. He found three fruits he recognized—light yellow guavas from a tree with white flowers and a nice dark clump of finger bananas. Green-encased coconuts that had fallen from the palm trees had stubbornly resisted being smashed against a rock outcrop, but Max wedged his spearlike shaft into a twisted tree trunk and slammed the coconuts onto the metal tip. They split, revealing the brown hairy coconut inside. He pierced a coconut's eyes and sucked the white liquid. Now that he had supplies, their chances for survival grew every

195

moment. Cutting and splicing palm leaves together, he made an efficient bag to carry the food he'd foraged.

Max bent down, scuffed aside fallen leaves and dug his fingers into the earth. There was moisture in it, which wasn't unusual—jungles were usually damp—but he knew rain squalls often hit this part of Central America. One of the noises that came out of the jungle was a creaking groan. It had taken Max some time to remember where he had heard those sounds before—it had been in a bamboo garden his dad had once taken him to. And bamboo held water. There was no choice: Max had to penetrate the darkened jungle, locate the bamboo, then find his way out again.

Flashes of color dipped and swirled through the branches as screeching birds clattered their way into the high canopy. Max moved carefully, listening to the rustling footfalls from unknown creatures around him. The pictures of his mother were still safe and dry in the wallet in his breast pocket. He saw her smiling face in his mind's eye, felt the warmth in his chest and imagined the melodic song of a jungle bird was that of his mum gently calling him.

Max eased aside the low branches and stepped inside a claustrophobic world that soon engulfed him.

14

Sayid watched as the people in biohazard suits carried a covered corpse out of the tunnel. They eased the orange-colored body bag onto a gurney and wheeled it to an isolation tent that had been set up on the platform, where another figure, also dressed in a biohazard suit, waited. Sayid could just make out what was happening inside. The body bag was lifted, slipped into yet another protective covering and replaced on the gurney. The side flaps of the tent were opened; regular paramedics took the stretcher and disappeared from view. For a moment, Sayid watched while the recovery team was washed down with what looked like a steam hose as they stood in a catchment tray. He was less interested in them than where Danny Maguire's body was being taken.

Sayid quickly manipulated the keyboard, found the cameras he wanted and watched as the body was loaded into the back of an ambulance. The area had been cordoned off by police. He had lost sight of the two men who had initially run after Danny, but now he saw a police officer wave a silver Mercedes through the security area. Sayid froze the frame and zoomed in on the car's window. It was the same two men.

A police motorcycle escort led the ambulance away from the station, and the Mercedes tucked in behind. The small convoy sped away into London traffic. Seconds later the tape went blank. Sayid keyed in a search for a London street map. He needed to work out which way the ambulance was going. And now that he had his program in place, he would be able to link into the CCTV street cameras that adorned almost every building and streetlamp in the city, watching like vultures.

Max followed the faint outline of an animal track through the undergrowth. He moved slowly and cautiously, always listening to the sounds of the jungle, muscles tensed, the length of the metal-tipped shaft in one hand, the crude ax in the other. The complaining bamboo was somewhere over to the right. Every twenty paces, he had tied a thin strip of salvaged cotton cloth on low-lying branches so he could find his way out. He tied the last piece round a branch exactly where he was to step off the animal track. It was so overgrown that unless he could take a mental picture of where he had walked, even the cotton strips could be lost from sight. The next dozen paces took him nearly fifteen minutes—pretty good going, given the density of the trees and vines. He bent leaf stems to help him find his way to the cotton strips but was wary of where he grabbed a handhold; some of those slender

198

branches were armored with vicious, needlelike thorns. If they broke off in flesh, they would fester, and tropical fever could soon follow. Then he would be a helpless victim of the creatures of the jungle.

Finally, the dense thicket of bamboo was in front of him. Each shaft was thicker than his leg and soared up into the canopy. He tapped one of the poles. It sounded hollow, but the next ringed section gave him hope. Using his shaft of wood as a spear, he pressed the point against the bamboo and leaned with all his weight. A small crack appeared and moisture seeped out. Now that the bamboo had been split, he aimed carefully and cut away more of the wood with his ax. Water poured out; he went down quickly on one knee and sucked in the cool, clear liquid. He did this two or three more times, and once he'd drunk enough, he filled the water bottle.

He turned round, searching for the way he had come in, but nothing looked familiar. It was just a mishmash of trees, vines and undergrowth. His foot caught a root and he fell back; for a brief moment he felt a surge of panic as he went under the claustrophobic foliage. Something bit his shoulder. Like a scorpion sting, it broke skin. Twisting quickly, he saw that he had landed on one of those viciously spiked branches he had been so careful to avoid.

For a few seconds, it felt as though the jungle and its heat encircled him, making it impossible to move. Sweat stung his eyes. Then, as if someone had turned off the volume, the jungle went silent. All his instincts were heightened. Somewhere behind him, the bushes shuddered and he saw a shadow mottled with yellow and black markings appear and disappear just as quickly. It was as if there was a tunnel through the tangled undergrowth barely knee-high from the ground.

Max gazed down through the green light until he saw the face of the jaguar. His eyes were on the same level as the big cat's. The jaguar made a small, snarling sound, baring its fangs, but it did not seem to be an overtly aggressive act. Max realized that he was nodding as if he understood—this was not his hunting ground; it belonged to the cat. A deep, almost unfathomable part of him recalled the time in Africa when a shaman had saved his life and endowed him the primal ability to project himself outside of his body and into the consciousness of other creatures. Like now.

There was another movement behind the big cat, and Max heard a softer snarl. It was a young jaguar, probably no more than a year old, still too young to provide for itself. It had to learn to survive in the jungle, but for now it was protected by its mother.

The burning pain in his shoulder snapped him back to reality.

He blinked. The tunnel was empty. The moment was gone.

Xavier made teeth-sucking noises as he squeezed out the thorns from Max's shoulder and muttered as he applied himself to the task. Max grimaced and gasped as the boy's nails dug into his flesh. A couple of thorns had broken off in his shoulder muscle. Max told Xavier how to get them out by using a flat piece of stone to drag the flesh upward until the ends appeared—squeezing embedded thorns could make them fester. But the stubborn thorns were in too deep; Xavier had to try forcing them out. All he got was blood that welled into the punctures.

Enough was enough. "OK, leave them, Xavier. We've got to push on."

"You sure 'bout that? It don' look too good."

Max nodded. They had to finish the raft. The pain would have to be endured, but the injury worried him. How long did he have before the wound became infected and rendered him useless? Now, more than ever, he needed some luck on his side if he was to survive. Instinct demanded that he strike out and get as far as he could upriver. Somewhere in this impenetrable world was the place where his mother had died. He had to know the truth about her death. And why his father had, by his own confession, abandoned her.

Riga studied his laptop screen as he followed the surveillance video of the firefight between the attacking helicopter and Alejandro's go-fast boat. It had taken the better part of the day for the secret report to reach him from Cazamind's contacts in a U.S. intelligence agency. The silent film offered no indication of the power of the guns as they hammered the boat into submission, but as Riga's analytical eye studied every movement of the desperate fight, he acknowledged an admiration for Alejandro's skill and courage. The film showed no evidence of the boat running away from the fight; rather, it was taking the fight to the helicopter. He saw bodies fall and watched as the boat zigzagged across the reef. There were moments when the boat was out of view, and it was these missing fragments of time that held his attention. He played the download time and again. There were clearly six people on the boat at one stage, and from what he had been told, Max Gordon was one of them. The helicopter had obviously overshot the boat, and when the camera focused again on the fight seconds before the boat exploded, Riga counted the bodies. It was possible that the boat's passengers had been killed and now lay out of sight or that they had fallen overboard in those missing moments, but Riga was not convinced. The boat had swerved for land, the angle had changed, the waves obscured an erratic maneuver and then, as the helicopter had gone past, turned and reengaged the men shooting from the speeding craft, there were only two men left standing. The exploding boat would have disintegrated them, or their bodies may have been thrown clear. The Coast Guard had reported recovering two bodies, both men in their early twenties.

Riga froze the frame where the boat had turned back from the shoreline, the angle the helicopter had as it turned to continue the attack. The shoreline disappeared. He zoomed in; there in the boat's wake were two small black dots. He released another frame and watched as the boat jerked its way out of view, and for a fraction of a second, white foam highlighted movement that looked like someone swimming.

Riga smiled: what were the odds of a teenager surviving a gun battle like that? This Max Gordon was proving to be a challenge worthy of Riga's skills, for he was convinced that if anyone had reached the shoreline, it would be the English boy. Riga picked up the satellite phone sitting next to his computer, pressed a button and heard Cazamind's voice answer.

"I think the kid made it," Riga said. "I'm going after him."

Max and Xavier looked ridiculous. Precious minutes were wasted in laughing at each other. Max had pulled one of the pieces of cotton onto his head—the torn fringe would help keep the flies and mosquitoes away—and jammed down on top of that was the crownlike headgear that Xavier had laboriously made, which would shield their eyes from the sun. As a final safeguard, Max had dug his hands into the nearby riverbank and smeared them both with foul-smelling mud in an effort to keep the vicious mosquitoes at bay. They looked like warriors from a long-lost tribe.

After a thorough check of the area, Max was satisfied that there was no sign of them having been marooned on the spit of land. If anyone did fly over, they would see only a narrow, unspoiled beach and the dense jungle fringed with mangroves.

The inflowing tidal current pushed them along, but it was a smooth ride, and as Max stood at the back of the raft using a straight branch to pole them around protruding boulders, Xavier sat as if he was on a pleasure cruise. The raft seemed to be strong enough for both of them, but as a precautionary measure, Max kept the white seat loose so that if anything happened Xavier had a flotation device. Within an hour or so, they had left the low, dense vegetation of the mangroves and floated between limestone cliffs that rose up each side of the river. Max was ever vigilant, watching out for the deep places where the current swirled and sucked around exposed rocks. Water shivered as the river tumbled over a shallow stretch.

"Hold on," Max warned as they bumped their way over the thirty-meter stretch. Xavier whooped with joy, like a kid on a small waterslide. But it was Max who was doing all the work, making sure the raft stayed as rigid as possible as he guided it over the broken water. He realized that anything more turbulent, like a real white-water ride, would tear them apart. Suddenly the river was deep again, running smoothly into calmer water. Max gazed up at the jungle that clawed its way across the forty-meter cliffs. Brightly colored birds swooped to catch insects; others sang, being answered by birds across the chasm. It was an unblemished paradise, wild in its majesty, untouched by man's hand. Max felt a strange contentment.

Riga sat in the open door of the Bell 222 helicopter as it thundered through the sky at 175 kilometers per hour, thirty meters above the ground. His feet were braced on the helicopter's skids, keeping him balanced precariously as he sat on the helicopter floor. It was an older model, but tough and serviceable, deliberately chosen by Riga because it was such a common aircraft and would not attract undue attention. Drug runners would have had the latest model with the most powerful engine, but this old 222 could travel at 240 kilometers per hour with a range of 600 kilometers, more than enough for the job at hand. Across his lap he gripped the wooden stock of an M14 sniper rifle. This, too, had been field-proven over the years and was still used by U.S. Special Forces, as the 7.62 mm round had enormous stopping power. He could have chosen any weapon, but Riga was, at heart, a simple man, who needed a simple, uncomplicated killing tool.

He mentally replayed the Coast Guard's pursuit. He had given the pilot the coordinates, and they weaved along the coast. The pilot brought the helicopter down to sea level a hundred meters offshore, just as the mercenary had ordered. Riga did not want to disturb any evidence supporting his belief that Max had survived. Riga pointed, waving his hand slightly, telling the pilot to move slowly from right to left so that they could get a clear view of the small beach and tree line. Nothing seemed out of the ordinary; there were no footprints, no sign that anyone had been on that beach. The helicopter edged into the estuary. The tide had moved into the mangroves, half submerging them, but again there was no sign of life. And no sign of any wreckage from the boat. As there should have been.

Riga motioned the pilot forward, and when they were fifty meters off the beach, he signaled him to hover. The skids almost touched the surface of the water, and Riga stepped down into the warmth of the lagoon. He was in up to his chest and held the rifle clear of the water as the helicopter's downdraft flattened the small waves. It banked away and held station a kilometer offshore, waiting for Riga's command to return. Riga walked out till he was ankle-deep in the water and let his eyes move across the sand and into the trees, looking for anything out of place; if Max Gordon and a second person had had any chance of survival, this was exactly where they would have come ashore. The lapping water reached up and gently sucked back across the sand, never going higher than the line of seaweed. Riga put the rifle butt onto his shoulder and slipped off the safety catch, ready to kill.

He spent an hour searching the immediate vicinity and saw no sign of anyone being there until he came across scuff marks on a tree trunk—not the gouged scratch marks of a hunting jaguar, but possibly made by monkeys. He squatted down, listening to the jungle sounds, and let his eyes find a way into the tangled forest. He picked a spot close by, then moved his vision inward another couple of meters and then repeated the action again until he had penetrated the forest to about fifteen meters, which was about as far as anyone could expect to see. There, at knee height, was a stem, not broken but bent backward. He stepped cautiously in that direction. It would take time, but he knew he would find more evidence of someone or something moving into the jungle.

Slowly but surely, he followed the almost invisible trail that Max had left by bending and breaking branches. Max had taken away the pieces of cotton, but he could not alter a few broken sticks that told their own story. Riga reached the bamboo thicket and saw the signs of Max's water-tapping. For a moment his guard was down as he knelt in front of the bamboo. A black mottled shadow unfurled itself from the jungle and crouched to attack.

The big cat had barely snarled its warning when Riga

brought the rifle to his shoulder and fired two rapid shots. In the couple of seconds it took for the jaguar to fall, roaring in agony, Riga didn't retreat but strode fearlessly toward the stricken animal and shot it once more, killing it instantly. He stood over the dead cat, whose breath still curled from its jaws. The amber eyes dimmed, and the muscle spasms stopped. Riga looked about him carefully—he had obviously stepped into the jaguar's territory. So, too, had Max Gordon, and Riga wondered if the boy had come face to face with the jaguar. It didn't matter—there was now only one hunter in this patch of jungle. Riga gazed down at his victim and felt neither sorrow nor exhilaration for the kill. It was what Riga did. Then he heard the softer and less threatening snarl of another jungle cat. He raised the rifle and aimed quickly at the young cub's head. He hesitated, though unsure why he did so. He decided to let it live; maybe it would survive on its own. Everyone had to learn to do that at some stage of their lives.

Retracing his steps, Riga went back to the beach, but now he looked more carefully. He soon noticed that a tree's fibers had been teased away from its trunk. Another had a shadow that curved upward, as if a clinging vine had been pulled away from it. Skirting the beach where the sand gave way to the jungle, his eye was caught by an oddly shaped clump of leaves in the undergrowth. He reached in and pulled out torn palm fronds. Someone had been trying to make something out of them, and their failures had been cast aside. So Max Gordon had found water and used a supple vine to tie or make something. The torn palm fronds gave him no clue, until he made a circle from one strand and saw that it could fit neatly over his head. Clever boy. Water and shade. But how would he have got away from this place? There was only one way and that was by river. That was what Max Gordon had done—he had made a raft and escaped.

Riga smiled. He had him. The boy was as good as dead.

15

Charlie Morgan might have been MI5 with the FBI on her side, but she did not have Riga's sources of inside information. She had scoured the town for any knowledge of an English boy who might have tried to rent any of the rooms available without any luck or word from the FBI. It seemed that Max had disappeared off the face of the earth. She could not know that Cazamind's influence hid even the news of the Coast Guard cutter's seek-and-destroy attack.

Charlie hated being inactive, and sat in her sweltering room beneath a creaking old fan with a map of Central America spread out on the floor. Beyond the small city were scattered settlements and the occasional speck of a town, but there were vast areas of dense forest and remote mountains where rivers cut through gorges and where it was probably impossible to survive for any length of time without proper equipment and supplies. Her finger traced the coast from

Panama up across the isthmus—the major drug corridor from South America to Mexico and into the United States—and then continued her search along the coast, up to the desolate Yucatán Peninsula. Borders merged into each other, and she knew that some of the countries had endured horrendous civil wars. Kidnapping and murder were still commonplace in various parts of Central America, and she could not imagine how, if Max Gordon had survived, he had managed to get down there. He had no money, no passport and probably only the clothes he wore; that was a pretty desperate state to be in.

Morgan allowed herself an amusing indulgence—her mobile ring tone. The unmistakable theme tune from *Mission Impossible* broke the sound of the whirring fan. She recognized the number; it was her FBI contact.

"Charlie, it's Tony. We've picked up something pretty strange from an intercept. One of our Coast Guard cutters in the Caribbean was involved in a firefight. We caught snatches of the pilot's voice transmission as he attacked a drug runner's boat. The whole thing is being locked down, and we don't have direct access to the intel on it. There are other agencies involved, and we're being told to ignore it."

"You're being kept out of the loop?" Charlie asked. "Is that normal?"

"Didn't you say your MI-Six guys leaned on your boss?" he answered.

"Right, yeah. So what do we have, a foreign operation under way, keeping out intelligence agencies inside your own country?"

"It happens. But there's more. Is it likely your boy Max Gordon could have any association with those drug runners who took him?"

"I don't know. I doubt it," she said.

"These guys run go-fast boats from Central America in and out of Miami. Maybe your boy wasn't kidnapped, is all I'm saying. Maybe he had contacts. We're just trying to figure it out."

"Are these the people Max got involved with in Miami? Was he on the boat your Coast Guard shot up?" Her heart sank as she thought of the carnage that would have occurred and that Max might have been caught up in it. He was only a kid, for heaven's sake.

"Could be. We don't know why it's being kept quiet. It must be something more than drug running. Anyway, the boat got taken out. There were no survivors. I'm sorry, Charlie, but if he was with those guys, I think your boy is dead."

Charlie's mind whirled. Was it that simple? Was *what* that simple? Max Gordon kidnapped by drug runners, or did he know them? Their boat attacked by the U.S. Coast Guard and all record of the operation, of the gun battle and the boat's destruction, kept secret. That wasn't simple—that was a complexity that needed unraveling and explaining. Ambitious as she was to be the one to bring the operation to a successful conclusion and take the credit that would enhance her career, she felt strangely protective of Max Gordon. This wasn't over. If he was dead, she wanted to know why. He was her case, her boy.

"Can you find out more? Can you get the transcripts of the attack? I'd like to get the coordinates and see where all this happened."

"We'll do our best, Charlie, but let's just say the impossible happened and your kid was dropped off on the mainland before these guys got taken out—where do you reckon he'd head for?"

That was the $64-million question. If Max's evasive tactics were to do with the death of his mother, then no one knew where she had died, but maybe questions were where Charlie Morgan had to begin. She had to get into those jungle settlements and towns and start talking to people. "I don't know," she said. "I'll try to figure something out. If my boy is on the mainland, I just can't see how he could survive. Try to pinpoint the location where the boat was destroyed."

"It's all restricted access, Charlie. We're not even supposed to have *this*. They just won't let us get our hands on it. I think it's a no-can-do."

"You're the FBI. And I always thought Americans had a can-do attitude. Or is that just a piece of Hollywood?"

She could imagine him smiling at the end of the phone. "You're a cruel woman, Charlie. Can-do is *what* we do. Though I'll probably lose my job."

"That's OK. Down here is a great place to retire. Find out what you can. I'm going on a bike ride." She closed the phone and hovered her attention across the map. Then, without hesitation, she touched the name of a town with her fingertip. She had to start somewhere—it might as well be a place that sounded appropriate: *Ciudad de las Almas Perdidas*, the City of Lost Souls.

* * *

The Bell 222 hugged the contours of the river. Max and his companion had a day's start on Riga, but the assassin calculated that they couldn't have got far on a makeshift raft. The wind buffeted Riga's face, and he could smell aviation fuel and exhaust. The clattering engine was an assault on his senses, and he enjoyed every moment of it. The helicopter's body shuddered, its vibration going through Riga. It was as if the beast were alive and he a part of it. He still cradled the well-worn stock of the M14 across his lap, and he debated whether he would shoot Max on sight or go down when he spotted the boy to hunt him on the ground.

When this whole thing had started, Max Gordon had held no interest for him, but now the boy was beginning to fascinate him. Like every good hunter, he had learned what he could about his prey. Cazamind had sent him as much information as they could find on Max. The boy had survived in Africa, and he had been involved in an enormous conflict in the French Alps, where he had taken on a powerful opponent and won. And then there was Max Gordon's father, whose reputation stuck in the throat of the people he had brought to justice, but he wasn't a threat any longer. In Cazamind's mind, everything now confirmed that Max's mother was the eco-scientist who had died in Central America years ago. Riga had questioned Cazamind; if Cazamind's clients had been involved, then Riga should know about them and to what extent they were implicated. Where exactly had Helen Gordon died? Cazamind had yielded little information. All he had been told was that Max Gordon should be stopped from proceeding any farther into the wilderness. Why not let the boy take his chances? Riga wanted to know.

Cazamind did not like the word *chance*; there was too much at stake. And now that they had discovered just what this boy was capable of, they should change their thinking. Max Gordon posed a threat—he was dangerous.

Riga felt a stab of resentment. All his life, since he was a boy, he had dealt with these faceless men who could change the course of people's lives—and of history—by issuing a command from the safety of their anonymity. Over the years he had obeyed their orders, done their bidding and killed whomever they wished him to kill. Perhaps he understood Max Gordon more than he realized. Riga had come face to face with him in the British Museum and had seen the look of determination in the boy's eyes. The English boy had given them all a good run for their money. There were times Riga thought that the likes of Cazamind should be dragged out and forced to face their victims so they could see and smell the fear and desperation of those being hunted, but he knew that their cowardice was entrenched. These men had no honor or courage, which was why they used people like Riga. It was a simple equation: money was power and power was control, and Riga was the instrument of their success.

At the end of the day, it did not matter what he thought of these men. His conviction was all that was important, and he was convinced of one thing: Max Gordon was no match for him.

* * *

Max heard the helicopter before he saw it, the blades' reverberations flattening the air. There was nowhere to hide; the limestone cliffs rose on each side, and boulders forced the water into eddies, making steering almost impossible.

Xavier watched as Max furiously dug the pole into the water and tried to find some purchase, desperately wanting to push them closer to the bank.

"Is it the Yanquis?"

"I don't know, but they'll be on us in less than a minute."

Max searched frantically for overhanging trees or anything that would give them cover. Xavier pointed. "Over there!"

There was a narrow cave on the other side of the river beneath an overhang, but it meant pushing across the current, which was running more strongly in that part of the river. They needed more power to get across.

"Take the pole!" Max shouted.

Xavier scrambled to his feet without question and took it from Max's hands. "Push the raft as fast as you can," Max told him, and slipped over the side into the water, kicking his legs and forcing the raft into the middle of the river. If he caught one of those swirling tongues of water, there was a risk of being stranded on the rocks, but if they could just get past them, he reckoned they would reach the cave in time. It was such a low, crevicelike slash on the waterline that they'd be lucky to get inside lying flat on the raft, but there was a good chance they would escape detection if they could reach it.

"Faster, Xavier!" he shouted. "C'mon!"

Max abandoned any thoughts of crocodiles being in the water. He reasoned, and hoped, that the swirling current and boulders would keep them at bay. His leg muscles felt as though they were being torn apart by the effort—the weight of the raft and Xavier together made it enormously difficult to push it across the current. The knot of fire in his shoulder felt like a hard-boiled egg beneath his skin, a small pocket of heat that would erupt at any moment. He kept kicking, shifting the angle of the raft, making it steer more easily. Xavier worked hard, trying to complement Max's strength by controlling the direction, jabbing the pole against boulders and riverbed as desperation fueled their efforts.

Max angled himself between the raft and the opposite bank; one more shove would get them out of sight. The front of the raft found its way into the cave; Xavier ducked, then lay flat as it went beneath the overhang and nudged into the chill half-light. The current pushed the rear end of the raft away, threatening to suck it out of the hole and take it back into the main stream. Max yelled, urging strength to transfer from his legs to his chest and arms as he made one last desperate shove to get the raft under cover. No sooner were they in the cave than Xavier screamed. A flurry of small bats, like a swarm of starlings, squeaked out of the cave. Max reached up and grabbed Xavier's shoulder. "Stay down! They won't hurt you. They're not vampire bats."

He could hear Xavier's smothered breathing as he buried his face in his arms. Max was less concerned about the bats and more worried about the swarm being spotted by whoever was in the helicopter, because now the thundering engine and whirring blades reverberated inside the cave as it drew level. Max saw the helicopter flash past, so low that the skids were less than a meter from the surface. Both doors were open, and he caught a glimpse of someone sitting on the other side, feet dangling over the edge. The aircraft was so close to the water that, had the man been facing the cliff wall where Max and Xavier were hiding, he would have seen them.

They listened as the helicopter noise receded and stopped echoing around the small cave. Finally, it went quiet. Now Max had to make a decision. They either stayed in the cave and waited a few hours, which meant they would be there all night, or they pushed back into the river and took their chances that the helicopter would not return.

Another five minutes, Max decided.

The tree-lined river edge blurred with speed, but Riga scanned everything. The helicopter had jigged ever so slightly to the left.

He pulled a headset and microphone off the bulkhead and spoke to the pilot: "What?"

"Nothing," the pilot answered. "Bats. We must've spooked 'em."

Riga thought for a moment. Maybe.

"Go back, half a click," he ordered.

The pilot pulled the helicopter up, banking in a fast, curving turn, then dropped it down again to just above the river, going back downstream for half a kilometer. Riga peered ahead, looking for any caves that might give the boy refuge. There was nothing obvious, but then he saw the slab of low overhang and the dark shadows of water that reached under the rock face.

"See that overhang? Stand off that—I want to look."

* * *

The cold air in the cave was welcoming at first, but now the water made Max shiver. Xavier still lay facedown as bats returned, seeking darkness. Then the unmistakable sound of the helicopter grew closer.

"Xavier. They're coming back!"

They were trapped. The water merged into blackness a couple of meters farther in, but there the ceiling of the cave would be almost on top of the raft—certainly no room to stay on board.

"We have to get the raft farther in, right into this corner, as far as we can. You have to get into the water. Come on."

Xavier shook his head. Going in the water was a fearful experience, but going into that inky darkness filled him with dread.

"You have to!" Max commanded, whispering as if his voice could be heard over the thundering racket of the helicopter that now hovered ten meters from the entrance. Then a searchlight danced beneath the overhang and lit the water.

Riga crouched low on the helicopter's skids as the pilot controlled the powerful searchlight into the narrow slit.

"Lower!" Riga ordered.

"We'll be in the water! There might be rotten trees and debris beneath the surface. We could get caught," the pilot told him.

"Do it," Riga said quietly.

Carefully the pilot lowered the helicopter so that Riga's legs went below the surface. Now the killer could bend down and look into the cave. If the boys were in there, he would see them.

Reflections from the water skittered around the walls as the power from the whirring blades created a spray across the surface. The thundering noise was deafening. Xavier covered his ears and screamed again as another swarm of bats fled the sudden terror and scraped across his back, neck and head.

Max reached up, yanked him into the water, pulled him spluttering from beneath the surface and clamped one of the boy's hands on to the raft. "Kick! We have to get in farther!"

Shocked and frightened, Xavier responded as Max took most of the weight of the raft, forcing himself to kick fiercely, ignoring the weight of his waterlogged cargo pants and boots.

Like a monster's eye, the light sought them out, but Max and Xavier had managed to shove themselves right into the corner. Their heads were barely above the surface as the water whipped into their faces. Xavier was gasping; Max could barely open his eyes. Holding on to the raft with one hand, he reached out with his injured arm and grabbed the back of Xavier's T-shirt, holding him up. "Hang on!" he yelled, but his voice was swallowed by the air-pummeling beat of the rotors.

*   *   *

Riga saw a swarm of bats escape the narrow gap. He stayed, eyes level, for another two minutes, knowing the pilot was struggling to keep the helicopter stable. The current was exerting pressure against the skids. Maybe they were pushing their luck. He didn't want the helicopter to be pulled into the river. There was nothing beneath that slab of rock except bats.

"OK. Take her up," he said.

The pilot eased the helicopter gently from the water and wished he had never been chosen for this journey.

The silence was as big a shock as the deafening noise. Their ears rang for a few moments, but then the darkness and still water settled over them. Max eased the raft out, still holding Xavier, until there was space for him to clamber back on board.

"OK? We made it," Max said cheerfully, despite the inflammation in his shoulder stiffening the muscles.

Xavier seemed exhausted, but opened his eyes and nodded. "We made it," he whispered. "Who were they?"

"I don't know," Max said. "Search and rescue, maybe Coast Guard. Maybe not."

"Who else could it be?" Xavier said.

Max didn't even want to think that it could be the people who'd been chasing him back in England. How could they know he was here? Right here, on this river, in this cave? He shook his head.

"We'll give it another few minutes and then we go."

"The bats will come back," Xavier said.

"We're the ones invading their home. How would you feel if you were fast asleep and some monsters came into your bedroom? *You'd* run outside screaming."

"Yeah, amigo, but when I go to sleep, I don' hang upside down in my bed. Let's get out of here."

The current, like a gatekeeper, rushed across the cave's opening, making it difficult to push free and have any degree of maneuverability. It would be like jumping into a slipstream; the river could whip them away onto boulders, which would shatter the raft. If they didn't get a big enough push into the river, into the deeper, slower-moving water, Max couldn't see how they could control those first few vital moments.

"Roll onto your back," he told Xavier, "use your feet against the ceiling and push us out. I'll shove from here. The moment we hit that current, you've got to get up and push us away with the pole. I'll get aboard soon as I can. OK?"

Xavier nodded. He didn't mind Max telling him what to do; it took away the responsibility that had always scared him.

"One, two, three—go!" Max yelled.

Xavier pedaled against the ceiling, giving the raft momentum.

They were clear. Max felt the tug of the current. He was now at the back of the raft and, instead of pushing, was now being pulled. His hands were slipping, the wood too wet to hold. He curled his fingers under the thin vine that held the raft together, still trying to use his body as a rudder to shape the raft's passage. Xavier was doing the best he could, but Max could see he was already losing control; he did not have the intuitive skill to nurse it into the best part of the river. The current pushed Max's body against the back of the raft, and he used it to help him clamber aboard.

"You OK?" he gasped.

Xavier nodded, pleased he could hand back the steering of the raft to Max. He shoved the pole toward him.

"That was great—well done, mate," Max said reassuringly.

Xavier grinned. He could not remember the last time someone had said he'd done something well. "Yeah? I do OK?"

"Better than OK. You saved us."

The boy smiled, wobbling as he kept his balance against the swaying movement, but there was an unmistakable look of pride on his face. Max knew how important it was to be encouraged when things got tough.

"Can you help me balance it now? The current's getting stronger—we have to be really careful. Whichever way I move to pole us, you go on the opposite side," Max said.

"You, the angels and me. We make a great team. ¿Sí?"

"The best," Max said.

As Max shoved hard to slip the raft sideways, out into the middle of the river and the calm water, Xavier moved carefully, concentrating on doing what Max had asked him. For the first time since he could remember, he was no longer a passenger.

Riga flew on for another hour. There was no sign of the boy, and there were a dozen or more small tributaries and offshoots like veins creeping into the jungle. Maybe he had got this far and gone off into one of them. If that was the case, it would take another couple of days of searching, and there was far more cover in those narrow rivers so he would be hard to spot. Riga needed more men, and another helicopter. He would call them in at dawn.

"Find a sandbank or somewhere to land."

The pilot glanced back. This was not something he was keen to do.

"Weather's shifting," he said, hoping it would change Riga's mind.

Riga checked the sky. He could smell the salt air being pushed upriver by the stiffening breeze. He nodded.

"I know. We stay as long as we can. The boy's out there somewhere."

"You think you missed him?"

"He has skills—and maybe luck—so we wait. Until morning, if the weather lets us."

The pilot nodded, knowing better than to argue. At least they had emergency rations aboard the helicopter. It might be a long night, but they could close up the chopper and keep out the mosquitoes, and they would have food in their stomachs, which was more than that kid would have. But he had seen these local weather fronts hit the coast before. This Riga was not local; he might think he could outlast anything. Not around here.

"It'll be difficult," he said, "what with the storm. We might have to get going in a real hurry."

"I don't care," Riga replied. He wanted to stay as close as

possible to the hunt. The pilot hoped this crazy man wasn't going to leave it too late for them to escape. He lifted the helicopter above the tree line and began searching for a landing zone.

Riga knew that if time was on his side, then Max Gordon might fall into his hands and make life—and death—a lot easier.

16

Danny Maguire's body was taken through the streets of London to one of the city's main hospitals in the East End. The men still escorted the ambulance, and Sayid had tracked them using more than twenty street cameras. He stored all the pieces of recovered archive footage in a compressed file so that they could be opened and viewed in sequence.

Sayid could see that the ambulance went to the rear of the building, where the body was off-loaded. The two men parked the car and walked in behind the ambulance crew. There was no movement for more than twenty minutes other than the ambulance leaving the hospital. Then a black, unmarked van arrived and also drove round the back of the building. The men who drove the van up to the mortuary entrance wore suits and looked like funeral undertakers. They unloaded a coffin, went inside and after another half hour came out again. It was obvious to Sayid there was now a body inside the coffin. As the black van drove away, the escort car followed it.

They drove for another hour, well south of the Thames, to an anonymous concrete complex no different from any of the other ugly, faceless buildings that surrounded it. When the van and a car emerged from the underground parking lot of the building, the two vehicles separated. It was at this point that Sayid stopped the surveillance. He was exhausted, but as far as he could see, Danny Maguire's body never came out again.

There was nothing else Sayid could do other than to get this information into the right hands. But who was that to be? If he told Mr. Jackson what he had been doing, he'd probably get booted out of the school and his mother would lose her job. He decided to contact the White Hat group and get their help to access cameras inside that building and send what he had to MI5. That was why he needed the best IT guys. MI5 could trace back the source of the information, but if the White Hats took it on with their sophisticated equipment, they could hide an elephant in a room and no one would notice.

Sam Keegan was a young desk officer at MI5. He was ambitious and pleased it was he who was delivering news to his boss concerning the ongoing investigation into Max Gordon.

"Sir, we had a bomb-burst message come through."

Ridgeway had been concentrating on something else and looked blank for a moment.

"It's a fragmented message sent from a hundred or more encrypted sources," Keegan explained.

"I know what it is. Show me."

Keegan swiveled Ridgeway's keyboard round to face him and made a few keystrokes. The screen showed a myriad of small windows that, after Keegan opened them, ran seamlessly into one screen.

"Someone has tagged together archive footage of Danny Maguire's death. This took some doing, but they clearly want us to see it."

Ridgeway gazed at the unfolding picture on his screen. "Can you trace this back?"

"Doubtful, sir. My guess is that there'd be a hundred dead ends."

Ridgeway nodded. It didn't matter, because whoever sent this was clearly asking for MI5's help.

"Can we identify this building?" he asked, pointing at the final frame of the concrete complex.

"It's south of the river, sir. When they sent it through, it had GPS coordinates attached."

"How very helpful of them. Well, whoever they are, it's a pity we can't get them to work for us. All right, Keegan, you'd better get down there and have a look. I just hope this isn't some tomfoolery and that we are the victim of somebody's sick sense of humor."

Keegan left his boss's office, neither man knowing that the mild-mannered desk agent would soon face a horror worse than his most frightening nightmares.

"Wake up! Get up! Now!"

Sayid jerked awake. He had been asleep for only a couple of hours, and the programmed alarm on his computer shouted at him like a housemaster. He was still fuzzy-headed as he sat down on a chair, hit the Return key and watched as a message came in from the White Hat hackers. They used his Web name:

Magician: you online, dude? bomb-burst delivered. guess they'll follow up. government morons won't find us. you take over the cameras live in that building, watch yourself. we'll be here and will monitor when you go in. dead bodies, Men in Black, not good news. could be tight if they attempt a trace on you. we'll block them as long as we can.

The screen imploded and then flashed up with more than a dozen CCTV camera feeds. Sayid popped a can of energy drink, shoved a handful of crisps into his mouth and washed them down with a swig. He had control of the cameras inside the concrete complex. He was spying in real time.

Wherever Max was, Sayid was still trying to help him. He just hoped his friend would contact him before too long and that Max was not in danger—but as the thought entered his head, he knew that was unlikely.

The storm gathered out at sea, hurled itself furiously toward the coast and then veered, scouring the coastline, doing its best to tear the landscape apart. Funneled by the estuary and deflected by the mountains, it lost much of its strength as it swept down the river, but it was still a force that demanded respect. The accompanying clouds clung to the peaks and dumped rain into the ravine-scarred hills.

Max felt the freshening breeze long before the storm pounded the coast. As he poled the raft on the calmer edges of the fast-moving current, he realized that fresh water had channeled into the river from somewhere—perhaps runoff from the steep banks—and that the water was no longer brackish. He remembered the River Dart at home when the tide pushed the salt water only so far, and then as water soaked downward from Dartmoor, the river became clean and fresh. Now the same happened here. They had made good progress in spite of the fast-flowing current, but the water had become deeper, the swirling eddies tugging at them, and he could feel the end of the pole being almost forced from his hand. There was no sign of the helicopter. Could they have given up the search so quickly? Max could see that as the river widened ahead of them and then twisted round a sweeping bend, the force of the water pounded the far shore. He would not have sufficient control to get them much farther upriver, and if the helicopter came back now, they would be exposed and vulnerable.

The approaching storm was a real threat, because the more rain that fell, the more turbulent the river became. Their flimsy craft was already struggling to cope with the torsion of the currents. They had passed two smaller tributaries, but Max had ignored them, wanting to push on as far as he could up the main stream, but now he realized that they could not get much farther.

"We need to find a side stream," he told Xavier.

Xavier was already gripping the white leather seat as the choppy water bounced the raft around. Like a child clutching a teddy bear, he hugged it to himself with one arm while gripping the raft's fraying homemade rope with his free hand.

"How do we do that?" he asked, his voice breaking with uncertainty.

"A miracle might help," Max said as he shoved all his weight against the pole, urging the raft to move toward the forested banks and into calmer water.

"I thin' we've used up all the miracles we had. You better talk to your angels, *chico*."

Max smiled. "There's always one more if you ask for it. Over there, see?"

Xavier was on his knees, the wind was freshening and he could feel that Max did not have the control he had had only a few minutes ago. As they approached the bend in the river, a small headland jutted out, masked by trees. Water gurgled, and in a lumpy, confused way, tore itself away from the main river.

"Right on cue!" Max yelled. "When I push to the right, get back here with me and put your weight behind me. You're going to get wet as the tail end of the raft goes under, but that's how we can slew it across. You ready?"

Xavier was nodding furiously and holding on for dear life. Max watched the current, saw the swirl of water and risked a glance over his shoulder, because suddenly the breeze was no longer a gentle whisper on his neck but an insistent, invisible hand pushing at him. The darkening clouds were pouring over the edge of the mountains like a breaking wave. A tidal bore—a churning muddy surge of water forced upstream by the sea—chased the raft. It would take less than a couple of minutes to reach them, and then all would be lost. Even if Xavier clung to the makeshift life belt, it was likely that the force of the water would tear it from his grasp and then he would drown, because Max would not be able to reach him in the turmoil.

"Now! Come on, Xavier! Get here, come on!" The wind was already carrying his voice away from the raft, swallowing it, muting his desperate command. Max jammed the pole into the riverbed, felt it bite into boulders and leaned, pushing the raft across the last stretch of troublesome water.

It was like being sucked down the drain. The narrow outlet pulled them out of danger, but the pole snapped in Max's hands. He nearly fell, but Xavier grabbed him, and they both clung desperately to the fragile raft as it jiggled, bent and twisted. It would not be much longer before it came apart completely. It was amazing that it had got them this far.

The helicopter pilot flicked the switches and mentally urged the propellers to wind up more quickly than they were doing. The sudden surge of water that came round the bend in the river had taken him by surprise, and he knew that if he could not lift the helicopter clear of the sandbank, they would be washed away. Riga was at the open door of the chopper, standing on a skid as he gazed downriver. If Max Gordon was hiding in the shallows or beneath overhanging trees behind them, this surge of water would have caught him and whoever was with him and flushed them out. But so far there was no sign of them.

The pilot was screaming at him. Riga wasn't wearing the headset, but he could see the man's mouth, spittle flecking from his lips in a silent demand that they get going now! Riga nodded, gripped the fuselage and felt the pummeling downdraft of the blades as the helicopter lifted clear. Boulders, trees and mud churned below the skids. Riga felt a twinge of regret—he did not want the storm to kill Max Gordon. The boy had tried his best to survive; he wanted him to live long enough so that he, Riga, could kill him face to face. It was a far more honorable way to die.

The narrow fork that Max and Xavier had turned down was a few kilometers from where Riga had waited in the helicopter, but the noise of the wind and the growling thunder of water as it pursued them stifled any noise of the aircraft they might have heard. Low clouds rode above the crested water like a phantom surfer. The violent wave had surged past the mouth of this channel, but the force of the water now turned its violence toward the two boys.

Max felt the raft begin to break up; the vine string and palm-leaf ties were simply no match for this kind of stress and strain. There were maybe two or three sections of the raft that might hold together, and it was these that Xavier clung to, with the leather seat beneath his chest. Max unrolled the length of rope and tied it to the middle of the metal-tipped shaft. He could see a small pool of water a hundred meters ahead, created by two boulders that made the river spurt its energy around them.

"Over there!" Max shouted. "That pool." He gripped the shaft, showing Xavier that he intended to throw it and snag the rocks. "The rope'll be long enough to take you close to the shore. You just hold on tight! Understand? It's the best chance you've got."

Xavier nodded miserably. Max knew he would have no choice but to go into the water and survive as best he could. If he was lucky, the tongue of water would push him into the undergrowth, where they might have a chance to climb ashore, back into the shelter of the trees where they would have to start their journey again on foot. A thrashing squall of rain caught them, then swept across and past them. Like bullets hitting the surface, the squall momentarily flattened the choppy water. If they were going to have any chance of reaching the bank, now was a good time to attempt it. He stood up, knees bent, balancing on what was little more than the width of a couple of surfboards. Grabbing the end of the metal-tipped shaft, he swung it in a flat arc, low across the water. His shoulder felt as though it had torn apart, the infection from the thorns protesting against the effort. He wrapped the end of the rope round Xavier's fist, hauled him to his feet and watched as the rope played out.

"Come on, Xavier, it's now or never!"

"Maybe never's better," Xavier shouted, but there was no choice in the matter as the last pieces of wood separated beneath them. The rope tugged, Xavier jumped and within a couple of seconds, Max tumbled into the water, plunging down hard and fast.

Max broke the surface retching, frantically kicking to stay afloat. He saw Xavier, still gripping the white leather seat and rope, his mind acknowledging that the boy was in smoother water and that he had a good chance of reaching the bank. Xavier was sorted. Max had his own problems. He was being pulled away by the current. Another squall splattered down, stinging his face, forcing him to close his eyes. Part of his brain was shouting at him to look downriver. He tried to shake the water from his ears, suck air and force his eyes wide open against the spray. What was that noise? It did not sound like the wind. More like an express train. A couple of hundred meters away, the mist phantoms were forced into the sky by a greater power. A curtain of spray that rose up from the river like steam. Waterfall!

He swallowed water, choked, gasping for breath, forcing himself not to panic. Whatever happened he mustn't panic; he had to stay in control as long as he could, but his strength was slipping away, and no matter how hard he fought, he could not beat this tidal surge, nor the fever that was swallowing him more quickly than the river. He had finally asked too much of his body, now weakened from battling the infection in his shoulder.

Was this what drowning was like? Everything fell silent about him. The wind and slushing water were muted. There was a lot of water in his ears—perhaps that was why he couldn't hear anything anymore. He tried to float on his back, arms outstretched, gazing at the cotton-wool-like mist and hoping his spread-eagled position would snag something, anything, to halt the unstoppable course toward the cliff edge. Was it a ten-meter drop or a hundred?

He bounced and bobbed; then a wave overtook him, washed across his face and forced his body down. With no time to take a breath, he simply closed his eyes and mouth and let the water spin him round. *Sometimes you can't fight it—just go with it, son. Find that place in your mind where it is quiet and where there's no fear.* How many times had his dad told him that the mind and body had to work together? It was like going through a door into a silent room where he could watch his body fight its own battle.

It was not his father that he yearned for in these final moments. This vein of river was the route to his mother's heart, and he called for her, crying out desperately in the darkness of his mind.

His face broke the surface, and he lurched upward, forcing his painful shoulder to raise him high enough so that he could see and breathe. It would take only a second for the water to tumble again, pushing him back down beneath the surface. He couldn't survive another thrashing. He was going to drown this time—better that way—before the drop.

For a moment he thought the helicopter had returned as a whirring hum of blades thrashed the air. The current spun him round; at least now he would not see the drop into the cauldron when it came, but the crazy image he saw took time to penetrate his mind. It was a big, flat-bottomed boat, and a man sitting on a high seat in front of a massive fan was pointing the boat directly at him. These killers just wouldn't give up!

A grizzled, bewhiskered man with a gold tooth, tattooed face and arms, an earring and a battered old straw hat with colored feathers shoved into it was mouthing something at him. This apparition stood at the front of the fan-propelled boat as it surged toward him.

Max almost laughed aloud: it seemed there were pirates of the Caribbean after all.

17

It felt as though he were tied to the riverbed, deep down in the dark, still pools where the sand was smooth and no turbulence could reach him. Seaweed had somehow wrapped itself across his body so that he could not move. He could breathe, which surprised him, and he forced his eyes open, trying to focus his blurred vision. He was not in an underwater grotto filled with bright colors of coral, fish and seaweed, but in a hut; its palm-thatched roof creaked as the wind rustled through it. The walls were made of thin slats of wood bound together, and the narrow-planked floor was worn smooth by years of bare feet moving across it.

A small, homemade wooden table bore scooped-out gourds, some fan-shaped seashells and an old-fashioned metal grinder clamped to the end. A drop-down bunk held by thin rope was cantilevered from the wall, and two or three lines, covered in skirts of different colors, were stretched across the room in place of wardrobes. Blue-dyed cotton with white stripes, orange-colored children's dresses, some T-shirts and green and purple homemade burlap bags, scuffed from use, hung on hooks. Max realized he was lying on a homemade bed similar to that on the wall, a soft straw mattress cushioning him from the slatted base.

He was tied down in the prone position, one arm stretched out and bent in front of his head, his wrist bound with what looked to be an animal-skin thong. He tried to raise himself, but he had been secured by similar straps to the bed.

A small girl wearing a crisp white dress embroidered with a bright red flower bent down next to his face. She gazed at him with wide eyes, like a fawn seeing something unusual in the forest. She smiled, then took one of the small gourds from a low table and put it on the floor next to Max. She dipped her fingers into the water and dabbed them onto his dry lips. Then she took a small cotton cloth, soaked it, wrung it out and gently wiped his face. Max nodded, as best he could, by way of thanks. His throat felt raw and parched, probably from swallowing and choking on so much river water. The girl smiled and got to her feet, and he heard her patter out of the hut, calling her father.

"Papa. Papa!"

Max knew someone had undressed him, and he could smell a gentle fragrance from his skin, so someone had washed him as well. He tried again to raise himself against the thongs that bound him, but they gave by only a fraction: he was well and truly secured. Then heavier footsteps came into the room, and the crazy-looking pirate he had seen on the river squatted down in the corner of the hut. Max could see him clearly in his limited line of sight. He had a long-bladed knife in its scabbard strapped to his calf over the tough cotton trousers he wore. There were two or three chains round his neck, some of them threaded through small pieces of coral and semiprecious stones, and the straw hat with the feathers was old and sweat-stained.

"You've been asleep for two days, my friend," the pirate said.

"Am I a prisoner?" Max asked.

The man smiled. Some of his teeth were missing, but the others were capped in gold. "You were nearly a prisoner of the river god. He would have tied you up, bundled you like a plucked chicken and sucked the marrow from your bones while you rotted on the bottom. I tied you down so that I could treat the wound in your shoulder. Those thorns had festered deep inside the muscle. It took a lot of effort to get them out, and I had to use my sharpest knife. We had to keep you like that so the dressings would not come off your back and shoulder. You want to get up now?"

Max nodded, uncertain how to engage his rescuer in conversation. The man spoke with a slightly unusual inflection— a gentle, clear pronunciation of his words. Max thought it might be an Irish lilt to his voice, though he looked as Latino as Xavier.

The man quickly pulled the knife from the sheath, leaned forward and cut the thongs. Max raised himself to his knees slowly and stretched out his muscles like a cat. He tentatively rolled clear of the bed and sat on the floor facing the man, feeling the pad of a dressing taped to his shoulder.

"Not too fast, my boy. You're weak. You need rest. Food and rest," the piratical man cautioned.

"I want to get up," Max said, forcing himself to combat the giddiness he felt.

"'How poor are they that have not patience! What wound did ever heal but by degrees?'"

Max stared blankly. What was he on about?

"You are schooled?" the man asked.

"What?"

"You go to school."

"Of course I do."

"Aha! An ignorant child."

"No, I'm not."

"But you do not recognize a simple quote from Shakespeare."

Shakespeare? Max's muddled brain tried to make some sense of the idiocy that seemed to have taken hold of his life. "Not offhand, no."

"Aha," the man said again, and settled the feather-stabbed hat more squarely on his head. "You feel strong enough, you come outside. We need to change the dressing."

"Where's Xavier? Is he OK?" Max asked.

"The sewer rat? You're a friend of that scum?"

Max thought about it. Yes, they had forged a kind of friendship over the last few insane days. Max nodded. "Yes, he's my friend."

"He's outside. You Western kids! You come here back-packing. You think you're on a big adventure because you take time off school; then you start playing around with drugs. Next thing you know, you're in big trouble. Let me tell you, boy, these drug runners will slit your throat, no questions asked, if you mess with them. And if the cops catch you, you go inside for a long time. You got bad friends."

The man leaned forward and handed him the gourd full of water. "Drink slowly—otherwise you get stomach cramps."

Then he walked toward the door.

Max called after him, "I don't know your name."

He stopped in the doorway and looked back hesitantly, as if debating whether to tell Max anything at all. "Your clothes have been washed and dried; they're on that rack. We can talk later when you've had some food." He went to a shelf and gathered up the photographs he had retrieved from Max's shirt pocket when he'd been brought ashore.

"The wallet saved them, but they were wet. I dried them out. They're a bit crinkled, but at least they made it," he said, handing them to Max. "My name is Orsino Flint. I am a plant thief, but I have nothing to do with drug-running scum. Your mother was my enemy, but she would have been ashamed of you, Max Gordon."

The shock of hearing Flint mention his mother took some time to wear off. His first instinct was to run after the man and grab his arm, demanding he tell him where he had met his mother and what he knew about her. But, as the man declared that he and Max's mother had been enemies, Max knew he had to tread very carefully.

He stepped out of the hut into a clearing. Half a dozen thatched huts built on low stilts stood around a central area shaded by low palm trees scattered among them. There were children laughing and playing, and beyond the central area, steps cut into the side of a hill went down to the riverside, which seemed to be little more than a narrow tributary and much calmer than the place where Max had been rescued. Half a dozen canoes were tethered to the bank, as was a small wooden boat with an outboard engine. The bigger, flat-bottomed boat with its huge fan had a camouflage net over it, which obscured it even more than the trees did. Obviously Mr. Orsino Flint did not want his pride and joy detected by the authorities.

Four men sat under the shade of a tree mending fishing nets while women dressed in white cotton smocks embroidered with hibiscus flowers brought washing up from the river. Others pounded corn in a mortar. Another fed a fire with kindling, stripping off leaves before allowing the flames to spit and flare. Max could smell pine resin—nature's fuel. What struck him was the abundance of flowers and plants growing everywhere, explosions of color climbing even into the trees. It was a small corner of paradise, accentuated by the shrill calls of red-and-green parakeets as they chased each other through the trees. Birds with white-ringed eyes, making them look as though they were staring directly at him, gave their strange cackling cry. An iguana, no more than thirty centimeters long, popped out of a hole in the ground. The small group of children screamed with delight as they gave chase only to lose sight of it again as it scurried under the bole of a tree.

Max gazed at the women: their rich copper-chocolate skin was smooth, the broad features of their noses identifiable as being Mayan. For the first time he was seeing the descendants of a great civilization whose kings and warriors were recorded on the stone lintels in the British Museum. He could barely remember when he had last been in London—it seemed a lifetime ago—but here at last, deep in the rain forest, were the very people his mother had worked among, the people he had come to find. If Orsino Flint believed Max's mother was his enemy, was there any likelihood these villagers might have known her, or even considered her differently? He felt some hope. They had not harmed him—quite the opposite.

Max watched the women working. One of them pounded roasted cacao beans and chili and maize, and he could smell vanilla pods as well as peanuts and honey as she mixed the concoction with boiling water. Ancient Maya drank their chocolate hot and frothy, and it appeared that these people did the same. The woman poured the dark liquid back and forth between two containers, creating a foamy mixture. The pungent smell of hot chocolate teased his senses.

Flint gestured to the woman, who spilled some of the dense liquid into a mug-sized container. He handed it to Max.

"It's food and medicine. It'll give you strength," he said.

Max let the beaten chocolate seep through his teeth. It tasted glorious. To be told that chocolate was good for him was a ticket to heaven, and the rich warmth sank into his stomach. Greedily, he finished the cup.

Flint nodded, satisfied. "Over here." He sat on a stool next to a small fire where another villager was frying something in a blackened old pan on the top of the low-burning embers.

Max joined him at the fireside. He could feel the sun's heat on his skin, burning through his shirt, though he could see from its position in the sky that it was still early. A quick glance at his father's watch, still clamped on his wrist, confirmed it.

Flint tapped the ground next to him with his long-bladed knife, and Max sat obediently. Despite the man's declaration of being his mother's enemy, he felt he wasn't in immediate danger. After all, this man had saved his life, so he was hardly likely to cut his throat now, especially not in the midst of this domestic setting.

The woman was shredding leaves, removing their stems and veins and then crumbling what was left into the pan.

Flint eased Max's shirt off his shoulder and slipped the blade beneath the dressing, teasing it from the skin. He could see it was still tender as the boy's muscles rippled in discomfort, but Max made no sound.

"So you think you're some kind of tough kid coming out here, do you?"

"No," Max said. "I'm just trying to find out what happened to my mum."

"Aha," Flint said. He nodded to the woman, who shook the pan, letting the seeds and pieces of leaf roast more evenly. "You know about the jungle? You ever been in a rain forest before?"

"I've been in the wilderness," Max said defensively.

"Wilderness is one thing; this place is more dangerous. It's not just wild animals, snakes, spiders and crocodiles that'll kill you; there are plants that'll get into your bloodstream and paralyze you, leaving you suffocating to death on the jungle floor. Then just about everything that crawls or slithers will come for you—that's if the ants don't get you first. There'd be nothing left of you after a couple of days. So, more foolhardy than brave, more dumb than intelligent. You kids have no sense. Like stepping into the lion's den and not seeing the lion."

"I told you why I came here. It's just that I hadn't planned on doing it this way," Max said, desperately wanting to find out what Flint knew about his mother but realizing he had to learn patience with this bizarre character.

"Your scumbag friend said you fixed his wound—said you got the infection out of him. You know about traditional healing, how to fix yourself in the jungle when you get sick or hurt?"

Max wondered where in the camp Xavier was being kept. They must have him locked up somewhere in one of these huts.

"No, not really," Max said. "I just learned a few things from my dad; he was a scientist and explorer as well, like my mum."

"Aha," Flint said.

"Please tell me about her. Why were you enemies? Did you hurt her?"

"No. Not me, young fella. But maybe we talk later. First things first. You want to get fixed, don't you?"

Max's impatience irritated him more than the sore itching of the wound in his shoulder, but he had to play this man's game, no matter how long it took. *Be patient, be patient*, he kept telling himself. He nodded, obeying his own instincts.

Flint gestured to the woman at the fire. "Fixing-up stuff. It's for your wound. Basil, clover, marigold and amaranth leaves. She's making up a couple of days' worth for you."

"She cooks it?" asked Max.

"You shred everything into a dry pan and keep stirring it till the parts of the plant are nearly burning. They've got to turn very dark. You cook it, you release the minerals. You unlock the healing ingredients from the leaves' ash," Flint said. The woman took the pan off the embers. She turned to a piece of white cotton where cooked leaves were cooling, then crumbled them until only powder was left. Flint reached out, took the cotton and carefully sprinkled the powder on Max's wound. From one of his side pockets he pulled a small roll of tape that could have been used for anything, from tying off frayed rope to strapping up an injured arm. Max felt the warmth of the cotton on his skin as Flint taped it into place.

Max smiled at the woman. "Thank you," he said.

She smiled back and carried on preparing more plants. Flint was on his feet, walking away as if uninterested in spending any more time with Max.

Max knew that despite the help he was being given, there might still be an underlying threat from this man. He needed to be careful, but he also needed information, foremost being finding out what had happened to Xavier.

"Where is he?" Max called after Flint, knowing full well he would know what he meant.

Flint turned. "Why do you care what happens to him? If I had known what he was, I'd have let him rot at the bottom of the river, and the crocodiles could have taken him when they smelled his stinking carcass. You have other things to think about, Max Gordon. You should forget him now. He'll turn his back on you the first chance he gets."

"I don't believe that," Max said. "I told you—he's my

friend. And he was trying to change. He wanted to get out of all of that. He's not all bad."

"'The evil that men do lives after them, the good is oft interred with their bones; so let it be with Caesar.'"

"Hey, I've done Shakespeare at school. I know bits and pieces of it—maybe not as much as you—so you can quote that stuff all you like. It makes no difference to me. Just tell me where he is," Max said angrily, wanting to show that he was not completely subservient. They had already turned round the corner of one of the buildings, and no sooner had Max spoken than he saw a bamboo cage built in the shade of a huge tree. And inside was Xavier, shackled by his ankle to an iron stake in the ground. There was evidence that he'd been fed, as well as a gourd that held water.

"Max! You OK? Don' trust these people! Look what they done to me! This guy is crazy—he should be locked up."

Flint kicked the cage. "No call haligetta lang mout till you done cross di riva," he said in a deliberate rolling accent that Max had little chance of understanding.

"Xavier?" Max said.

"He's Creole, mixed race. It's patois. He said not to call the alligator long mouth until you get across the river—he's just telling me that I shouldn't insult him while he still got me in a cage. Well, I won't be here forever, and when my people find out, then we see how many teeth he'll have left in his big mouth."

"Shut up, Xavier. You're just making matters worse," Max said.

Flint had walked away, leaving the two boys together, knowing that Max had no chance of releasing his friend.

Xavier spat on the palm of his hand and reached out his arm through the cage. "I told you we were partners," Xavier said.

Max took his hand. "He saved our lives, Xavier. Don't forget that. We owe him."

"You owe him if you want. Me, I just wanna get outta here."

"Well, if you learn to shut up once in a while and think before you say anything, then you might have a chance." Max turned to go after Flint. "Leave it to me. I'll sort something out. Don't go away."

"I was gonna go for a walk and pick some flowers. OK, I'll stay. You talk, I sit, then we run." Max was already farther away. "And, hey, find a map. We gonna need a map to get outta here. A big map. Yeah? You can do it. You just ask one of your angels."

The Angel Killer himself swept low across the treetops, shattering the stillness of the jungle in his voracious hunt for Max Gordon. Now that the weather had cleared, the turbulent river had settled to a more docile state, allowing him to put men on the ground. Three helicopters had been deployed with four men in each, and they had rappelled into the jungle in a triangular search pattern with the waterfall as its baseline.

Riga had spent two days scouring the river and decided that Max must have taken one of the forks that splintered away from the main stream. Broken fingers of water clawed into the dense rain forest, and each of those small rivers had offshoots of its own. At first he had been doubtful that Max would have chosen the river that ended in the seventy-meter waterfall, as the thundering gorge could be seen from where the river escaped from the main stream. Then he realized that the storm and the low cloud would have obscured that fatal plunge. He had positioned four of the men at the bottom of the gorge where the water churned through massive boulders and then softened to a more manageable flowing river. It was they who had found splintered wood, a couple of pieces of which were tied together by creepers and a twinelike binding made out of stripped palm leaves. There was no doubt that it was the remains of the raft, especially once a white leather seat cushion was found wedged between two boulders at the base of the falls. He had concentrated all the men, flanking both sides of the falls, to search for any bodies washed up farther inland. So far nothing had been found. He sent another group of men to search every small island and inlet that the broken forest allowed. If by any chance Max had survived, and Riga was beginning to think it highly unlikely, then the boy could not be far from the river.

He knew there were remote settlements deep in the forest, some of them depending on local fishing and hunting to survive, but as he examined the maps, he could see that no one on foot, or swimming for that matter, could have reached them. If by an outside chance fishermen had been in that area, an ordinary boat would not have been able to negotiate the river on the day of the storm. No boat, no rescue. Logically—if he was alive—Max Gordon had to be within no more than a kilometer of any of these river offshoots.

The manpower that was now being employed made little sense to Riga, but Cazamind had insisted that no effort be spared to ensure that Max Gordon was indeed dead. In fact, Cazamind had insisted that if his body was found, it must be brought to him personally. Riga could taste the paranoia that came from the twisted psyche of the Swiss mastermind. He was beginning to think of him as a demented cuckoo-clock maker and imagined that when the small door opened and a cuckoo appeared, it would be a horrendous caricature representing the suppressed demon in the man's soul. Riga had no such conflict within himself. All he wanted was a clean kill and to be done with this job.

Irritation crawled across his skin like prickly heat. Max Gordon was beginning to represent failure. He hoped the boy was down there beneath the jungle canopy, because then he would be found, and Riga could finish the job himself.

The helicopters had not included Orsino Flint's hamlet in their search pattern; it was too far north and west, and there was no chance that Max Gordon could have reached there. Had they known about Flint's fan-powered boat, they would have swooped like vampire bats and savaged everyone.

"They're still looking for you," Flint told Max. "They haven't stopped, so you must have upset somebody in a big way, or you have something they want. Which is it? You know something you shouldn't?"

"Boats or helicopters?" Max asked.

"Helicopters, three of them, far away from here, but we know about them. You live out here all these years, you know when a bird falls out of a tree. They want you bad. Why?"

Now it was Max's turn to hold back. As much as he

wanted to squeeze information out of Mr. Orsino Flint, he needed to know more about who the man was and why the avowed enemy of his mother had sheltered him.

"Have you seen those helicopters before?" Max asked him. "Are they military or police, something to do with the government?"

"You think the government is chasing you?" He studied Max's face for a moment. He could see how the boy's eyes might shine with laughter if the occasion was right, but he also recognized an almost detached, cold determination in them that he had once seen in Helen Gordon's eyes.

"Over several years, half a dozen ecologists have been murdered in Central America, mostly by people with illegal logging interests. Some of the do-gooders ran into drug smugglers, or so it is thought, and their bodies have never been found. The kind of work your mother and father were doing here attracted some bad people who did not want their activities exposed."

Max felt that squirming in his stomach, a sign of fear, a sudden anxiety that was a forewarning of bad news. "My father? You knew my dad was here? With my mum?"

"Everyone knew about Tom and Helen Gordon. They were a pain in the ass. Saving the rain forest is one thing; telling people how they should or shouldn't live is another. What gave them the right to stop people making money as best they could—poor people, people who lived on and farmed the land the best they could? And what do I fish out of the river? Their brat! And bringing trouble with him. Is that some kind of genetic disease in your family? Causing trouble? I'd have left you to drown if I'd known who you were."

"I don't think you would have. You're not like that. You said you weren't responsible for my mum's death, and I believe you, but you know something, don't you? Do you know what happened to her? How she really died?" Max grabbed Flint's arm unthinkingly and felt the skin tighten on his shoulder wound. Flint easily squeezed and twisted Max's wrists to release their grip.

"'Do all men kill the things they do not love? Hates any man that thing he would not kill?'" Flint made a small dramatic gesture, acting a role that Max was beginning to find very irritating.

"I reckon you need a television out here. What's the problem? Just one *Complete Works of Shakespeare*, is that all you've got on the shelf? Get a life! No one talks like that. It's the twenty-first century—or hadn't you noticed?"

Flint took a step back from the verbal onslaught. Some of the women stopped what they were doing in the background and turned to watch. Max noticed they were smiling. Obviously no one had challenged Orsino Flint, plant thief and pretend pirate, like this before.

Flint seemed duly chastened. He nodded and walked away. Max ground his teeth in frustration and, after a moment, strode after him. "Look, Flint, all I want is to find the truth behind my mother's death. Help me. Why did you hate my mother? What did she ever do to you?"

Flint stopped at the top of the track that led down to the river and gazed at the flowing water for a few seconds before answering. "My father was Tyrone Hickey Flint. An outcast from Ireland. The greatest exponent of the Bard there ever was. He trod every termite-ridden board from Patagonia to the Mexican border for nearly fifty years. Not once was his name put up in lights. Not once. He craved the fame of recognition, but he ended up going from village to jungle town to share his love of Shakespeare for a meal and a bed. And my mother, a Creole woman, went with him. Never complaining, fetching and carrying, making him feel like a great man. I could never be my father's son—but I could be my mother's. He beat the words into me, and she lovingly taught me every flower and plant in the jungle. I'm the greatest plant thief there is, and your mother found out about me and destroyed my life. Now I survive on a fraction of the money I used to get—I'm too notorious to do business with. Your mother and her tree-hugging friends saw to that."

"Then do you know how she died?"

"No. But I think I know where."

18

Sayid watched Keegan skirt the building. Heavy steel doors barred his way, but then he made his way down the ramp to where the van had taken Maguire's body. There was a keypad there, and Sayid watched as Keegan, glancing over his shoulder to make sure that no one was around, swiped a card and then stepped back as the door moved upward. Keegan ducked under quickly when it was only a meter off the ground, and then Sayid saw it roll back down to its original position. He quickly fingered the keys to select another CCTV camera from the dozen or so others on his screen. By the way the man acted, inspecting the building first and then finding a way in, Sayid realized that this man had to be from MI5 and that they were responding to the surveillance files that had been sent to them.

Sayid manipulated the lens of the camera inside the first area. No natural light found its way into the tomblike building. Sayid watched as the man turned on a small but powerful torch, searching the walls for a light switch. That was going to be very helpful to Sayid, but he thought that maybe it wasn't a great idea for the man himself. How did the man know that the torch was not going to set off a light-sensitive alarm? Maybe he was inexperienced. Or scared. Did MI5 people get scared? Sayid felt nervous enough being a fly on the wall as the camera lens tracked the man down the corridor.

All the walls inside the building seemed to be made of brushed stainless steel or thick opaque glass, and Keegan edged along warily, hands moving across the walls, trying to find a doorway or an opening of any kind, because where there were frames within the glass, there seemed to be no handles to indicate that a door or entrance of any description could be there.

There was an uncanny silence in the corridor and a chill that reminded Keegan of a mortuary. It was not his imagination—even the walls felt cold. There was an elevator at the end of the corridor. He pressed the button and the doors opened; there were only two floors to choose from. First floor and work up? Second floor and work down? He pressed the first-floor button, noticed that his breathing had become more ragged, more fearful, but could not deny the thrill of danger that squirmed in his stomach. The doors closed on him.

He would never see daylight again.

* * *

Sayid was as edgy as Keegan. He watched a dozen cameras on-screen, but they all seemed to be focused on corridors, empty and cold-looking, bare and unwelcoming. He could see the MI5 man standing in the lift, gazing up at the camera lens—right at him. Sayid suddenly felt a tremor in his hands as he manipulated the camera. It was as if the man knew he was there, but then he glanced back down. Obviously this camera was behind a panel and not directly in view.

It was like being a ghost, standing right next to someone, almost able to touch them, going with them on their journey but being invisible. Sayid thought he seemed very young to be a spy and looked to be in his early twenties. As if he had not been out of university for long. He looked cool. Jeans, shirt hanging loosely, black jacket and canvas trainers. His hair was chopped in a modern style. Just an ordinary-looking bloke you wouldn't glance at twice in the street. Exactly what a spy should be, Sayid reasoned.

The lift doors opened.

The low-lit area Keegan had stepped into was ultramodern. A number of small screens were strategically located along the wall, evenly spaced, as if there were rooms behind those thick, dull panels. Fingerprints were required to access whatever lay behind these opaque glass screens. As he stood at the end of the corridor and gazed along it, he realized it was wide enough for him to reach out both arms and almost touch the walls on each side. Wide enough for what? A hospital trolley maybe? A full-sized wheeled bed? Was this some kind of private hospital or clinic? It smelled like it.

He remembered when he had gone round the building outside how the narrow alleyways had run far back. This building had a lot of depth, and the internal space must be used to store something, but what? It had to be really important, because only a privileged few gained access to this second stage of security—you had to have the correct fingerprint. How could he get round that?

Sayid watched the man move back toward the lift. He stood in front of the doors for a moment and studied the framework next to where the call button was located. His fingers seemed to trace the area around the stainless steel, and then he took something from his pocket. Sayid changed camera angles, choosing one that sat high in the corner of the corridor and included the lift doors. He used his mouse to pinpoint the camera's control panel that sat on his screen and tweaked the direction of the lens. Sayid zoomed in. Now he could see that the man had a square of what looked like acetate in his hands. He peeled the back off it and pressed it against the frame, then lifted it off carefully. Keegan turned and moved back down the corridor.

Sayid changed camera angles again. He was just to one side, and high up, but he could look down at what the man was doing—placing the sheet on a small screen. It was a fingerprint swipe. Clever. He had lifted a fingerprint to gain access. These guys were good, Sayid thought. No wonder they were MI5.

The opaque wall panel slid back, exposing a broad, tiled room. Immediately to one side were stainless-steel coat stands, purpose-designed to hang a biohazard suit on—and there were four of them suspended now, just like the ones Sayid had seen worn in the Underground tunnel.

But the man had barely glanced at the suits, because set square in the middle of this room was a glass cage with a stainless-steel table in the middle. Like a postmortem examination room. The glass cage was a completely sealed unit, and if Sayid could have viewed the room from another angle, he would have seen that there was a special entrance built through an air lock at the back of this cage, where a medical team could enter and exit safely once they had hooked up the oxygen line for their biohazard suits.

Sayid watched as the man pressed some console buttons on one wall. A series of screens appeared, half a dozen individual frames, as if they were an integral part of the wall, just as a hospital examination room would display images from a scanning machine. Sayid could not see what the images were, but he watched as the man put a hand to his face in horror and then staggered back a few paces, banging into one of the biohazard suits. He spun round, completely disoriented, and then bent over and vomited on the cold tile floor. Whatever was on those screens must have been horrific.

Sayid saw movement on his monitor. Someone else was in the building. He quickly keyed in different camera angles. Two men he had never seen before. They were in the downstairs area stepping into the lift. Another angle—they pressed the button. The first floor. They knew there was an intruder in the building. Sayid couldn't see the faces yet; they kept their chins tucked low. They knew there were cameras. Sayid keyed to his angle back in the examination room; the man was leaning against the wall, wiping his face with his sleeve.

He seemed weakened by what he had seen. Why didn't he get out? If what was on those screens was so terrible, why didn't he get out?

Sayid shouted at the images, "Run! Get out now as fast as you can! Hurry! *Hurry!*"

A warning flash bleeped loudly on Sayid's computer. It was insistent, demanding his attention. The men were getting closer to that examination room; the doors of the lift were opening. Sayid pressed the key that highlighted the warning signal. It was from his White Hat group. The text was in capital letters: they were shouting a warning at him.

SHUT DOWN, MAGICIAN. SHUT DOWN. THEY'RE TRACING YOU! WE CAN'T HOLD THEM OFF. THESE GUYS ARE POWERFUL. SHUT DOWN. GET OUT NOW. GET OUT!

Sayid felt a wave of terror engulf him. He clicked back to the screens. The man was backing against the glass cage, his arm raised as if trying to shield himself; then he went out of sight, because one of the two intruders stood in front of him and was extending his arm, pointing at him. Pointing or aiming?

Helplessly, Sayid yelled at the screen. "Leave him alone! Leave him alone!"

Suddenly his vision was blurred. A hand had reached up and pulled the camera lens downward. One of the intruders looked right at him. Right into his eyes. He pointed a finger. And smiled. The screens went haywire. Sayid ripped the power cable out of the wall.

And then there was nothing. Sayid sat in stunned silence

for a couple of seconds. With a surge of fear, he pushed the chair back from the desk. It felt as though the man were in the room with him. What had happened in that building was connected to Max, and so were those images that Keegan had seen.

What were they? What horror was Max facing?

Faces with gaping mouths screamed in silent terror. The clay pottery masks with their empty eye sockets gazed blindly into Orsino Flint's hut from where they hung on the walls. Animal skins were stretched across the wall and floor; rare and exotic plants, dripping with moisture, were tucked into corners, competing for space with a collection of spears, shields, bows and arrows. It was a museum of jungle living. More face masks, but this time of wood, crudely carved and decorated with brightly speckled garish paint, hung on another wall as if in a gallery. They looked like representations of various jungle animals.

Flint pointed to a place on the floor. "Sit there," he said as he began to rummage in a corner where rolls of maps and charts were stacked like a woodpile.

Max could barely curb his impatience. Where had his mother disappeared to before she died? He could not rush this strange character; he was there because of Orsino Flint's goodwill. His own fate had not yet been decided. One thing was certain: Max could never escape from this jungle hideout. He needed Flint on his side. He did as he was told. "What are all those masks?" he asked, trying to divert his attention from the more pressing questions he had.

Flint kept his head down, looking at the rolls. "The Maya call him Balam. Jaguar. Don't you know anything? The jaguar is revered here."

Max's heart thudded. Instant recall. The memory of the big cat in the jungle as its eyes met his own, penetrating the depths of his consciousness—a moment of raw power when the two entities, animal and human, met.

The image broke as Flint unrolled two old maps on the floor, holding the corners down with a selection of rocks, pots and a monkey skull.

"People like you and your parents come here, and how much do you know about the Mayan culture? Not a lot, is my guess. You come here to save them; they don't need saving. They are the people of the earth and sky—and the jaguar. Thousands of years ago, they were plotting the stars and planets; their temples were built in position so that precise observations could be made. They worked out that there were 365.24 days in the year. Not bad for a Stone Age people, eh? They were craftsmen, farmers; they traded jade across Central America. They were warriors who fought fierce hand-to-hand battles. They took prisoners and they sacrificed them—that was their way. Dying under the knife was a privilege. Bloodletting was essential to appease the gods: it brought rain and good harvests. Even the kings and queens pushed sea-urchin spines through their tongues to collect blood. And then along came the Europeans and showed them what barbarity really was: slaughtering them with muskets and disease."

Flint sat back on his haunches and made a roll-up cigarette.

Max was not going to be bullied. "I'm not taking responsibility for the downfall of a civilization. I'm a schoolboy looking for his mum, so don't lay a guilt trip on me. And as far as I know, they died because there were too many of them— there wasn't enough food to feed them all. Isn't that right? They lived off corn? The seasons changed and they couldn't feed themselves. Fat lot of good slaughtering people did."

Flint stared at Max. "You got a mouth, son. Just like your mother. Maybe you should bite your tongue once in a while, eh? OK, so you're a smart kid. You think you're educated, do you? I didn't go to school, but I'm the only man who can spend months in the jungle and get out alive, right back to where I started. I'm still the king of plant thieves. Who finds the ghost orchid? Me."

"And my mother stopped you. I'm glad she did that. She hated thieves and people who hurt others."

"I don't hurt nobody. I save things," he said as he puffed on the cigarette and gazed down at the sweat-stained maps and drawings. "I saved you, didn't I? Why do you think I was near the river? I was finding the ghost. You cost me time and money, boy. You're damned lucky, 'cause if I wasn't a plant thief, you'd be croc bait."

Max knew it was foolish to antagonize him. He softened his tone. He needed the man on his side.

"I'm grateful, Mr. Flint, but I don't want to hang around here any longer than I have to."

"Son, no one calls me Mister. You keep it simple—Flint will do. And I want you and that drug merchant out of here. You could bring me big trouble."

"Xavier tried to get away from all that. He wanted a new life."

"Aha. Listen, boy. If you don't ever take on board one single word I say, you remember this: that kid out there is a drug merchant. He and his kind kill untold numbers of people with what they do. If he made a deal with the devil to save his own skin, then that's what he'll do again. He will betray you at the first opportunity he gets. Don't you ever forget that."

Flint returned his attention to the maps on the floor, his finger tracing a line through the jungle. The maps were old and probably something Flint never needed to use anymore, but he touched a large darkened shape that looked to Max like a mountain range. "You don't know how bad this jungle can be. I reckon your mother went into the most forbidden place of all."

"Where the illegal logging is being done?" Max said.

"That's one of the most *dangerous* places. What I said was *forbidden* place. Get those pictures of your mother out," he said.

Max eased the photos from the folder. They were dry and hard to the touch, the colors faded by the water, but other than that, there was little damage. Flint's grubby hands took them carelessly and threw them down in front of Max like playing cards, but he had thrown them down in some kind of order.

"This one here," he said, stabbing one of the pictures, "this is called Xunantunich. This whole area was once heavily populated, a huge city, but it means nothing—it's where the tourists go, so why would your mother be there?"

"I don't know. I suppose she was just taking some time out."

"Aha," Flint said, and then pushed the other photographs

into place across the maps. "This second one here, you see this stone relief she is standing in front of? That's an ancient Mayan king, and next to him is what?"

Max studied the photograph more carefully. He had seen the pictures so many times, and although he had understood that the stone carvings on the lintels were similar to those he had seen in the British Museum, he had not identified the creature. It was a dragon-type monster with a crocodile head, but it had the ears of a deer, and where its claws should have been were deer hooves.

"I don't know. It's bizarre."

"Only to those who can't see beyond the ordinary. That's called the Cosmic Monster." Flint kept his finger on the photograph. "It represents the planets across the star fields; it's the path between the natural and the supernatural worlds. And that figure there is the jaguar sun god."

Max took the picture from him and looked at the fine detail of the carvings, something he had simply not comprehended before. "So does this mean something?"

There were four more photographs laid out on the maps, but Flint ignored them for the moment and kept the first one taken at Xunantunich. "Did you have any other pictures from the jungle?"

"No," said Max. "These were all I ever had of her on her last field trip."

"I think she was pretending to be a tourist in this one," Flint said, the cigarette dangling from the corner of his mouth. "In case anyone was following her, because someone like your mother would have known these places. In each of these photographs, your mother is moving to different ancient sites. Most of these are not known to outsiders. Maybe a few archaeologists and the local people who have ventured into the jungle as their guides, but these places are not where tourists go. She was going deeper and deeper into the jungle."

Max was fascinated more than ever by the pictures of his mother, because now she was telling him a story. "Do you think she was trying to tell me, or somebody else, about where she was going?"

Flint shrugged and flicked the soggy, extinguished cigarette away. A rattling cough accompanied the shake of his head. "I don't know." Then he went through the remaining pictures, touching each one as he explained their location to Max and the meanings of the cut-stone panels. "These carvings with the bird feathers, they're priests, shamans. They did all the blood sacrifices. These here, these are Serpent Warriors."

"Serpent Warriors?" Max said. The image of twisting snakes coiled about their victims leapt into his mind. "Did they use snakes when they fought their wars?"

Flint reached out and took a spear that leaned against the wall. "No. That's just what the warriors were called, but you spend time out here and you'll see boa constrictors take wild animals, crush them and swallow them whole. You'd better hope you don't tangle with one of those." He handed the spear to Max. "This is one of the weapons the warriors used."

Max felt the weight of the spear and fingered the flint head—a heavy blade, its edges flaked to slice into the enemy's flesh.

"They were called teeth of lightning, those spears. And

264

they also had stone knives cut into the shape of a jaguar paw. It was a mean way to fight, but they were warriors who fought face to face—you have to admire that. Fight or die. Simple choices." He held the photograph up. "See these carvings?"

Max took it from him. The picture showed his mother standing next to the remains of a temple where the jungle had swallowed most of the building, but she held her hand against a stone carving, her face turned toward the camera. Max looked hard at what her hand rested against. One of the images was of a figure Max took to be some kind of holy man or chief. He sat on a stool, emblems on his arm, and he wore a headdress, but his elbows were bent, offering something in the palm of his hands. It was a severed head.

"The stool is made from the bones of sacrificial victims," Flint told him. "That's where the head came from." He pressed his finger onto the map. There was no sign of any village or town or anything that could be called a settlement. It was in the middle of nowhere. And it was very close to the dark, shaded patch on the map.

Max was uncertain if what he felt was nervous excitement at finding the route his mother took into the jungle or an increasing sense of doom. Were these pictures shot shortly before his mother died, or had she gone on alone, deeper into the jungle, to meet her fate?

"These must have been taken by her guide," Max said. "Do you think we could find him?"

"Perhaps. He'd be Maya, and there wouldn't be too many who could go that deep into the mountains. And not this place. Nobody goes in—or comes out. I believe in the old ways. There are *wayob* in there. I'd bet my last dollar on it."

"*Wayob?*" Max asked.

"Jungle spirits. Shamans can create animal forms. *Wayob.* You can't kill them, but the bad ones—they can kill you."

Max had learned from his time in Africa never to deride ancient beliefs. There was no reason to doubt that shape-shifting could serve evil purposes as well as good. One of the photographs showed his mother standing next to carved images of a sacrifice. Danny Maguire had told him that on the khipu. OK. *Think it through,* he told himself. Danny Maguire could not have been with his mother—his mother's death had happened too long ago—but he might have met the guide. Maybe that was where he got the information that he sent to Max. Danny was doing his own research and came across the guide and heard the story of his mother's disappearance. That had to be it!

There were other carvings: young children, bound together like slaves. "Was this a war party? Were these the children of the people being sacrificed?" Max asked, remembering Danny's message.

"You're beginning to get pretty good at this, son."

"It had to be a dangerous place for one reason or another. Someone I knew sent me a coded message. I don't understand why she is there, or why she is touching this particular stone carving."

Flint pointed at an area on the map. "Twenty years ago a vast biosphere reserve was created to help save the rain forest and the animals and plants, but that's always under threat because of oil pipelines and the need for slash-and-burn farmland. That's where environmentalists have been killed. Illegal logging and oil both bring wealth to a poor country and power to a few." Flint began rolling another cigarette, busying himself, spilling tobacco into the paper, but he had one eye on the boy. Waiting.

Max studied the map and saw a dotted area colored light green, the small word *biosphere* barely visible.

"My mother was involved in trying to protect the rain forest and plants for medicines—I know that. She was really brave, my mum. Could she have got into trouble there?"

Flint stayed silent and laid the last photograph on a dark, shaded area. The picture had a plume of smoke curling upward in the background. Max already believed this to be near a volcano. His eyes sought out the contour lines on the map. The dark mass was nowhere near the biosphere. He pointed at an area. "Is that where this photograph was taken? There's another reserve, isn't there?" Max asked.

Flint smiled. The boy had a brain, and he knew how to read a map. Maybe there was hope for him after all.

"Aha." Flint licked the edge of paper, smoothing the wonky roll-up. Max plucked it from his fingers and put it behind his ear.

Flint was surprised. "Bad habits stay with you a long time."

"I don't want a lecture, Flint; I want answers. My mother went here, didn't she?" he insisted, touching the dark mass that spread like a virus across the paper, its edges creeping into the forests. "What is it?"

Flint gave up cigarette making and circled the darkened area with his hand, as if drawing out mute information from the creased paper. "No one really knows, but it was established as a place of special scientific interest, whatever that might mean. It was the same company that set up the biosphere reserve, so their intentions were good."

"Who are they?"

"Zaragon."

Max knew that name! It resounded in his memory—but from where? He could not place it. It would come, in time, and that might give him another clue to the mystery surrounding his mother's death.

"The area is prone to earthquakes," Flint continued. "An active volcano sits in the middle of the reserve, and every now and again it bursts through the lower cracks in the mountain. Lava spills down through the ravines but then gets swallowed up by the huge underground caves. There are old, hidden ruins, but no one's been in that jungle for thirty years, maybe more. It's a place where the Maya are allowed to live as they have always lived, without outside interference. No one else is allowed in. It's a forbidden zone," Flint said.

Max felt the shiver of anticipation. He was sure this was where his mother had gone. He almost whispered, *Why?*

"They say it is the place of the jaguar god of the underworld," Flint said.

Max looked at Flint, who averted his eyes. What was he thinking? What was he unable to say to Max's face? If his mother had gone into this forbidden zone, was Flint telling him that she may have been sacrificed? The thought sickened him, images too appalling to even think about flashing through his mind. He shook his head. "You can't be sure she went in there."

"No. It just seems she was heading that way. People die out here. Snakebite, injury, disease, it doesn't have to be anything more suspicious than that. Maybe that's what happened to your mother," Flint said a little more kindly.

Max tried to remember everything he knew of his mother's disappearance. Why had his father run away? Was it because he had been frightened of something? As far as he knew, his mother had died and been buried somewhere in the jungle. What was it that was so terrifying it had made his father run away?

"Have you ever been in there?" Max asked.

"Not me. There are stories of people who tried—they never made it. In or out. They were destroyed by the hummingbird god. There are so few ways to get inside there. I've been close, maybe a couple of Ks, and on a calm day you can hear him. Those mountains are like an island—I'm talking thousands of square kilometers—and I tell you something else. There's a logging strip round half of it, and there are armed guards. Private. That place is bad news."

"I bet there are some amazing rare plants in there," Max said.

"You're crazy. You're not going to get me anywhere near the place. Nowhere near."

"Then can you get me close? I have to find out what happened. I have to, Flint, don't you see? It's why I'm here. How long do you think it'll take those men chasing me to finally come to this place? If they're that determined, they are going to check in an ever-wider circle. As you said, I could bring you big trouble."

Flint stayed silent for a few seconds, shaking his head as if discounting his thoughts, but then he sighed, giving in to the inevitable. "There is one way in, maybe. The Cave of the

Stone Serpent. None of the locals would ever go near it." Flint got up and took down a carved figure from the wall, a skeleton draped in ornaments of bone and skin covered in black spots.

Max pointed to the necklace on the carving. "What are those?"

Flint handed it to him. "Eye sockets, a symbol of the underworld. The cave is where Ah Puch lives."

"Who is Ah Puch?" Max asked.

"The Mayan god of death."

19

Max sat with Xavier, who was still in the cage. He handed the cigarette through the bars, and Xavier took it like a thirsty man grabbing a bottle of water. He smelled it and muttered something in Spanish, then said, "You're a good friend, Max Gordon. But you would be like my family if I could light it."

Max held up a match. He struck it against a rough piece of bamboo and held it for the boy, who sucked the smoke into his lungs, then coughed until finally he eased himself back against the bars. "You can be my cousin," he said, smiling. "My first cousin."

Max sat with his back to the cage, upwind of the smoke that funneled out of Xavier's nose, as if he were a baby dragon. "Flint is going to get me out of here. He knows that whoever was searching for me will come looking sooner or later. But I don't know how far you want to go along with me."

"I go with you as long as you want me to go. Maybe I can

help you when we get to a town. People know me. I know people. We can get away and never be seen again."

Max could see Flint and another man talking. Flint was pointing to the fan-driven powerboat; the man was shaking his head, obviously not wanting to go to the notorious cave.

"Listen, Xavier. I'm not going into any towns or villages. I'm going into the mountains. I still want to find out what happened to my mum."

Xavier nodded. "OK. Then I go with you and I help you."

"Maybe you'd better think about it."

"I no need to think, *chico*."

"I'm going to the Cave of the Stone Serpent."

Xavier choked. He leaned forward, grabbing Max's arm through the bars. "Max, amigo, don' go there. I heard about that place, man. They been telling stories about that cave since forever. There's a snake in there bigger than a river. It takes you and it swallows you, and that is not a nice way to die."

Max could see that Xavier was really frightened. "That's just a legend. It's a story to keep people away," he said, trying to convince himself without much success.

"Then it works. Maybe I'd better think about it."

Max knew he would be going in alone. It was probably better that way. There were fragments being drawn together in his mind. He had remembered the name Zaragon. When he had once visited the London office of Angelo Farentino, the man who had betrayed his father, there was a sign on the building next door—ZARAGON. Was there a connection even way back then? Farentino, once an influential supporter of the frontline eco-scientists, had sold his soul to a mysterious organization that wielded enormous influence. It now seemed likely that on other adventures, Max, without realizing it, had faced their terrifying power. Somewhere in the background, like a spreading stain of evil across the face of the earth, greater forces than Max could imagine were wielding power, manipulating governments and multinational corporations.

A small cog shifted in his mind. When Farentino had told Max that his father had run from his mother, how could he have known that? Max's dad would never have confessed such guilt to anyone. So, Angelo Farentino had information from someone involved in this area. Max did not believe in coincidences. Zaragon, those faceless men and women, must be the power behind many of the international eco-disasters his mother and father had fought so hard against in the past.

Were these the people Max's dad had run from, leaving his mother to die?

There was never any question in Max's mind of turning back, of going home to the safety of school and friends. He was getting closer to finding the real reason behind his mother's death and his father's cowardice.

He shuddered, his own fear of going through the Cave of the Stone Serpent tormenting him like a small devil on his shoulder, whispering its terrifying warnings, embedding them like fishhooks in his mind.

He stood up and called to Flint. "I'm ready!"

Charlie Morgan's 250cc motocross scrambler bike, which she'd bought in a broken-down garage, had taken her a few hundred kilometers north of the city, over red clay tracks, through villages that were little more than shacks on stilts, where scattered banana trees were the main source of income. And then she had reached the City of Lost Souls, which was little more than a frontier town with dirt streets, a couple of bars, some rough accommodation and a small marketplace where worn-out diesel buses choked the air as they brought people in from the surrounding countryside to sell what little produce they had grown. It was a bleak, forbidding place and aptly named.

What she wanted was a cold beer, and what she did was go into the roughest-looking place in town. She never gave a thought to the fact that she was a woman traveling on her own. She had always been able to look after herself, no matter what the circumstances. The tattooed men with bandannas pulled across their heads could barely believe their eyes when she pushed into the dimness of their bar. She ordered a beer and drank straight from the bottle without pausing for breath. The heat prickled her skin and sweat ran down her back, but the sharp point of a knife at the base of her neck felt like a small wasp sting. Everyone was looking at her. And then the man with the knife moved round to the front of her, holding it under her chin. He was shorter than she was and had stained teeth, bad breath and pockmarked skin. He pouted his lips—he wanted a kiss.

Charlie did not flinch. "You understand English?" she asked.

He had not taken the knife from under her chin. "I speak it. I understand it. I went to school. You think we are savages here?"

Everyone in the room laughed.

"Then tell me why a handsome man like you would need a knife to get a kiss? All you have to do is ask politely," she said.

The man smirked at his friends in the bar, then lowered the knife and looked at Charlie. "OK. I would like to have a kiss, please, pretty lady."

Charlie smiled at him and lowered her face slightly. "This is called a Liverpool kiss," she whispered quickly, before snapping her head forward and breaking his nose with her forehead. The man went flying backward, smashing into a table and chairs, where men scattered. Charlie stood her ground, tapped the bar counter with the bottle, gaining the attention of the barman, who, like everyone else, was watching the stricken man staggering to his feet, pushing away helping hands.

"Another beer," she said, "to go."

She would ask questions later. Right now she had what she needed.

Respect.

Max was ready. Flint would help him get to the cave through the back streams and rivers of the mountains where the shallow water could take no boat other than his own.

He now had a spear, food and water and a leather satchel made by one of the women. A curved panga-type knife for cutting through foliage, better than any machete, Flint had told him, sat firmly in a scabbard on his belt. But what Max really needed, Flint said, was a specialized weapon to take into the hostile environment. In particular, a frog. A small blue frog.

Orsino Flint tiptoed quietly, barely disturbing the ground beneath his feet. As fast as a striking snake, his arm whipped out and caught the small creature. He gestured for Max to join him and eased a slim wooden dart along the frog's skin. He did this with another four darts. "You use these in the blow-pipe; it's a neurotoxin. It'll kill an animal and put a man down in a couple of minutes. You won't kill him, but it will disable him for a couple of hours. Be careful how you handle them."

He gave them to Max, who put them into a thin wooden tube used for carrying the blowpipe darts. He knew about in-digenous people's poisons from the time he spent in Africa with a Bushman boy. He tucked the tube into his waistband; the meter-long blowpipe was already nestled across his back on a thin cord. Flint handed him four small bunches of herbs wrapped in cotton.

"This is jackass bitters," Flint told him, opening one of the packets. "You sprinkle the powder on any sores you get. You already know how bad an infection can get. And this"— he opened another small square of cloth—"this is if you get a wound."

Max had put his nose to the crushed leaves. It was a mix-ture of subdued smells. "What is it?" he asked.

"Red clover and marigold with basil and amaranth. It's what we put into your shoulder, remember?"

Max nodded. Everything you needed to survive in the jungle was there if you knew where to look, but there were plenty of things ready to cause you harm if you did not.

"OK. Time to go," Flint said.

It was a wild boat ride. The propeller chopped the air and whirred them along at breakneck speed. Xavier had had no choice other than to accompany Max—Flint did not want him in the village. The boy had yelped with excitement for the first couple of minutes as Flint bent them round blind corners and skimmed vast flatbeds of green weed. And then Flint had opened the throttle and shown them what real speed was on a narrow, curving river that grew narrower with every kilometer that flashed by. Xavier fell silent, gripped the handrail and at times closed his eyes.

Max's attention stayed glued to the blurring river. He was spotting exactly where Flint was taking them. Figuring out in his head, in split-second bursts, where the boat could founder and his quest could suddenly end. But Flint knew every river and its tributaries. He was as much at home in the jungle as the jaguar.

The river turned into smaller side streams, then into what were little more than shallow creeks. The tree canopy created a tunnel of cool, gloomy shade. The engine slowed and then the huge fan whirred gradually to a stop. They had been traveling for almost five hours, and now, as their hearing returned, they could hear the birdcalls again.

Flint let the boat's momentum carry it onto a mud bank. "There are no crocs here. It's too far upriver. Watch out for snakes and spiders." The boat stopped. Xavier's legs were shaky from the ride, and Max helped steady him as he climbed out of the boat.

Flint tied the boat's mooring line to a tree and pushed on through the jungle, finding natural breaks, and the boys followed. It was hard going on the steep, muddy bank, but Max reckoned this would probably turn out to be the easy bit.

After twenty minutes, drenched in sweat, lungs heaving from the exertion, Flint stopped and sank down onto his haunches. Xavier, who Max had had to pull up the last few meters, guzzled the water Flint offered him, spilling a lot of it down his chest. Max reached out and steadied his shaking hand. When they had all drunk and their breathing had settled, Flint crawled on another few meters and then pulled back a low branch.

Beyond this fringe of trees lay a wasteland, half a kilometer of cleared land, a deep red scar across the landscape.

"Armed men patrol this area.. They have tree-cutting machinery; it chews the jungle, keeping it back, so they can see anyone who shouldn't be here. No one is gonna get in there unless they are lucky, or unlucky."

"Why? Just what is it that they don't want people to see?"

Flint wiped the sweat from his face and shook his head. "I don't know. But it ain't worth dying for, that's for sure."

Max's eyes scanned quickly across this devastated area to the soaring cliffs. Beyond the slashed land, dense forest blanketed the approach to the low foothills and stretched up to the higher peaks, which were almost bare of vegetation. The mountain range, two or three thousand meters high, swept beyond Max's vision, but its curve told him that on the other side of those peaks was an amphitheater. A hidden place— forbidden, as Flint said.

"That's it, isn't it?"

Flint nodded. "You can't see the volcano today. There are

often clouds sitting up there. Lot of waterfalls make the rock wall impossible to climb."

"You really gonna do this, *chico*? Goin' up there? Man, I don' think even your angels are gonna like that," Xavier said.

Flint unfolded a piece of cloth that had a rough plan, simple but clear, drawn on it. "There's no way in or out except three or four places, and that's where people die." His finger touched the map and then pointed to sections of the jungle-clad mountains. "That's where the hummingbird god destroys them."

How much to believe of ancient customs and legends? Max wondered. Something was killing people, but a bird god? It didn't matter; from what Flint had told him, he'd chosen to take an even worse risk. "Where's the Cave of the Stone Serpent?"

Flint pointed. "South, beyond this open area, into the forest. In those trees are lots of small creeks. No more than a meter deep. The mud'll suck you down, but the big snakes lie in there. You understand me? They'll crush you to death and swallow you. You have to get through there fast. It's no more than a kilometer until there's a sheer ravine. You watch out—it falls right out of the jungle, sixty meters down into the river. It's fast; you can't get a boat down there, but you stay on the low bank and when you hear the waterfall, you know the cave is there. It's an open jaw, Max. It breathes smoke. You can smell the dead. . . ." Flint's voice trailed off. His gaze held the cloud-topped mountains for a moment longer before looking back, regretfully, at Max. "I can't go in there with you, son. You know that."

Max nodded. He had to concentrate to keep his fear at bay. If he thought about what might happen, what could happen, through wild imaginings, he would not be able to get to his feet and go on. "What are the prevailing winds here?"

"Wind?" Flint asked.

"Look," Max said, tugging out one of the pictures of his mother. "That's the volcano behind her in the distance. The smoke's curling to the right. If the wind comes from the west or the north, then this tells me she was in the southern part of these mountains. She might have even gone through the cave."

Flint nodded. "Of course. Yes. This time of year, the north. But inside those mountains it can veer around. So, who knows? We get storms off the sea as well. The cave is south of the volcano." He shrugged. Nothing was predictable.

Max put the picture back. "OK. It's a start. Let's get going."

"I need a cigarette," Xavier said.

"No more smoking," Max said. "If there are men in there, they'll smell the tobacco on you. We can't take the risk."

"Hey, cousin, I don' wanna take any risk here. I wanna go home. You know, I got family, too, yeah?"

Flint offered a farewell handshake to Max. "I don't want him. He's yours."

Xavier scowled. "Blood fall vein," he said in Creole.

"What did he say?" asked Max.

Flint spat to one side, partly to rid himself of the small fly that had settled on his lips, but mostly in disgust. "Blood follows vein—he means relatives look out for each other." Flint snorted. "Good luck, son. I'll wait until you're across; then

I'm out of here. But I'd watch my back with this one," he said, looking at Xavier.

Xavier dared to point a finger at the grizzled face. "You bush crazy, you know that, plant man? You got weeds growing in your brain. This boy is my friend. I wouldn't wanna stay with you even if you asked me nicely."

Flint smiled at Max. "'How sharper than a serpent's tooth it is to have a thankless child!'"

Xavier pleaded with Max. "You see? This guy has been smokin' stuff that's bad. An' you trustin' him to send you in there?"

"It's Shakespeare."

"I don' care what it's called—I just hope there was none of it mixed up in that cigarette you gave me."

Max smiled but felt a stab of uncertainty. There had been moments when being with Orsino Flint was the safest refuge he had had in days. Now he was going back to a violent environment. The moment passed. Fear was a good thing—it would keep him alert and alive along with the inflamed energy of anger he felt for his dad. *He would not run away.* That thought drove him to his feet, and he ran across the barren, exposed ground.

Xavier was startled by Max's aggressive burst of energy. The boy looked primal, caked in sweat and dirt, armed with blowpipe and bush panga, carrying the flint-headed spear, hair plastered to his head and with a wild look in his eye. It made Xavier think twice about following him. Orsino Flint grabbed his shirtfront and pulled his face close to his own.

"Get out of here, drug scum. You ever come back, I make you croc bait." He shoved Xavier out of cover. Like an uncoordinated bird fallen from the nest, Xavier stumbled, arms floundering, but then gave chase to Max, who was already halfway across the wasteland. More than anything else, he did not want to go where Max was going, but he could not stay with Flint.

Max did not look back. He wanted the safety of the trees and prayed hostile eyes were not watching his pounding approach. He made it to the edge of the forest and ran in a couple of meters before stopping, turning and looking back for Xavier. He saw the gangly kid run across, and in the distance Orsino Flint eased back a tree branch and disappeared. As Xavier ran, Max saw him turn his head to one side. He faltered, and fell, sprawling into the dirt.

He got to his feet, confused, and then ran on, looking wildly for where Max might be. His uncertainty made Max step back into the open. He raised his spear arm, and the boy swerved to run toward him. As Max grabbed him and yanked him into cover, Xavier coughed and wheezed, shaking with exertion. "There's someone comin'!"

Max pulled him down. "Don't move. Stay absolutely still, whatever you do. There may be men in the trees as well."

Now Max could hear the sound of a pickup truck approaching. He moved position slightly so he could see down the wasteland. At first he saw only the plume of dust from the vehicle, but then, as he raised his head slightly through the cover, he saw the open-backed 4x4. Two men in the front, two more in the back, all of them armed. Maybe this was a routine patrol, but it was very bad timing as far as Max was concerned. The pickup truck slowed. A man in the back was pointing at something ahead of the vehicle. And then they stopped almost opposite the place where Max and Xavier were hiding.

"What they doin'?" Xavier whispered.

"I don't know," replied Max, keeping his eyes on the men who now climbed out of the vehicle. One of them was pointing to something on the ground. He bent down and picked up something that glistened in the sunlight. It took Max a second to realize what it was, and as he did so, Xavier's hand went to his neck.

"My gold chain," the boy muttered.

The men were studying the ground. Max could hear them talking, and then they looked up toward the trees. They had seen the boys' tracks. No sense in hiding now; they would be caught in a couple of minutes. Max grabbed Xavier's shoulder. "Come on. Run for it!"

The boy faltered. In that brief moment, Max saw the fear on his face: he did not want to run into the jungle, but then he smiled. "It's OK, it's OK! I know a couple of those guys. They've worked with my brother. Max, you go on—I'll be OK here. They can take me back with them. I won't say anything. I'll cover for you. I can get home now."

Xavier's smile broadened. He squeezed Max's arm. "I can keep these guys off your back, *chico*. You get outta here. Go on! I'll never forget you, cousin." And before Max could stop him, Xavier ran out into the open, waving and calling to the men. In an instant, weapons were raised to their shoulders and Xavier had the good sense to stand still and raise his hands above his head. "Ronaldo! Alonso! It's me! Xavier Garcia!"

All the men lowered their weapons except one, who kept

an eye on the jungle, the butt of a pump-action shotgun on his shoulder. Max held his breath. The men had reached Xavier, and they seemed to be smiling. He heard them greet each other and embrace, and then Xavier began telling his story, never looking back to where Max lay hidden.

Orsino Flint's words came back to him about not trusting Xavier and that he would sell him out at the first opportunity to save his own skin. Max was desperate to believe that Xavier would do no such thing, and for a few brief moments his faith in the boy held out. But then one of the men gently pushed Xavier against the side of the truck. They did not seem happy with the boy's explanation. Xavier was protesting too much. As one of Xavier's "friends" held him, the others turned to stare toward Max's hiding place. These men might have known Alejandro, but now they were working for someone else, and that someone must be paying them big money not to take anything at face value. Max ran. The men saw the movement. The chase was on.

20

There were no tracks to follow in the jungle, so Max ran purely on instinct. Keeping his head down and his shoulders hunched, he brushed aside many of the low branches. If he couldn't see any tracks, then neither could the men following him, but they would hear him crashing through the undergrowth, and that would lead them to him.

Before he plunged into the undergrowth, his last sight of the three in pursuit was of them running in a V formation. That was clever. It meant that Max's arc of escape was in a confined area.

He tried to keep a sense of direction and run in a straight line—almost impossible in these conditions—but he knew that if he could, he would reach the ravine and hopefully find the entrance to the cave. The going was hard, and already the heat and difficult terrain were sapping his strength.

He crouched, wiped the sweat from his eyes and tried to

slow his breathing. If he could not see his pursuers clearly, then the same was true for them. He waited. These men were clumsy, just pushing through the undergrowth. There was a rustling movement nearby—one of the gunmen. Max lay flat.

He concentrated on his breathing—it sounded so loud. The man was less than three meters away.

Max eased the blowpipe from his back and, with agonizingly slow movements, loaded a dart. He got the blowpipe into position, brought it to his lips and in his mind's eye pictured the man's route.

The jungle floor rustled with insect life, and the largest spider Max had ever seen emerged from the twisted growth. Its long, prickly legs must have spanned almost twelve centimeters and supported a hairy, misshapen body. The legs picked their way through the debris and came straight for him. The spider's fangs for biting and poisoning its prey were clearly visible, and its globular eyes seemed to be focused on his own. The man's footfalls had obviously flushed it out. Max froze. The spider straddled the blowpipe, and with silk-like softness walked across his hands.

Max's heart thumped into the ground. He squeezed his eyes shut and felt the spider clamber across his face. Every part of him wanted to scream and jump clear.

His back muscles quivered. The spider picked its way across his hair and onto his neck. The way Max was lying meant his shirt collar was pushed up. It crawled underneath.

Like a tickling piece of cotton, its hairy legs touched his spine. It seemed to hesitate. Did it think being under his shirt was a safe refuge? Should he roll quickly onto his back and crush it? Impossible. He'd be dead. Certain death from the gunman or from a fatal spider bite. Neither was a happy solution.

It crept its way along his spine, and then he felt it move out from beneath his loose shirt.

The moment its weight left the back of his legs, Max jumped up, leveled the pipe and aimed at the man, who had gone past by four or five meters. It was a clear shot—the gunman's shoulders were above the low undergrowth.

Max spat breath down the pipe—and missed.

The man half turned. He must have heard the dart cut into the branches. He stopped and listened for any other movement. Max already had another dart loaded. He deliberately took his time, aimed the pipe, took a deep breath and blew.

The man yelped as the dart struck the muscle over his shoulder blade. As he twisted round to feel what had bitten him, Max ran.

The man shouted. An answering voice called from a distance away. And then Max heard the howling of a high-revving engine. He knew it couldn't be the pickup—this was some kind of machinery that had been started. Max dodged through the undergrowth, ducking and weaving as gunfire raked the branches, but it was high, way too high. Max risked a glance back. The gunman was down on his knees, the AK-47 spraying the air. Then he fell facedown.

Max dropped to his haunches, trying to see if there were any animal tracks or paths that would allow him an escape route—nothing. Now the sound rose in intensity as a churning, slashing rending of the forest came closer and closer, as if a huge beast was on the rampage.

In places the jungle was lighter, less dense, and that was his best way forward. He pushed on, but still that sound grew closer and closer. He turned and looked at the canopy. The leaves shuddered and shook. He could feel the vibrations coming up through the ground, and for a moment he thought some trick of his imagination was conjuring up an earthquake.

The noise surrounded him. He felt a moment of blind panic but refused to yield to it, because then he would be helpless. He turned and ran, ignoring the whip stings of branches on his face, determined to put distance between himself and the ever-increasing roar. And then he saw the monster. Its teeth devoured the forest before it.

It was a tractorlike machine, its operator sitting in a mesh safety cage as he drove it forward. Whirring blades with clawlike teeth reached out ahead of the machine, their power ripping and tearing every living thing in their path. If Max made the wrong decision and became entangled in the undergrowth, he would be shredded.

But could he outrun it?

He turned his back on the howling, thrashing noise. The ground leveled out before him, and he looked for where the light penetrated the canopy the most. He used the shaft of the spear to push away some of the low-lying branches in front of him and dared, once, to look behind him. There was no sign of the other man who had come into the forest, but the one driving the machine had obviously spotted Max and was increasing the revs, speeding up as he focused on the retreating boy.

It took twenty seconds to break through the next dense

patch, and in that time Max was out of sight of the pursuing killer. A muddy bank suddenly gave way to a sheet of rock. Max slipped, grabbed at roots and stopped himself slithering over the edge of the sheer drop that lay camouflaged beyond the curtain of trailing branches and vines.

As he hauled himself to his feet, the machine burst through the undergrowth. All he could see were its vicious blades, blurred with speed, bits and pieces of root and leaf caught up in its teeth like a carnivore's incisors after a kill.

He saw the man's eyes through the mesh cage, glaring in anticipation of a gruesome kill, and the unmistakable push of his arm as he shoved the throttle lever forward. He knew he had Max. The surge of power that went into the tanklike treads churned up the ground.

The man saw a boy frozen in fear.

Max saw a man smiling in victory.

Then, dropping his spear, he reached up onto a vine, grabbed a couple of handholds higher, bent his torso and pulled himself out of harm's way.

The blades chewed the dangling vine trailing below him. The rush of air from their vicious, lacerating spin caught the back of his legs—it passed barely a handbreadth below—and then it fell away.

In seconds the machine had disappeared. The engine raced without the traction from the ground, and Max knew that suffocated in that cacophony was a man's scream as, trapped in the cage, he plummeted to his death.

There was a distant crash as metal tore on rock, and then, except for the cries of alarmed jungle birds, there was silence.

Max dropped to the ground, retrieved his spear and, using

it as a staff to steady himself, peered over the edge. The over-hang hid what must have been a sheer drop. He had to skirt round it and find another route down. But the third man was out there somewhere. Max focused and ran, hoping his peripheral vision would allow him to spot the enemy. Now the silence was uncanny. Death had stalked the jungle and won.

Small gullies, a couple of meters wide, crisscrossed in front of him. He leapt across one, turned and followed the narrow strip of water that ran away to one side, convinced it had to lead to the river and the ravine. The blood pounded in his ears, and his smashing through the undergrowth muted the sudden slashing of the leaves. It was as if someone was using a thin flexible stick to lash the greenery around him.

This ripping sound was immediately followed by the hacking chatter of an automatic weapon. The things snap-ping angrily around Max's head were bullets!

He jumped into one of the water-filled gullies. It was waist-deep and the bank allowed him some cover. Trying des-perately to control his breathing, he peered into the thick jungle, looking for any sign of his enemy's approach. Reason cut through his fear: these men were not jungle fighters; they were armed thugs paid to control the outside area. This gun-man was shooting blindly. Max smiled to himself, the hunter's instinct rising from his belly into his chest—a differ-ent type of energy now, the need for survival putting him on the offensive.

Keeping his eyes on the jungle and letting his breathing calm so his hearing could pick up every sound, he scooped mud from the low bank and smeared it across his face and shoulders. Then he crawled into the low undergrowth, using ferns for cover, and pressed himself against the broad roots of a big tree.

Max could smell him.

Stale cigarette smoke, sweat and alcohol settled on the air like the scent of a pungent flower. His pursuer was fairly close. No matter how skilled the man might be—and he wasn't— it was impossible not to make any noise. Max closed his eyes and listened. About five meters away, the man's heavy footfalls and stumbling approach were as good as shouting out his location.

Max felt for the darts. They were gone. He must have dropped their holder during the chase. He refocused, looking for anything that would help him defeat his pursuer. A couple of meters away, a large brown clay ball of a termite nest clung to a trailing vine. No sooner had Max seen it than the man's face appeared through the foliage. Acting purely on instinct, Max threw the spear and heard it thud into the target. Inside the ball a honeycomb swarmed with termites, and as the clay dome shattered, it fell across the man's head and shoulders. Suddenly engulfed in thousands of small biting insects, the man floundered and the AK-47 fell to his side, held by its strap, as he tried to beat them away. He yelped and swore.

It was a momentary diversion; Max knew the man would recover quickly, but the few moments it might buy him were vital. Max still needed his weapon, and he ran hard, skirting the man, to retrieve his spear. The gunman reacted as quickly as he could when he heard the sound of the crashing undergrowth. One hand went back to the AK-47 while the other tried to brush the termites from his eyes and face, but as he swung an arc of gunfire, he spun on his heel, and the combined effort of shooting and beating at the termites made him lose his balance. He fell backward into the shallow gully, which gave Max enough time to reach his spear. He yanked it from the ground, turned and powered on, knowing he had to get farther down the watercourse. He hoped the stream would take him to the ravine's edge. The man dragged himself from the water, gasping, still plucking insects from his eyes, but his anger had given him the energy to scream what Max took to be a full-blooded threat. One very angry man with one very lethal weapon meant Max had a long way to go before he was safe.

He jinked left and right. Another stream, another gully, and then he could hear tumbling water. Roots of trees crept into the low banks, and he realized that the water had become shallower, so he would make quicker time. He just had to be careful not to run blindly over the edge; he had to find a way down.

His pursuer had recovered quickly and could be heard splashing through the shallows; he, too, had realized that this was the easiest route. Suddenly there was no place to hide. The man came round the bend of the gully, and he was in plain sight. If Max tried to move now and clamber back into the undergrowth, he would be spotted immediately, and a burst of gunfire would rake him to death.

The gully's low overhang was his only chance of concealment. With any luck, the man would be looking ahead and might bypass the dark shadow that was Max unmoving among the tree roots. There seemed to be no choice. He lay down on his side, feeling the mud suck at his clothes as he eased himself backward until the bank pressed against him. Bits of tangled root and leaves offered some camouflage in front of his face, and he hoped he could settle his breathing—right now he felt as though the whole world could hear him gasping for breath.

A huge snake, five meters long, stirred. Alerted by movement, its muscles flexed. At full length it resembled a dead tree trunk, its mottled-brown shaded patterns camouflaging it almost to the point of invisibility. Heat-sensitive pits on its head guided it toward the creature that had blundered into its territory. It had not eaten for a couple of weeks. The deer it had crushed to death and swallowed whole had taken that long to digest.

Max had no idea that the shivering turbulence along the stream's bank was one of the jungle's most lethal creatures. Its jaws, lined with small, hooked teeth, would grip its prey as it rapidly coiled itself about its victim. Within moments the massive strength would crush bone and suffocate lungs; then the jaws would unhinge, allowing it to swallow its prey. No one was strong enough to fight a boa constrictor of this size once they were held in its coils.

Death was certain.

Now it would eat again.

Sayid had paced the floor, back and forth, eventually sitting on his bed, head in hands. Had his intrusion into the building been traced? He half expected to hear someone pounding on his door at any moment, so powerful was the fear of discovery. What to do? If he admitted hacking into all those cameras, then one thing would lead to another and they would know that he was involved with Max from the very beginning. But if he did not warn the authorities that a man might have been killed or captured, he would never be able to live with himself.

By the time he had made his decision, he found himself already knocking on Mr. Jackson's door.

"You're absolutely sure that this is exactly what happened?" Fergus Jackson asked him moments later.

"Yes, sir. I think they held him at gunpoint, and after that they pulled the camera off the wall. It's all a bit of a mess, sir. I hope I haven't made matters worse by sending the information through to the people at MI-Five. That would mean I was responsible for whatever happened to that man."

Mr. Jackson nodded and put a hand on the boy's shoulder. "Well, you've done the right thing now, Sayid. We have to bring in the authorities," he said as he picked up the phone.

"I really don't want to hurt my mum. And I'm scared."

"I'll make sure nothing happens to you and your mother." Jackson turned away as he spoke into the phone. "Hello, Bob, I think there's something you should know."

The White Hat hackers were safe; Sayid had seen to that. They had left absolutely no trace of their involvement and had created a spaghetti junction of unfathomable complexity to cover their tracks. Robert Ridgeway and another man had landed in the helicopter an hour after Mr. Jackson made the telephone call. Now he stood back as the young man with him keyed information into Sayid's computer. He turned and nodded, and Sayid could see that he had reconnected to the CCTV cameras in the building.

"The boy's telling the truth, sir. He was logged into the security circuit." He adjusted the screen so that Ridgeway, Sayid and Mr. Jackson could see. A dozen camera views flitted through the building, and Sayid could see men and women in every area. They were searching, testing for fingerprints and recording everything on cameras.

"One of our men is missing, and those are my people searching for him. You are certain you saw nothing other than what you've told us?" Ridgeway asked Sayid.

"I've told you everything. I was the one who alerted you in the first place. I sent you the building's location."

"Yes, well, we'd really like to know how you did that. That's a major security breach as far as we're concerned." He glanced at Jackson, who shook his head gently. He did not want any threat leveled against Sayid and his mother again.

"But perhaps that's a conversation we might have at another time," Ridgeway said, pressing a button on his mobile phone. They watched as, seconds later, one of the agents on the screen answered his own phone.

"We're watching," Ridgeway said.

The man looked up into one of the cameras, speaking directly to them.

"Boss, there's no trace that Keegan was in the building. No prints, no fibers. Nothing. This is a private hospital. Half a dozen rooms behind each security door. It's also a mortuary. It's genuine; we've checked it out. It's run by an independent medical group called Zaragon that uses it for their international clients based in London. Postmortems are done here at the request of a patient's family. There's nothing suspicious, so what do we do now?"

Sayid pointed at one of the screens. "There were monitors on that wall where that stainless-steel table is, and your bloke saw something that was really horrible."

"Did you hear that?" Ridgeway said into the phone.

The agent nodded. "We've checked already," he replied. "They're viewing screens. So far all we found was a computer library with postmortems recorded. Keegan isn't the toughest of blokes, with all due respect, sir. Anyone could cringe at an autopsy."

Ridgeway looked at Jackson. He was stymied. The only evidence he had was that Sayid Khalif had hacked into the building's cameras and had sent the location to MI5 in the first place. If it were not for the fact that Keegan was missing, he would write this off as a schoolboy prank that had got out of control.

Ridgeway stared at Sayid. "There's nothing I can do about this, unless you can give me something more to go on. Did you see these men hurt my agent?"

"No, sir, but I think one of the men pointed a gun at him."

"Then is there anything else at all that can help us find out what happened to him?"

Sayid couldn't think of one thing. He gazed at the screens and let the computer mouse click on each one. He stopped in the tiled room with the stainless-steel examination table. Then he panned the camera round slightly. Something was different. What was it?

He pointed to the room. "There was something like a

clothes rack there. It had special suits hanging on it. They were biohazard suits. Now they're gone."

"Biohazard?"

"Yes, the same kind I saw in the tunnel when Danny Maguire's body was found," Sayid told him.

Ridgeway considered this information for a moment and then put the phone back to his ear. "Lock that building down and bring in a full forensic science team."

They saw the agent nod. Ridgeway looked down at Sayid. "I can't see any reason why you would make that up. You've convinced me something's going on in that building. Well done, son."

The snake coiled rapidly, twisting round his body. It happened so quickly he had no time to scream. Barely a gasp of fear was possible as it slithered from the mud, caught his ankles and then in a smooth, lethal turn entwined his body. One hand was free, but he couldn't reach a weapon. If he could have grasped his knife, he'd have slashed at the ferocious head that now stared into his face, its tongue flicking out to touch his bursting, sweating skin.

It crushed him. Steel-like bands of coiled muscle contracted, exerting a force that squelched his organs and made his eyes bulge with horror as the needle-toothed jaws opened.

From a place of darkness, somewhere deep inside his body, Max's primal scream echoed through the jungle.

* * *

That horrifying sound was almost inhuman. It froze the blood and rooted Xavier and his guard to the spot. The fight in the forest had played back to them in all its heart-clenching terror. Xavier reacted first. Breaking free from the man's grip, he sprinted down the path looking neither right nor left, determined never to run into the jungle again. He zigzagged, but he was an easy target. The man raised his weapon.

"Stop!" Orsino Flint yelled, bursting through the edge of the forest.

The gunman turned and fired. Flint dived into cover.

Xavier stopped, turned and shouted in surprise. "Flint!"

The gunman twisted back and fired at the boy, who forgot his fear of the jungle and plunged into the undergrowth.

"Don't shoot!" Flint shouted again as he ducked into the open, and back again, getting ever closer to Xavier.

The gunman could not cover both at the same time. He waited, the AK-47 sweeping left to right, ready to fire again. He was scared. The scream from the forest, the failure of his companions to return, all brought home the fact that he was alone and vulnerable. There was a sudden flurry at the edge of the jungle. He fired, the bullets chopping the leaves, but Flint had moved farther down the forest edge and run across the strip.

He gripped Xavier's neck as he pinned him to the ground, the bullets snapping the air above them. "Stupid! You're so damned stupid!"

"You said you were leaving!"

"I saw your dumb stunt, and I couldn't believe it! Come on! He's reloading."

Xavier was dragged to his feet. He saw the gunman fumbling for another magazine, but Flint had already yanked him into the trees.

Which was worse? The gunman or whatever lay in the jungle?

Max burst from the muddy water, powering himself upward, his mouth still wide open from the scream, but now he was snarling as he attacked. He held the spear in both hands and lunged.

The gunman's bulging eyes were glazing over, the breath had been sucked from him like vacuum-packed meat as the snake still twisted round him. His swollen tongue protruded, and in the last few moments of consciousness, he saw the blurred movement of a mud-streaked demon lunging at his head with a spear. Max thrust the spear into the snake's jaws and shoved with all his might. He felt the recoil as the snake's muscles spasmed and swirled, lashing in ferocious death throes. Max leaned on the spear, pinning the snake to the ground, jamming one foot onto its writhing coils. Dripping with sweat, he desperately sucked in air as he overcame his fear. He closed his eyes, gripping the shaft of the spear, concentrating all his strength and energy, making sure that the terrifying snake could not survive and attack him.

Light faded as thunder ricocheted across the mountains from the low-lying clouds. Max was oblivious. He hunched over the writhing snake, clasping it with foot and fist, the flint blade like a big cat's claw. Max's teeth were bared with exertion as he growled with primitive savagery against the thrashing snake.

Finally, he knew the snake was dead and sank to his knees. He gazed at the magnificent creature and for a brief moment regretted its death. The man who had tried to kill him lay on his back in the dirt. Max tried to find a pulse, but there was none. His effort to save the man had come too late.

A steady pattering beat the forest leaves as a rainstorm broke. Max tilted back his head and let the fresh water wash the grime and sweat away, tasting the sweet liquid that his adrenaline-scoured body so desperately needed. Nothing else moved. A distant, muted bird trill and a gentle plopping call of another was all that could be heard.

The downpour ended almost as quickly as it had begun.

The rapid beating of the rain gave way to the steady sound of dripping leaves. A small movement caught his eye— a blue morpho butterfly opened its wings, its deep iridescence startling against the greenery. A brief moment of beauty in a place of death.

Max yanked out the spear and turned for the ravine. He had fought one snake; ahead lay another unknown peril—the Cave of the Stone Serpent. Like a jungle cat, he bent his body and sought a path beneath the low foliage. Some of the big leaves reflected the dull glint of rain, but a mottled form shifted in the shadows, and Max could smell the dank odor of wet fur. Without another thought, he chased the shadow. His senses altered, and like radar, his sense of smell and hearing took over. He ran bent low, ducking beneath curved branches as he found the animal path opening ahead of him. The rustling branches and the sound of paws on the ground led him through a dim, twisting labyrinth where light barely reached the forest floor. His feet hit mud, and he slithered onto his side, brought to a halt by a rotten log across the path. His shoulder slammed into the crumbling bark, and as he reached up to pull himself clear, he gazed into the eyes of the creature that had led him this far. Four meters away, smudged in camouflage, the jaguar gazed at him; its panting breath reached his nostrils. Max blinked. The jaguar was gone. Had he imagined it? He saw tracks in the mud. Surely it could not have been an illusion? The big cat had guided him here. Max looked to one side; the cliff had turned into a steep, muddy descent. Imaginary or not, he had reached a place where he could get down to the river.

Max could hear the sound of a waterfall. Using vines as ropes, he slithered his way down to the river sixty or so meters below him. It was broad but shallow, and he could see that, with care, he should be able to cross without being swept away. But what held his attention was the gaping hole in the rock face on the opposite mountainside. It looked as though someone had carved a mask into the mountain, and the cave gave the appearance of snarling jaws with jagged pinnacles of rock as teeth. Fetid, breathlike mist eased out of the opening. From where Max stood, there could be no doubt that it resembled the head of a snake. This was it. He had to enter the Stone Serpent's gaping jaws.

Another ragged rain cloud curled down the mountainside at the far end of the valley, snagging on forest limbs like sheep's wool on barbed wire. Max felt the first gust of wind and sting of rain as it urged him across the shallow water and onto the lower slopes of the mountainside. It seemed insistent on pushing him into the unknown.

Something splashed out of the mist into the stream behind him. He spun round. It was the driver of the bush-cutting machine. Blood streaked his clothes. Somehow he had survived the fall—maybe the cab's roll cage had saved him. He staggered toward Max, pulled back the action on the shotgun he carried and brought it up to waist height. Max was exposed. There was no cover. There were one or two deep pools, but how far underwater could he dive to escape those lethal blasts? How long could he hold his breath until the man gave up? It was not an option.

In that moment of hesitation, the man stumbled into deeper water. He raised the shotgun, but it was more for balance than for aiming at Max.

A cry of pain ripped from the man's throat. He had dropped the shotgun, beating the water with his fists. He screamed when the surface fluttered as if struck by hailstones, then fell facedown into the turmoil. Max was rooted to the spot. In less than a minute, the man was shredded. His blood had attracted the most ferocious of predatory fish—piranhas.

A stupid thought flashed through Max's horror. He hadn't known there were piranhas in Central America.

He did now.

Fragments of the man's shirt floated past him.

Max gazed up into the huge, frightening cave that awaited him, but after the punishing terror he had experienced, it offered the illusion of a place of safety.

Could his mother and father have traversed this very

route? Somewhere in the amphitheater of these mountains, on the other side of this cave, had they faced danger and death? His mother had died; his father had run. There was only one way to find out the truth.

Max stepped into the darkness and let the serpent's breath smother him.

21

Riga was not the kind of man to sit idly by as events unfolded around him. He had studied maps and satellite photos while he waited at the abandoned airfield for word of the missing boy and the likelihood of his survival.

Cazamind's determination to destroy Max Gordon was such a high priority that, for the first time in his career, Riga wanted to know why a target's death was so important. Using his own contacts in Russian intelligence and with others who worked like himself, he began to feel the uneasy presence of Cazamind's shadow world. There were rumored links to a network of power brokers whose secretive global influence was staggering. It was like a huge octopus, with Cazamind sitting squarely between the eyes of the beast. Cazamind knew everything. Riga had never had any sense of self-importance. He knew his place in the world, and as long as no one ever double-crossed him, or gave him incorrect information that stopped him from doing his lethal work, then Riga had no complaint. He could take his inquiries into Cazamind's activities only so far without raising suspicions. The Swiss control freak would not like him probing. Riga had been careful, choosing only those men he knew would never mention his query. If he had asked anyone else, his questioning could seep out into the world like blood into sand. There was no sense in jeopardizing his own position just because the fate of a schoolboy had aroused some interest in him.

He had also listened in to the radio chatter of the various people who patrolled the strip zones around the rain forest and forbidden mountain kingdom, and as he heard the sporadic radio calls in the background, he studied air-reconnaissance photos of the area.

Riga looked through a stereoscope's eyepieces, shifted the photos slightly and saw the aerial images of the sheer mountain walls lose their flat perspective and become three-dimensional.

Now he could identify clefts in the mountains, but he knew that no one would survive going through there, not with the security measures Cazamind's people had put in place. He scanned the riverbed and saw what looked like smoke but knew it to be the vapor from a waterfall. These photographs had been taken on a clear day some years ago, but the physical features had not changed. Riga heard excited shouting of men on the ground through the radio set. He spun the chair and fine-tuned the channel. The excited shouts were too difficult to follow, and, besides, Riga did not understand Spanish well enough to follow the fast, disjointed speech. He went to the door and called out through the rain to the pilot, who ran the few steps from his helicopter into the hut.

"What's going on here?" Riga asked, pointing at the radio.

The pilot listened for a few moments. "There's some kind of trouble. There's been shooting; three of the men are missing. The guy's saying there were strangers down there. They've escaped. Something scared him pretty bad."

Riga turned to a map spread out on the table. "Speak to him. Get his position. I want to know where he is. Exactly."

The pilot lifted the microphone, thumbed the Call button and spoke quickly in Spanish. He had to shout once or twice to calm the excited man at the other end of the radio link. He moved next to Riga and the map, tracing his finger along the rain forest that nudged against the curved river. He dragged his finger south onto the scarred landscape where the forest had been cleared. "He's about here."

Riga could read a map like others could watch a movie. Every line, every mark was a picture in his mind's eye. He pulled the aerial photographs next to the same area. "Tell him to stay there. Fire up the chopper."

The pilot looked horrified. The low cloud base obscured the mountain slopes down into the jungle. No one could fly in this. "It's not possible, *señor*! We would crash into the mountains or the forest. We have to wait until the clouds lift."

Riga was already pulling a backpack from the floor and picking up his rifle. "We fly between the forest and the mountains, along the river. And we fly low and we fly fast."

He was already moving out of the door with the pilot

begging at his side. "Señor Riga, I do not have the skills to fly like that. It cannot be done. Please, it will be dark soon; tomorrow will be clear."

Riga looked at the frightened man.

"Your life is in your own hands."

The meaning was clear. The pilot had to find the ability within himself to fly the machine in treacherous, almost suicidal conditions—and survive—or disobey Riga and die where he stood. The minuscule odds of survival flying blind in terrifying conditions at least gave him a chance.

He started the engines.

Max gazed upward. The cave looked about a hundred meters high, the limestone bleeding into stalactites that seemed to hang precariously from the roof. Max could not help but think of the needlelike teeth of the boa constrictor. As he looked down toward the darkness at the end of the cave, it felt like he was moving down the creature's gullet.

There was very little light inside the cave, and the mist added to that made it an eerie, unwelcoming place. Max knew his imagination could be his worst enemy. The mist was being drawn from the river and had penetrated only so far into the gloom. Max reasoned that this had nothing to do with any breeze from outside, but rather that there was air sucking it down the tunnel—so there had to be a way out. It just meant going into the pitch-darkness and feeling his way beneath a mountain. And Max hated confined spaces.

He dropped the various pieces of wood and dried root

he had gathered before moving into the cave. The kindling and resinous branches from an ocote tree would help get him deep under the mountain without darkness smothering him.

Using the panga, he shaved the pine into flakes and wrapped them in the supple roots he had ripped from the forest floor. Slowly but surely, he built a torch, allowing each layer of air to breathe. The dank, sticky atmosphere would smother a flame without these pockets of oxygen. Finally satisfied, he laid the sturdy torch at his side and sat, small and insignificant, in the cathedral-sized cave. He opened the vine-wrapped food Flint had given him at the village and chewed, on what he did not know. Then he unwrapped a pod, like a small egg, licked it and with undisguised delight bit into it. It was pure cocoa—a fast and delicious energy fix that also gave him a psychological boost. Swilling his mouth with water, he held the liquid for a moment, letting it smother his taste buds, hoping it would slake his fear-induced thirst.

Kneeling in the limestone dust, he hit the panga's blade against the flint-tipped spear. It sparked three or four times, and then the shards of fire found the resin chips. The torch began to burn. Max blew on it, more for luck than necessity, and held the shaft above his head. The flickering flame spluttered in the damp air, but as he moved forward into the darkness, cooler, drier air allowed it to crackle with life. Fire, the most basic of human needs, gave him comfort as he pushed deeper into the cave's embrace.

The height of the cave did not seem to diminish as he moved farther into the darkness, but then, with the glow casting giant shadows around him, stalactites bore down as the roof curved and narrowed. Like snakes' teeth. Easy to see how legends were born. At least, that was what Max hoped.

It was impossible to gauge the depth of this mountain range, or how long it would take to get through to the other side, but as he moved forward, he felt something crunch beneath his feet. Lowering the torch, he saw the dusty outline of bones. He knelt down and gently brushed away some of the dust from the remains. The bones crumbled under his fingertips. Perhaps these were ancient, but as he looked more closely, he could see that the victim had been trying to crawl toward the cave's entrance and that there was a broken clay pot within reach of the bony fingers. Had this been someone trying to escape? Was the clay pot the last of their provisions? Had they succumbed to the terrifying darkness?

There was no telling whether Max would get so far and no farther, or whether he would be able to return if he got trapped in narrow spaces. It was like a huge tomb, and Max did not want to die alone and in the dark—because sooner or later, the flame of his torch would fail. His mind kept questioning his courage. Could he go on? The heavy silence and limestone-dust floor absorbed the sound of any footfall or movement. He could imagine the fire flickering and dying, leaving him in absolute blackness, being unable to move forward or go back, being forced to curl in the rock face, lost and forgotten, with no one knowing where he was. That was where he would die. And one day an explorer might find *his* bones.

"Shut up!" he yelled at the corrosive voice in his mind. "That's not going to happen! So do us all a favor and SHUT UP!" It suddenly felt better to have screamed a defiant warning to himself. After all, there was no one else to do it.

The distorted echo bounced off the walls and rock faces, and then there was another sound—muffled at first and then sharper. Someone was calling his name.

Orsino Flint snatched a breath, the exertion from clambering across the rugged cave floor taking its toll. "You move like a damned mountain goat," he complained, his own fire torch adding to the flickering glow.

"An' you don' smell too good, either, cousin," Xavier said.

Max smiled. "It's my special jungle fragrance," he said, his morale boosted now that there were others who would share his dangerous journey. "Things didn't work out with your mates, then?"

Xavier shrugged. "You can't trust nobody these days."

"How did you find me?"

It took only a few minutes for Flint to lay the blame at Xavier's door. The Latino boy argued as best he could, but it was obvious, from the fact that his brother's friends back on the road were now working for someone more powerful with more money, that old loyalties no longer existed. The trail of destruction in the forest had not been difficult to follow, and Flint had picked up Max's trail past the dead gunman crushed to death by the snake. It was obvious that Max had killed it. There was nowhere else Max could go other than the cave, and it seemed that Orsino Flint, as reluctant as he was, had to follow, because he expected the jungle roads to be swarming with gunmen sooner rather than later.

"The man at the truck had a satellite phone. He'll be calling others," Flint told him.

Xavier shivered. Max realized it was from more than the cave's chill. "Let's keep going while we have light," he said. "There's fresh air ahead. I can smell it." He smiled at Xavier and put his hand on his shoulder. "It's good to see you again, cousin."

"You too," the boy said without much conviction, staring nervously into the encircling darkness.

Flint settled his feathered hat on his head, looking around warily at the cave that carried such frightening legends. "Can we forget the family reunion and try to get out of here?" he said, the grizzled face yielding no sign of humor. "When we crossed the river, I could have sworn I heard a helicopter. They might be bringing people to the cave."

"You goin' crazy, old man. That was thunder. No one could fly in conditions like that," Xavier argued.

"They won't come after us in here, Flint. They know the legend of the Stone Serpent. They'll be too scared."

"I'm scared, and I'm here," Flint told him. "I'm telling you, someone with more guts than I'll ever have was flying a chopper down the valley. And there's only one place they could be heading."

Riga was not immune to fear. He had taken part in many vicious campaigns where his daring had been tested, but now even he felt a lurch in his stomach as he gripped the steel handrail in the helicopter. The pilot was soaked in sweat, his eyes unblinking as he gazed into the near-invisible way ahead. He prayed as the helicopter lurched when he threw it to one side, then swore, pushing hard on the rudder pedals and making the helicopter do an almost acrobatic movement it was not designed for. He had just missed the face of a cliff. Riga's knuckles were white, but he showed no other outward sign of fear. The helicopter's skids nearly touched the river, the blades thrashing through the tree-hugging clouds and mist. And then suddenly the pilot pulled back on the control stick and the helicopter veered sideways. He had reached a hairpin bend in the river, and he had not seen the trees in time. Riga felt the helicopter shudder as the skids tore at the treetop branches, and the screaming engine, pushed beyond its capabilities, began to falter. By a miracle, it lifted free of the treetops and seemed to dance across the top of the canopy. In the swirling confusion, Riga saw a pickup truck on the ground and a man waving a crimson flare.

It was a hard landing. The helicopter skidded and bounced and finally ran into tree stumps, veered round on its axis and came to a shuddering halt as the pilot fought the twisting impact and switched off engines and fuel supply.

Riga's arm and shoulder ached from the exertion of gripping the handrail, but he jumped onto the ground, casting a glance back at the pilot, who sat slumped over his controls. Maybe the man had snapped his neck on impact. But then Riga saw him shudder. He was crying, sobbing with relief at surviving the hell of the journey.

The gunman threw the flare to one side and began to jabber at Riga, hoping his failure to stop Max and the others would not cause him to be punished. Riga ignored him and clipped the earpiece of his satellite phone in place as he turned for the forest. He had studied the maps and photo-graphs and knew exactly where to go, but first he was going to tell Cazamind. Whatever lay inside those no-go mountains was dangerous enough to scare everybody. Riga needed to be prepared to face that threat if he was going in after Max.

They went farther into the labyrinth. Climbing across obsta-cles of rock and crumbling crevasses, they became increas-ingly exhausted, but Max knew they had to push on as far as they could for as long as they could. The others wanted to stop and sleep for a few hours, but Max argued that they had to keep moving while they still had torchlight.

The cave became a twisting tunnel, a corkscrew whose smooth-sided rock face became more and more treacherous. If they slipped, the steep gradient would hurtle them down to the unknown. Max felt a gust of air on his face, and the torch flared as he reached the edge of a black hole, no wider than a man's body. Somewhere below he could hear water. Xavier and Flint caught up with him and knelt, looking into the abyss. Max leaned forward, holding the torch as far down as he could, and they saw the funnel curve out of sight. It was probably climbable, like a smooth chimney, but at some point that shaft would give way to a drop. How big a drop was the unknown factor.

"I think we have to sacrifice one of the torches—mine hasn't got long to go anyway." The worried look on Flint's and Xavier's faces reflected his own trepidation at slithering down the last curve of the Stone Serpent's belly.

He dropped his torch. It flared and reflected the twisting

chimney. They could hear it clattering as its light reflected upward for a few seconds. And then it went quiet. Max counted in his head: a thousand and one, a thousand and two, a thousand and three, a thousand and four—then they heard a splash. Max had counted four seconds exactly. He didn't know how to work it out, but he guessed that that had to be about a fifteen- to twenty-meter drop. Into what? Shallow water that would smash their legs or deep pools with currents that could suck them under and drown them?

There had to be another way down. He just didn't believe his mother would have come this way and taken such an un-calculated risk as to drop down this chimney into the un-known, no matter how brave she was. And there was also the skeleton that had been crawling toward the cave's entrance. That person could not have suddenly got from river to cave by levitation. There had to be another way down.

"We have to backtrack," Max told them. "We can't risk jumping through there. Flint, you lead the way. If we're above an underground river, there might be some kind of pathway down to it."

No one had wanted to drop through the hole in the floor, so Flint and Xavier nodded. Xavier licked his lips. "*Chico*, you know I don' float so good. Maybe we should go back the way we came—back to the forest. At least we have a chance out there."

"That's up to you," Max said as Flint moved away toward the cave's walls. There was nothing he could do if Xavier wanted to make his own decisions. He kept his eyes on Flint, who made cautious progress through jagged stalagmites.

The soft light from Flint's torch cast its shadows. Xavier studied the boy next to him. His knuckles were scraped, there were scratches on his face, he was smeared with dirt and grime, his hair was matted and he gripped the spear like a prehistoric hunter. Max Gordon did not look like any schoolboy Xavier Garcia had ever known. He looked dangerous.

"That was some snake you kill, eh?"

Max nodded. He didn't want to talk about it. He would never be able to erase the horrible image from his mind.

"OK. Maybe I stick with you. You're gonna get us out of here."

"I wouldn't bet on it," Max said.

"I would," Xavier said. "You gotta have faith in your angels, cousin."

Flint yelled. "Over here. There's a way down."

Xavier smiled. "I could make money on you, Max Gordon."

They moved quickly to where Flint held the torchlight above what looked like a huge open stairwell. At some stage, perhaps thousands of years ago, someone had hacked rough handholds and steps into the cave's walls leading downward.

The steps were just about wide enough to accommodate the width of a body. Max took Flint's torch. "All right, let's see what's down here."

They took no more than a couple dozen steps, twisting down, when Max stopped them. Something was wrong. The rising air was suddenly acrid. Their eyes stung and ammonia fumes choked them.

Max felt the shock wave of air. A surge of energy ascending from the bowels of the cave. And then he heard them. It was nothing like the fluttering sounds he had experienced in the river cave. These squealing screams were as if someone had taken the lids from the coffins of the undead.

Vampire bats.

Cazamind drew blood. It hurt and he winced, sucking his finger, hoping the pressure of his tongue would ease the insignificant wound. It was the small things that seemed to hurt the most—a rose thorn, a stubbed toe and this, a torn fingernail. Riga's crazy cuckoo-clock control freak had developed a bad habit. He bit his nails. It was unsightly, it was unhygienic and, as in this case, painful. It had started when Max Gordon had evaded all attempts at assassination. Then the private hospital had been compromised by someone hacking into the security system, and that had to have something to do with the Gordon boy as well. And now MI5 had taken it upon themselves to examine every inch of the place. Luckily his own cleanup crew had effectively destroyed or altered evidence. His friends in government would soon stop them investigating any further, but it was all getting dangerously close to secrets being exposed. Who could have imagined when that interfering eco-scientist Helen Gordon had stumbled upon his secret in the rain forest all those years ago that her son would now be posing as big a threat? If Cazamind failed his masters, he would bear the full responsibility—and he did not wish to die. Now the situation had just worsened. He listened to the satellite link from Riga. He was on the boy's trail, right behind him, and was convinced he could finish the job. He was asking for information about what lay in the amphitheater of mountains that for years had remained of no concern to anyone. Cazamind paid gangsters and former drug runners to be his mobile guards; he had stripped back the rain forest, sheltered illegal loggers, dissuaded and even killed environmentalists, all to disguise what lay in those forested mountains. Riga wanted information. Wanted to know what was in there.

Death was what lay hidden there.

"Leave him," Cazamind told Riga as he fumbled a Band-Aid onto his torn nail.

"Let him go?" Riga answered, his voice crystal clear on the satellite phone.

"Yes. He can't survive in there. He can't do us any more harm."

"He hasn't done too badly so far," Riga said.

"I don't want you going in there," Cazamind said. It was an order. He could not risk any outsider getting inside, especially not one like Riga, who had the skills to get out. No outsiders—that was the golden rule. You go in, you stay in.

There was a moment's pause. Riga was obviously considering what to say next, which surprised Cazamind. His brain focused, the finger forgotten. Why was Riga hesitating? Why wasn't it a quick *Yes, sir*? End of story. Paid. Money in the bank. Mission terminated.

"All right," Riga said. "Understood."

Cazamind ended the call. The man's inflection was wrong. Another fear tugged at his nervous system. He had not believed Riga's compliance. His assassin was going to ignore his orders—he was convinced of it. Riga was going in alone to satisfy some irrational professional desire to complete the kill against an elusive enemy.

Cazamind was being driven to ever more desperate measures to ensure that one of the world's biggest cover-ups stayed covered up. He had to ensure that it all ended now. He needed to be in absolute control. He would have to make very definite assurances that all was as it should be. He could be in Central America in under twelve hours. His finger hurt when he pressed the button on his phone console.

"Eliminate Riga," he said coldly.

Dense clouds of bats, their bodies no longer than Max's thumb, with twenty-five-centimeter wings, unfurled from the darkness and smothered Flint and the two boys. It was a frenzied attack. Unlike legend, the bats did not suck a victim's blood; their razor-sharp incisors slashed skin while an anti-coagulant in their saliva kept the blood flowing as their tongues lapped it up.

Max pushed his back against the rock, swinging the flaming torch back and forth, trying to beat them off to allow the others to move lower down the rock-hewn steps. But everyone was trying to cover their face with their arms to stop the painful attacks from the pug-faced creatures.

Torchlight shadows leapt, creating their own monsters in the mayhem, and then, screaming, Xavier fell. Max watched as he tumbled into the swirling mass. He immediately tossed the burning torch after him, desperate to see the boy. As the torch fell, Max's gaze followed it down. Xavier's legs bicycled

318

in the air, his arms flailed and he still screamed. There was no choice. Max leapt into the darkness, following the diminishing light. Not knowing if Flint had seen him jump, he yelled the plant thief's name as he plummeted downward.

A couple of seconds later, he heard Xavier's body splash into water, followed rapidly by the hissing torch as it was extinguished by the river. His mind told him he had a couple of seconds before he, too, hit.

And then he was underwater, all the air pounded from his lungs. He kicked hard and quickly broke through the surface. Within moments he could see light glimmering in the distance. "Xavier!" His voice echoed across the smooth surface of the river, reverberating around the cold rock face. No sooner had he called the boy's name than he heard a mighty splash a few meters behind him. Orsino Flint had jumped into the void to follow him. Max cried out again, "Xavier!" And this time he heard the boy's cry for help.

Max was surprised to find he still gripped the sturdy spear shaft, and within moments used it for support in the silted riverbed as it grew shallower. Then he saw Xavier's bedraggled figure clinging to a boulder in the slow-moving water. He had been lucky. The deep pool had broken his fall, and the gentle current had washed him quickly into shallow water. But his foot had become wedged beneath a rock, and even though the water was shallow, he was forced to raise himself on his elbows to keep his face from slipping below the current.

The light was brighter now; they were near the river's exit into daylight. Max heard splashing behind him. It was Flint, his straw hat soaked but still firmly in place.

Max could see that, despite being dunked in the river, blood still flowed from Xavier's face and neck, and he knew that he, too, was still bleeding. But his main concern was for Xavier. He could see that his leg was not broken, but the awkward position of his ankle meant that if he tried to drag the boy free, he could damage it. Ramming the spear shaft under the rock, he levered his weight down.

"Pull yourself free!"

It wasn't enough. "Grab his shoulders, Flint. Ready?"

Max grunted with effort, found a rock to push his legs against and levered downward. In a slush of water and silt, Xavier was yanked free a moment before the spear shaft snapped. Max fell back into the water, but he was unhurt.

Released from the underwater trap, Xavier hugged Max like a long-lost brother. He gabbled something furiously in Spanish. Max eased him away from the embrace. Flint wiped his face with his hands and looked at the smears of blood.

"He said . . ." Flint sighed. "You don't want to know what he said. It's embarrassing." Then he pointed at Xavier and said something to him that made the boy look guilty. "I told him you jumped after him. To save him, again. And I told him he wasn't worth it. Now let's get out of here and get rid of all this blood."

"Check his leg first. I'm going to look outside," Max told him.

He trudged through the shallows toward the gaping entrance where the river spilled out. A sheet of rock like a huge split tongue jutted out from the cave's mouth. The gently flowing water spilled over in a gossamer waterfall. Max stood on the rock's edge, with water swirling past his ankles, high enough above the tree canopy to look across the vast expanse of encircled rain forest. Wisps of cloud and mist were being tugged from the treetops by the breeze, and the amphitheater's mountaintop was ringed in a circle of fire from the rays of the sinking sun. Piercing a cleft of rock, a laser beam of sunlight etched across the craggy peaks, broadened into a spotlight and washed the waterfall beneath Max's feet into a crimson veil.

Max felt as though he had stepped into an unknown paradise: trees and flowering plants swayed in a gentle breeze, the silence broken only by the whisper of the waterfall. The mist was lifting, and in the far distance, as if revealed by a giant hand, the volcano's smoke drifted lazily away.

He was in the forbidden land.

The warrior's eyes watched him from the jungle below. It was his duty to guard the Cave of the Stone Serpent—a portal to the underworld, the place of death. But now he gazed with increasing fear.

In the legend of time, the Spearthrower clans had been defeated in great jungle battles because they could not throw their lances in the dense undergrowth. A new clan had emerged carrying shorter, flint-headed stabbing spears. They were brutally effective in close-quarter battle.

He saw a figure step out of the Serpent's jaws and stand on its tongue. He carried the weapons of a jungle warrior: a blowpipe, a knife and a stabbing spear. Blood streamed from his head and face, washing into the river, causing the waterfall to turn red. Blood was sacred to Mayan life and war. Seized by a primal fear rooted in thousands of years of memory and legend, the warrior ran into the jungle. He must report what he had seen.

The Serpent had created a projection of its own being in another form, its *wayob*, and sent it into the world of man—it was a manifestation of death.

22

They clambered down and moved across the shallow sand-banks into the edge of the jungle. Flint made them wash the blood away while he went foraging in the undergrowth. He soon returned and gave Max and Xavier a handful of leaves. "Chew these into a pulp, then put them onto the cuts," he instructed them, shoving some into his mouth. Within a few minutes of dressing the wounds, the steady flow of blood from the bat cuts stopped.

The shadows were deepening, and a moment of silence fell across the forest before the night sounds started.

"We need to get out of the open and deeper into the jungle in case anybody sees us," Max said.

"There's no sign or smell of anyone. It's been a tough day; we need food." Flint took the straw hat off and ran his fingers through his long hair, pulling it back behind his ears. He was looking over the terrain.

"Where would you choose?" he asked Max.

Max looked around. There were slabs of rock that reminded him of a tor back on Dartmoor. Prehistoric man had once made his campfires on those rocks and used them for lookouts and shelter. He pointed with the broken spear. "I'll climb up there and see what I can find," he said.

"What do I do?" Xavier said.

"You come with me and I'll show you how to catch a snake. Then you can skin it," Flint told him.

Xavier's face said it all. "I go with Max," he said with a grimace.

As Flint turned away and quickly disappeared into the jungle, Max clambered up onto the rocks. Xavier had no desire to be left standing alone, so he exerted himself in trying to match Max's mountain-goat agility.

When Max finally reached the top, he found he could see deep into the forest, and looking back to the river and the cave mouth, it was obvious they were on the bend of the river. The rocks sheltered a now overgrown clearing, in which stood an abandoned hut. Xavier was bent double from the exertion.

"Down there," Max said. "It's perfect. Out of sight but with a clear view of these rocks and the river beyond."

"I've stayed in better slums," Xavier said. "But after hanging out with you, that place is like a hotel."

Xavier began to move forward, but Max reached out his hand and stopped him. He pointed with the spear. "Look at that," he said quietly.

Xavier turned to face Max's line of sight. The sun had already disappeared below the mountain peaks, needles edging against the dark sky, but far away in the jungle, a curtain of mist was drawn across the valley. And it was bloodred. They stood for a few moments trying to understand what they were looking at.

Flint, huffing and puffing with his smoker's cough, climbed up behind them, a dead snake in his hands and fruit tucked into his shirt. Max recognized the diamond-shaped head of the snake, one of the deadliest pit vipers in the tropics. Without a doubt, Orsino Flint was an expert survivalist—no one tackles a three-meter fer-de-lance without knowing what they are doing. He turned back to look at the veil of blood. Flint's eyes squinted. The breeze was picking up. He sniffed the air. "Aha. You smell that," he said.

Max nodded. He, too, had caught the slightly disgusting smell of sulfur on the wind.

"That's an open stream of lava. The rising mist is from the damp jungle. This whole area was once an active volcano. Now it's just that one mountain bleeding into the land. The mist is the lava's reflection," Flint said.

"Dangerous ground. I don't want to go anywhere near it," Max said. "At first light, we'll find a track and see where it leads us. The pyramids and buildings in my mother's pictures are out there somewhere. We find them and I might find out what happened to her."

"And then?" Xavier asked.

Max shook his head. He wanted to go home, but the thought of facing his father again twisted something inside of him. He felt no compassion or understanding for what his father had done. Max knew his dad had failed to beat his own fear about something out here. He was determined to find the truth about how his mother died, but there were moments he wished he had not embarked on such a torturous journey. From the very start, it had caused pain and hurt, and the truth of his father's actions tore at him.

There was no point talking about it. He didn't want his own fears bubbling to the surface. Best no one saw that.

The embers of the fire burned in the stone hearth that Max had made in the hut. They had grilled and eaten the snake, and even the reluctant Xavier had admitted it wasn't so bad and that it tasted like chicken. But now the breeze began to blow through the hut's windows. As Max peeled fruit and handed it to Xavier, Flint began closing the wooden shutters.

"It's already hot in here," Max said. "We need some air."

"It is not good to have the night wind move across your body when you sleep," Flint told him as he fastened the shutters. "Some winds are malevolent; they are night spirits. You understand that? Your *ch'ulel*, it can be attacked."

"*Ch'ulel?*"

"*Ch'ulel* is your life force, your spirit," Flint explained. "It is vulnerable when you sleep. We're intruders here, but our presence will be known. There are different ways of stopping us. Shamans can take on the form of animals and travel on the wind."

"The *wayob?*" Max asked.

Flint nodded. "The windows stay closed."

Xavier pulled fruit strands from his teeth. "Y'see, *chico?* Peasants. These people live in the forest and they start thinking like monkeys."

In an instant, Flint had a knife at Xavier's throat. Xavier

choked. Max's reactions were just as quick as he gripped Flint's knife hand.

"Flint! Stop it! We're in enough trouble as it is. Leave him."

Flint pulled back but gestured with the knife. "Do not insult a man's beliefs, drug scum. They sit more deeply than the heart."

"Apologize," Max told Xavier, who stared at him in disbelief. "Go on," Max urged him. "If he wanted to kill you, he could have. I couldn't have stopped him. He was warning you. If I were you, I'd apologize."

Xavier grimaced as if the fruit had been sour. "OK. So . . . so you believe in evil spirits. OK. That's cool, amigo. It was a joke. OK? I was joking."

Flint muttered and backed himself into a corner, where he lay down with his back to the wall. "You are the ignorant one, boy. Your *ch'ulel* has already been corrupted. The dark ones took your childhood. You should ask for forgiveness and one day, maybe, you will understand what it means to live like a human being instead of a cockroach."

Xavier flinched, and this time Max's hand restrained the boy. "Leave him, Flint. Xavier tried to start a new life for himself and his brother. He'll come right."

Flint grunted, rolled a cigarette and let it smolder in his lips as he pulled his hat down over his eyes. He gave a rattling cough, his lungs struggling with the smoke. Both he and Xavier settled down. Max gazed into the fire. He knew about shamans and the creatures they could become. The shaman in Africa who had saved his life had taken him through a terrifying experience. Max understood what it meant to feel your body turned inside out, to experience the sensation of becoming an animal. Some things you can't explain. The subtle energies that moved through his body were a mystery, but he had stepped into that maelstrom on more than one occasion. If he were able to, he would beckon it at will, but it was beyond his capability. Something triggered it—he didn't know what—so he accepted Flint's explanation. The room was stiflingly hot, but he closed his eyes and let the exhaustion take him into the fractured world of dreams.

Outside, the jungle bristled. Max and the others had been seen by more than the cave-guardian warrior.

A hundred pairs of eyes gazed through the darkness toward the hut.

As daylight broke in the City of Lost Souls, it was the women who came to Charlie Morgan. Half a dozen pickup trucks with armed men had torn up the muddy street as they headed toward the jungle. Charlie wiped the sweat from her neck, tugged her clammy T-shirt away from her body, swallowed the last of a cold drink and crunched ice between her teeth as she waited for the dozen women who had gathered in front of her to speak. They were nervous. One nudged another forward, but the women seemed either shy or afraid. Charlie smiled. Time to be nice.

"¡Hola!" she greeted them.

"You are English?" the woman asked. There was no trace of hesitancy. Obviously, Charlie reasoned, they had all been educated.

Charlie nodded. That seemed the right answer, as if it comforted and reassured the women.

"No one, no woman, has ever stood up to the men."

"Well, there's a first time for everything. Slimeballs need a bit of housecleaning once in a while."

The women hesitated, seeming uncertain, until their spokesperson translated this into what Charlie assumed was Mayan. The women smiled, nodding. Charlie didn't usually get on that well with other women, but this seemed to be going OK.

"I'm looking for a boy," she said. "An English boy."

"Yes. He said someone would come after him."

"Max Gordon was here?"

"We do not know his name," the woman replied.

Charlie tugged out Max's picture. "Is this him?"

The picture was quickly passed around, and the accompanying shake of their heads answered Charlie's question.

The woman handed the picture back. "The boy had long hair. He was tall. He had heard of a woman who had gone into the rain forest four, maybe five, years ago."

Charlie nodded. "His name was Danny Maguire, and he was looking for a scientist called Helen Gordon."

The woman shrugged. That part they did not know about. "And this boy you are looking for?"

"Her son," Charlie said. She watched their faces register what it must be like for a young boy trying to find his mother. "The boy with long hair—Maguire—did he go into the jungle?"

"It is forbidden," the woman said.

Charlie had to tease the answers out of them. "So is standing up to violent men," she said.

They smiled again. "Yes, the boy got inside, but he became very sick. There is a place where they take supplies through. The man who drives that truck—he is a farmer—he helped him. The man is not like the others. He is Maya. He understands the old ways. He does not like the way these Creoles have been bought by Westerners."

"Westerners?"

"Sí. They come into the mountains in their helicopter. They are important, and they have bought the men here who run drugs, who kill and threaten us, but there is nothing we can do. You should not stay here. We came to warn you. You have shown how strong you are, but they will not forget. The reason they have not killed you is because they are unsure about you. No one has done to them what you did."

"Where have the men gone?"

"We do not know. They do not tell us."

"But something has happened. They've pulled out in a hurry. Are they after someone, do you think? Did they chase the Maguire boy when he was here?"

"We took a big risk when we helped that boy escape. Some of us were beaten badly, but we did not tell them how we got him to the city."

"So they *were* after him?"

"Sí. They are paid to kill."

"And Helen Gordon?"

"Some years ago, we heard of a woman who passed through one of the villages. She said she was looking for old ruins, but everyone knew she was an environmentalist. They live a dangerous life. We do not know what happened to her."

Charlie Morgan considered her options. She was so close to unraveling the mystery and knew that Max Gordon had to be out there somewhere. He was close. All her instincts told her that. But they also told her that she, too, could "disappear" once she ventured away from this town.

But imagine if she pulled it off. How cool would it be to find Max Gordon, to dig out the mystery and find out what Danny Maguire had discovered? She might even uncover the truth behind Helen Gordon's disappearance. That would be a real coup. But could she do it on her own? She felt her heartbeat quicken.

"Can you take me to the man who drives the supply truck?"

The women fell silent, and then each of them shuffled past her; they touched her arm, as if they were already grieving at someone's funeral.

"We can take you," the woman said. "But we do not wish to be responsible for your death."

Riga used a handheld flare when he ran into the cave. It helped him to see the tracks made by Max and the others. The grotto of saw-toothed images absorbed the light and became a snarling creature. Riga was not afraid of the shadow-riddled cave. He had never believed in myths and legends; they were lies told by storytellers to scare people or to make them feel good about themselves and create false heroes. Life was not a story. It was hard and unforgiving, and if you did not think for yourself and make your own decisions, then you became one of the followers, one of the herd. If you did not test yourself, you might be easily deluded into thinking you were better than you were. And that was where so many men entered the realm of fantasy. Riga had tested himself time and again. If he failed, he learned the lessons and became better; if he felt fear, he faced it, controlled it and mastered it. No one was going to make Riga a loser.

But the gunshot took him by surprise.

Searing pain creased his leg muscle and he fell, which saved him from further bullets that impacted dully against the damp walls. He rolled instinctively, found cover behind a stalagmite and saw the muzzle flash as his attacker kept firing blindly and stupidly at where he had been. The flare had distorted Riga's body with shadow, and the gunman had shot wildly. They were the actions of a scared man, who betrayed himself as someone who thought he could kill without stealth.

Riga closed his eyes—it was nothing to do with the pain; he wanted them to adjust quickly to darkness when the flare he had dropped spluttered and died. Lying still, he listened for every movement. A boot crunched the limestone gravel floor thirty or forty meters away. He did not open his eyes. He saw the man's approach in his mind's eye. He had stopped and turned slightly, checking the area, his boots twisting into the grit; then he moved again. Riga could hear the man's breathing. He opened his eyes and gazed into the darkness, his night vision clear, the subtle tones of black showing the dark-smudged features of the cave.

He knew he could not move quickly enough to take the man with his hands and make him confess who had ordered the attack. That was obvious enough. None of the gunmen used to patrol the forests would want to enter the Cave of the Stone Serpent, and none would dare attempt to kill Riga unless they faced something or someone more threatening.

Cazamind.

Riga lifted the rifle to his shoulder, waited, saw the slightest of changes in the darkness and fired. One shot. A body fell. Another couple of seconds and he heard the man's last breath. He waited again.

A second man, who must have stayed still, fired at his muzzle flash. Riga felt the snap of air next to his head. He did not flinch but, with an instinct born of years of close-quarter battle, returned fire. There was a cracking splat of bone and blood and the hard, sudden thump of a body thrown backward onto the ground.

A rush of air caused a vibration, an almost imperceptible fluttering of dust, as a figure rushed from the darkness. This man was better than the others; he had waited, using animal cunning to get close to his adversary, which meant that he would use a knife. Riga silently took all the pain as he bent down on his wounded leg, his lower profile fooling the attacker. He came in high, found only air, then felt the agony of death as Riga dispatched him with one blow.

Riga quickly calmed his labored breathing. He listened. There was no one else. But others would come.

He pulled the tab on another flare and examined his leg. The bullet had torn across his thigh, but no bone was broken, no artery damaged. Butterfly clips would not hold a gash like this, especially with the exertion he would be placing on the leg. He would stitch and bind the wound. It would slow him down and there would be pain—though he was no stranger to that—then he would continue his pursuit.

And find out why Cazamind had turned on him.

Max acknowledged that Flint was the rain forest expert and at first light allowed him to lead the way into the jungle. Flint found the line of least resistance through the trees, and using the animal paths, they made good time.

Xavier was insistent that he go in the middle. Flint could lead the way, but Xavier wanted Max behind him; there was no way he was going to bring up the rear. He had seen plenty of movies where the man at the back always got taken out by whoever was hunting them.

As Flint moved forward intuitively, Max kept his eyes on the jungle. He could see no movement, and yet there was something out there that worried him. The dank smell of the undergrowth filled their nostrils, but Max was convinced he could smell the sweat of men. He whispered a gentle hiss to Flint barely ten paces ahead of him. By the time Flint and Xavier turned, Max was on one knee and gesturing them down. They dropped to their haunches at once. Xavier's eyes were wide with fear, and Max put a finger to his lips to make sure the boy did not speak. Flint had not moved as he concentrated on the surrounding jungle. He would not question Max's caution; the boy had good instincts.

He shook his head. Max nodded an acknowledgment. Maybe, he thought, the warning sensation was simply a state of heightened tension. Like a wary animal, Max felt a nerve-tingling threat. A sixth sense was at work. They moved on carefully, but within seconds Max's fears were realized. It was as if a million butterflies had flapped their wings at the same time and created a fluttering current of air that jostled the leaves—a wave of unseen energy rushed toward them. They no sooner felt it than the jungle floor erupted.

Flint and Xavier were swept up into the air by a net, their bodies slammed together. Xavier yelped; Flint cursed. Their arms and legs were caught up in the rope weave. It had happened so fast. Max was barely a step behind them, but he twisted round, fully expecting someone to complete the attack. He was too late. As if from nowhere, dozens of spears angled at his chest and throat. He was surrounded by urchin-like children, some of them about ten or eleven years old, others no more than Max's age. They were Maya, they were armed and they had Max trapped.

And they weren't smiling.

23

Moments after the attack, Flint shouted at their attackers in Mayan. After a minute of uncertainty, they cut the net trap, thumping him and Xavier to the ground. The children stepped back, lowering their spears, but they stayed on guard as Max went to help Flint untangle himself from the net.

"They wanted to make sure who we were. I told them we were searching for your mother," Flint explained as he got to his feet. "They're like feral kids; they have to stay out of sight of the warriors."

"The Serpent Warriors?" Max asked.

Flint nodded. "They're scared of them, and they want us to get out of here now."

This was no time for Max to start asking any more questions. Prompted by the sharp points of the spears behind them, Max, Xavier and Flint started running. They ran at a pace that nearly killed the older man. On and on they went, through barely perceptible gashes in the undergrowth, across crevices and streams, uphill and down. The high humidity made them gasp, and the heat attacked them like another enemy. Flint's smoke-raddled lungs could not take in the oxygen he needed to keep going. Max and Xavier supported him and managed to keep up with the fast-running children.

They finally came to a makeshift camp, and it was obvious to Max that these children were not part of any formal settlement. The lean-to huts offered basic protection from the elements, like a forest shelter that any Boy Scout would make—branches, twigs, leaves and moss on a simple frame. Max realized they also offered good camouflage against any searcher who did not look carefully enough.

Four hours of grueling travel had taken their toll. Xavier gulped water offered to him by a young girl and then crumpled, exhausted, against the base of a tree. Max watched as some of the children helped drag the half-conscious Flint into the cooler air of a lean-to. These kids seemed organized. A young girl bathed Flint's face; another fanned him with a big leaf. Once he had drunk more water, he seemed to recover quite quickly. Obviously the plant thief could endure jungle conditions. It had been the hard pace that caused him problems.

Max stayed on his feet, still wary of what was going on. If he needed to make a run for it, he would do so in an instant. One of the girls approached and offered him a gourd full of water. She smiled at him, nodded and said something Max didn't understand. "It's OK. They won't hurt you. You're safe now. Drink," Flint translated.

Max spilled water over his face and felt his belly distend with a satisfying swig as one of the boys stepped forward and threw the broken-shafted spear and his blowpipe at his feet. He said something to Flint.

"He wants to know if I'm telling the truth about you searching for your mother," Flint said.

Max made no attempt to pick up his weapons. He looked directly at the boy and girl and nodded. Dare he hope these wild-looking children knew anything about his mum?

The boy looked at him intently. They were of equal age and build—perhaps the jungle boy was sizing him up, wondering if Max posed a challenge. It seemed he was the spokesman for the group. Again he said something to the girl. She looked uneasy.

"When white people come here, they bring trouble," Flint said quietly. "But they saw a Serpent Warrior run from the cave's direction, which meant something had frightened him. It had to be you."

Max looked directly into their eyes. Even if they did not immediately understand his words before Flint translated, he wanted to convince them of the truth. "We were attacked on the other side of the mountains before we came through the Cave of the Stone Serpent. I don't mean to bring you any trouble."

He extended his hand to the boy, reasoning that there was a hierarchy in this group and the boy should be greeted first.

"My name is Max Gordon. Yes, I'm trying to find out what happened to my mother."

The boy ignored Max's gesture and spoke again, looking to the girl, who said something in her gentle voice. She smiled and Max felt a seldom-experienced tenderness. She was beautiful.

"Boy's name is Tree Walker, and she's called Setting Star. They're brother and sister," Flint said. "Son, don't you go all soppy on me now. She's a pretty girl, but we're still in deep trouble here."

Max blushed. He hadn't realized he had been so obvious. The boy gestured him toward the center of the settlement. He noticed there were no fires, but there was fruit laid out on broad jungle leaves that served as plates. Flint's whiskers were already covered in yellow juices as he smothered his face like a dog in its feed bowl.

"Flint, you eat like a pig at a trough."

"Aha. Eat as much as you can as quick as you can. I got a feeling these kids are gonna be on the move again, and soon. They're scared. These Serpent Warriors are out there somewhere, and from what I can tell, they're gonna be coming for you." Flint sank his teeth into a huge slice of mango and sucked like a drain. In between slurping gulps, he translated as Tree Walker and Setting Star spoke quietly but with a sense of urgency. As if eager to rid themselves of painful memories.

"These kids've been separated from their parents for years. Before that they lived a simple life, mostly farming and fishing the rivers. The volcano causes them problems, like she's bubbling now, and they expect her to rumble any day. These are bad signs. Lightning storms and volcano activity, and now you've appeared." He hesitated. "I think this is as far as we go. They don't want us with them; we're bringing them trouble."

Max was not going to be pressured by Flint. He looked around the camp; these youngsters had survived without their parents for years. If they could do that, then so could he. He needed to stay with them as long as it took to find the truth about his mother's death.

"Flint, you can ask them to take you wherever you want to go, but I want to stay with them until we find out how my mother died and what's happened to their parents."

"Son, you don't hold any sway over these people. You don't mean nothin' to them. They don't want us around. Let's just try to get out of here in one piece."

Max knew he had to convince Tree Walker and Setting Star. There was only one way to do that. He had to tell them what he had experienced when he was in Africa. What he had told no one before. They needed to know about the shape-shifting and his animal instincts. What he did not know was whether this would frighten or anger them. Could his experiences be some kind of insult to Mayan beliefs?

"I need them on my side, Flint. Tell them my *wayob* is good and it is strong. Tell them it runs with me through the night."

Flint nervously licked his lips. "You start talking about the spirit world, about things supernatural, and you're pushing a stick into a hornet's nest. People like me and them, we take that kind of thing seriously. Don't fool with it; it's dangerous."

There was an uneasy moment of silence as the children looked to Flint and then to Max. They sensed uncertainty and perhaps discord. Xavier realized Max could be stepping into a world he knew nothing about and for the first time sided with Flint.

"Max," he said quietly but pointedly, "listen to Flint. He's right. You can't mess with that stuff. I know what I said last night, but you tell these people somethin' like that and they're gonna expect you to show your hand. That's shaman stuff; you can't pretend with that. Come on, *chico*, let's get out of here."

"You tell them that I have gone through the tunnel of death. I have been to the other side and I came back. I have flown as an eagle and run as a jackal, and I have touched the spirit of the jaguar. My *wayob* calls me Brother of the Night."

Xavier was stunned into silence. Flint got to his feet, as if to strike Max. He held his ground because something told him this strange English boy who had survived in this lethal wilderness was telling the truth. It was in his eyes.

"Tell them," Max said.

As Flint spoke of Max's shape-shifting experiences, the children fell silent and the looping calls of the jungle birds were all that could be heard. It was Setting Star who spoke first. She faced her brother and then the other children who got to their feet. Perhaps, Max thought, it was Setting Star who had the voice of the group.

"She says she believes you are a shaman and that they will help," Flint said. "Their own parents were taken by the Serpent Warriors. Somewhere beyond the hummingbird god. It's already killed a couple of the kids who tried to escape through the mountains."

"Ask them about my mum. She was around here somewhere." He gave the pictures to Tree Walker and his sister. "Was my mum with them? Was she taken as well?"

Flint asked the questions again and Tree Walker answered. Max listened to Flint's translation.

341

"There's a story about a white woman. She came in with a guide, but the woman got taken to the pyramid temple."

Fear and hope mingled in Max's heart. "Flint, don't you see? That has to be where she was. You've seen the pictures."

Flint shrugged. He did not want to tear apart Max's hope. He glanced at Xavier, who sat listening.

"Cousin, it's time for a reality check. Best thing we can do is get out of here. There has to be a way. We can't go back through the cave—those guys will still be there. We gotta let these kids help us, yeah? There's some really bad guys in here."

Setting Star held one of the photographs toward Max. Her voice held regret. Max took the photograph back.

"She says this is near a temple of the Serpent Warriors. If your mother was there . . . then . . . well, then she wouldn't have survived. That's where they sacrifice anyone captured."

Max felt the flutter of panic in his throat and chest. Terrible images of ritual killing flashed in his mind. And Mum. No! Was that why his dad had run?

"I don' like the sound of these Serpent Warriors, cousin," Xavier said.

Max's hand trembled as he tucked the photograph away. He spoke directly to them as Flint translated. "My mother is dead. I know that. I want to know what happened to her. I need your help. I will not leave until I find the truth. Nothing else matters to me."

As Flint translated, Tree Walker still seemed unconvinced, but he nodded when Setting Star touched his arm and answered Flint.

"They can take you only so far. They won't go anywhere near the temples," Flint said.

It was a small success. Max felt a surge of victory.

Three heartbeats.

One—Max saw a jaguar at the far edge of the clearing; then it disappeared into the forest.

Two—the birds fell silent.

Three—bloodcurdling screams shattered the stillness.

Then a sudden cacophony of conch-shell horns and wooden trumpets blasted the air as bass drums, like heart-stopping thunder, rolled through the trees. The forest edge shivered and changed shape as hordes of warriors yelled their battle cries and charged into the clearing. They were terrifying. Faces painted red and black, they wore plumes of feathers on greenstone-studded helmets and god masks of jungle creatures. All were armed with shields and flint-tipped weapons. Shrunken heads of victims slain in bygone wars dangled from their embroidered, sleeveless cotton jackets. It felt as if demons from hell had been vomited from the underworld.

Children screamed in panic. Tree Walker and Setting Star ran four meters in front of Max and stood firm, gripping their spears and bravely awaiting the charge—it was obvious they were going to defend Max.

Xavier ran, stumbled and tried to make himself small. Flint chewed through his cigarette, pulled his knife and awaited death. The blurred unreality of it all spilled across Max's vision.

The horde of warriors surged forward, and Max did not flinch. Was it a moment of insanity? He was the eye of the storm. Still. Unmoving.

And then he yelled, "Don't run! Don't fight!"

Tree Walker and Setting Star turned at the sound of his voice. They did not understand his words, but the way Max stood—arms extended in a pacifying gesture, feet planted firm—told them everything. He was like a tree: rooted, unmoveable. Doubt momentarily crossed their faces. Then they shouted their commands. The children, and Flint, looked back to Max.

Somehow it all made sense. Why Max had stood his ground no one knew—perhaps pure instinct—but battle warriors would find no honor in killing someone who did not resist. Bloodthirsty slaughter may have been part of their heritage, but Max's action stopped their leader from his advance. The surge stopped. The drums and trumpets fell silent.

Tree Walker and his sister ushered the children into retreat behind Max as a phalanx of warriors strode closer. Then they, too, stopped. The cave guardian pointed to Max, and a well-muscled warrior, who was obviously their leader, tentatively came a few paces closer. He lifted the wooden jaguar mask from his face and stared at Max.

The energy of the charge had eased into an uncanny silence. The warriors from the forest rippled as if the breeze brushed them. It was anticipation. Would their leader try to kill the Stone Serpent's *wayob*?

Max's fear seeped away. He felt strangely in control of his emotions. His legs had trembled when the attack started, his hands had sweated when he lifted the spear shaft, and his throat had dried seconds before he had spoken.

These were the Serpent Warriors—and they would know about his mother—and if their superstitions were intact, then they would take him as a prisoner to the temple pyramid.

344

The warrior signaled his men. They herded the children away from Max and began tying them with rope round their necks, ankles and hands. A dozen warriors surrounded Max, but he did not move. His back muscles prickled with the expectation of a spear being thrust into him, but he forced his mind—and his eyes—to stay locked on the devilish face of the Serpent Warrior in front of him.

The warrior reversed his spear and nervously bobbed forward, jabbing Max with the end, like someone scared of a corpse coming to life. Max was the unknown—how powerful was he?

Without the blood surge of the bellowing war cries, it was down to the warrior's cold courage to determine whether Max could slay him with a look or a touch.

Max faced him down.

Keep your fear to yourself, son. You show you're scared and you've given your opponent victory.

Dad's voice. Uninvited. Contradicting his own cowardice.

Being frightened is natural, Max. We all go through it. See it for what it is. Be brave even when you don't feel it.

Mum. Warm. Comforting.

This was all he could do. Everything else was out of his hands. Max stopped himself from saying something really stupid, like *Take me to your leader.* No sooner had the ludicrous thought flashed through his mind than he laughed aloud.

The warrior flinched. This boy-spirit had bared his teeth like a snake about to strike, in defiance of any fear. He raised his spear in an attacking thrust. And then nature saved Max's life. The ground shook, rippling like a small wave, swaying trees, buffeting the grassland like a horse's mane.

Earthquake.

Warriors and children flung themselves to the ground. The minor earth tremor threw those left standing to the floor. Except for Max. The shuddering energy below his legs made him instinctively brace himself. It felt like being on a snow-board running across uneven, broken ground on a ski run. He kept his balance. For a few brief moments, everyone lay face-down around him. The warriors looked up to see this mani-festation from the Cave of the Stone Serpent standing above them—like a king. This *wayob* had power. He had laughed at their most ferocious warriors and then caused the earth to strike them down to the position of lowly servants, lying be-fore him in subservience.

The tremor passed. The warriors got to their feet and— with a respectful distance between themselves and Max— gestured with their weapons that he should walk. Surrounded, he did as they wanted and followed the child prisoners into the forest.

Max felt an almost overpowering sense of anticipation. Every step now took him closer to finding the truth of his mother's death and his father's betrayal.

24

Ridgeway was collating his resources, calling in favors owed from civil servants and cabinet ministers, as well as discussing his fears with retired senior military officers. Someone had cleaned that private mortuary so well it raised suspicions to the point where he had instructed his team to go beyond their usual fastidious checks. He wanted to know what had happened to his man, Keegan, and why that building was shrouded in such secrecy. And the more he reached out for information, the greater the pressure that came from MI6. It would be a battle of wills between the two security services whether the truth was exposed or buried. One thing he was absolutely certain about was that his government, or rather the key people within it, were involved in some kind of cover-up.

Ridgeway sat with Tom Gordon in his room. Marty Kiernan hovered in the background as the MI5 man unfolded a large map of Central America across the table. He knew he was risking Tom Gordon's health and mental stability by coming here, but he needed to pinpoint where the explorer and scientist had been with his wife when she disappeared. The room was tense with silence, and Marty could see the prickled sweat on his patient's forehead as he gazed at the map.

"I have one of my people in the jungle. She has contacted me in the last few hours and believes she is close to an area that is exceptionally dangerous, guarded by armed men, and where your wife might have been before she died so tragically. Thanks to your son's friend Sayid Khalif, we had sufficient information to convince us that an illegal covert operation is taking place. My agent volunteered for this. She wants to go in. She has no legal backing from me or our government, and I do not want to risk her life needlessly. There is a British Army training team based in the mountains of Belize, where our soldiers are taught jungle warfare. Right now there is a company of Gurkhas there, and if I have to, I will put my job on the line and get those men in to support my agent. But I have to know if this is the place."

Max's father gazed at the contours of the map, each swirl a memory of steep climbs and rugged terrain. Like a badly edited video clip made on a handheld camera, snatches of pictures flashed through Tom Gordon's mind.

Ridgeway spoke quietly. "The boy who died on the London Underground has been identified as having gone there, and his death is still a mystery. But we believe that it's the information he gave to your son that triggered Max's disappearance. And if Max has survived, then I'd be surprised if he wasn't in the same area. So these troops would be put at risk to save your son and help my agent," Ridgeway said.

There was absolutely no response from Tom Gordon. His eyes were locked onto the map; he was in a world of his own, letting his mind reveal whatever memory could be recovered.

"Was this the area your wife had been in? If Max is there, we think time might be running out for him."

Tom Gordon's finger traced a route on the map. "A runner found me. . . . He came from the mountains, through a cave. He was frightened. He took me to my wife. I tried to save her. I tried . . . She was so ill. . . . No doctors . . . no one . . . That's why I ran."

Ridgeway saw that Tom Gordon's hand had covered the area where Charlie Morgan was sitting on the edge of violence as volatile as an unstable volcano. He knew he could squeeze no more from the man's ruined memory, but it was enough. He shook Tom Gordon's hand and turned to leave.

Marty Kiernan escorted him to the door. "I know this has to be something big for you to be taking these risks, sir, and if there's any likelihood of Max being in that area, then he'll be there. The boy's got guts and stamina—he's proven himself before. I think there's a better way of getting armed men on the ground—unofficially—and if anyone can help your agent and Max, then these are the people you need."

Marty Kiernan had spent a few hours on the telephone. The British government might well have a training team of specialists in the jungles of Central America, but to use them for a live operation could cause a diplomatic incident. If there was a chance to save Max, and if there was fighting to be done, then Marty knew who to call.

Over the years, British soldiers who had trained others in

the specialist art of jungle warfare had stayed in the area, married local women and settled down to raise families in the environment that was second nature to them. Most had served fifteen to twenty years in the army and now received a modest pension to supplement whatever work they did. In the modern world of warfare, they would be considered too old to go on active duty—but when the call came from Marty, each of the dozen men went to that special place in his home where he kept his well-oiled and trusted weapons hidden.

Charlie Morgan winced. It was a ragtag army that arrived at the rendezvous point Ridgeway had instructed her to reach. Battered old pickup trucks, ex-army Land Rovers and a quad bike cut through the mud and bush. Some of the men were still close friends; others hadn't seen each other for a few years, but the more she looked, the more she realized that these were hard-nosed veterans, their skin tanned mahogany from years in the sun. They might have been older than your regular squaddie, but she could see that the men had an understated, deadly efficiency about them. By the time they'd introduced themselves, made a few passing cracks about her being young enough to be their daughter and then started asking for tactical assessments of the target, she knew she was in business. These were the men who had taught others how to fight.

Charlie Morgan, ever practical and self-confident, believed she now had the resources, no matter how meager, to take on the gunmen and whatever else lay in that forbidden zone. Now all she had to do was find Max Gordon in that twisted jungle that ensnared its secrets like a poisonous spiderweb.

Like startled birds, two of the children ran. Somehow they had freed themselves. They ducked and weaved as warriors threw their spears and gave chase for a couple of hundred meters. The kids sprinted for some boulders where bushes hid what must have been a way through. Cries of encouragement turned to alarm, and then screams. Tree Walker and Setting Star tried to break free in their anxiety, but a Serpent Warrior yanked the rope round their necks and pulled them back in line.

"Why have they stopped chasing them? What's wrong?" Max asked Flint.

"There's a hummingbird god up there. These kids are too young to know about it."

Tree Walker gave a final scream of warning—but it was too late.

Max saw the two escaping children suddenly thrown to the ground as if a massive invisible hand had slammed them down. Everyone fell silent.

It made no sense. What had killed those children? He stepped forward; the warriors threatened him with their spears, but he continued walking slowly. They kept him encircled but moved with him, calling for instructions from their warrior leader.

"Don't be crazy. Boy! You ain't no jungle god! They'll kill you if they have to," Flint warned him.

The Serpent Warrior's leader ran forward and shouted a command. The spears jabbed closer. Max stopped. He had pushed his luck far enough. But now that he was closer to the children, he could hear a gentle hum of something in the trees.

The children's bodies were scorched. Red welts across their arms, chests and legs. Max realized that the hummingbird god was an electrified fence hidden from sight. There was a power source somewhere, fueled by what? Was a generator powerful enough? Maybe there was something hidden underground or in one of those caves he could see. Whatever it was, it had nothing to do with ancient superstitions—this was modern-day technology being used.

Hours later, after stumbling along pathways hidden by the high canopy, a broad expanse of cleared forest, trapped on each side by mountains, opened up before Max and the others. Layers of mist and smoke hung in the air, seeping upward to escape the treetops. Shafts of sunlight angled into a collection of pyramid-like buildings. Max had been pushed through the trees into a lost city.

He scanned the ground as quickly as possible. How to escape when the time came? Water channels that led down from the mountainside to irrigate fruit and vegetable gardens seemed the best bet. Get across those, through the trees and climb! Young legs, fear and desperation could take you a long way in a hurry.

As the procession of captured children was stopped by the warriors, they saw women—also tethered—tending the vegetable garden and looking at the war party's victims with expressionless faces. Their half-raised eyes told Max they dared not look too closely. It was fear that kept them under control.

Like bullying nightclub doormen, the guards chivied the children toward an overgrown entrance, an archway that looked like a short tunnel. Its stonework was intact, but, like an unrelenting virus, the jungle clawed at every stone, slithering across the limestone buildings, strangling them in a relentless embrace.

Max was still surrounded by his captors, so he was first through the archway, followed by Flint, Xavier, Tree Walker and Setting Star. Younger children were crying but were being comforted by the older ones. Max could hear the gentle, soothing tones of the Mayan language, which suddenly stopped as the prisoners emerged from the tunnel.

The main area was bigger than a couple of football fields. To the left and right were sloping stone walls, dotted with scowling gargoyles: squashed faces of ancient gods that reminded Max of the totem pole he had climbed in the British Museum—a couple of lifetimes ago, it seemed. Above these walls, steps rose up to create a low, flat-topped building. At the end of the field was a stepped pyramid that Max reckoned was fifty or sixty meters high. Smoke curled from the top, obscuring the summit. There were other buildings, most of them so ancient they were little more than ruins. The complex must have once been very impressive, with its brightly painted colors on smooth lime-plastered walls, but they were now worn away to reveal the underlying blocks, the structures subdued by the elements and the jungle. He could not recognize any of them from his mother's photographs. Despair squeezed his insides. He had to shake off any soul-destroying depression, or he would be helpless. There must be other buildings he had not yet seen.

Howler monkeys bellowed their supernatural-sounding cries from the dense vegetation that skirted the buildings, like gatekeepers to hell welcoming the condemned.

Max kept looking, scanning each building, each frieze or sculpture depicting scenes from ancient life. He wanted one of the stone-frozen figures to point out where his mother had stood, had her picture taken—had smiled.

The prisoners were brought to a halt. Max's guards moved away, leaving him separated from the main body of children. Flint was close to him and spoke quietly.

"These were sacred cities. All these buildings were aligned to the heavenly bodies so they could pinpoint planetary cycles. Y'see that smoke up there? That's where the Vision Serpent is. That's where they make sacrifices. They spill enough blood, it releases the *ch'ulel*. Then the shaman goes into a trance and sees the smoke take shape. He summons up one of their gods from the underworld." He took a wheezy breath. "The Maya sacrifice prisoners of war by cutting their hearts out."

Max gazed up. A figure stood at the top of the pyramid's steps. Iridescent feathers plumed out from his clothing, swathed in bands of color. He held a staff of some kind from which swung an incense-laden censer, like a priest in a church. A dull ache spread across Max's chest. He had brought this on himself in an effort to find the truth; now it stared him in the face—he was going to die.

A chattering flock of red macaws darted across the open

space, like droplets of blood splattering against the forest green. Something was happening next to one of the buildings. Other warriors had moved forward, like an advance party, but Max could not yet see who was following them.

He heard a whisper. *"Chico."*

Max dared a glance over his shoulder and saw Xavier huddled amid the others. His bound hands were raised slightly, trying to point at the new arrivals.

"Not all these guys are Mayan warriors. You see those tattoos? They're gangster tats. No way these fellas have been here a long time."

Max looked hard at some of the approaching men. Xavier was right—they looked more like gang members than tribesmen. Before he could give it any more thought, three or four men and a boy who looked very important, flanked by more guards, emerged from one of the darkened passageways between the buildings and walked toward them. They were dressed in a more refined manner than the men who had attacked them in the forest. Swathes of cloth, folded and tucked like skirts with leather belts, were wrapped round their waists, and they each wore what looked like a turban held by a leather thong, studded with green stones and decorated with bird feathers that half hid their shoulder-length hair.

A dozen or more men danced around these important newcomers. Flutes and chest-high drums vied with the shrill cry of clay whistles as ankle rattles whished like dry sand on a tin roof.

The royal-looking group kept their distance, staying about ten meters away from Max and the other captives, but one of the warriors had approached the newcomers and knelt before them, and was explaining something. There was a look of concern on their faces. And then Max heard Tree Walker shout out to them in Mayan.

Flint heard him as well. "He's telling them you are Eagle-Jaguar, that you cannot be harmed or it'll bring great misfortune to this place. He's trying to save you."

Max looked into Flint's eyes and knew that being saved was probably not going to be an option.

A guard moved quickly forward and hit Tree Walker with a stout stick across his back, knocking the boy to his knees. One of the fancily dressed people raised a hand and said something. Almost immediately, a young man ran into the arena carrying a ball slightly bigger than a basketball. The guards took over again, separated Xavier, Setting Star and Tree Walker and cut them free from the others.

Max looked at the boy who was with the dignitaries. He was probably a couple of years younger than Max, but there was something about him that he just couldn't figure out. It was a brief moment of disbelief.

Max called out, "You! Wait!" The celebratory music stopped. He ran a couple of steps toward the younger boy but was stopped by guards who pounced, kicking his legs from beneath him. Max fell hard onto the grass and suddenly felt a spear against the base of his throat. He pointed up toward the boy. "That's my mother's," he said. "Flint! Tell them that the necklace the boy's wearing is my mother's!"

Flint hesitated and saw the simple chain that bore the symbol of the sun. "You can't," he said. "They think you're some kind of supernatural creature. They're going to give you a chance to live. If they know you're just like the rest of us, they'll take your head off right now!"

But the younger boy stepped forward, waved aside the guards and ignored a rebuke from the man who seemed to be the boy's father. He knelt next to Max and spoke quickly, barely above a whisper. His fingers touched the small sun disk at his throat.

"Before I was brought to this valley, I was taught in a school. I understand you. I speak English. This was your mother's?"

"Yes," Max said.

The boy looked stricken. "I cannot help you unless you win the game. Stay silent or they will kill you now."

He got to his feet before Max could ask any more questions. The boy pointed at Flint and spoke in Mayan. Then he turned and joined the others, who walked back to the archway. As Max got to his feet, the boy looked back once and then turned away again.

Max felt a surge of hope. There was someone here who might help him but, more importantly, who also knew of his mother.

Xavier and the others had been pushed into the arena as Flint explained what he had been commanded to tell Max. They were in what was called a ball court, and what looked like a basketball was solid latex. The hard rubber was heavy, and it would bounce high and fast. In this game it was forbidden to use hands or feet—only knees, shoulders, chest and elbows. This ancient game had one purpose—to choose a victim. Once the game started, it would end only when somebody allowed the ball to touch the ground. Then that person would die a horrible death by having their heart cut out.

Flint gazed back toward the pyramid. They could see that the boy and the others had joined the shaman. *"Chac Mool,"* Flint said. Max stared to where the group stood next to a reclining sculpture that looked like a creature sitting back on its haunches and elbows, its stomach a broad flat surface. Max realized the stains that colored the ancient limestone were blood. "That's the sacrificial stone," Flint said.

" 'Into the jaws of Death, into the mouth of Hell rode the six hundred . . . ,' " Max muttered quietly.

"That's not Shakespeare," Flint said, a little uncertainly.

"No. But it'll do," Max replied.

Then someone blew a whistle. The game of death was on.

Riga had followed the tracks that Max and the others had left. Every scuff mark told a story, and when he heard the war cries and drums, it was as easy as a stroll in the park to locate the boy he hunted. Skirting the river, he gained high ground, ignoring the discomfort of the wound in his leg, letting the pain be something to beat at every step.

He saw the curtain of bloodred mist that rose from the valley floor as the hot lava sizzled through the wet ground. Like a dragon with bad breath, it continued its hissing roar unabated, as if its tongue were licking the jungle floor.

By the time the warriors had tied their captives, Riga was almost in sight of them. The earth tremor had caught him unawares. Some rocks around him were shaken free and went smashing into the gorge below. It happened so quickly he nearly tumbled from his precarious perch. Pain shot through his thigh, and blood seeped into his trousers—the jolt had torn a couple of stitches. He knew he should not let the wound become infected; it might easily prove fatal in this tropical heat.

If he went back through the cave, he could find a way out and get medical help. But then Max would escape him forever—a thought he considered for hardly an instant. He could find plants to keep the wound clean.

Using a small pair of binoculars to track the warrior group's movements, he watched as they disappeared under the rain forest's canopy. It seemed they were heading for that scalding river of fire.

Tightening his sweat rag across the wound, he gripped his rifle and made for the dragon's tongue.

The ball bounced. Xavier ran like a midfield player and took it on his chest as if preparing to drop it and kick a long pass, but the weight of the ball thudding into him forced the boy to crash down onto his back.

"Don't let it touch the ground!" Max yelled as he ran forward.

Xavier squirmed, arching his hips, pushing his face into the pungent-smelling rubber that now felt as though it was crushing his rib cage. Max was right there and saw Xavier push his body up with his hands and feet, keeping the ball clear of the ground and trying to flick it toward Max's uncertain stance. How to stop it from touching the ground? As the ball came clear of Xavier's body, Max went down on his knees, felt the grass burns cut into his skin, ignored it, caught the ball on his shoulder and pushed himself up as hard and fast as he could, forcing the ball onto the sloping walls, allowing the others to run and take the rebound.

Tree Walker, more muscular than Xavier, used the top of his bicep to hit it back on the sloping wall toward Setting Star, who pivoted like a gymnast, took the ball onto her knees, fell back and flicked it above her head. It was too low, its weight making it impossible to move with any great degree of skill. It would not be long before trying to push the solid ball of rubber would exhaust or injure them.

Guards and warriors whistled and cheered. They beat drums and blew conch-shell trumpets. Their yelling faces and thunderous roars broke through in waves to Max as he fought the deafening sound of pounding blood in his ears. It was like a ribald crowd at an FA Cup final, only there was more to lose than the cup—and there would be no medal for the runners-up.

Xavier had football skills, and if anyone could keep the ball off the ground, he could. He outran Max and Tree Walker, his skinny frame sluicing sweat, his long hair flicking droplets to the ground as he twisted and turned, and on more than one occasion saved each of the others from dropping the ball.

It was, Max realized, an amazing achievement for the slightly built Latino boy. How much longer could any of them keep going in this crippling heat? Who would be the one to die?

Max could see Xavier was tiring. He had retrieved the

ball and, in what had to be a near impossibility with a ball that size and weight, bounced it from knee to knee. He cried out, "Max!"

With an effort Max would never have expected of the boy, he got the ball high enough onto his chest, dropped it again onto his knee and then hefted his scrawny leg upward so the ball was in place for a header. He jumped, making contact, and aimed the ball directly to Max.

Then Xavier sank to his knees. He was out of the game. It was down to Max and the other two now. Max struck the ball with his shoulder, and it felt as though he had been punched by someone twice his size. Muscles and tendons would not be able to last much longer. Faces blurred; Max felt giddy. He saw the children screaming, watched as Flint waved his hat and roared encouragement, as the guards in their war paint became a surreal and macabre tapestry.

The ball!

It was in the air. Tree Walker had kicked himself against the side of the wall, powered into it from a low angle and struck it with his elbow. His arm snapped. He writhed in agony.

Setting Star was too far away. She ran like a sprinter out of the blocks. The rising cacophony became deafening. Tree Walker would die. He was the last to touch the ball. She dived in a hopeless attempt to catch the ball and amazingly got an arm to it. It skidded against the side wall, caught the pockmarked face of a gargoyle and spun away into no-man's-land. None of the players would reach it. Setting Star would die for her brother.

In a startlingly brief moment, Flint saw Max's face. The whole world stopped for that one blink of an eye as, in some kind of shocked understanding, he realized something about Max had altered. Every muscle in his body had contracted, a surge of power gathered down his back, his shoulders hunched, his eyes narrowed, and his teeth bared into a snarl.

Orsino Flint knew he was looking into the *ch'ulel* of the beast.

In three catlike strides, covering a huge distance, the ragged boy from England launched himself and leapt like a predator toward the stricken girl and the ball that was now only inches from the ground. There was a collective gasp from the crowd at the shock of seeing the impossible.

Silence fell.

Max's attack, for that is what it was, never wavered. He stretched out; his sinews demanded he stop. The rush of air told a part of his brain that he was still off the ground.

He was too late!

The ball was on the ground.

Almost.

Max's fingers curled like a jaguar claw and caught the edge of its weight. No human hand, let alone a boy's, could stop it from rolling onto the grass. But Max's did. It dug into the impenetrable, it squeezed the uncrushable, and it threw the ball of death clear from the girl.

The children cried out. The guards and warriors bellowed their approval.

They had their victim. The ball rolled away.

Max Gordon had sacrificed himself.

* * *

Riga clawed his way forward. The cheering had stopped, but now the jungle exposed the hidden city, and he followed the watercourses down the hillsides toward the blind side of a high pyramid where smoke and incense swirled across a small group of men who stood before a sacrificial stone.

The tumbling water would obscure any noise he made— not that he intended to make any—and he could see that one of the channels fed a waterwheel in a building adjacent to the pyramid. It had no doors, but the entrance was pitch-black. No light penetrated it. Maybe that was the way to get into this ancient settlement without being spotted.

Riga was no stranger to house-to-house fighting. He made his way down, scanning the ground for Max.

And then he saw him.

The guards had quickly surrounded Max and, as he staggered to his feet, made it clear by pointing their spears that he should move forward toward the huge steps of the pyramid.

Flint ran forward and helped the exhausted Xavier to his feet. "You did well, boy."

Xavier nodded, grateful for the compliment from the man who had always been an enemy. After a moment, he got his bearings, watching the children run to Tree Walker and Setting Star. Max was already thirty meters away, sur-rounded by the grinning, joyful warriors. Now there would be blood.

"Max, no . . . ," Xavier whispered.

"We can't help him now, son. We have to find a way out

of here. There might be a chance when they're distracted . . ." Flint did not allow himself to finish the sentence.

"When they kill Max, you mean? No, no, we have to do something. We *have* to," Xavier insisted.

But the brief thought of bravely trying to rescue Max was cut short as the guards turned back to Xavier and the others. They were to be herded along as witnesses to the sacrifice.

Max began the long climb upward. The steps were chest-high, and he had to lift himself up with his arms and drag himself up each level. This alone, without the exertion of the ball game, would have exhausted anyone. Perhaps it was designed so that the victim would have no fight left in him once he reached the sacrificial stone at the top of the pyramid.

He had to concentrate! He had to use every breath to feed his body, to hold on to his remaining strength. And each time he climbed higher, he looked around him. If nothing else, he would get to see the surrounding countryside, the other buildings, places his mother might have been. Perhaps she, too, had escaped from this terrible place. The thick curtain of crimson mist was beyond the perimeter of the buildings, and he felt the air grow hotter from the molten lava. The jungle sizzled and he could hear rocks cracking as the lava cooled.

Water tumbled down the hills through the trees and disappeared into the ground. There was no sign of any escape route. The sun was blistering; Max was weak from lack of food and water, and he was desperately thirsty. His knees and elbows were badly grazed and painful, and he could feel the bruises forming where the ball had struck his arms and chest. It felt as if he had been beaten with a baseball bat.

He glanced down and saw the others, under guard, watching him. He did not want to die like this and hoped against hope that at the top of the pyramid, the boy who wore his mother's necklace might reach out compassionately and save him.

Crunching fear twisted his stomach. Had his mother been sacrificed? Was this the terror his father had run away from?

If you've got one breath left in your body, then you have a chance. Don't die like a lamb to the slaughter, Max. Keep fighting, son. It's your life. Don't let the killers and the thugs take it easily from you.

Dad's voice. Why hadn't *he* fought?

Two steps left.

He looked around. The panoramic view showed the mountains, the river, the smoldering, troubled volcano and the far horizon, where another world lay hidden beneath the rim of the earth. A crease in the tree canopy looked wrong. It was a strange shape, a gaping hole in the natural curvature of the treetops. He wiped the sweat from his eyes and stared into the glare. It was a camouflaged satellite dish nestling in the tree line above a partly exposed smaller building.

The breeze caught his face. It had changed direction. The incense and smoke cleared. He looked up into the eyes of the waiting men. Any thought of fighting his way clear and finding an escape through whatever lay at the back of this pyramid was snatched away. The shaman wore a painted wooden animal mask, some kind of mythical creature whose curved open jaw exposed vicious teeth like a snarling wolf. Even the boy wearing his mother's pendant looked frightened. And, unexpectedly, there were four other men in attendance—

guards. The shaman lifted the sacrificial knife and pointed it at Max. There was no need for him to climb the next couple of steps. Two men jumped down and hauled him up.

Max shuddered, fear rippling through him.

A lamb to the slaughter.

This is how they killed lambs. They cut their throats. Did they feel fear? Did they smell the blood of others? Max felt revulsion as he thought of the times he had seen lambs playing in the fields around Dartmoor High, because, like them, herded to the slaughterhouse, he was now helpless.

He could smell the men's sweat, and the sweet, cloying incense stung his eyes. It was a nauseating mixture. The shaman was chanting something quietly beneath his breath. The guards waited, ready to do his bidding the moment an order was given. The others sat on stone benches awaiting Max's execution, a cruel entertainment to satisfy an ancient ritual.

Only the boy stood. Max's mouth was dry from the exertion and the heat, and now the smoke scratched the back of his throat. He needed to buy time. Every single second was vital now, because the longer he could delay the inevitable, the greater the chance of escape—somehow.

He gazed at the boy. "Don't let them kill me yet. Please, before I die, tell me what happened to my mother."

The boy turned to his elders, spoke quickly to them, and Max saw them nod.

Hope restored.

And then it got better. The boy offered Max an animal-skin water bag. Max grabbed it before anyone could change their mind and gulped as much water as his breath would allow. That water was high-octane fuel to his starved body.

The shaman snatched it away and commanded the guards, who then grabbed Max's wrists.

"Wait! Not yet!" Max shouted.

Skin scraped from his back as they manhandled him onto the stone sacrificial table, his wrists and ankles held by the four men. The shaman put his hand on top of Max's chest—to feel the heartbeat. Max squirmed. There was no need to feel for his heart as far as Max was concerned; it was banging so hard it would burst out of his chest of its own accord.

The shaman recoiled, pulling back his hand as if burned, said something to the other men, who looked scared, and then took a step backward.

The boy spoke again. "He says you are a creature of power and that he must call on all the forces of the Vision Serpent to destroy you. He will take your heart and burn it. It is the only way your *ch'ulel* can be sent back to the otherworld."

Max twisted his head, trying to appeal directly to the boy, wanting eye contact. "Don't let him kill me! Come on, mate. Help me out here! Come on!"

"I cannot," the boy said, lowering his face to Max's. His mother's pendant swung close to Max's eyes. Max struggled, but the men held him firmly. It couldn't end like this!

"Your mother came here, by mistake. She was going to join your father on the other side of the mountains. At the sea. Have you seen the ocean?"

"What?"

"I have never seen it. Your mother told me many stories about it. I was sick. Your mother helped me. I was only a boy."

Max had to concentrate more than he ever had before. He *had* to understand what was going on—what had happened.

This wasn't a nightmare he was going to wake up from. This was moments before his own death.

Max cried out in despair and fear. He could not move a muscle. Now the men put their weight on his legs as he bucked again. The shaman said something to the boy, but he responded with a stinging reply, and the shaman obediently waited for the moment when he could plunge the knife into Max and cut out his heart.

"My mother! Tell me!" Max begged.

"Before the people came here and took the children's parents away, everyone lived together. We are the last royal family of the Maya. We are descendants of the great kings. Many of those warriors do not belong in this valley. They were brought here by the outsiders. They made us their prisoners. It is because our people have something in our blood these men want."

The boy gazed away across the darkening sky, as if seeking a way for his memories to escape. He quickly slipped the pendant over his head and curled it into Max's open palm, his wrist held tight by the shaman's henchmen.

"Your mother got sick. She saved me, but we could not save her. There was a white man here, the one who controlled everything. He had a helicopter, but he would not take your mother. He left her to die. He did not want her to speak of him. Two of our people took her through the Cave of the Stone Serpent, but only one survived. Your mother told us that if we could find your father, he would get her to a doctor."

"My father?" Tears welled in Max's eyes.

The boy nodded. "She said he was beyond the mountains. Your father carried her for days through the jungle. He ran until he could run no more. At the place where the white stone stands at the ocean. That is where he buried her. That is all we know."

Dad ran. He ran to save her! Farentino lied! I got it wrong. Dad had run to save her!

The boy touched Max's forehead. "It is the time we call blood sun, when the sacrifice must be made. Go to your mother. She is waiting for you in the otherworld. Do not be afraid." He stepped back.

This was it.

The shaman raised the knife, the light glinting on the blade; a wave of sound came from below as the children, Flint and Xavier screamed for Max's life.

Max lifted his head. Tears stung his eyes. He gripped the pendant until it cut into his skin. *Mum, Dad. I'm sorry! Please help me.* Then that moment of pure love and desperate fear deserted him.

Anger erupted like a volcano unleashing its power. He would not die like a lamb; he would not show how scared he was—he wouldn't! He would leave them with the foul taste of a curse in their superstitious lives. Thunder rolled around the mountain peaks. The air was still. He sucked in a lungful and spoke each word with as much force as he could muster. "I am *wayob*! I am Eagle-Jaguar! And my father will kill you all!" he snarled.

He spat as hard as he could into the shaman's face. The shaman's head snapped back, blood splattered the group and the guards released their grip.

The sacrificial priest was dead.

25

Riga lowered the rifle. No one but him was going to kill Max Gordon, and the kid deserved a better death than having his heart cut out or getting a long-range bullet through the head. The gunshot had been swallowed by the rolling thunder and torrential streams that splashed down the hillsides. Riga moved; his injured leg slowed him down, but he had figured out that Max had only one escape route.

On top of the pyramid, Max was the first to react. The shock of seeing the shaman's blood splatter across their fine clothes stunned the group into silence. In the past, Mayan kings saw death as an honor and offered their own blood to appease their gods, but for these people to hear a shouted curse and see one of their own die threw them momentarily into disarray. Had the *wayob* struck the shaman down?

Max realized what had happened, but there was no time to work out who had shot the priest. Maybe Flint had broken free, found a rifle. From where? It didn't matter. Max was alive.

The guards were the first to recover. Whatever they believed about the supernatural, they did not lack courage. They were there to defend the boy and his family. Max was already on his feet. There were no weapons to hand except the shaman's censer. He swung it. The incense plumed and the men ducked back, shielding their eyes. He felt it connect with one of the guards' heads. Like an ancestral killing when bodies were thrown down from the top of the pyramid, the man tumbled into space, his cry cut off abruptly as his bones shattered on the steps and his rag-doll body fell limply toward the bottom.

The rod holding the incense burner snapped. The men lunged at him, but Max sidestepped and grabbed the boy, whose look of confusion turned to fear.

Max yelled at the men. "Stay back!" He felt a pang of sympathy for picking on the boy who had tried to help him, but he was all Max had as a bargaining tool. The guards ran at him, but Max's snarl as he half pushed the boy over the edge made his intention clear—*Come for me and the boy dies.* Max held him over what was almost a sheer drop. His heels slipped; he nearly fell. One of the elders raised a hand and the guards stopped. Max wasn't sure what to do next. He would not be able to manhandle the boy down those steps, and the moment he released him, the guards would be on him.

The boy whispered fearfully, "Behind you."

Max looked. There was a narrow arched doorway with

steps inside leading down. He pulled the boy with him and entered the cool shelter of the pyramid. The stone stairway twisted downward, and he pushed the boy in front of him until light from another doorway spilled into the building. They had quickly reached the first level of the pyramid, where the kings of old would have entered and moved up to the top, showing themselves to the people, convincing them that they were descended from the gods. No more than a magician's trick.

But there were no tricks that could make Max disappear; he would have to make a run for it on his own. He held the boy away at arm's length, letting him feel the security of the wall against his back, then released him. The boy may have told him about his mother, but he had also been prepared to stand back and let them cut out Max's heart.

One last question. Max pointed toward the satellite dish. "Does that belong to the men who came here, who imprisoned everybody? The man who arrived in the helicopter?"

The boy nodded. "We cannot go there; it is where they take our blood. It is protected. No one can go there."

Max had to know if that place held any other answers to his mother's death. He couldn't see an obvious way in through the jungle; it seemed to be blocked by a jagged scar of a ravine.

"What sort of protection?"

"They took one of our people and sent him through that place to show us," the boy said, pointing to the building next to the pyramid. "It is the Razor House. We heard him scream before he was cut to pieces. Go. You must run. I will tell the guards you have gone toward the jungle."

No more questions. Max turned away and began the long run down, hoping the boy would do as he said, or he would still have to avoid the warriors on the ground.

Riga followed the turbulent water that channeled down toward the compound. Max Gordon had his wits about him. He had got this far. Did the kid know anything about this place? Cazamind wanted Riga dead because he had disobeyed him and entered this forbidden killing ground. His secret was here somewhere. Did Max Gordon know what it was?

He saw children and an old man being herded away by warriors. They had been spooked by what they'd seen on the sacrificial site. Riga could have shot a dozen of the men before they knew what hit them, but they were unimportant, and he did not have time—a shadow lengthened down the side of the pyramid. It was Max heading for the building where the water hurtled in a torrent of power through a narrow sluice. What was there? He wasn't going to get down in time before the English boy reached the building's entrance.

Riga flung himself into the water chute.

Max could see Flint's feathered hat jostling amid the crowd of children. He knew Xavier would still be with him, but there was nothing he could do to help them now. The tendons and muscles in his legs screamed for rest. This was worse than any sports training he had ever done, but there was something else driving him now—something that felt like revenge. He had doubted his father. How *could* he have thought his dad was a coward and had abandoned his mother? So why did he feel this surge of vengeance? Who was it against? As he pounded downward, he realized it was against himself.

He hit the ground running. Sprinting through the shadowed alleyway between the pyramid and the Razor House, he felt a low rumbling in the ground beneath his feet. Another earth tremor? He braced himself against a wall, but there was no surge of power rolling through the ground. This was coming from below the building. Running to the end of the passageway, he could see that the ball court was being cleared of the prisoners, and the guards moved in the opposite direction. The Mayan boy had given him a chance. He turned the corner quickly and stepped into the gaping cold shadow of the doorway. Dust sprinkled from the ceiling; the walls trembled with a slow, grinding vibration. He moved farther into the chilled interior. The light from the entrance was too far back to penetrate this deeply. He closed his eyes, wanting the sunlight from seconds ago to seep away so he could see into the gloom. Something moved. It whispered. The air brushed his face. He stopped.

Whoosh.

Stale air wafted past his face.

He waited, caution reining in his urgency. The Razor House? Blades?

Whoosh.

Like a fan.

He took a step back, opened his eyes and concentrated on the darkness.

Wooden poles, like fallen sticks, crisscrossed the narrow passage that led through the building. It was an ancient but

intricate design to obscure and obstruct any further movement. The sour taste of nausea caught his throat. It was no
fan that cut the air—it was hundreds of flint blades attached
to wooden arms bound to those turning poles. Razor-sharp.
They were like a meat grinder. With more angles than the
face of a diamond, any one of those flints would snag clothing
or flesh and churn their victim into its shredding jaws—like a
boa constrictor's teeth.

Max backed away, lest the mesmerizing machinery draw
him in. One more step forward and it would snare him, then
slice and hack him in a terrifying and painfully slow death.

If he wanted to get through, he had to find what drove
the stone-wheeled machinery and destroy it. He turned. A
shadow stretched in front of him. A man, water dripping from
his clothes, stood silhouetted in the entrance. His leg was tied
with a sweat rag, a rifle gripped casually in one hand, his
backlit face in shadow.

Max knew without a doubt that if he saw this man's eyes,
they would have the same cold, penetrating gaze of the man
who had nearly killed him in the British Museum.

"Hello, Max," he said. "My name is Riga."

Charlie Morgan and her convoy of ex–British Army jungle
fighters had pursued the men from the City of Lost Souls.
The old man who drove a battered supply truck in and out of
the jungle stronghold had scraped the route map into the dirt,
showing there was only one entrance, which lay between
rugged boulders.

She had been relegated to the back of the convoy,

because the men knew the action would be ferocious. As much violence as the ex-soldiers could muster would be inflicted on the mercenary *banditos*, as the old man called them. The Brits had age and experience on their side, but the defenders of the jungle stronghold outnumbered them at least three or four to one. Charlie Morgan was trained to fight, but she had never seen this type of intense and determined action before. Her ex-soldiers moved in pairs, fire and maneuver, gaining ground, calling out to each other, working the terrain to their advantage.

The enemy's heavy machine gun, mounted on the back of a pickup truck, laid down wicked fire, shattering tree trunks and flailing branches and leaves. It was slowing her men's flanking attack. Within moments they would be forced to find dead ground beneath the killing fire, and their momentum would grind to a halt. A failed attack meant a failed result for her. And she wanted success more than anything.

She got behind the wheel of the old Land Rover, slammed it into gear and floored the accelerator pedal. The 4×4 bit into the mud and chewed undergrowth as she wrestled the wheel left and right, avoiding other vehicles, tree stumps and gullies. She was going for the gap, and the machine gun turned its attention to her speeding approach.

As the gun swung and opened fire, her men on the ground took advantage of the brief respite and moved forward. She had created a diversion that allowed the attack to regain momentum, but Charlie was now staring down the barrel of the machine gun and saw the spent cartridge cases spinning away as the line of fire tracked her approach on the red dirt road.

The last thing she remembered was throwing herself

down as the windscreen shattered. The careering Land Rover plowed off into the undergrowth and immediately became ensnared like an animal in a trap.

Max stood, unable to react for a moment, his thoughts shattering against the wall like water splashing on a rock. How had this man got to him? All this way? After all this time? Had he been the one pursuing him downriver in that helicopter? It was like a dark angel standing in the entrance. And yet he made no move to raise the rifle. Clearly it had been he who'd killed the shaman. What did he want?

Even now Riga had little to say. He reached out to the wall with his free hand and hauled down a wooden lever. There was a sudden gush of water as if a small waterfall had been blocked.

"Water powers a wheel that spins all those blades. We're both looking for answers now, Max. You're a hard boy to kill. You've earned the right to live awhile longer."

The poles creaked in the waterwheel and finally stopped. Water dripped somewhere; each drop like a small, echoing threat that the power could be unleashed again.

Max had not moved. He knew that, even with the poles unmoving behind him, he would not be able to make a quick escape. Trying to get past those blades would be like edging through razor wire. "Who sent you? Did you kill Danny Maguire? Why are you after me? Tell me!" The questions came quickly. He wanted to buy time as well as get answers.

Riga did not move from the entrance. He was not going to give Max, with his speed and agility, a chance to escape.

He shrugged. "Why not? It makes no difference now. There's a man called Cazamind, and he runs this project—whatever it is. This is his secret. Danny Maguire caught some stinking disease that chewed up his body and sucked out his brain. Blood poured out of every pore, even his eyes. When he fell on the high-voltage rail, it fried everything and stopped it spreading, but Cazamind had him cremated, just in case. And this place is connected with it. That's why Cazamind didn't want you getting close. In case you found things out."

Max's stomach lurched as he thought of his mother. Had her beauty drowned in blood? But Riga, why was he here now? Why had he not killed Max already?

Riga looked at him, sensing the question flitting through the boy's mind. "I came here to kill you—but Cazamind tried to kill me. He didn't want me to find out his secret either."

Max's mind raced. He was on the brink with Riga. In a second he could kill Max. Why hadn't he? He knew the answer!

"You think I know what's going on here and how to get my hands on that secret," Max said.

"Maybe."

"Not maybe. Definitely. Otherwise you would have killed me by now. Well, I do know that there's something going on. . . ." He hesitated. This wasn't good enough. He *had* to convince Riga. "My mother left me clues," he lied. If he could stay alive long enough to reach that satellite dish, he might find a way of calling for help.

"What kind of clues?"

"Photographs."

378

Max saw something cross Riga's eyes. Recognition? Understanding? Belief? "You know my mother was here."

"OK," Riga said, "he told me that."

Max nearly winced. This Cazamind *knew* his mother had been out here. Had he been the man who'd refused to airlift her to safety? "You need me. I know where to go," he bluffed.

Riga studied him. Max stared back, desperately hoping his lies would not flicker through his eyes.

"Through here?" Riga asked, nodding toward the blades lurking in the darkness.

"Yes. It's the only way."

Riga thought about it. "All right. You take me there."

"What happens then—between you and me?"

"A contract is a contract. But when the time comes, I'll give you a chance. You have my word. You deserve that." Riga smiled. "You remind me of myself when I was a kid."

"I'm nothing like you," Max said. "And if I get out of here, I'll do everything I can to make sure you're caught."

"It's a deal," Riga said. "Now get over here and help me with this lever or we'll never get through those blades."

Max moved cautiously, but he knew he had no choice. Riga could have killed him then and there and hadn't. So now the assassin and his quarry would work together to reveal a secret whose keeper had tried to kill them both.

The wooden handle quivered under the weight of the water that was building up. The lever had to be jammed into position. Riga leaned his weight down onto it and shoved his rifle into Max's hands. Max could see exactly what needed to be done. He settled the butt of the rifle onto the lever and its barrel into the wall so that the pressure of water could not force it upward and start the blades spinning.

Riga took his weight off the lever; the rifle took the strain. "OK. Go," Riga said.

Max looked at the vicious obstacle course and then at the manhunter. "You first," Max said.

Riga laughed. The kid had guts, but was he a killer? Would he yank the rifle away and unleash the water pressure when Riga was in the middle of all those blades? He had answered that question once before; nothing had changed. Max Gordon was no killer. He shook his backpack free and pulled out half a dozen small flares. He ripped the tabs clear and threw each one as far as he could, clattering them through the blades and poles into the darkness. Their crimson glow dabbed the blades' tips.

He moved into the labyrinth. Max gave him a couple of seconds' head start and then followed. His eyes quickly adjusted to the flickering light, and he bent and twisted his body like a contortionist through the sharpened flesh shredders. He could see a couple of the points had nicked Riga's skin as he bent and stooped his way around the lethal obstacles. Riga had made no sound, as if impervious to pain. Max winced; his concentration had flagged watching Riga's movement, and one of the blades had scraped into his back. He felt the warm trickle of blood ooze like sweat. But he knew they were almost through, because he could see light seeping through from the other end of the building. Another four or five meters and they would be clear.

He wanted to move more quickly, but the blades snagged

his shirt and trousers like barbed wire. He had to pick his way clear. Riga seemed to be making better progress and was almost through.

And then Max's legs trembled. He felt the panic rise quickly and almost reached out to grasp one of the blade-tipped arms for support. He twisted his upper body to balance the movement under his boots. Another earth tremor.

Riga was nearly out of the deadly traps, but one of the poles twisted from the vibration, and like a cog in a wheel, it shifted into its normal stationary position. The bladed arm swung in a lethal curve from behind Riga's right shoulder down toward his left leg.

"Behind you! Look out!" Max yelled, desperately keeping his own balance, eyes darting left and right, hoping none of the blades was shifting toward him.

Riga's reactions were remarkable. Keeping his feet firmly planted, he twisted from the waist, raised his left arm above his head and turned himself clear of the cutting blade. The tip caught his shirt, ran beneath his ribs and bit into the shoulder holster. Max heard the clean ripping cut as the blade severed it from the shoulder strap. Max's warning, Riga's fast reaction and the shoulder holster had saved the killer from a lethal wound. The chrome-plated semiautomatic tumbled away beneath the blades.

Riga was clear. He caught his balance and turned back to watch Max's progress through the last few meters. "Come on, kid, that lever might not hold. Hurry!"

Max could hear the poles creaking and saw the blades quivering. Another earth tremor snaked beneath his feet. He almost fell. And then he heard a sound from the other end of the building. It was metal scraping against rock. The rifle was being forced along the rock wall under pressure.

Riga watched Max trying to move more quickly. It was like observing a fly trying to escape from a spiderweb. Sometimes the fly got lucky.

"Come on! Do it!"

And then they both heard the crash of the lever breaking free of the rifle's restraint; the sound of rushing water echoed through the chamber. The poles groaned back to life. Behind him the blades were already turning, and Max felt the exertion force itself out of his lungs. He gasped as he tried to get through the last couple of meters before the teeth around him spun into life and devoured him.

He was not going to make it. And he knew it. He raised his head to look into Riga's eyes less than a meter away—but the blades spun. Riga snatched at one of the moving arms, jammed his foot onto another and threw his weight backward. The sudden counterbalance on one of the poles slowed the blades that had not yet reached full speed.

Max saw the narrow space between the blades, like a gap through a bramble hedge. Throwing himself forward, he felt them nick his clothing. He hit the earth floor, rolled and came quickly to his feet. Even Riga's strength could not have held back the blades any longer, and Max saw them wrench free of the assassin's grip.

Max looked at him. How did you thank a killer who had just saved your life but had promised to kill you later? You didn't. It was already a debt repaid.

"Where now?" Riga demanded.

Max saw the location of the satellite dish in his mind's eye. He turned and ran for the opening that led into a green umbrella covering of forest. "This way!"

They were no sooner clear of the claustrophobic building than they could hear the muted staccato of what sounded like firecrackers somewhere in the distance, the harsh sounds swallowed by the dense jungle.

"Gunfire," Riga said. "AKs, M16s, others. Two or three clicks away."

Max kept running and noticed Riga kept pace despite his injured leg. He was one of those unstoppable guys, Max thought. People like him will keep coming for you until they die. Max had never wished anyone dead before, but Riga was different.

It was a world away from the stark, heat-seared ball court. No blue sky penetrated the overhanging tree branches and vines.

It seemed like an artificial corridor of foliage, as if a gardener had created a massive tunnel out of the greenery.

"Camouflage," Riga said. "Deliberate. This whole area is hidden from view."

"There has to be another way in here," Max said. "The Razor House kept everyone out from that side."

The ongoing gun battle came no closer, but one or two echoes became more dominant. Who was doing the shooting? It wouldn't be the warriors fighting, so it had to be police or army. Were they coming here? Max heard the roaring cries of howler monkeys moving away and sensed rather than saw birds' alarm as the air beat somewhere above the green tunnel. He had no idea how far they had run, but the ground was clear of any major obstacles. It looked as though it had been cleared by machinery. Then it dropped away, and a vine-covered stone building, most of it below ground level, was just about visible through the undergrowth.

Riga ran his hands over the limestone blocks, then edged round to the side, trying to find the line of the building, but there was nothing else. This wall was all that existed. Anything else must be underground. Max rubbed his hands across a stone lintel. He gazed at the shapes and figures of mountain monsters that had been cut into the building, probably more than a thousand years ago. He did not have to bluff now.

"It's a temple. An ancient temple," he said.

"How do you know that?" Riga said.

"It's in one of my mum's photographs." He looked around. "None of this camouflage was here then. There's an entrance somewhere." Max's heart felt a squeeze of regret. The photographs in his pocket were his insurance against Riga killing him. He dared not look at his mother smiling in front of the old temple. She had been right here. On this spot. He could almost feel her.

Max traced his hands along the wall. Behind where his mother had stood, there should have been a small entrance. He thrust his hands into the dense undergrowth.

"Here, pull this away."

Riga unsheathed his machete and hacked at the ropelike vines that dropped down the temple walls. A small window-sized opening was visible, recessed into the depth of the stone. It was covered in steel mesh.

"I don't know too much about Mayan culture, but I know they didn't have windows like that."

Riga looked at him. "All right. So you know where you're going. Good."

He pulled Max out of the way and kicked hard and fast against the corners of the mesh. It gave way on three sides, and Riga pushed his weight against it. The corner snapped, the mesh window dropped, and they heard it clatter onto stone. Riga climbed in. There were steps going down. They were in a dark corridor of an ancient temple, which was obviously unused and which had been sealed to stop anyone clambering through the small window. Riga moved forward, the back of his hand running along the wall to guide him. Max followed. The fetid air made their labored breathing the only sound in the heavy atmosphere. The passageway angled left and right and then opened out into an antechamber. It would have been pitch-black this deep inside the building except for a hairline crack of light seeping around what appeared to be a door. Max reached out and his palms met the smooth texture of a wooden covering.

"Can you smell that?" Max asked.

"Chemicals," Riga said. "OK. We're out of options. This is where we go in." He rammed the tip of the machete's blade between the wood and stone, forced it back, felt the wood ease slightly. He kept the pressure on it. "Kick it!"

Max twisted his body, balanced on one leg, grunted with effort, side-kicked the door and heard wood splinter.

"Again! Come on! Harder, kid!"

Max put all his power into the kick, and, with Riga's shoulder aiding his efforts, the wood gave way.

They gazed down three meters into what looked like a hospital laboratory. A polyethylene tent took up most of it, but Max and Riga could see the main room had a sliding metal door opening to the outside. In the enclosed area, two men in biohazard suits were loading spill-proof vials of blood-colored liquid into specially padded containers.

Half a dozen suitcase-sized boxes were being manhandled outside the tent by two men wearing jeans, T-shirts and bandannas. AK-47s were slung across their backs. This was some kind of cleanup operation. Like flash photography, it was a frozen picture of shock and fear as Riga and Max smashed through into the room and jumped down. Then the gunmen dropped the containers, and one of the men in biohazard suits screamed at him. His voice was muted by the visor, but clearly they did not want whatever was in those cases to be damaged. Their reaction was a natural response to something terrifying.

One of the gunmen leveled his AK-47. Riga shoved Max aside and pounded toward the two men. Rolling on the ground, he dived beneath the spray of gunfire. For a moment Max thought thunder was reverberating across the valley. It was no gathering storm Max had heard: the other gunman had fled outside and hauled the metal door closed behind him, trapping them all inside.

A man yelled, then screamed. By the time Max got to his feet, the remaining gunman was down on the ground and unmoving. Riga sheathed the bloodied machete and reloaded the dead man's weapon. He yanked one of the doors—padlocked. There was no way out.

"Get out here," Riga commanded the laboratory workers. The men stepped out of their polyethylene tent, zipped the area behind them and pulled off their head covers. The clatter of gunfire from outside grew closer as Riga grabbed one of the bareheaded men. "How toxic is this stuff?" It was obvious Riga was wary of getting too close to the containers. And it was obvious to Max that he thought it was something that demanded enormous respect.

Max lifted a line of cord off the ground. He let it slip through his fingers as he moved forward; then he saw the packed blocks of plastic explosive. "They're going to blow the place up!" he yelled at Riga. "We have to get out of here!"

Riga threatened the men. "What is it back there?"

"Genetically modified bacteria," one of them said nervously.

Riga looked at Max. "That's what your friend died of; it has to be some kind of slow incubator." He turned back to the men. "High voltage or fire destroys it, right? That's why this place is wired."

The men nodded. Riga raised the submachine gun.

"Don't kill them!" Max yelled. "My mother was here! Years ago. Was she infected? Did this stuff kill her?"

The man babbled, desperate to save his life. "It's nothing to do with us! Mr. Cazamind took everything. He has all the data."

"Cazamind is *here?*" Riga demanded. He grabbed the man. "Where?"

The scientist could barely speak for fear. "Helipad. A kilometer north of here."

Max barely listened. His attention was fixed on the metal doors as he desperately tried to yank them open. The man had barely finished speaking when a shock wave threw them all to the ground. This was the most severe yet. The unstoppable force of nature whiplashed the room. Part of the wall collapsed. The metal doors buckled and screeched as they were torn from the walls. The lab men ran for their lives. Riga let them go—he was looking at the damaged laboratory. Even high-security containers could not withstand that kind of tremor. One had fallen from its cradle and was spilling liquid. Just how lethal was it? Riga backed away. Aftershocks made the ground shudder.

Max was almost shoulder to shoulder with Riga as they made a break for the open door. Explosions followed almost immediately as a chain reaction of powerful detonations came from somewhere in the jungle, ricocheting toward them. The timed demolition ripped the forest apart. A vast area of hillside erupted, dirt exploded, trees disintegrated— the shock wave sucked the moisture from their throats, pounded their ears and flung them to the ground. A ten-meter wall of fire raced down the tree line and reached the temple, which erupted in a massive explosion. There must have been other chambers below, because as the temple disappeared in the debris, the ground collapsed and absorbed most of the shock wave. If it had not, Max and Riga would have died then and there.

Riga was getting to his feet, searching groggily for the AK-47, but it had been blown out of sight. Max choked and spat out soil; his eyes stung, and his eardrums hurt. Deafened by the blast, he staggered uncertainly for a couple of steps, then fell again. Like an old man, he managed to get himself onto his knees. They had been lucky. Ash and dirt caked their skin, and rivulets of sweat tracked through the grime on their faces, creating grotesque masks. Their shirts, already snagged and ripped by the flint blades, now snared fragments of earth and leaves. They looked like creatures from hell, and the inferno that swirled around them was the devil's playground.

The explosive chain reaction had wrenched the ground apart, exposing a long wall of mountainside. Even Riga stood momentarily stunned at what came pouring down the sheer rockface toward them. A lava flow had erupted from beneath the surface and was incinerating everything in its path.

Max's ears popped. His hearing came back. That was when he heard the unmistakable sound of a helicopter's blades starting up. But he was almost too exhausted to care. The air thundered with a raging fire that swept across the edge of the forest. Smoke and dirt swirled; it felt as though the world were ending.

Riga yelled at him above the firestorm. "You want the man who let your mother die? He's getting away. Get up!"

Max could not move. There was no strength left to fight with. The explosions had battered him. He tried to drag himself to his feet.

Riga grinned. "You know you won't make it out of here."

"If you don't stop me, I will."

"You just never give up, do you, boy? OK. It's not over yet," Riga said. "Here. You need a weapon." And he tossed the machete toward Max.

Max stared at the man paid to kill him. He was giving him the final piece in the puzzle about his mother's death. "I want him; you want him. And he's here," Riga said.

The assassin extended his hand to help him up. Max knocked it away and staggered to his feet unaided.

He had to see this through.

Riga looked meaner than Max had ever seen anyone look before. There was a beastlike quality to his face. It scared Max more than he thought possible. Riga nodded at Max in unspoken admiration for his determination.

"Payback time, kid."

26

Cazamind sat in the helicopter, with the pilot waiting nervously to see which way the flames would turn in the wind that blew unpredictably from different directions. Two muscular bodyguards, men from eastern Europe, stacked the last of four sample cases into the helicopter's hold. These were Cazamind's own people, brought in to make sure that he had the best chance of survival should those in power doubt his ability to keep matters under control.

Cazamind's chewed and torn fingernails hurt. He had no idea whether Max Gordon had reached the ancient Mayan site or whether he had perished in the jungle. But he had every reason to be fearful. Riga was still on the loose. Between him and the boy, Cazamind's life had taken a turn for the worse. He had ordered the usual thugs from the City of Lost Souls to secure the area, had offered them a huge bonus to kill anyone who tried to get through the supply route. He could hear that the gun battle was now little more than sporadic gunfire, a mopping-up operation. But who were the attackers? And who had won the battle?

The slightest breach of security, or even the threat of such a breach, had demanded a complete shutdown of the operation. These were the orders given to Cazamind by his "people." The faceless men in power were not sitting here in the shuddering helicopter in the stinking heat, soaked in sweat, while an inferno raged around them. And he knew, even as he recovered the blood source material from the jungle laboratory, that others were searching his own private databases and bank accounts, in fact every scrap of his personal life, in case he had made copies of what he knew to be as explosive as that huge tree that had just disintegrated. The pilot yelled at the men to hurry the hell up because they had to get out of here. Now!

Cazamind felt the handcuff bracelet bite into his skin. The slim aluminum briefcase, barely the size of a small notebook computer, held half a dozen sheets of facts and figures and the breakdown on a computer disk of those he knew to be involved in this massive conspiracy. It was no use trying to hide it in electronic databanks—those people would root it out. Even if they only suspected that their loyal servant had covered his back, then he would stay alive as long as nothing was discovered. When it came down to good old-fashioned safety nets, handwritten testimony was always the best bet. He hugged it to him.

Another explosion made him wince. The charges had

gone off prematurely because of the unexpected volcanic activity, and now the whole world seemed to be on fire. The helicopter had been hidden in one of the caves, and when they brought it out onto the plateau where the small helipad was located, the ground was already shuddering, threatening to plunge them down into the scalding valley. Cazamind wiped the sweat from his face. The storage compartment door banged shut; the men were getting into the helicopter. He would soon be safely away.

And then he saw the apparitions.

Two filthy, sweat-streaked creatures powered up the edge of the plateau as if they had risen from the underworld. One of them he recognized as his rogue killer, Riga. The other was a boy whose tattered clothes clung to him like a second skin. The flickering light from the wall of fire behind him made his ash- and dirt-covered body look like a jungle cat, head down, muscles rolling in a seemingly effortless movement of attack. Cazamind wiped his eyes and looked again. It was no jaguar; it was Max Gordon. And Riga had let him live. That meant they shared one purpose. They were coming for him. One of the bodyguards was still trying to clamber aboard when Cazamind screamed the command to take off. The man fell to the ground; the other slammed the doors closed. Survival was the main thought on all their minds.

The heat was intense, but Cazamind felt as cold as if he were on the ice face of a Swiss mountain. The helicopter lifted slowly and hovered momentarily as the pilot fought the gusting wind. Cazamind allowed a sigh of relief. But there was something wrong. The helicopter lurched.

*　*　*

Riga was stronger and faster than Max and had pushed ahead, but his injured leg meant he was less agile, and Max could see that they were not going to reach the helicopter before it lifted off. The man who had tried to climb aboard had fallen badly, tumbling down the slope. Riga shouted for Max to be careful of the rotor blades, but Max was already beneath the swirling dust. He could have reached up and clung to the helicopter's skids, but instead he looped a wrist-thick ground vine round its leading edge, yanked hard and twisted it round itself, so, at least for a few seconds, the helicopter would not be able to take off. It was up to Riga to do something.

Max felt the monster falter. If he did not let go of the vine, the helicopter would slam back down onto the ground and crush him. It swung crazily, as if trying to rid itself of whatever held it earthbound. Max rolled clear but saw the nose sideswipe Riga, who fell heavily.

In an instant Max stood alone as the helicopter ripped itself upward. Its nose tilted and he gazed up at the monstrous bug. A man sat in the backseat, leaning forward, commanding the pilot and pointing toward Max. The nose tilted farther and the rotor blades began to thrash the swirling smoke. They were going to hack him to death.

Riga was pulling himself away, but Max had nowhere to run. In a desperate but determined gesture of defiance, he threw the machete at the high-tech monster that was trying to kill him.

It clattered into the rods at the base of the rotors, and over the din of the whirring blades, Max heard the satisfying *graunch* of metal against metal. The helicopter shuddered. Max saw the fear on the pilot's face. The men inside were mouthing shouts of panic. And then the rotor blades tore into the dirt, the helicopter slammed into the ground, cartwheeled over and landed on its roof. The blades twisted and screamed as they were wrenched from the body. Lethal shards of metal hissed through the air as Max flung himself facedown, clawing his fingers into the dirt and praying that the hurtling metal would miss him as pieces slashed into the few remaining trees, the impact splitting their trunks.

Riga had backpedaled as fast as he could from the crashing helicopter. The destruction settled quickly. The beast of a machine was dead. He looked toward Max. Unbelievable. The boy had destroyed a million-dollar aircraft with a machete worth a couple of dollars. The men inside the aircraft hung upside down from their seat belts. The tough-looking one recovered quickly, kicked open the door and helped to drag the man in a suit, with the attaché case chained to his wrist, out of the crash. Cazamind.

Riga went for him. The bodyguard blocked his attack, and Riga had a hard fight on his hands. Riga was a lethal opponent, but the other man had not endured what the assassin had gone through these last few hours. For a couple of minutes he got the better of Riga with hard, muscle-tearing blows.

Cazamind stumbled away. Max tried to see him through the smoke, but then the ground shifted and began to break up. Like liquid, the earth slewed a few meters. Max kept his balance. There was a thrill of fear—he had been in an avalanche before and knew how terrifying it was—but when half a mountain moves, there is little chance of survival. The ground beneath his feet steadied, but the far side of the small plateau started to disappear.

The helicopter began to slide, metal screeching against rock as it was slowly dragged ever closer to the edge and the plunge down to the river of lava that cut through the valley floor. Cazamind panicked, lost his footing and managed to scramble away from the machine. Max saw that he had fallen and that the chain of the attaché case had snared itself on the helicopter. It was going to pull him down. He would be fried. Max ran forward and saw the man desperately trying to un-lock the handcuff. The helicopter groaned as it slipped away. Any moment now it would slide rapidly into the furnace. The crumbling earth would not bear its weight much longer.

Max felt the heat from the flowing lava blistering his skin, even though it was a hundred meters below him. He got down beside the man, who looked imploringly at him and gestured with a small silver key that was attached to a chain from his belt. He could not reach the handcuff.

"Help me, boy, help me! For God's sake, don't let me die. Don't let me die! Please!"

Max's mouth was so dry he could barely speak, but he pushed his face close to the man's. "My mother needed help. She was dying, and you refused to help her."

The man shook his head desperately. He was crying, a horrible death only moments away. He begged. "I had to! It would have exposed our plans."

"Did you infect her? Is that how she died?"

Cazamind shook his head. "No, no. We hadn't started the program then. She just got sick. It was the jungle that killed her. Not me. I swear. The case! Everything is in the case! She found out—"

The helicopter slithered another meter. "What?" Max screamed at him.

"Save me! I beg you!" Cazamind would barter the world to save his life. "Your mother . . . the rain forest . . . we were buying the rain forest . . . thousands and thousands of hectares . . . It's all in the case!"

"Who gives the orders? Is it Zaragon? Is that who you work for?" Max yelled.

Cazamind's face scrunched up in fear and self-pity. He shook his head. Tears leaked into the creases around his eyes. "Please . . . please . . . don't let me die. . . ."

There was no more time. Max ripped the key chain from him, fumbled with the lock, his hands sweating. The helicopter lurched. Cazamind screamed. Max got the key into the small lock. He hesitated. Cazamind looked horror-struck. Was the boy tormenting him? Was he going to let him die after all?

"The case's combination. What is it?" Max insisted.

"All sixes! HURRY!"

Max turned the key and released the handcuff. The terrified man fell clear and rolled away as Max grabbed the attaché case.

He wanted revenge for his mother's death, but he could not let the man responsible die in such a horrible manner.

Riga had no such sensitivity.

As Cazamind got to his knees, Max could see him mouthing, *Thank you, thank you.* And then Riga appeared out of the smoke and hauled him to his feet. Cazamind's face distorted into a mask of terror. He knew there was no compassion or mercy to be had here.

Riga had the bodyguard's handgun, which he leveled at Cazamind's head. Max saw that he tried to beg, and there was a brief look of surprise and relief as Riga lowered the weapon, but it was a cruel act of false hope—it was all over in a second. Riga threw him backward. Cazamind's scream was lost in the roar of fire. His body hit the downward slope and then tumbled over its edge toward the lava that had just consumed the helicopter.

Max could not avert his eyes from the horrific sight. Cazamind's body flared into a fireball and then disintegrated as it hit the molten lava.

It seemed to Max that, no matter how injured or exhausted he was, Riga was unstoppable. The killer turned toward him, kept his eyes on the boy and bent down to retrieve the attaché case. His blackened, bloodstained face was like a Mayan war mask. Max was too exhausted to resist when he took it from his grip.

"This," Riga said as he picked up the case, "is everything."

They faced each other. Was he going to kill Max now?

"End of the road, Max. Go home. Be a schoolkid, like you're supposed to be. Stay out of trouble."

And without another word, Riga moved away down the far side of the slope into the trees, which looked as though they had been flattened by a bombing raid. Max was safe from the killer now. He had been reprieved. All he had to do was get home—somehow. So why did he hesitate? Why did he turn and search the smoke-filled hillside for the assassin?

Because in trying to save the rain forest, his mother had

stumbled upon a greater evil. Others could suffer a vile death like Danny Maguire, and the evidence of corruption and inhuman experimentation was in that case. He went after Riga. It was what his dad would have done.

Charlie Morgan's superficial injuries from the crash had been patched up by her men, and when they broke through the narrow defile, there was virtually no further resistance from the gunmen. She saw the fire mountain move and watched smoke churn in a rhythmic swirl that could only be caused by the draft from a helicopter's rotors. Her binoculars showed her fragments of the conflict on the hillside more than a kilometer away. The smoke and flame obscured much of what was going on, but she watched for a few moments longer while her men were regrouping and heading for where they had heard cries from a vast hidden compound that held the captive Maya. She wasn't interested in who they were or why they were there—what held her focus on the distant hillside was that there were two survivors. The larger of them had taken something from the smaller, who had the look of a boy. At last she had found Max Gordon.

The man moved away and it looked as though he carried a small case. That case was important.

She ran.

Max unclenched his fists. His fingers, caked with dirt and ingrained black ash, curved into claws. A strange stillness embraced him, distancing him from the roaring fires and exploding trees. The fractured land still tore itself apart in a determined act of self-destruction, but Max did not move. He gazed across the layers of smoke, saw the sun throw spears of light through the clouds, pinpointing the running man—who then disappeared into the smoke-shrouded forest.

Instinct took over from reason. Max would have to risk moving down the slithering hillside and jumping across the breaking ground to reach him. It would take the predatory skills of a jaguar to move that quickly and sure-footedly in pursuit.

Max's thought process had moved to another level. He was beyond rational thought; he was sniffing the air, finding the man's scent, and he was running.

Rain clouds that had clung stubbornly to the mountain peaks edged down toward the inferno and released a tropical downpour that began smothering the flames. The ghostly haze rolled into the broken land, twisting its way through branches and undergrowth. Moisture dripped from the broad leaves as the ash-blackened rain pounded the forest.

Memory told Max he had run to the farthest part of the valley where the lava stream's curtain of crimson mist still rose, though now it was being sucked into the forest, making it an eerie netherworld of twisted shrouds.

A flicker of movement caught his eye. A woman, tufts of hair the color of fire, was running hard along a path in the partly obscured distance. She disappeared from view. Max hunched down. The footprints of his prey scuffed the earth; his senses tasted the man's smell. A slab of ground broke free, earth tremors and rain forcing it away from the clinging roots of the forest. Trees tore, snapped and crashed down, carried by the force of the landslide. Creatures ran, birds screeched, monkeys howled.

Max leapt onto a tree trunk, gripping and ripping its bark as in a seamless bound he stretched across the void and found the safety of pockmarked boulders next to water cascading down a ravine. A natural channel from the high peaks, its roar was louder than the depleted firestorm in the distance.

A surge of water splashed against rock, dousing Max. He gasped as if plucked from a dream. His hands stung from dozens of scratches and thorns—as though he had been running on all fours. He refocused.

Less than two hundred meters away, wind sculpted the mist, twisting the crimson curtain into a monstrous smoke ring—an oscillating halo—and in its midst lay the body of a man beneath a fallen tree. He was facedown in the mud, one arm outstretched, the other trapped beneath him. A short distance away, the attaché case lay on the ground. It looked as though the assassin's luck had finally run out and the landslide had killed him.

Riga lay in the path of the young MI5 agent. How did she get here? It made no difference. Max realized that the tree under which Riga lay was an old deadfall, not a casualty of the earthquake, and that water sluiced beneath it in a shallow runoff, so the ground was gently scooped out. Max gazed at the body. Something was wrong. Riga's head rested close to his trapped arm, so the water trickled around it; otherwise the man would have drowned were he not already dead. Riga had a breathing space. He must have seen the girl approaching and crawled beneath the tree. His face was turned in Max's direction, away from the girl, making the situation more inviting, less threatening for her.

His eyes were open.

It was a trap. The girl was going to be dead in a minute.

It was no good shouting a warning. The waterfall would swallow the sound of his voice. Max had to make sure that Riga saw him and that when he did, Morgan would be alerted.

And that Riga did not gun him down.

Sweat stung her eyes, and the rain felt like driven sand, but she moved steadily upward, gripping the semiautomatic in her hands. She slipped and stumbled a couple of times on the slimy ground, but maintained enough balance to watch the unmoving body. Her eyes were on the briefcase a few paces away from him. What was in there that was so important? She would know soon enough. Ambition drove her on. She could almost hear Ridgeway's praises, could see the commendation, knew her future was assured and that high rank would be hers for the taking.

She was almost there. Her hand trembled, more from anticipation than fear. She kicked the body. It did not move. She carefully took a couple of steps away, then bent forward to retrieve the case. A figure was running flat out from the top of the hillside, slipping and sliding, waving his arms, mouth wide open, screaming a silent yell. The boy was sliding down the mud bank as the mist curled in on itself, a small bloodred wave that made him look like a demonic surfer. She lost sight of him momentarily; then he reappeared, directly level with the body now. Max Gordon. He must be terrified, desperate to be rescued.

And then she realized that he was charging at her, rather than simply gaining her attention. He was warning her.

She threw herself to one side at the exact moment the man's body twisted, coming up with a gun in his hand. He fired rapidly three times. The numbing pain crashed through her body. She fell. Riga had hit her with every shot.

He turned, leveled the weapon. Trained men don't aim; they point and kill. He pointed at Max—a demented kid who looked like hell, cut and bleeding, blackened from fire, who swung a piece of wood like a club, who was attacking. Attacking a man holding a gun! There was something gloriously insane about it. But not something Riga would consider worth saving the boy's life for.

Max saw the moment when Riga leveled the gun, when his eyes looked beyond the weapon and locked on to his own.

Riga fired twice—a double tap that would pierce heart and lungs.

Max fell, his body sliding, momentum carrying him into Riga. The angels were still with him—the bullets had barely missed him as he threw himself backward half a heartbeat before the killer squeezed the trigger. He kicked out at Riga's injured leg. The heat and exertion would have taken its toll on the wound. With the massive kick and impetus from the slide, Max hit his target.

Riga cried out in pain and tumbled back across the fallen tree into the mud, the handgun slipping away into the slime.

The killer's body had cushioned Max's impact. He clambered across the tree trunk, swinging the piece of wood, uncertain whether the red mist in front of his eyes belonged to the forest or to his own rage. Riga was on his knees reaching for him; if he pulled Max down into the mud, he would kill him. The club connected with the side of Riga's head, and he fell back onto his twisted, injured leg. Max stood above him panting like an ancient warrior who had brought down a beast of the forest. Danger heightened everything. Each grunting breath was confirmation of his victory as he stood over the beaten enemy, never taking his eyes off the fallen assassin.

Max was in the zone.

The rain was heavier now. Sluices of blood-colored mud exposed the bone-white limestone mountainside. It would not be long before the ground gave way and swept debris and boulders down into the valley below.

Max dropped the club and went over to look at Charlie Morgan. She lay where she had fallen, and had it not been for the splashes of blood on her rain-drenched clothes, he might have thought she slept. He carefully eased her arms down to the sides of her body, then straightened her legs. He could see the dark blood still oozing where she had been hit. He eased open her shirt. There was a wound in her side, another in her upper chest and a third in her leg, but the bone had not been broken. She was alive. He took off his tattered shirt, ripped it into bandages and then dug into his cargo-pants pockets and pulled out the herbs Orsino Flint had given him.

The downpour washed the blood from the wounds. He dabbed them dry as best he could, then, using his thumb, pushed the herbs carefully into the punctures. He bound each wound with the strips from his shirt.

He was still on his knees, wiping the flecks of dirt from her face, when he felt the forest change. The rain eased, the crimson mist shifted slightly in the wind, and the dense jungle undergrowth a hundred meters away fell silent for a moment. A shadow figure, the rosettes on its skin barely noticeable, had made the disrupted light alter. Max gazed through the foliage, into the dark patch that was unmoving. Two amber eyes gazed back. They blinked; small tufted ears twitched.

The stare was intense.

And then the jaguar bared its teeth.

Slushing rain and mud disguised the sounds behind Max.

But the vibration in the air had changed. His sixth sense was heightened, the link between jaguar and boy almost tangible. Max spun round in time to stop Riga's lunge.

Like two beasts they grappled, rolling in the sliding mud. Neither spoke, neither yelled, both grunting in their fight for survival—and Riga was still by far the stronger. Max had a blurred memory of clawing the man's back and trying to bite and scratch his way clear.

He reached out blindly for anything to strike Riga. His hand delved into the mud for a weapon, but all it found was tangled roots. And that saved his life.

The ground slid away, the force of the water creating a mudslide that swept Riga from him. Max clung to the roots, but he saw Riga's face. A look of disbelief as he gazed into Max's eyes. The killer knew he could not survive. He smiled. Max Gordon had won.

Max pulled himself clear, onto drier, firmer ground, and looked down the mud slurry to the valley thirty meters below. There was no sign of Riga's body; it must have been swept farther away into the turmoil of the broken land.

In the end, the forces of nature had beaten the killer.

Max pulled the case to him and thumbed the beveled locks. All sixes—666. The mark of the beast. There was a handwritten notebook inside, as well as dates, numbers, names, a computer disk and a small picture clipped to an environmental-impact report. Max's mum. This all started and ended with her. He placed the file back in the case with her picture still attached and closed the lid. Others would now know how she had triggered the unfolding events.

As the locks clicked back into place, it felt as though he was laying his mother's memory to rest. And in this jungle hell he had found the truth about his father.

He slipped the attaché case's handcuff onto Morgan's wrist. If she lived, she could have the glory. He eased her body onto his shoulders. Then, grabbing her arms across his chest, forced himself onto his feet. He was surprised at how light the agent's body was, not thinking for a moment that he had gained extra strength.

He looked into the jungle.

The jaguar was gone.

Max began a slow, loping run.

The authorities declared the forbidden valley a disaster area, but as so few people were involved in the confined and protected area, it was decided to send only medical teams and a few troops to clear out the last of the Serpent Warriors. The Maya resolved to stay in their villages, away from the ruined temples where cruel men had ruled their lives by fear. The imprisoned adult population that Charlie Morgan's jungle fighters had found were the forest children's parents.

Among the medical teams were British and American undercover intelligence officers, whose investigation into events in the reserve would confirm information contained in documents brought out of the disaster area by a young, courageous MI5 officer, who survived three gunshot wounds at the hands of a known assassin.

No one understood how Max Gordon could have run so far carrying her body. Paths were blocked, the land had shifted and the heat from the lava flows had increased dramatically. How anyone could have found their way through the dense jungle using barely recognizable animal paths defied logic. But Max Gordon had run, and had kept running, beyond exhaustion, until he found Charlie Morgan's jungle fighters.

It was an amazing feat.

Robert Ridgeway could not disclose to Fergus Jackson what had actually happened in Central America, nor the connection between events in London concerning Danny Maguire. Neither could he mention that the remains of one of his officers, Keegan, had been found in a private hospital. Sayid had been sworn to secrecy, an oath he would honor to ensure his mother's safety, but he would later share the information with his closest friend.

For years scientists had been hunting down organisms capable of triggering new diseases among the human population. Biosphere reserves such as the one in Central America had been set up by pharmaceutical companies to examine the often unknown healing qualities of the rare plants found there. There was now evidence that an independently run arm of the international company Zaragon had discovered a rare blood type among the adult population in the forbidden zone. Their blood carried the antidote for a genetically modified disease, created by scientists in express violation of the international treaty banning biological warfare weapons. Whoever controlled both the disease and its cure would wield unlimited power. Once Cazamind's documents had been examined, governments moved swiftly to dismantle any laboratories located in their country. The computer disk in Cazamind's attaché case revealed horrifying footage of other unknown victims who had died and whose bodies had been examined in the private hospital's mortuary before being cremated. It was these images, Ridgeway reasoned, that Keegan had seen on the monitors before being killed.

How many others had died over the past few years was difficult to ascertain, but when hospitals had been closed because of uncontrolled and unidentifiable infections, Cazamind's evidence revealed that a dozen or more victims had been taken to the private hospital and isolated before they died.

The mutated bacteria took the form of a worm that devoured its host.

The research on the bioengineered microbial agents secured enough information for the British chief medical officer to announce that new vaccines would be available in the next couple of years to destroy the hospital superbugs such as MRSA and the terrifying flesh-eating disease called

USA300, traces of which had been discovered in the privately run hospital in London.

Important figures in MI6, the CIA, British and U.S. governments, U.S. drug enforcement agencies and big business quietly retired from their careers earlier than expected. Biological warfare was not to be mentioned. It was all hushed up. But the real power brokers, those men who lived in a shadow world and who had ultimately controlled Cazamind, they would never be discovered. Even he had not known who they were.

Finally, the MI5 report revealed that the assassin's body had been found by search teams. It had been identified by tattoos on his wrist: *Kunnia—Velvollisuus—Tahto*. Honor—Duty—Will. It appeared from the claw marks on his body that he had fought with a jaguar, the sacred animal of the Maya—and lost.

27

Max's physical wounds healed quickly. A few more scars creased white lines across his suntan, but the warm ocean soothed him. He walked out of the deep blue onto the bright sand. A U.S. Coast Guard cutter stood offshore as a Zodiac boat made its unhurried approach through the reef.

Sunlight glinted on a bling bracelet as a skinny kid raised a glass with a small umbrella stuck on the top.

"They're comin', *chico*."

"I see them," Max said.

"Maybe we should stay here, cousin?" Max took the drink Xavier offered. Their towels were laid out under the palm trees. "We got room service from them navy people; we got everything here. We kings, man, of all we behold. You been good to me, cousin. I don' forget that. Not ever."

Max smiled. Xavier shrugged. "That crazy Orsino Flint.

He taught me that when we got put in a cage while you went off and destroyed half the world."

"You think he survived?"

"He said he was stayin' 'cause he was in a secret valley, that there'd be all them orchids and things he could smuggle out."

Max nodded. Orsino Flint would make a small fortune.

"Those kids. Y'know, Setting Star and her bro, they got back with their parents. They were all prisoners. I dunno why, maybe 'cause they didn' wan' no one findin' out what was goin' on in there."

"It had something to do with their blood. The bad guys needed it."

"Like vampire bats?"

"Worse," Max said.

Xavier made the sign of the cross.

"It's good the kids found their parents," Max said, and did not deny himself the sense of warmth from the memory of Setting Star.

"You better now? Y'know, you thin' you find out about your mother an' all?"

Max nodded. "She discovered they were buying every scrap of rain forest they could get. Huge no-go areas that protected them from what they were doing. Now it'll be saved."

The Zodiac boat was getting closer. "What about you, Xavier? You'll miss your brother."

Xavier nodded.

"Have you decided what you're going to do with your immunity and new identity?" Max asked.

"I dunno yet. Bein' an honest citizen might take some get-tin' used to. But, y'know, since I been in the jungle with you, I might open an exotic pet store. These creepy things? They don' bother me no more."

"What about driving around in fancy sports cars?"

"I was thinkin' maybe that'd draw too much attention from the wrong people, yeah?"

Max finished the drink. "Yeah. Good thinking."

"That's right. Get smart, *chico*, I tell myself. After this loco trip. Get smart."

The boat ran ashore. A sailor jumped into the shallows.

"Are you ready, sir?"

Xavier pulled his sunglasses on top of his head and ges-tured for the man to wait. "Y'see, Max, now they call me sir." He smiled. "OK, cousin, I won' be able to tell you where I'm going or my new name—witness protection an' all that—but you ever want any birdseed, you look up Alfredo's Pet Store in L.A."

Max and Xavier hugged each other.

"You gonna be OK?" Xavier asked.

Max nodded. "The Royal Navy is coming for me in a cou-ple of days."

"No, I mean . . . inside. About everything."

Max nodded and gave him a reassuring smile. "Bye, cousin."

The ship eased from the bay, a brief blast of farewell from its siren, and then it was gone, leaving a rippled blemish on the calm water. The sky sucked in the light as a purple glow edged the horizon. The sunset would soon flutter and die be-neath the surface.

Max knew there were still questions to be answered. Somewhere in the world were threads connecting his mother and father to a force that wielded enormous influence and control. Like an invisible disease, these people had penetrated positions of power throughout the world.

And Max had been drawn into it all.

Two rows of footprints led toward the white rock jutting out into the bay that he had found a few days earlier. A few meters into the jungle, a small area had once been cleared and sun-bleached stones collected to make a grave. The handmade wooden cross was strong and had already survived four years—his father's hands had seen to that.

He gathered flowers from the jungle, then cut down and placed on the grave a traveler's palm frond whose base held fresh water, in which he arranged the flowers. Then he carefully entwined the pendant around the cross. The disk glinted as the blood sun reached out its beams like a mother's arms enfolding her child.

A jaguar sat on the white rock, deepening shadows disguising her presence, as Max felt himself drawn into the sun's embrace.

Anything else could wait for another day.

AUTHOR'S NOTE

The volcanic-rock carving of the jaguar in room 24 of the British Museum does not exist. Everything else is as described, but the beast lurks only in the shadows of my imagination.

Ach Puch in Mayan is pronounced with the *ch* sounding like the letter *k*. The location Max's mother visited, Xunantunich, is pronounced *shoo-nahn-too-nic*, and means "Stone Woman" or "Maiden of the Rock."

ABOUT THE AUTHOR

David Gilman has worked as a firefighter, a professional photographer, and a marketing manager and served in the British army's Parachute Regiment Reconnaissance Platoon. He lives in England and has traveled the world, gathering inspiration for his Max Gordon novels along the way. Visit David at davidgilman.com.